Bells for Eli

Susan Beckham Zurenda's exquisite debut novel transports readers into the small-town South of a supposedly simpler time and place where tragic circumstances and malicious consequences shouldn't happen. With genuine emotion and a mastery of atmosphere and action, *Bells for Eli* is a consummate story of determination and love prevailing in a world where cruelty and exclusion threaten to dominate. Stories of the heart don't get any better than this.

—Mary Alice Monroe, award-winning
and *New York Times* best-selling author
of *The Summer Guests*

Bells for Eli is a compelling coming-of-age tale set in a South Carolina small town during the 1960s and 70s, an era rife with rebellion, passion, and change. Zurenda's skillful writing and depth of characters swiftly pulled me into this unique story and didn't let go until its heartrending final pages. A memorable, atmospheric novel of love, friendship, and bonds that surpass all reason.

—Kristina McMorris, *New York Times*
bestselling author of *Sold on a Monday*
and *The Edge of Lost*

"Susan Beckham Zurenda is a vibrant new Southern voice. *Bells for Eli*, her debut novel, will remind readers of Pat Conroy's rich storytelling. Vivid and beautiful. The book will capture the hearts of those who love the South and in particular South Carolina."

—Ann Hite, award-winning author of the
Black Mountain series and
*Roll Away the Stone: A Family's
Legacy of Racism and Abuse*

Bells for Eli

A NOVEL

Susan Beckham Zurenda

MERCER UNIVERSITY PRESS
Macon, Georgia
2020

MUP/ H988

© 2020 by Mercer University Press
Published by Mercer University Press
1501 Mercer University Drive
Macon, Georgia 31207

9 8 7 6 5 4 3 2 1

Books published by Mercer University Press are printed on acid-free
paper that meets the requirements of the American National Standard for
Information Sciences—Permanence of Paper for Printed Library
Materials.

Printed and bound in the United States.

This book is set in Adobe Caslon Pro.

Cover/jacket design by Burt&Burt

ISBN   978-0-88146-737-6
Cataloging-in-Publication Data is available from the Library of Congress

For my cousins Emma and Jeannie

and in memory of their brother Danny

Yes, there are two paths you can go by but in the long run there's still time to change the road you're on.

—Jimmy Page and Robert Plant (Led Zeppelin)

Think, when the bells do chime, / Tis angels' music: therefore come not late.

—George Herbert

In Franklin's tower there hangs a bell
It can ring, turn night to day
It can ring like fire when you lose your way

—Robert Hunter (The Grateful Dead)

ACKNOWLEDGMENTS

I am grateful to the many people, both directly and indirectly, who have encouraged and assisted me in bringing *Bells for Eli* into the world:

To my phenomenal agent and friend Marly Rusoff, who offered invaluable advice, suggested important revisions, and never wavered in her belief that this novel would find its place.

To the team at Mercer University Press: Director Marc Jolley, Publishing Assistant Marsha Luttrell, and Marketing Director Mary Beth Kosowski for their expertise and tremendous support.

To my friend and associate at Magic Time Literary Publicity, President Kathie Bennett, whose exceptional talent and enthusiasm as a book publicist has introduced me to extraordinary authors and readers. I am grateful she loves my book and that I am an author she advocates.

To poet and teacher Peter Schmitt whose patience, expertise, and evaluation of each chapter helped shape and sharpen my work. I call him my MFA (Magical Fiction Advantage).

To my early readers and friends, Carolyn Hooker, Meg Hartin, Donna Dornes, Malinda Tulloh, Julie Garrett, Marianna MacIntyre, and authors Cassandra King Conroy and Ashley Havird, for their honest and helpful remarks.

To gastroenterologist Dr. Gordon France and retired gastroenterologist Dr. Mitchell Allen for their willingness to guide my medical understanding of my character's condition and its effects.

To my husband Wayne for his unflagging support, and to my daughters Kassie and Susanne for their encouragement.

MERCER UNIVERSITY PRESS

Endowed by

TOM WATSON BROWN
and
THE WATSON-BROWN FOUNDATION, INC.

To author Rosa Shand who taught me a graduate class in creative writing many years ago and then became my dear friend. It was an honor when she began asking me to read her drafts and offer feedback after tirelessly reading and remarking on mine.

And to my late parents who nurtured in me the love of stories, those created in our family and those read in books, from the time I was old enough to listen.

Bells for Eli

PROLOGUE

AUGUST 1978

I am one of those people for whom physical activity is a tonic for darkness. It doesn't make the gloom go away, but, like aspirin for a brutal headache, it sometimes softens the hard, throbbing edge. Today, I'd walked about four miles past the outskirts of town in the thick August heat to assuage my spirit and also to escape my hovering parents.

This summer at home in Green Branch—my small South Carolina town situated on a natural ridge between the Broad and Catawba Rivers—I'd done not much more than live out my days, and for the most part my folks had let me be. Other than, from time to time, Mama proclaimed I ruminated too much. She called it "paralysis by analysis." And my father—who is not by nature demonstrative— touched me often, sometimes with a light arm across my shoulder or a quick stroke on my arm, as though he might ask an important question.

But now, since the start of August, I had begun to feel a shift in my parents. Not exactly overt, but it was there—an unspoken plotting about how to get me back to school. I'd left just before exams in the spring, my senior year at Tulloh College, an all-female school about two hours from Green Branch. My current status, thanks to a sympathetic dean, stood at Incomplete. My parents were anxious for me to return and finish. Who could blame them? And I had no desire to worry them. But I also had no desire to return to school.

I pounded the sidewalk in heavy steps—sweat dripping from my eyebrows—as I turned the corner at Stapleton Avenue and approached the Green Branch Town Cemetery on my right. I stopped to unscrew the top of my old Girl Scout canteen and take a swig of warm water. I'd found it at the back of my closet and liked carrying it slung across my chest when I went out walking, not just to quench my thirst but also for the nostalgia. Swiping my hand across my eyes to clear the sting of salt and unfog my vision, I heard voices and looked toward the direction of the graveyard.

About 30 yards behind the spiked steel fence I saw Miss Inez Wilson with an entourage of women. I knew they stood at the site of the Lauderdale graves because I am connected to these people through my cousin Eli and know where they are buried. I turned and advanced toward the open gate.

"Adeline Green, what in heaven's name are you doing here?" she called when she noticed me. Everyone knows Miss Inez, and she knows almost everyone too, especially someone like me with the Green name because I am a member of the founding family of the town, at least according to her research. She interviewed my father and wrote us up in her *History of Green Branch* the University of South Carolina published umpteen years ago.

"I'm out walking," I replied.

"Why are you walking in here?" she asked, bossy.

"Why not?" I answered. "It's cooler in here where there's grass and shade. No disrespect, Miss Inez, but why are *you* walking in the cemetery? It's pretty hot out." Though I knew full well why because of the five aged ladies who stood behind her. I knew she was conducting one of her famous tours of the graveyard, so old it contained soldiers from the Civil War and generations even before. From my approach, I had an excellent view of six sets of stony legs, skin mottled and puckered, veins prominent, that no hot nylon stockings could hide. It made me sweat even more to think about that clinging mesh.

"I've walked to this spot to discuss the Lauderdale family and show the graves to these ladies from the DAR branch in Ridgewood," Miss Inez explained, clearing her throat uncomfortably. "So if you don't mind." By then, I was standing near our esteemed town historian. She sighed heavily, obviously embarrassed on my behalf, a girl dripping sweat in cutoffs and a Ziggy comics T-shirt in the graveyard, not to mention the anachronous canteen.

I've no doubt that people in our small town wondered about me, the girl who had exiled herself at home. The girl without plans. And the sight of me strolling into the cemetery on this blazing day must have been a curiosity to these daunting ladies Miss Inez wanted to impress.

She looked at me quizzically and then decided introducing me was best. "This is Miss Adeline Green of the Green family who founded our town," she announced abruptly. She swept out an arm of jiggling flesh toward me. I knew what she was thinking. How unseemly of me to interrupt her tour in my unkempt way.

"Uncanny that you should arrive," Miss Inez said with a toothy, overdone smile, her tone shifting into genteel. She pulled herself up tall to her full five feet, having suddenly remembered her breeding in front of her important assemblage. "I was just saying how the Greens and the Lauderdales are an excellent illustration of the different paths of antebellum families in this area." She directed a short index finger at me.

I nodded to the ladies, then looked toward Miss Inez's motoring mouth.

"They both started out prosperous families in the early 1800s. Both farming King Cotton. But the devastating effects of concentrating on a one-crop system, coupled with the effects of the War, changed history for the Greens."

"My folks were mill people," I blurted out to the group. "My grandparents worked shifts at the Bratton Cotton Mill. They bought their food with tokens only good in the company store."

"My goodness, Adeline," Miss Inez remarked. She pulled at the collar on her silk blouse and crooked her long, puckered neck jerkily like a crane.

"Just helping with the history lesson," I said, bowing slightly.

"The Lauderdales," Miss Inez broke in, "held on to their land with a fierce tenacity. They rotated crops and took up cattle farming. The land is with them still."

"What she's saying is my cousin Eli's folks were shrewd and we weren't," I said. One of the ladies tittered. Another fanned her face with a tissue she pulled from her purse.

"Adeline's father, William Green, is one of our prominent citizens," Miss Inez gestured determinedly from me to the cluster. No doubt they found this hard to believe, having heard my family statement. "He crossed those metaphorical tracks from the mill village on the GI bill and is an engineering executive at Bratton. His wife

Jeanette was his childhood sweetheart."

My parents grew up in neighboring bungalows in the Bratton Mill village and were each first in their family to graduate from college, but I didn't bother elaborating for the group.

"So how," a timid question surfacing from the assemblage, "are Miss Green and the Lauderdales related?"

I looked about to determine which of the ladies had asked the obvious question, but all mouths were closed. I couldn't tell.

Miss Inez and I spoke at the same time. She prevailed. "Adeline here," she pointed at me yet again, "her mother is Jeannette Winfield Green whose brother Eugene Winfield married Mary Lily Lauderdale, daughter of Mary Margaret and John Macon Lauderdale. Both of Mary Lily's parents are buried here." She gazed toward the graves. Only the year before in the spring, the azaleas and dogwoods blooming, Mary Margaret—I called her Mimi—had died. She was not my grandmother by blood, but she might as well have been. She was grandmother to my cousin Eli, who was Aunt Mary Lily and Uncle Gene's only child and Mimi's only grandson. I loved her just like he did.

Eli and I had approached Mimi's coffin together—I'd never seen a dead body before and didn't want to look—but he said we were supposed to. I resisted, but in the end he convinced me. Mary Margaret lay in a soft blue dress, her yellow hair coiffed around her face. Not unlike she had been in life: dignified and stately.

"Uncle Gene was a war hero," I interrupted Miss Inez's lecture again. "He fought the Germans in the Battle of the Bulge and earned a Purple Heart and a Bronze Star."

"Yes, indeed," Miss Inez agreed. Nothing further about my uncle was said. I didn't say he had become only a salesman who sold cellophane-bagged cookies to grocery stores out of a Delton Cookies truck. That he was a man my aunt Mary Lily married against her parents' wishes. That he was often hard on Eli.

Miss Inez went on to explain the whole Lauderdale family history starting back before Green Branch even got its name. I stood until they left. I was just reclining on the grass beside the Lauderdale plot to rest a little before I started back up my walk when I saw Miss Inez looming over me, her protégés now in the distance, headed the way they'd come.

4

"I want to say, Adeline," she started. I stared hard at her and she halted.

Then Miss Inez Wilson reached down and touched my face, startling me. "In time, the sadness," she said and paused, I'm sure, because I rudely scowled at her. She adjusted her pocketbook across her arm. "Please tell your folks I send my regards. Lovely people."

I nodded and watched her retreat toward the waiting group. I lay back and looked up at a day full of August sky. Even with some mottled shade from an oak tree nearby, the starchy grass beneath my arms felt hot enough to kindle stones. The sun blazed white, and I squinted against its brilliance. My arm across my face to shield the heat, I thought about school, about not graduating *magna cum laude* as I was supposed to back in the spring. I wasn't trying to be difficult. I simply couldn't do it. I was fully aware of my parents' gift in paying for four years of education, still am.

I must have dozed, for the sound of the noon bells from the clock tower jolted me, though it shouldn't have. I heard them every day. Green Branch is famous for its clock, supposedly the oldest working public clock in the country, erected in the center square in 1832, the year the town was named.

The clock has a set of eight bells in its tower that ring the Cambridge Chimes every hour except on the stroke of noon, when the chimes peal for five full minutes. Eli learned on a peal of eight bells, 40,320 changes are possible. He was mathematical like that.

I roused myself from the grassy spot where I lay beside Lauderdale graves. I wiped the back of my dusty wrist across my wet forehead and then onto my shorts, creating a gray smear. I stood reluctantly and looked toward the street. I considered the walk back to Congress Street, to our house at the end, the last one to be built, a Dutch Colonial constructed of blue granite in the 1940s from the quarry outside of town. It took a century to create the menagerie of houses on our block—Gothic cottages, imposing Mansard Victorians, bungalows, Queen Anne Gingerbreads, and lots of Early American Revival.

Eli's house, across the road from ours but farther back off the street, is the oldest and grandest, a late Victorian ennobled by a turret and surrounded by an ornate, wrought-iron fence. A wedding gift from Mary Margaret Lauderdale for her daughter and son-in-law. Its crowning glory is a triangular window of stained glass set into a large front gable. A window that both colored and obscured the childhood paradise within: the attic junk room where Eli and I contemplated the mysteries of our world.

1

JUNE 1959

The day before Eli's third birthday, in early morning with the heat yet
bearable, Mama and I dug in the soil along the stepping stones to our
front door. She wielded a spade and I dug with a spoon. On June 4, it
was late in the season to plant summer flowers, but I wanted them, and
my mother surrendered. The day before—Mama has told me the
prophetic story many times—I picked a stalk from white, feathery
wildflowers in the corner of our lot and walked across the street to show
Mary Lily. My aunt was working among her flowering perennials—
phlox, columbine, and salvia—the names exotic and the blossoms
alluring.

"Oh, Adeline," she exclaimed, "you have Queen Anne's lace
blossoming early this year. There's not a wildflower that grows more
beautiful." I imagine her sweeping her arms open in that way she has,
as though she is gliding through water.

She told me then a legend of the dark purplish red in the center
of Queen Anne's lace. That it formed when a magic queen spinning
lace petals onto the flower pricked her finger and spilled a single drop
of blood. I was sad that such a lovely creation bore this stain, and she
soothed me by saying the blemish was the heart of the flower's beauty.
"I want to grow flowers like you," I told Mary Lily. She called my
mother that evening, and the next morning we made a trip to the
garden store.

Some people can retain early memories, but for me, this is not
true. For me, the day of the marigolds is my only detailed memory
during the year when I was just over midway to my fourth birthday. I
can close my eyes and still see the half-planted row of robust orange
plants laid out along the stones—the only flowers I've ever known my
mother to put into the earth. The other half remained undisturbed in
their little plastic cartons.

I am exactly seven months older than Eli. My birthday is

November 5. Had I been born several days earlier, I would have been a grade ahead of my cousin. Instead, by missing the November 1 deadline, I was the oldest in my class. We thought those few days connecting Eli and me according to grade were a fortune of fate. It was our parents who put the idea in our young heads, for they knew how a moment changed everything. How devotion might be born from catastrophe.

I was patting dirt around a seedling while Mama held the fragile stalk steady when a loud and alarming cry shook us from our task. We looked up to see Pot—he'd been working in the yard—run from the side door of the Winfield house with Eli in his arms. Mary Lily stood on the front porch watering ferns, and I watched her wide skirt fan out into a circle as she nearly stumbled in her haste down the white wooden steps toward Pot. Her straw hat flopped down low over her forehead.

Mama pulled off her gardening gloves, and I tried to dash across the street, but she caught me. "No, Delia," she said. Her hands were tight on my shoulders.

"Something's wrong with Eli," I wailed.

"Whatever it is, we don't need to hamper them," she said. My mother shoved the new gardening gloves into the waistband of her blue-checked pedal pushers. I liked seeing my mama relaxed in her pedal pushers because in those days she nearly always wore a dress. She wasn't so fixed up as June Cleaver, but she did wear, perpetually, the same shirtwaist dresses, cinched with a narrow belt, coupled with an apron around her middle.

Mama took my hand. Hers was damp. Together we hurried to the edge of our front yard, close enough to hear, but we did not cross the street.

Pot had caught up to Mary Lily at the bottom of the steps. We were in hearing range, but he talked so fast I had to grasp at phrases. Pot Hawkins works for the Winfields, but to say he's their gardener hardly begins to identify his place in their world. His family has been connected to Mary Lily's maybe since the end of slavery. All I know is he and his mother Caro have lived in their little house out in the country on Lauderdale land all my life.

"That Red Devil Lye in the Coca-Cola bottle Mr. Gene done left on the back stoop," I heard him say. "For them balloons." And then for a while I could not follow the words until I heard, "Mister Eli drunk some of it."

I heard Eli breathing, even from across the street. I thought he was choking because his face was contorted, his cheeks sucking in.

"My God. Oh, God. Help me, Pot. Get Ellison into the house. Milk. He needs milk," Mary Lily screamed.

My mother began to run toward our house, pulling me by the hand.

"What is Red Devil Lye?" I sputtered as I slipped and staggered alongside her, trying to keep my arm in its socket. But she didn't answer.

Inside the house, she made a call and I heard her say the name of our street. Then she sat with her head in her hands.

"What is Red Devil Lye?" I asked again.

"It cleans drains, but my brother must have been using it to blow up balloons for the party."

"Did Uncle Gene hurt Eli?" I asked.

"I'm sorry, baby," she said, and smoothed my hair. "I can't explain it. I have to be quiet and think what to do." She picked up a pencil and paper and began to write.

The next thing I remember was the deafening shriek of the ambulance siren and Mama jolting from her chair. Again, she grabbed my hand and began to run. I kept up better this time, and unlike before, we crossed the street. Yet we stood back, waiting.

I watched terrified as two men in white, waist-length coats brought Eli out on a stretcher. His arms bent in at the elbows and stuck out like wings. I saw his mouth opening and closing and then he vomited on himself. I heard him heaving. One of the men took the bottom of the sheet covering Eli and wiped away the yellow spew.

Mary Lily hurried behind the stretcher, but before she climbed into the ambulance, she looked toward Mama. She was crying while she talked. "Call Dr. Crawford and tell him we are on our way to the hospital in Columbia, not Green Branch." My mother and about everyone else in town worshipped Dr. Crawford. He had stayed with my mother the whole twenty-four hours she was in labor with me, napping on a cot nearby.

As a child I loved our doctor, but I feared him, too, for visits to his office often resulted in a painful shot of penicillin. Even with a temperature of 103 degrees and a throat so swollen with pus I could hardly swallow without tears, I was never so sick that I didn't dread the needle burning into my hip. So at the mention of Dr. Crawford, I knew Eli must be very sick.

The ambulance turned on its siren again and pulled away from the curb. Mary Lily and Pot and Eli were all inside. Suddenly, the vehicle stopped and Mary Lily opened the back door and leaned out, calling to Mama. "Dear God, Jeanette. Find Gene. Tell him." And then the ambulance was gone, carrying Eli away in a loud blur of wheels and warning bells.

"Tell him what?" I asked Mama.

"Tell him Eli has had an accident," she said. Her face pulled taut with something like reproach, or maybe it was only sorrow and fear. I was too young to define it. Yet I remember the way her eyes stared out at nothing, her mouth open and grimaced. And knowing somehow she was thinking about both Eli and Uncle Gene.

"What is wrong with him?" I asked. Her head snapped around.

"The lye, it's likely burned everything in its path through his body," she said.

"He's burned like in a fire?" I asked.

Maybe there was fear in my voice because Mama clamped shut and would say nothing more. She looked at me curiously, but she didn't speak. Young as I was, I recognized she had told me a gruesome truth she hadn't meant to tell her child.

Mama had to go inside to make calls to find her brother. "Let me stay out here," I said.

She looked at me sternly but relented. "Don't dare leave this yard. I'll watch out the window," she said.

I thought about my cousin Eli. How poison going down your throat would feel if it burned everything on its way. Like fire, it would turn things black. Your tongue. Your throat. And maybe your veins would turn from blue to black. I'd seen what weed poison did to plants in Mary Lily's garden. Pot never let us come near when he sprayed, but I'd seen afterward what it did to once-green life. It turned things brown and dry, then black like ash, and then they were dead.

I stared at the spot where the ambulance had parked. I wiped at my eyes. But when I noticed the arc of blue, green, and violet spread in the road, rainbow oil lying slick in a thin puddle settled in a dip in the street from a thunderstorm during the night, I felt consoled. Because I knew the meaning of rainbows. I would not imagine Eli turning to black ashes inside, even as my own throat clinched, feeling charred and dry.

2

NOVEMBER 1959

Eli did not die. But he almost did. His esophagus and windpipe were severely burned, the trauma and inflammation threatening to block his breath, so a tracheotomy was performed immediately after he arrived at the hospital in Columbia. It might have been the critical care nurse with a snug twist of white hair wound beneath her black-striped cap who really saved Eli's life. A few hours after his surgery, she spoke privately to Mary Lily in Eli's room, saying she was risking her job by her disclosure: she didn't believe Ellison would live more than a week unless he was transported to a children's hospital specializing in poison cases. She suggested Boston. Her formal, forthright manner, and perhaps even her authoritative starched cap, convinced Mary Lily who then convinced Uncle Gene.

Eli stayed in Boston Children's Hospital for six months. I remember asking my parents over and over, week after week, when he would come home, why he wasn't home, and being told very little. My parents determined—and maybe they were right—the less I knew the better. It was many years before I understood, mostly from my mother, the rudimentary facts of my cousin's life in the hospital and his early years at home.

The food issue was extremely problematic, for Eli could not swallow. His team of physicians determined he must have an operation to make a direct entry—a gastrostomy, a word still heavy and foreign in my head—into his stomach. The hole was kept shut with a plug. When it was time for Eli to eat, the plug was removed and food was inserted straight into his belly.

Repeatedly during his hospital stay and for the years afterward on his return trips, a rubber dilator was pulled to and fro through Eli's stomach and up through his throat to keep his damaged esophagus open. The dilation was accomplished with the aid of a string running through his body, starting in the stomach opening and threading upward through my cousin's nose, then behind his ear where it was secured behind his neck.

When I first saw Eli after the accident, the string both fascinated and puzzled me. It looked like ordinary white, cotton twine, often slipping from its place tucked behind his ear and falling across his lower cheek. I asked questions until my mother relented and tried to explain. The doctors in the hospital tugged on the string in Eli's nose to pull the tube through his gastric tract to his throat, she said. Then they reversed the course by pulling on the other end of the string stationed at the hole in his stomach. "Why?" I asked my mother.

"The poison caused scar tissue. And other things I don't know. The doctors have to keep everything open," she said.

"Does it hurt?" I asked.

"They give him medicine so it doesn't hurt as much," she said.

Her explanation made little sense to me. I didn't know what scar tissue meant. I was too young to envision it. And I had never seen— nor would I ever see—the bottom end of the string.

I could, however, imagine the pain of an object in Eli's throat, since I had once tried to swallow an aspirin. The hard, solid pill made me gag. It terrified me, and I refused to try again. So whenever I needed it, Mama mashed up aspirin with the back of a teaspoon in Coca-Cola, and I drank it from a cup.

I learned much later the doctors in Boston recommended my aunt and uncle put Eli in an institutional setting and predicted he would never be able to live at home. Mary Lily and Gene refused to believe them.

When they brought him home, Mary Lily had learned how to feed Eli. She ground his food in the blender, removed his stomach plug herself, and inserted the pureed mush into his stomach with a turkey baster. After each meal, she taped the plug back in place.

Eli's parents could not, however, maneuver the dilator on their own. So, routinely, Eli returned to Boston Children's Hospital. The trips were costly and disruptive. And Eli hated each one. Finally, toward the end of second grade, when his esophagus was bigger, an alternative was proposed. Eli could swallow a flexible tube weekly instead of having the procedure in Boston. He was promised the permanent removal of the string as incentive to learn how to swallow the dilator and pull it back out himself.

I never witnessed the swallowing, but I well recall seeing the ubiquitous nightmare tube in its coiled position on the bathroom counter, a grotesque pink mockery of human intestines. Uncle Gene first swallowed the two-and-a-half-foot length. He coated the tube with Vaseline and with much gagging and regurgitation learned to swallow it so he could teach his son. I cannot imagine how Eli, so young, swallowed and endured the pain of the torturous object that expanded the thin, fragile passage down his throat.

✍

On November 5 of the year Eli was confined in the Boston Children's Hospital, I turned four in Green Branch, the occasion celebrated with a splendid birthday party in my backyard. It was a mild afternoon, and we wore only sweaters for wraps. The decorations were designed by nature, a multitude of red and gold leaves on the oak and maple trees. There were no balloons, and at the time I didn't notice, didn't miss them. Odd, though, how I vividly recall us drinking Coca-Colas through paper straws out of green, six-ounce bottles.

Eight little girls plus Mary Lily—home for a few days to check on things—attended. Uncle Gene was traveling.

To my dismay, I do not recall missing or even thinking of Eli in the hospital that day. I was a small child, absorbed in myself.

My parents gave me a jungle gym that birthday, and my father had finished piecing it together late the day before the party. We must have been a sight: nine little girls hanging upside down on multi-leveled monkey bars, dresses and crinolines covering our heads, our legs and white-laced panties turned up to the sun.

After gifts and cake—maybe to kill time until mothers retrieved their daughters—my mother asked each guest to tell a story. Nealy Simmons' narration fascinated me most. She told of owning a magic carpet, as tall as a door. I can see her now, hands lifting for emphasis. I don't recall if she actually did lift her hands, but it has always been a grand gesture of hers, so I imagine she did. She described a blue rug with thick, red fringe. It stayed under her bed, she said, until she wanted to take a ride. She claimed it had taken her around the world.

14

Right then, I wanted to ride with Nealy on her magic carpet. It wouldn't have to be far. Just a spin around Green Branch where I could wave to everyone below while we flew among the treetops.

After the party, I could think of nothing else but Nealy and wanting to fly. I talked Mama into letting me invite her to spend the night with me. I believed if I could offer something as exciting as my friend's magic carpet—I had in mind one of my daddy's scary stories— she would be impressed and take me for a ride. Nearly every night Daddy read to me from my mother's frayed college book of children's literature, and for Nealy, I asked him to read us "Little Orphant Annie" because it was a poem full of mystery and excitement.

Listening to Daddy read this poem was like someone tickling the bottom of my feet. If I was in the right mood, I had the nerve and stamina to withstand it, and it was exquisite. But at other times, I couldn't bear it.

That evening, he sat at the foot of my twin bed while I lay curled on my side facing Nealy, who sat upright against the headboard of the other twin bed. In his slow, expressive way, Daddy became the old backwoods Hoosier speaker in Riley's poem. He dropped letters, swallowed words, ran the sounds together. He paused expectantly in certain moments, his voice rising and falling with the rhythm of the lines. At the first refrain, "An' the gobble-uns 'at gets you / Ef you / Don't / Watch / Out," Nealy yelped like a frightened puppy. My father didn't falter but continued on. At the end, he quietly closed the book and folded his glasses back into his shirt pocket. He was maybe thinking of what he should do next when Nealy bounded across from her bed to mine. Her eyes in that moment looked like big brown bubbles eclipsing her whole face.

"Oh," Daddy said, "is everything all right?"

Nealy squeezed up beside me. I felt my heart pumping. She was scared—and so was I—but for me it was a good kind of scared.

"There's nothing to be scared of," I lied, "they aren't coming here," because, of course, I wanted her to believe they were. Being scared meant being amazed. And that meant matching the exhilaration of her magic carpet.

"Have you ever been as bad as Annie?" I asked. "Made fun of all your 'blood and kin.'"

"No," Nealy muttered. She squinched her eyes shut and put her head down.

"That's enough, Adeline," my father said. I understood this tone and stopped.

"Those goblins aren't real," Daddy said and told Nealy please not to worry. I imagine he swiped his palm back and forth across his head—prematurely balding until soon it would be a smooth dome surrounded with only a dark fringe of hair—a habit he falls into when nervous. She didn't look up.

"Read us the 'Quangle Wangle's Hat,'" I suggested.

"Maybe it's time to settle down," he said instead. "Why don't you girls both sleep in Delia's bed? I'll lie down on this other bed and rest until you fall asleep. Sweet dreams until the morning light." He kissed the tops of our heads.

I woke the next morning to Nealy bumping my ribs. She was in a rollicking mood now in the daylight. At breakfast she brought up the goblins in "Little Orphant Annie" and the little boy who disappeared because he wouldn't say his prayers. "It isn't real," she said. She looked at me.

"How do you know?" I asked.

"Because it isn't. Because you can't see goblins."

"It doesn't matter if you can't see something," I said. "It can still be there."

"I made all that up about my magic carpet," she said. "I don't really have one." I saw her open mouth full of mushy cereal and milk.

The words felt like a wind blowing me backward, the kind of strong gust to make a child lose her balance, and for a moment I couldn't speak.

"Are you sure?" I finally said.

"Oh, yes," she responded with glee. She put down her spoon. She grinned at me and pushed at her sleep-tangled hair falling into her face.

"I didn't really believe you anyway," I said defiantly. I set my spoon down, too.

And so we were even, our friendship begun through the great perils of illusion and fear. My mother, cheery, seemed to appear from nowhere. Had she been at the stove behind us the whole time? Most likely, that was the case, for she produced a slice of pound cake, toasted with butter, already cut in two exact halves for Nealy and me. It was her own favorite treat, consumed with coffee and the newspaper after Daddy left for work, and until then, a luxury I'd never been allowed.

3

DECEMBER 1959

Eli came home in mid-December. I didn't see him right away, not until a few days later when my parents invited Gene, Mary Lily, and Eli for dinner. My mother served me early since Eli could not eat. We would play while the grown-ups ate.

They tried to prepare me, explaining Eli breathed through a hole in his throat where the air went in and out just as air did in the holes in my nose. Still, on first seeing him—I tried not to—I stared. A child barely four years old is drawn to such a sight. In the hollow of the raw, wrinkled skin of his throat was a silver disc with two small holes, held in place with white tape. While Eli stood still in front of me, I must have grasped the valley of my own neck because I recall my father reaching for my hand and pulling it down to my side. The rest of Eli that I could see, disregarding the string running strangely through his nose, looked like Eli, but the silver plate—emitting a thin trickle I would soon understand was the same as when I had a runny nose—bewildered me.

Caro came with the Winfields to watch after Eli and me to give our parents some time to themselves. She was staying in town with them while Eli settled in. She must have been nearly seventy then, but Caro had the energy of a much younger woman. Under her arm she carried the board game Candyland. She bent down to me and whispered, "Master Ellison"—as she referred to him back then, often in a weirdly mixed tone of unease and admiration—"he run short of breath easily. We having quiet games."

We spread out on the rectangular, flowered rug in my bedroom. Caro folded at her knees, her long legs crossing under her. I remember her heavy black oxford shoes poking out beneath a long, printed house dress. She announced the rules required the youngest player go first. I knew Eli should be the one to go first anyhow because he was sick.

It looked like I would win until I drew the Peppermint Stick

Forest card and had to move my pawn nearly back to Start. Then Eli drew the Lollipop Woods card and moved forward a long way around the board, far ahead of Caro and me. He landed at the Candy House to win while I was only halfway there. I was a competitive child, yet I recall a feeling of strange relief when Eli won.

After the game, Caro read to us. I sat across from Eli during Candyland, but now he sat close beside me, and I smelled his curdled scent. I didn't know then that the odor emanated from the hole in his stomach. Even with the hole plugged and taped, the fetid smell of decomposing food was always present.

I noticed also the husky sound of his breathing, a sound like Mama's coffee pot percolating. I became so aware of the inhale and exhale of his breath that the timing of my own breathing fell into his and unsettled me. I tried not to pay attention so I could return to my own rhythm. But I couldn't. I could not break away.

After a while, Eli lay on the rug. He'd hardly spoken all night except for his hooting hurray when he won at Candyland. I had looked in panic at Caro, believing Eli was choking when he spoke, for he first took a deep, wheezing breath and covered the disc in his throat with his index finger. "It gonna be all right," Caro had said, caressing my arm. "Master Eli is covering that hole so his breath can go out the right way through his mouth and nose to make his vocal cords work better. Let him be."

I didn't realize he'd fallen asleep until Caro stopped reading and lifted him onto my other twin bed, turning up the bottom corner of the green spread in a triangle shape to cover my cousin.

I didn't want to sleep. I asked to see my parents, and Caro yielded. I heard Uncle Gene's gruff laugh as I approached the blue haze of cigarette smoke hovering around the dining room's open door. In those days, it was the exception for an adult not to smoke. My mother was the exception in this group.

All four adults looked toward me when I appeared. Though dinner was over—the empty dessert plates in front of them on the table—the glasses still held wine. When she saw me, Mary Lily gasped and laid her cigarette on the brimming ashtray near her. She stood.

"Adeline," she said, "where is Ellison? Is he all right?" Dangling gold earrings connected in three linked hoops swung from her ears.

Even under the cascade of her gold wheat hair—not bound behind a hair band or shaped into a French twist that night—I caught their gleam. Most mothers in Green Branch didn't have pierced ears, at least not then. My own mother didn't approve of pierced ears. But I longed to be beautiful and exotic like Mary Lily.

"He's asleep," I said.

"Y'all had a good time, didn't you," Gene said, looking at me. He beamed one of his big, wide grins. I loved my uncle Gene, but even then, I often felt ill at ease in his presence. You never knew what he was going to say or what his mood might be. He was a bit shorter than Mary Lily, but thick and strong like the men in muscle magazines. His hard-angled flattop—a relic from his military service—heightened the suggestion of his tough-guy manner. He once told me he didn't own a comb, proclaiming such an item was for sissies.

"We played Candyland," I said.

"Good for you," he said. I told him Eli won, and he grinned again.

"It's time to go," Mary Lily said. She remained standing. "Please carry Eli," she said to Gene. I watched him drink the remainder of his wine in one long swallow before stepping toward my bedroom.

"We're going to have a surprise at Christmas," he called to me over his shoulder as they left, Eli's head dangling over his back.

Days leading up to Christmas were the best days. The anticipation of magic, the grand imagining of gifts left mysteriously in the night beside the fireplace—these things enthralled me. On Christmas Eve that year, Mama claimed she heard sleigh bells on the roof and said if I weren't in bed, Santa would pass over our house. But I wanted to hear the bells, too, so I lay my head on Mama's green hairbrush, the bristles piercing my scalp, in an attempt to stay awake. I failed. I missed the great elf deliver the gifts on my list.

Among the things I had asked for—a gun and holster set, a cowboy outfit, a record player—I had a surprise, too: the doll named Marybel, Madame Alexander's "doll that gets well." She characterized the romanticism of convalescence. It wasn't until years later I realized whenever I'd removed the measles spots from Marybel's rosy cheeks or unsnapped her leg cast, the subliminal message was always there: Eli was a child who would get well.

℘

I wondered what Santa brought Eli, but his family had left to have Christmas dinner with Mary Margaret out in the country. And in the middle of the afternoon, Mama packed the supper she'd been cooking all day to take to Grandmama Loula's in the mill village. My only living grandparent, my father's mother, stayed mostly confined at home because she was sick. Back then, it was called mill fever, but now we call it brown lung—a disease that develops when a cotton mill worker breathes too much cotton dust for too many years.

Daddy's brother and his wife and their twins a year older than I, Nancy and Glenn, were there from Norfolk, Virginia. I looked forward to seeing these cousins on holidays, but in truth, we never knew quite what to do with each other. It wasn't like being with Eli. Maybe the distance was partly to blame, but deep down I knew it was more than that.

The next morning I begged to cross the street to see Eli by myself because Mama was busy undecorating the Christmas tree and Daddy had returned to work. When she said no, I stomped my foot at her. She sent me to my room. Fifteen minutes later, post confinement, I returned to hover and rebuke my mother for taking down our beautiful tree so early. Winding a strand of pearls from the branches around the spread fingers of one hand, my mother responded calmly that leaving a tree up after Christmas was bad luck. The truth was the minute Christmas day was over, my mother wanted her house back in order. I must have continued to pester her because the next thing I knew, she was on the phone with Nealy's mother asking if Nealy could come over to play with me.

My friend arrived just after lunch with her new Betsy Wetsy doll. After a while, all Betsy's diapers were wet, so we fed her the bottle and watched the water drip from between her legs. It was a funny sight, but when I laughed, Nealy pouted and went off by herself.

With Nealy sulking, my mother's plan to occupy me while she put away Christmas backfired. She had no choice but to step in and figure

21

out how to direct us.

I saw my opportunity and jumped at it. I told Nealy there was some kind of surprise at Eli's house and we could find out what if Mama would only let us go. And suddenly, we were on our way, each of us holding one of Mama's hands as we exited the front door.

We climbed the steps to the Winfields' porch, really three porches wrapped around three sides of the house beneath the first-floor eaves of lacy, ornamental woodwork. I heard piano music from inside. Mary Lily was a graduate of the Juilliard School. She had played the piano from the time she was very young, and her parents thought her talent deserved the best of music schools. They also believed if they sent her to a school far away from Green Branch, not only would she return an even more accomplished musician, but the distance would dissuade her from Uncle Gene, her high school sweetheart. The second part of their plan did not work.

Mary Lily's family was above ours. My family labored in the cotton mill to survive after the Civil War. We'd been left with only a name and a family Bible authenticating our pre-war station. The Lauderdales, however, had an ongoing genteel and moneyed history, evident in all that surrounded them except my uncle, who brought the Winfield name into their midst. But more than snobbery, I believe what prompted Mary Lily's parents to separate her from my uncle during their youth was his reputation as a wild and unpredictable boy, a boy who once rode a horse into the high school just to be outrageous. Two siblings could not have been more different than my uncle and my mother, and I have often wondered to what extent she is aware of her efforts to balance the scale in her constant aim for the highest propriety.

In the end, Mary Margaret and Eli's grandfather, John Macon Lauderdale (dead from a heart attack a few months before Eli's birth), couldn't stop their daughter. Uncle Gene came home from World War II a hero, and Mary Lily, having written him hundreds of letters overseas, was more smitten than ever. They eloped, not quite so romantically as Mary Lily climbing down from a balcony bedroom window, but by her sneaking out of the front door on a moonless, January night, shortly after her Juilliard graduation. She wore the taupe lace suit purchased for her senior recital and carried an overnight bag with cosmetics and a change of underwear for the 35-mile drive to

Columbia, a journey from which they returned married the next day.

In their escape, they traipsed down the long, magnolia-lined drive of the Lauderdale house, aptly named Magnolia Manor, to Gene's Plymouth Coupe he'd bought before the war with his long-saved earnings as a bag boy after school at the A&P. He had parked the car on the dirt road no one much used anymore because of the paved highway running parallel.

Now, standing on the Winfields' porch, Mama rang the doorbell, and the music stopped. Mary Lily opened the door and swept her arms open.

"Oh, Adeline," she exclaimed. "And here's a friend with you. Paul and Linda Simmons' little girl, I do believe." She wore a blouse with the shirttail out and black Bermuda shorts underneath. Her teardrop silver earrings swung unimpeded by her ponytailed hair.

"Hello, Mrs. Winfield," Nealy politely said.

"Oh no," Mary Lily said. "Call me Mary Lily. And Nealy, is it short for something else?" That was an odd thing about Mary Lily. She was the most informal of women in the manner she wished to be approached, but the most formal in her expression toward others of any adult I knew then or now.

"Is it?" I turned to my friend and asked. It had not occurred to me Nealy might be a nickname.

"Not really," she said. She twisted a finger in her hair.

"Why, I'm sure it is," said Mary Lily. "And for a beautiful name, I'm sure. Do tell us."

Perhaps it was the sureness of my aunt's tone and bending down to her at eye level that made Nealy reveal the truth.

"It's Cornelia, my mother's middle name."

"Oh, how enchanting," Mary Lily said. "Did you know Cornelia was a famous Roman mother of twelve children?"

Nealy gave a slight shake of her head, the kind where you don't know whether a person is saying yes or no. But associating herself with a famous mother made her smile, for mothering was what she loved.

"Come in, all of you," Mary Lily said, gesturing toward my mother. "Ellison will be so happy. He has something to show you, too. Ellison," she called out. "Come along," she said when Eli didn't answer. "He's back in the solarium with Eugene." She swept her long, elegant

23

hands about. "Girls, you've come at a most wonderful time to see the surprise out back."

I skipped ahead of Mama and Nealy. I arrived at the entry of the solarium to see Gene and Eli gazing into the yard from the back panel of windows.

This magnificent room grew out from the back of the house. Mary Lily called it her sanctuary between nature and people. The room rose to the full height of the second floor in a curved ceiling supported by arched wooden beams. The walls were mahogany panels separated by wide plates of paned glass, so that dark and light continuously confronted one another.

Gene turned around toward me, but Eli remained facing the windows.

"Why is his daddy home?" Nealy whispered when she caught up a second or two later. We stood in the doorway with Mama.

"Maybe because of the surprise," I said, "and maybe because it's Christmastime," but in truth Gene was often home. My daddy worked five and a half days a week at Bratton Mill, but Gene's job was different. He seemed to work when he wanted to. I came to understand—Mama made no secret about it, always in her tone of disapproval—her brother didn't really have to work because of Mary Lily's money.

"Ellison," Mary Lily said, making the syllables of his name a melody, "you have company. See?"

He finally turned, saw it was me, and sprinted toward us as well as he could for Eli. "Hey, Delia, see what I got?" When he spoke, he moved an index finger to cover the hole in the silver plate on his throat. The gesture allowed air to flow outward through his mouth, not through his throat, so that his vocal cords could operate better. Even then, his voice strained and wheezed and scratched at the words.

"What?' I exclaimed.

"First, here's someone for you to meet," Mary Lily said to Eli. She stepped aside and motioned us into the room, introducing my friend. Nealy and Eli barely spoke, so I started up again.

"What is it, Eli?" I demanded.

"A pig. A real live pig. Like on a farm," he said. "Come on."

"A pig? Why did you get a pig?"

"Because I wanted one," he said. "Right, Dad?" Eli returned to the window and patted his hands on his knees. He was happy.

"Right, boy. Damn right." Gene waved to us to come close to the windows.

"This is Nealy," I said, walking over to Uncle Gene.

"Why, I thought I was seeing double," he said. "But I see there are two of you taking pretty pills." He winked at us.

"Wanna go outside and see him?" Eli asked. "His name is Fred." His excitement made his words catch.

I couldn't wait to see Fred. I thought maybe Gene would take us outside, but it was Eli who led us, with Nealy and me behind, flanking Mary Lily.

Fred had arrived only two days before, but already the yard smelled sour, and in places, I felt something slick beneath my feet.

The pig noticed us at once. He was a baby, but he looked awfully big now that we were in the same space. As we continued to walk toward him, he walked, too. Then, suddenly, he hurdled toward us. He bypassed Eli and came at Mary Lily, Nealy, and me. I don't know how she did it, but my aunt swooped up Nealy and me, each in an arm, just as Fred arrived at her feet. I reached down and touched him, then pulled away, his tiny stiff hairs and tough skin startling me. Nealy had drawn herself into a ball under Mary Lily's arm and wasn't studying about touching Fred.

"Go on, go on now," Mary Lily exclaimed to the pig. She shook her foot at him. But shaking her foot was the wrong thing to do. It got Fred really interested. He rooted his snout around her feet. Then, he bit down on the bow of her patent leather shoe. Mary Lily tried to run, but we were too heavy in her arms. Fred pulled off the bow, and the force caused the pump to slip off Mary Lily's foot. She ran backward wearing one shoe and with us still in her arms. Eli trailed behind.

From inside, we watched Fred chewing on the bow. "Well, it doesn't matter. It doesn't matter a bit," Mary Lily said, but I felt bad. On our account, she had gone out in the muck to brave Fred, and he had ruined a good shoe. My mother stood looking at Mary Lily's naked, dirty foot, dumbstruck.

And then Uncle Gene started laughing, not a little, but fiercely. It seemed a mean thing to do. He laughed until he had Eli laughing, too. Nealy made a couple of little squeaking sounds, but it wasn't laughter.

I don't know what it was. I remained quiet, caught between the harsh laughter and Mary Lily's brave look. "My brother thinks giving his son a pig can appease his guilt," I heard Mama mutter under her breath to no one. I looked over at her, at her face rigid with disgust.

It wasn't long after Fred's arrival, just a few weeks, before the neighbors directly behind the Winfields on Baylor Street complained to the city about the noise. Fred had to leave, in spite of Uncle Gene's protests. I never asked where he went.

4

MARCH 1962

My baby sister Helen arrived in the early spring of my first-grade year. I'd been an only child for a long time with my parents' full attention and hardly knew what to make of her. I would walk in her room when she was sleeping and peer into the bassinette. I thought of her as a baby chick submerged in a nest of white netting. One evening just after dinner, she was so still and quiet in her bassinette, I couldn't resist the urge to pinch her leg. She awoke screaming and Daddy rushed into the room. "What happened here?" he demanded.

"I don't know," I lied. I didn't fully know why I pinched her and didn't know why I lied. In my conscious mind, I thought of it as an experiment, to see what the baby would do. Unconsciously, of course, I was jealous. Daddy lifted Helen from her bassinette and felt her diaper.

"Are you sure?" he asked again. I nodded. Mama arrived, her hair drawn roughly behind her ears so that I could see the roots of silver. Prematurely gray, she persistently colored her hair its natural dark auburn to hide the fact. I suppose with Helen's birth, she'd gotten behind in her schedule. She and Daddy began to whisper. She took Helen from his arms and sat with her in the rocking chair. They glided up and back, and Helen's crying immediately ceased.

"You come with me," Daddy said. His voice was stern but kind, too. We watched *Mr. Ed*, one of my favorite shows. Afterward, I brushed my teeth and Daddy read one of our favorite stories, *And to Think That I Saw It on Mulberry Street*. Before he left, we knelt on the floor beside my bed to say my prayers. He put his hand on top of my head and patted my hair. Always at the end, I was supposed to pray for the specific people and things on my mind. That night, for the first time, I added my sister to my list.

"And God bless Helen," I said. "She's a tiny baby and can't take care of herself."

"That's a nice prayer, Adeline," Daddy said.

~

The next day after school, I learned I would spend the weekend at Eli's house. Looking back, I realize my parents needed to separate me from the baby for a little while, and they knew I'd be happy at Eli's. My backyard had a jungle gym, a whirligig, and a swing set with a sliding board. But Eli's yard was far more appealing. Mama always had one eye on me at home, while at Eli's we roamed free.

There were Mary Lily's gardens with paths to wander and hidden spots for make-believe, especially the six-sided gazebo where Pot or Mary Lily served us tea parties on the old wicker table with its curlicue legs. Often, we played house there. Eli always got to be the father, and I was the mother unless Nealy was with us; then we had to take turns being the mother. The one left over had to be the child.

The four of us—Gene, Mary Lily, Eli, and me—sat at the dinner table Friday evening discussing what Eli and I would do on Saturday. Eli never seemed to mind watching the rest of us eat.

"How does Eli eat?" I asked, as though he weren't sitting beside me, and though I already had a general sense of the answer from my parents.

Gene coughed and picked up his can of Budweiser. Mary Lily set down her fork and looked directly at me.

"Of course, you must wonder, Adeline," she said. Then she looked at Eli before she continued.

"Ellison ate a little while ago before you arrived, the same thing we are eating right now." On my plate were a pork chop, yellow squash, and fried okra.

"Why can't you eat with us?" I asked Eli directly, but Mary Lily answered for him.

"He eats differently from us," she explained. "You chew your food and swallow it. Ellison's food is ground another way and goes directly into his stomach without swallowing."

"Oh," I said. I wanted to ask if I could watch him eat, but I didn't.

I knew what my parents would say.

"Let's talk about what you two will do tomorrow," Mary Lily said.

Eli spoke. "Let's invite Nealy over," he said. Eli didn't have many friends besides me because, for one thing, he didn't go to school. He had a private tutor for first grade because he didn't have the stamina to go to school all day. He could play in the yard and do most things, but his energy wore out quickly.

"Why, that's a lovely idea," Mary Lily agreed. "I'll call Linda after dinner to see if she can bring Cornelia to play."

While we were watching *The Flintstones* in the den, Mary Lily came in to tell us Nealy would arrive in the morning. Eli was ecstatic.

Mary Lily brought me an enormous fluffy white towel and washcloth and instructed me to take my bath in her bathroom when the cartoon ended. She explained when I was clean, she would tuck me into bed in the room I liked with the pink chenille bedspread and white lace curtains.

"What about Eli?" I asked.

"Oh, he's going to get clean, too," she said, nodding and grasping her long, straight fall of hair into a ponytail. Eli grimaced. I knew he couldn't sit in a bathtub the way I did. I didn't know how he bathed, but I knew the holes in his stomach and throat could not go underwater. But he had his own bathroom connected to his room, an amenity I couldn't imagine. At my house, while Mama and Daddy had a small bathroom with a makeshift shower stall connected to their bedroom, we all shared one tub in the hall bath.

I enjoyed Mary Lily's bathroom, with its delightful slightly lemony scent of her. And my bath, piled with bubbles. But I couldn't completely relax, as I dreaded going to bed.

Until I was much older, I feared sleeping in any bed alone if it was not my own bed in my own home, even in a place I knew as well as Eli's. So when I'd asked about Eli, I'd really been asking where he was going to sleep. I wished Mary Lily would offer to let me sleep in his room, or at least let him sleep in the room with me. Eli made me feel safe. I hinted around, saying I would fall asleep faster if I slept with Eli. "You'll be more comfortable if you spread out in your own bed," my aunt countered.

After Mary Lily left to run my bath, I asked Uncle Gene if Eli could sleep in the bed with me, but he was noncommittal. "That's not my department," he said. "I don't see a problem, but it's up to your aunt Mary Lily."

"Don't be a scaredy-cat," Eli admonished. "Nothing's going to get you."

"I'm not scared," I shot back. Though, of course, I was.

I lay awake under the soft spread for a long time, staring at the ceiling. I tried to concentrate on a small dark spot I could make out in the dim glow provided by the hall night-light. I did not let myself look at the windows because any crossing shadow—the limb of a tree swaying or the rare passing set of headlights—frightened me. Twice, I climbed out of the bed and looked under it, and also behind the door, to make certain no one was waiting to jump out at me.

At some point, I did fall asleep, clutching the second bed pillow to my stomach. The morning light coming through the thin lace curtains woke me, and I leaped to the floor in joy.

≈

We'd just finished a tea party of limeade and sugar cookies in the six-sided gazebo. Eli, of course, only pretended to eat. If Nealy wondered why, she didn't ask on that warm spring Saturday afternoon when one of my mother's many sayings—three is a crowd—happened.

We had decided to play house. We were sitting at the old wicker table, my feet crossed around one of its ornate legs, when Eli suddenly stood, raised a white china saucer above his head, and declared whoever reached it first would get to be the mother that day.

"That's not fair," I screamed. "I'm not tall enough, and Nealy was the mother last time."

"It is fair, Delia," Eli responded. "All's fair in love and war. Don't you know that?" (It was a phrase he'd heard somewhere, maybe from his father; I don't know, but the idea gave him a sense of power.) "Come and get it," he taunted me. Nealy towered over me by probably three inches on her long, skinny legs. I stood no chance of grasping the saucer. Jumping would only make me look stupid. Torn between pride and desire, I stood watching my cousin turn the little plate back and forth in half circles above his head.

Nealy moved away from the table and stepped toward Eli. Her hand stretched up toward the plate while she looked at me, wondering, I guess, if I was really going to give it away so easily. I remained stoic.

"You're jealous, Delia, because you're short," she said.

"It has nothing to do with being short," I said. "Y'all aren't playing fair."

"Oh, she's going to get upset now," Eli teased. He set the plate on the table. "Be a good sport, and be the baby."

"No," I said. "I don't want to play." I knew he was only showing off for Nealy. He never acted this way with just the two of us. I backed away toward the screen door of the gazebo.

"Yes, yes, yes," he said and came toward me twirling his fingers like crawling spiders.

"Go away, Eli," I demanded. "I don't want to play."

"You need pigtails if you're going to be the baby," Nealy declared.

"Ha," I responded. I shook my head back and forth, my long hair swinging around. "You don't have any rubber bands."

"Oh, yes, I do," Nealy said, grabbing at her own hair, which was pulled into a high ponytail with a navy blue ribbon. She untied the ribbon wrapped around a single rubber band. "A rubber band for one pigtail and a ribbon for the other," she announced gleefully, tossing her own hair about.

"You try, and I'll get you back," I promised, even as they both headed for me.

"Hold her so I can make the braids," Nealy said to Eli. "Then Delia can play in her playpen." She pointed under the table inside of the chair legs that would serve as the bars of my confinement.

Eli put his arms around my torso, but I flailed until I broke free, slapping his hands away. He gestured to Nealy, who happily joined him. Together, they tackled me. I screamed and spit, but they wouldn't stop. Sweat trickled down my back and into my underpants.

"I hate both of you," I managed to sputter between my screams and spasms.

All of a sudden, Eli stopped. Nealy kept trying to get at my hair, to pull it more than anything else, but it was easy enough now to kick her and push her away.

"Ouch, that hurt," she said. She bent over and held her stomach.

"You kicked my bones."

"No, I didn't. You don't have any bones in your stomach." But she persisted in bending over until her thin shoulders nearly touched her bare knees.

"I'm sorry, Delia," Eli said. "You know I wasn't going to hurt you."

Nealy poked her head out from her crouched position, her hands on her hips. He saw she felt betrayed and backtracked to impress her.

"But you make a good baby," he said. His lips spread wide, the smug smile of victory. My nose stung inside.

"I don't make a good baby. But you do. You couldn't beat up anybody if you wanted to. You wouldn't have the breath." I pronounced my words evenly and slowly. We never talked about Eli's condition. But we all knew it was there. I watched him carefully. His chest still rose and fell heavily from the exertion of tickling me. Sweat ran down his cheeks. He reached up and ran his fingers along the string, pushing it firmly behind his ear.

Nealy forgot about her stomach. She looked at me, and her pale lips opened into a perfect circle.

I wished I could take it back, but I didn't know how to say or do anything to offset my cruelty. Young as I was, I still knew it would sound like mockery to say I was sorry. My words lay all around us, invisible blocks to stumble over. I'd said he was weak and different, and in shaming Eli with the truth, I'd shamed all of us. Because I didn't know what to do, because I'd been mean, I turned and walked out the screen door.

I did not walk far. I stepped into one of Mary Lily's spring flowering perennial gardens and sat on a half-moon wooden bench. Grape hyacinths bloomed in clusters around my feet. Their velvet beauty made me feel more miserable. I put my head in my hands. While my eyes were closed into my fists, I heard a noise and looked up. I thought I saw a shadow like a big hunched monkey a good many yards away, back near the gazebo, but that wasn't possible. I sat very still. I was afraid to turn around.

I fingered the blooms at my feet, trying to work up my courage. But before I could stand to turn around, I heard my uncle's voice a short distance beyond me. "Delia, is that you I see sitting over there? Where are the others?" He walked toward me.

"They're in the gazebo," I said, surprised to see my uncle in the garden.

"Sure enough?" He touched the top of my head gently. And all of a sudden, I knew he was the shadow monkey. That he'd been outside the gazebo listening to us. I felt heat rise in my cheeks. I didn't want Uncle Gene or anyone to know Eli and Nealy had tormented me. I didn't want anyone to know I had shamed my cousin.

"Let's pick some of these for your playhouse back there with Eli and Nealy," he said as he gestured toward the hyacinths. He bent down on his knees so that his wide, flat back paralleled the bench and the side of his head was at my knee. I could see his white scalp beneath the thinner part of short blackish bristles wet with perspiration in his crown. He looked up at me, and I smelled the alcohol on his breath. I'd only recently learned to identify this odor, likely from the cocktail hour before dinners at Eli's house, but I don't know if that's really true. What I do know is the sour, sweet, strong smell repulsed me that afternoon, and I stood to get away from it.

In a minute, my uncle rose with a fistful of flowers in his broad hand. "Come on," he said, patting his hand on my shoulder and flashing one of his Uncle Gene grins. He rapped dramatically at the gazebo door, though of course Eli and Nealy could see us through the screen. Eli opened the door. I wondered what game they had played without me. At our entrance, Eli pulled his arms around himself in a downcast posture so that I knew then they hadn't played anything fun at all.

Gene whispered to Eli for what seemed like several minutes, until Eli unwrapped himself and took the bouquet of flowers from his father.

Then my uncle spoke. "So, see here, son," he began. "You're the man of this house, right? It's your job to take care of the ladies." He poked his thumb out toward me. "Here, I found one outside where there might be danger." Nealy giggled at what she thought were Gene's attempts to enter the world of make-believe with us. He reached his hands to my shoulders and nudged me forward back into the group, and for a moment, one of his feet caught slightly behind the other and I thought he would stumble.

Back then, it made no sense why Uncle Gene would be out following us. Not then. Now, I know that was the first day I knew.

That he was prone to follow Eli and direct him afterward. Not to safeguard his delicate son so much as to encourage his determination and daring. Uncle Gene was resolved Eli's accident would not defeat his son. He wanted to overcome the calamity and make his son strong for both of them. In Uncle Gene's terms.

"Remember what I said." My uncle turned toward Eli. He looked at his father, and his father returned a piercing stare. It seemed we all stood suspended for a time, watching Gene, but surely it was only a moment until Eli spoke.

"Here, Delia," Eli said and offered me the bouquet. "These are for you. You're the wife today."

Back at the house, I put the bouquet in a mason jar filled with water, wishing Eli had picked the flowers of his own free will for me. I wondered what Gene had whispered to him. I would never know specifically, but it is easy now to surmise my uncle's advice to his son on how to manage girls.

5

SEPTEMBER 1963

Though Eli was strong enough by second grade, Mary Lily didn't want him to attend Chesterfield Grammar School and had secured the private tutor's services for another year. That is, until Eli and I heard Uncle Gene arguing with her just days before the opening of school as we sat in front of the television, side by side on the sofa, watching a morning rerun of *The Real McCoys* in the Winfields' den. We'd been absorbed in Little Luke's distress—mocked at school for being different, a hillbilly among the townsfolk—until we heard Uncle Gene yell from the kitchen, "God dammit, he's normal and he's going to school."

Eli stood and walked across the room to the television, twisting the volume knob on the console all the way down, though he didn't need to. We could hear everything loud and clear, his parents surely forgetting in the heat of dispute that we were close by. "You don't know what other children will say, how they will react. He's safe here," Mary Lily countered, her voice a high pitch I was unaccustomed to.

I rose and walked to Eli, hovering over the television. I tapped him on the shoulder. "Sshh," he whispered. We looked at each other in silence.

"Are you listening? He doesn't need safe. He needs normal," Uncle Gene's snarling voice boomed around the wall between kitchen and den.

"You don't need to worry about the money for his schooling," she said.

"To hell with your money," he said. "It's been a long time, hasn't it? Maybe since…that you thought I'm good enough for you. You blame me for everything with your silence. But I can take care of my son, no matter what you think."

If Mary Lily responded, she was quiet because we didn't hear her. But she didn't need to. We knew Uncle Gene had won.

ॐ

On the morning before we began second grade, my cousin's first day of real school, Eli and I stood together beside the wide-trunked water oak shading the front gate of his yard for a photograph. Uncle Gene snapped the shot with his Kodak Instamatic. It remains framed both on Mary Lily's Steinway Grand piano and on the wall of family photos in my parents' bedroom.

We were expectant and excited that sunny morning. I wore a checked jumper over a Peter Pan-collar blouse bought for the occasion, and Eli sported new slacks and a wide-striped green and white knit shirt. I remember how the green stripes matched his eyes. I stared at how beautiful he was, his canvas book bag slung on his back. I gripped my new leather satchel loaded with supplies: fat pencils, skinny pencils, erasers, a ruler, writing tablets with wide-spaced lines, and a 64-count box of Crayola crayons with a built-in sharpener.

Mama and Mary Lily walked us the several blocks to Chesterfield Grammar School. In first grade, Mama had accompanied me to my classroom door where my teacher took me by the hand to my seat. But this year our parents were required to leave us at the big double-door entrance where sixth-grade safety patrols escorted the younger students.

A plump boy with kinky blond curls motioned to us and asked what grade we were in.

"The second grade," Eli answered confidently. His voice had become sweetly froggy over the years since the accident.

We followed our safety patrol to the auditorium to the second-grade section. Eli sat on the end of a row, elbows resting on his knees, pretending nonchalance. I sat next to him, my legs dangling, too short to touch the floor from my hard wooden seat. I looked straight ahead at the stage where skinny, gray-haired Miss Crockett, our principal, stood at a podium, class rosters in her hand. The room buzzed with the energy of hundreds of school children awaiting their fate.

Eli and I were called to get in line with young Mrs. Hamell, newly married over the summer. The name Winfield came last in the lineup, and it quickly became clear that no one after Eli would be lucky enough to have the adored Mrs. Hamell. A slight but audible groan reverberated through the other second graders still waiting for the call. No one wanted pitiless Mrs. Cousar—everyone knew she made you fill up the board in small-print apologetic "will not's" after school for one infraction or another—or Miss Folks, an old maid who rapped the knuckles of unruly children with a yardstick.

School policy separated siblings, cousins, and even best friends (if Miss Crockett could identify them) from being in the same classroom. So I knew, in spite of the rules, plans had somehow been arranged for Eli and me to be together and to be in Mrs. Hamell's class. I also knew this was for Eli's sake.

Our tall and willowy teacher directed our line to her classroom and instructed us to unpack our book bags and get organized while she called us one at a time to her desk for our textbooks. Eli took a seat on the row to the right of me, next to the door. A boy named Willard Timms who'd been in my first-grade class plopped down behind him. Willard had been in the slow reading group. And once he had to wear the dunce cap for ten minutes for doing something stupid I couldn't remember. But I did remember feeling sorry for Willard because almost no one ever had to endure the humiliation of the dunce cap.

"Hey, what's that string behind your ear for?" he whispered. When Eli didn't answer, Willard reached out and tugged on the string. Eli gasped and rose up off his bottom, an effort, I was sure, to relieve the pressure of the pull.

"Let go," I hissed at Willard.

"It's slimy," Willard said, letting go. "What is it?" He was no longer whispering.

Eli turned about halfway in his seat, not quite facing Willard but not avoiding him either. He took a deep, gasping breath and covered his throat with his index finger—a gesture I hardly noticed anymore—so that his words would come out stronger. "None of your business," he uttered.

"What's the matter with your voice? Why's it so scratchy?" Willard asked.

Mrs. Hamell looked up from dispensing books to the student standing at her desk.

"What is the disturbance?" she called out. No one answered. I raised my hand.

"Adeline, isn't it?" she said.

"Yes ma'am," I answered. But then I didn't know what to say. I didn't want to risk being a tattletale and make things worse for Eli. Instead, I willed Mrs. Hamell to look at Willard. And she did.

"Willard," she commanded. She already knew his name without confirming. "Have you unpacked everything and put your supplies in your desk?" The hinged tops of our desks housed a storage area underneath. "Or do you need something else to do?"

"No ma'am," he said. Willard got busy doing what he was supposed to do. And Mrs. Hamell went back to the task at her desk. Eli never looked over at me. He stared forward.

Once she had distributed all the books, Mrs. Hamell directed us to open *Friends Old and New*, our Dick and Jane reader. She walked around the room, directing each of us to read aloud. She must have realized at once that it was hard for Eli to speak for a prolonged time, because after two paragraphs she told him he'd read enough. Afterward, she divided us into three reading groups. Eli and I were placed in the top group, the red group, though I couldn't read nearly as well as Eli. His voice might be scratchy and weak, but he knew more words than any of us.

Recess arrived at 10:00 am, and I bounded out of the building, forgetting about my cousin. I was eager to meet up with Nealy, to find out whose class she was in. And to see Gloria Banks, my friend from first grade I'd not seen since school let out in May. We three had become friends the previous year from our fondness for walking the circular periphery of the playground in what we thought a grown-up sort of way, chatting about anything on our minds. They stood near one another in line at the sliding board. When I called to them, they jumped out of line and ran to meet me.

They had been assigned to Mrs. Cousar's class and proudly announced they, too, had been chosen for the red reading group. I didn't want to be in Mrs. Cousar's class, but I did envy my friends being together without me.

We assembled at the back of the line for turns down the slide. The metal was blazing hot. "It burnt my fanny through my panties," I proclaimed when my feet bumped the ground.

"Ooh, it would be awful to be in one of the dumb groups," Gloria said, ignoring my comment as she flew down behind me. Gloria was a beautiful, baby-doll girl with high pink cheeks and butter-colored hair, held in a clip at the nape of her neck that day so that it fell in a smooth plane down her back.

"Yeah, but we wouldn't have as much homework," Nealy said. "That wouldn't be so bad."

I heard a commotion and looked toward the tetherball pole. No one was playing at the pole, but a group of boys had gathered there.

Instinctively, I knew Eli was somehow involved. "Come with me," I said to my friends.

We arrived to see Eli and Willard standing in the middle of a circle of eight or nine boys.

"What's this?" I heard Willard say to Eli as we approached. He pressed his index finger to the silver disc in Eli's neck. "Yuck, it's wet." He pulled his hand away.

Eli didn't respond. He took a step back.

"What's wrong with you?" Willard asked. Still, Eli didn't answer.

I pushed my way into the circle. Nealy and Gloria stayed on the outside behind me.

"It's how he breathes," I screeched.

"How he breathes?" Willard jeered. He turned toward me. "What's wrong with his nose?" He reached out to Eli's face and squeezed his nostrils together.

I was starting to yell for him to stop, when the bell rang across the yard for recess to end, and everyone scurried toward the building.

Willard started it all that first day. The boys wanted nothing to do with Eli. They mocked his breathing; they mocked the way he spoke; they never chose him for a kickball team because of his inability to run fast enough. They said he was a pretty boy, and he was. His skin was soft and white as vanilla ice cream, and he had his mother's wide-set olive eyes, laced with heavy lashes. His nose was nearly perfect, straight and slightly tipped up, like a Walt Disney movie prince. But beauty made Eli's situation worse. It made him seem like a sissy.

The girls said he stank, and sometimes held their noses when they were near him. Partly, I think, they were jealous because Eli was smarter even than all the girls. His only advocate was me, and on the playground, sometimes Nealy and Gloria. "I know he's your cousin, but he does smell bad," Gloria admitted to me one day when our walk ended and we sat together on an outlying bench. "He smells like puke."

"The smell is because his stomach has a hole in it," I said. "And none of that matters to me. It wouldn't to you, either, if you really knew him."

Eli did not go to the lunchroom with us. He stayed in our classroom, and while our peers thought he received special treatment and was the teacher's pet for being so smart, only I knew the truth.

"A hole?" Nealy exclaimed. She had been around Eli for enough years to know his limitations, but she didn't know the reason or the extent to which his body was compromised.

"Yes, it's how food goes into him, but you can't tell anyone. Promise?"

"What keeps his food from dripping out? Why does he have to eat that way?" Gloria asked. I'd slipped out a piece of truth trying to defend him, and now I had to explain everything the best I understood and hope they would keep his secret. It terrified me. For the first time in my life, sitting on a cement bench with my friends, our shoes toeing the bare dirt of the playground beneath us, I told the story of Eli's accident.

At the end of my account, the three of us sat quietly, dumbfounded in the moment—I from the telling and they from listening—waiting for the recess bell to call us in.

ə

We'd been in school more than a month with Eli enduring day after day of being both taunted and shunned on the playground, when on our walk home one afternoon he said, "I'm going to show them."

"Show them what?" I asked.

"Show them they can't mess with me anymore."

The girls, more interested in their own intricacies than in the oddities of Eli, typically left him alone now, but the boys were relentless. Eli had no friends beyond Nealy, Gloria, and me, yet he remained stoic, fending off the taunts of the other boys, mostly by ignoring them.

"What are you going to do?" I asked.

"You'll see," he said. "And I'm going to ask Mama to drive us to school tomorrow instead of walking." I didn't ask why, and never would have guessed the reason.

Before school officially began each day, the students remained in the front yard at Chesterfield, overseen by the safety patrols and by a few teachers on duty. Only if it was raining were we allowed to sit in the auditorium. Many mornings Eli and I walked to school—the weather not yet turned cold—but sometimes one of our mothers drove us, as Mary Lily did that day. She dropped us off about ten minutes before the bell, waving enthusiastically from her open car window as she pulled away.

Eli wasted no time. He trotted in his measured way toward a group of second-grade boys standing in a knot near the flagpole, and I followed him. The gathering reminded me of the first day on the playground when Willard poked at Eli, drawing everyone's attention to his visible abnormalities.

"Look here," Eli called out when he arrived at the group, holding his finger over his throat. Collectively, eyes turned toward him. My cousin pulled up his shirt, exposing the red rubber plug in his stomach. Then, he ripped away the clear tape and pulled out the plug. The contents of his stomach spilled down his pants and onto the ground. It looked like lumpy beige soup.

The smell was immediately strong and sour, and I realized he hadn't wanted to walk to school so his stomach would be fuller.

"Get away," someone shouted, and there was mass hysteria as boys scrambled. Miss Parker, the school's PE teacher, scurried over to us.

"Oh my God!" she broadcast loudly. Then she caught hold of herself, remembered she was a teacher, and held Eli around the waist. "Oh, goodness, what in the world, honey? Let's go inside and get you cleaned up."

"Freak," someone yelled as Miss Parker guided Eli toward the front double doors of the school.

"Gross, weirdo," someone else called out before Eli was through the doors and out of earshot.

I didn't see Eli again that day because—as I learned when Mama collected me from school that afternoon—Miss Crockett called Mary Lily to take him home. I was glad he had gone home because I'd heard

41

him called every ugly, repulsive name anyone could think of during that awful day.

Uncle Gene rarely took us to school, but he did the next day. We rode in the cookie van, and he talked nonstop to Eli. I was silent in the back seat while he ordered his son not to take any "bullshit." He was trying to make an impression by using bad words, even if he used them a lot of the time anyway. "You fight back, you hear me?" he commanded when he pulled to the curb. I shuddered at the thought.

࿂

When the bell rang for recess, Mrs. Hamell tried to keep Eli and me in the classroom by saying she needed the erasers and chalkboard cleaned and would appreciate our help. But Eli wanted to go outside and asked if he could help her after school instead. I saw the worried look on Mrs. Hamell's face.

"All right then, you and Delia stick together," she said. She was a sensitive teacher, calling me already by the name she'd heard my classmates use. Mrs. Hamell usually went outside at recess, along with the other teachers whose classes had recess at the same time, but none of them mingled with us on the playground. They sat under the covered walkway near the building and chatted about teacher things, watching from afar.

I asked Eli what he wanted to do, if maybe he wanted to walk with Nealy, Gloria, and me.

"Let's swing," he said. We walked over to the long line of canvas-strap seats. Most of them were empty, so we had our pick. I could see Gloria and Nealy in the distance, walking the perimeter of the playground, but I couldn't join them. I had to stay with Eli.

Our legs pumped hard; we were in an unspoken competition to see who could reach the highest point, when three boys stepped in front of us. One of them was Willard Timms.

"What's sissy boy doing? Swinging with his girl cousin?" Willard said. He reached out and caught the chains on Eli's upswing and brought him to an abrupt stop. They faced each other, Eli sitting—his breathing labored from his exertion on the swing—and Willard towering above him. The other boys, Jimmy Watson and Joe Cribb,

42

stood nearby.

"You're nasty," Willard said. "You know that?"

"You're the one who's nasty," Eli responded. I stopped my swing quickly by lowering my feet and dragging them in the dirt. Every muscle in my body grew tense.

"Let's see who's nasty," Willard said. He looked over at Jimmy and Joe. Eli stood up from the swing, facing Willard.

I wanted to run for Mrs. Hamell but there wasn't time.

Willard swung at Eli's face. Immediately, a thin stream of blood appeared, trickling from Eli's nose. But Eli did not fall and he did not so much as whimper. He stood erect, his nose bleeding down his lips, and kicked as hard as he could into Willard's groin. My heart squeezed with pride when Willard screamed in feral pain. I imagined a phrase Eli sometimes repeated going through his head: All's fair in love and war.

Jimmy and Joe stepped up, ready to pounce on Eli, but by then everyone on the playground had tuned in, including the teachers. Mrs. Cousar arrived first and separated the boys. She grabbed Willard's ear, twisting it until he was forced to lean into her. With her other hand she yanked Eli's arm and dragged both of them to Miss Crockett's office.

Our greatest fear at Chesterfield School was Miss Crockett's paddle, drilled through with symmetrically lined holes for more stinging power. A visual deterrent, it hung in plain view on the wall in our principal's office. In reality, it was rarely used. But it was put into service that day. From what we heard, Willard took the brunt of five hard hits. A fifth-grade office worker filing papers in the outer office where the secretary sat claimed to have heard Willard crying, and that's the story we believed. Eli received two licks, which he claimed he could hardly feel.

6

OCTOBER–NOVEMBER 1963

Miss Crockett notified Mary Lily and Gene of Eli's scuffle, and of the resulting two licks with the paddle. She told them about Willard and his cronies, too. But according to Eli, he didn't get in trouble at home for the incident. In fact, his father clapped him on the back and praised him for "hitting Willard where it counts." I didn't know then what such a hit meant.

Instead of Mama or Mary Lily driving us to school on the days we didn't walk the short distance, Uncle Gene began taking us. When he dropped us off at the flagpole at the bottom of the walkway, more than once I noticed his van pull forward and pull back into the curb farther down. If Eli noticed, he never let on as we made our daily advance into the crowd of students, the weather still mild enough for students to stay outside until the bell rang.

Uncle Gene was spying, still the shadow monkey, but hiding now in the cookie van and looking from the rearview mirror instead of listening outside the gazebo. How did I know this when Eli seemed oblivious? Or maybe he did know and didn't think I would notice. That Uncle Gene watched, hoping to see his son steer away from me and join the boys—huddled in their cliques, flailing out their arms at nothing, kicking sneakered feet into the dirt, buzzing with their restless morning energy. Eli never did.

On the afternoon of Halloween as we left the school building, passing under the breezeway onto the grass of the side lawn, with no teachers in sight, Willard and his sidekicks caught up to Eli and me. We were walking home from school that day, and as we usually did, cut through the side yard because it was a shorter way. Unwittingly, we'd never considered how this exit hid us from the front of the school where all the cars and people were.

"He doesn't need a costume, does he, Joe?" Willard's taunt exploded suddenly behind us.

"Nah, 'cause he's already wearing his freak suit," Joe said, sniggering. I turned just enough to see Joe bent over laughing, amused with himself.

"Don't turn around, Eli," I cautioned. I tried to take his hand to hurry us along, but he shook it off. Still, thankfully, he didn't stop. He kept walking, and I stayed at his side.

"Hey, turn around. What's the matter, fraidy cat? Scared 'cause no teacher is here to save you?" It was Willard talking again. "We've seen your daddy in his van. Watching over you. Where's your daddy and his cookies?"

Eli couldn't bear it—the human need to defend himself triumphed—and he turned. I turned with him to see Jimmy and Joe mocking my cousin by holding their fingers to their throats and pretending to wheeze.

Eli took a step forward. Willard took a step forward also and held up his fists. I started to run for help, and then out of nowhere, perhaps as he might have jumped in rage from a foxhole to charge at three enemy Krauts, Uncle Gene appeared amid the standoff. But instead of an M1 rifle, he held a grayed-out ax handle.

"I'll show you a fraidy cat," he yelled, brandishing the old handle back and forth in front of his chest. The smell of alcohol poured off of him and permeated the air.

I shrieked. I twisted from the scene in front of me, toward the school. I didn't know what to do. Whether to run back into the building and look for a teacher or stay at Eli's side. I remained, unable to think clearly in the moment that there was nothing here a second-grade girl *could* do.

Willard backed away, but my uncle kept coming. Eli stood mute, too shocked I guess to move. I don't think Uncle Gene intended to hurt any of those boys. He intended to scare them, but he was too unsteady in his movements. The three boys backed up a few steps at a time, huddled in unison, trying to maneuver themselves as a unit to pivot and run. But they couldn't achieve the momentum because Uncle Gene impeded them, continuing to swing the ax handle just inches from their fused bodies.

"Come on, man up," Uncle Gene yelled. "You're tough. Who's first?" He swung wildly forward and lost his balance, pitching onto his hands and knees. The heavy end of the handle flew forward too and connected hard with Jimmy's kneecap. He fell, screaming in pain. The other boys lost their balance and toppled onto him.

"Oh no," I said, no shriek this time but a whimper. Eli still stood mute.

Uncle Gene righted himself and sat on the ground. He picked up the ax handle and set it in his lap. The stiff black bristles of his hair gleamed with sweat in the sunlight as he shook his head back and forth, as though trying to understand what had happened. Willard and Joe stood and ran. Jimmy did not move.

Miss Crockett called the police who took Uncle Gene to jail. Then Jimmy's parents arrived, and his father lifted him into the back seat of their car. Though it didn't look too awful—a patch of raw red ringing his knee rather than blood gushing from the hit—still Jimmy could not stand and it seemed clear his kneecap was broken. Mama arrived to retrieve Eli and me. Mary Lily had ridden with her to drive the cookie van—parked out of sight at a haphazard angle on the other side of the softball field—back home before she called the magistrate. My father was at work.

"What's the matter with Uncle Gene?" I asked Mama on the way home. At first she wouldn't answer.

"My dad wants the boys to like me," Eli answered instead. "He wants me to be like them."

And then my mother spoke. "I'm sorry, Eli. Your father loves you so much he got carried away. It's hard for him." I wasn't sure, but I thought I heard her murmur something else at the end, something like, "hard being responsible."

The magistrate released Uncle Gene at Mary Lily's request. She waited until the next morning to pick him up. Trying to collect herself, perhaps. And likely to rebuke my uncle, even if uncharacteristic of her. Jimmy's family did not press charges. Perhaps both the law and Jimmy's parents felt sympathy for the Winfields. Or more likely, the matter was dropped as a testament to Lauderdale clout.

❧

After the calamity, things quieted down for Eli at school. In some ways,

Uncle Gene's frightening encounter with Willard and his pals succeeded. All the boys left Eli alone, perhaps fearing Miss Crockett's stiff paddle or perhaps a return of Uncle Gene. If they called him names, they did so behind his back. They spurned him completely.

I wanted my cousin to make friends, but I didn't see how it was possible. So much had been done that couldn't be undone. Occasionally, Eli walked with Nealy, Gloria, and me at recess, but he cared little—and who could blame him—for second-grade girl talk. President Kennedy had signed the Equal Pay Act in the summer, and that fall Gloria's mama bought her Mattel Inc.'s response to the new law: Barbie's Executive Career Girl outfit, a two-piece gray tweed suit and matching hat. Collecting Barbie clothes had become the rage, and Gloria acquired the coolest of them all.

On one of our walks, I thought of things I could trade with Gloria for her new ensemble, but even my offer of Barbie's red velvet and satin evening gown didn't tempt her. Walking between Gloria and me, Eli tried to charm her for the outfit on my behalf, but she remained stalwart. "I'm sorry," he whispered to me, his lips brushing my ear.

Perhaps I wanted this outfit because early on, expectations for my future were established—albeit subtly—by my parents, particularly my father: to make good grades in school, go to college, and stand on my own two feet.

It would become ever clearer as I grew older: my father cared not so much for my finding a husband as for my finding a living. His outlook both pleased and frightened me. "You can do it," he said one night, patting my shoulder during a tearful episode in ninth grade when I sat at the kitchen table, not understanding my Algebra II homework. "You're a smart girl," he insisted while I stared, frustrated, at the incomprehensible problem before me.

Somehow, I'd ended up in advanced math when I despised math and desired no more than the minimum requirement to graduate. I wanted out of advanced math. I pleaded with my father. "I'll marry Mr. Right, who can do finances and figure out all the formulas," I said. It was not the right thing to say. My father became furious, something he rarely did.

"You are responsible for yourself," he shouted. "You learn to take care of yourself. You and no one else."

My mother doesn't make a living, I wanted to shout back at him, and I nearly did, but I stopped myself. Instead, I slammed my book and ran to my room. Mama had stopped teaching elementary school when I was born. Not because my father asked her to teach or not to teach. In truth, as far as I knew, my father never questioned her decision not to work, one way or the other.

Daddy tried tutoring me in the evenings after dinner, but it didn't work. He was a human calculator and didn't understand why simple formulas confounded me. I screamed and he fumed. Mama stepped in.

"Let her be, Will," she pronounced, emphasizing my father's name and pounding her hand on the kitchen table between us. "We will hire a tutor, and she'll get through this. She doesn't have to love math." In the end, my mother did hire a tutor, and I figured it out well enough to progress to geometry the next year.

By the time my eighth birthday came, making me again another year older than everyone else in my class, I had moved on from Barbie's generic career ensemble and yearned instead for her Flight Stewardess attire, perfectly suited for my sophisticated Bubble Cut Barbie. I adored this gift from my parents, the set including a tailored navy cotton suit with metal wings pinned on the lapel of the jacket, a pert hat, black purse, and zippered flight bag with the American Airlines logo.

On our walks at recess, my friends and I fantasized about careers for ourselves. I would travel the world. Gloria would become a fashion designer for women like Jackie Kennedy. Nealy would teach children (maybe because she could control them, I thought, amusing myself). Eli rarely entered our chatter. He merely tolerated our conversation, for he wanted nothing more than to be with his own kind, whatever kind that might be.

More and more, he stayed inside at recess. Sometimes, Mrs. Hamell stayed with him. She encouraged him to read book after book. He escaped especially into space books. He loved *You Will Go to the Moon* and must have read it 100 times. If my fantasy was jetting to Paris in a sleek navy sheath skirt, his was flying to the moon, weightless.

Eli was the first among us to learn of the president's assassination that November Friday, for he was in the classroom during lunchtime listening—as he was allowed—to the radio Mrs. Hamell kept in the coat closet, just for him, I secretly thought. Sometimes he came to the cafeteria because he could drink milk, but he still couldn't eat regular food. Kids had mostly stopped asking questions, but sometimes they still looked at him strangely when he didn't eat. Mostly, Eli preferred staying alone in the classroom.

I looked up that day, passing a basket of yeast rolls, to see him standing in the doorway of the cafeteria. I try to imagine how we must have appeared, aligned in our seats along the long rows of tables, eating nonchalantly from our compartmental plastic lunch trays, our three-cornered milk cartons marking our places. In my mind's eye it seems every head—students and teachers—swiveled toward his unfamiliar presence.

"Something happened to the president," he said. His voice was low, but we heard him as we had quieted when he materialized at the door. At first, I thought my cousin was pulling a prank for attention. Perhaps the teachers did, too. For several seconds, the cafeteria remained dead quiet. "I'm telling the pure truth I heard," Eli declared into the silence.

The teachers, who ate together at the head table, reacted like scared hens, their heads flapping back and forth at one another. Finally, it was again Mrs. Cousar who approached him.

"Young man," she said, though she, like everyone else, knew who Eli was—after all, she had retrieved him on the playground. "What are you saying?"

"Something is wrong with the president." His voice became defiant, and he coughed in the effort. He threw his shoulders back, put his hand over his throat.

"Come with me," she said, and continued toward Eli, still standing in the doorway. When she reached him, she put her hand on his back, turned him, and guided him forward. They walked away out of sight. Our teachers stood and walked to the fronts of our long tables. It wasn't time for lunch to end, but we lined up anyway.

In our classroom, we sat at our desks, and Mrs. Hamell turned on the radio. A little before 2:00 pm we heard Walter Cronkite say

President Kennedy had been shot. By the time school dismissed at 3:00 pm, there had been an official announcement: the president was dead. Eli had told the truth. Everyone marveled how he had been the first to know something was terribly wrong and told the school. For one shining moment, Eli was our hero and he basked in the glory.

Children are fickle, though, and as quickly as it arose, the attention paid to Eli disappeared. I remember the following February, on Valentine's Day, he delivered a valentine into each of our classmates' boxes, as we were expected to do. In return he received two cards in the shoebox he'd covered with red construction paper and adorned with white hearts during art period. One valentine from me and one from Mrs. Hamell; that was all. My box, painted pink and bejeweled with gold glitter, was full.

Eli didn't take his box home to show it off to Mary Lily and Gene. He threw it into the tall metal trash can at the end of our hall as we were leaving school. The halls had mostly cleared. The sound made a hollow thud in the empty bin. "I hate them," he said. Of course, he could see my box tucked under my arm. I was sorry it was too big to fit in my book satchel so he wouldn't have to see.

I shifted my box under the arm holding my book bag, leaving my left hand free. I reached out and took Eli's hand. At first his fingers hung limp in mine, not consenting to my gesture. Then finally his grip tightened. We walked that way until we exited into a cold, clear day. He dropped my hand in front of the building where the cars picked up children. He didn't want anyone to see him holding on to me.

On our walk home along the sidewalk, I remarked on the bare winter trees, how they looked like skeletons. He zipped up his coat, not really answering, but nodding, more or less. He was a proud, lonely boy. I loved him.

The next year Mary Lily planned ahead. She signed valentines with question marks and expressions like, "Guess who?" She gave them to me, and I slid the stack into the slot of Eli's valentine box as I passed my own cards into my classmates' bright boxes. It made me sad to feel the cards slide easily into Eli's box, proof there was no bulk hidden beneath the lid. Surely he knew, but he never said. He seemed grateful to hold the cards in his hands.

7

JUNE 1966

Just before his tenth birthday, Eli's tracheostomy was removed at Boston Children's Hospital. Eli did not talk about it, but I knew Mary Lily both dreaded and anticipated the day. You could see it in her conduct. You could hear it in conversation between her and Mama. She was giddy, floundering back and forth among all her fears one minute and her excitement over Eli's new life the next. Her heavy, blonde fall of hair swung all around her as she talked. For the first time, her son would look normal. He would breathe through his nose. He would swim like a regular kid, though Eli's ability to keep his neck above the water line when he swam was nothing short of amazing.

Eli's stomach tube had been removed the year before. Now he ate any kind of soft food, but the stomach tube was small potatoes compared to the trach. Without the trach he would eat what everyone ate and breathe as everyone breathed. Dr. Crawford consulted with the doctor in Boston to start the process for weaning Eli from breathing through his throat. It began with a trial in Dr. Crawford's office where he put a cap on Eli's throat. I was terribly frightened at the prospect, for I wondered how Eli could suddenly breathe through his mouth and nose when he didn't know how.

"It's not like that," Daddy assured me when I asked him the night before the capping if Eli might suffocate. He'd finished reading the Uncle Remus tale of how Br'er Rabbit was too sharp for Br'er Fox, and was turning out my light. I could read the stories myself, but Daddy did it because he liked for Helen and me to hear stories together. And though I wouldn't have admitted it, I liked hearing him read them.

"Breathing is a natural process, but it will take some adjusting for Eli," Daddy said while he picked up my four-year-old sister and flung her over his back. She rubbed at Daddy's head—nearly bald by then with only a dark circular fringe above his ears—lifted her face, squealed, and stuck out her tongue as he carried her away to her room. I returned the gesture. She didn't know it, but Daddy would be back to check on me. She didn't have him all to herself.

The next morning, waiting with Mama and Gene on the Winfields' porch for Eli to return, I still didn't see how it would work. And then I saw with my own eyes a red cap covering the hole in Eli's throat. Uncle Gene sprang mid-pump from the porch swing where he sat with Mama—Helen on her lap—when Mary Lily parked at the curb. He jumped so quickly the back slats rammed into the porch rail, leaving Mama to catch herself and keep both her and Helen from falling out. I sat safe in a rocking chair out of range of the flying swing.

Gene ran to Eli walking up the path to the porch, grabbed him around his middle, and whirled him into the air. Eli's face transfigured. He became all eyes—brimming green pools—staring out at us. His hands grasped at the red cap. I thought he was scared he couldn't breathe and soar aloft at the same time. I stood. I looked up at my cousin. He smiled at me. I understood then that, though he might have been scared, his eyes were liquid happy, too. I watched him breathe in and out of his mouth. He hadn't quite gotten the hang of his nose.

Each day, Eli wore the cap longer until he stretched to all his awake hours breathing through his mouth and nose. Capping during sleeping would not be done until he arrived at the hospital in Boston where special nurses would monitor him in case he experienced what Mary Lily called "airway distress." I didn't have to be told "airway distress" meant he could die.

Gene, Mary Lily, and Eli were gone for two weeks. The first night in the intensive care unit with Eli's trach capped while he slept, he didn't have airway distress exactly, but he was restless and his oxygen level dipped too low. Uncle Gene called Mama and gave the report. She informed me Eli's trach could not be detached the following day as hoped.

I tried to imagine what it felt like. I sat on my bed and covered my nose and closed my mouth except for a thin slit. I lay back on a pillow for as long as I could stand it. It was maybe three minutes, but it felt like an hour. I began to sweat and suck hard to pull in air. Helen walked into my room about midway through my experiment. "What's the matter, Dee?" she asked, at four still calling me the name she used when she first began to speak. It had become her form of endearment, and it caught on. Even now, I am Dee. I didn't answer but continued to hold my nose.

She ran from the room screaming to Mama. I believed I loved my sister, but she often drove me crazy with her electric energy and histrionic nature. Not to mention she wanted my company constantly. I prefer to think it was because I was so much older that I did not as much yearn for hers.

Mama appeared at my bedroom door. By then, I'd ended my simulation and sat on my bed among my mod orange and turquoise daisy pillows. My sister coveted those pillows. "Delia," she demanded, "are you all right? Helen says you're holding your breath." Her hands held tight to her hips and a dish towel quivered on her shoulder.

"Eli must be terrified," I responded.

"Oh," she exclaimed and dropped onto the bed beside me. Helen—pigtails bobbing—followed, grabbing my biggest flower-power pillow to her chest, swinging her legs off the side.

"You saw him with the cap on many times before he left."

"Yes, but when he was asleep, his oxygen was low."

"You just said it," Mama surmised. "He was asleep…so he didn't know. He wouldn't be terrified if he was asleep. He wouldn't know." She rubbed her hands down her culottes skirt across her thighs. It meant her palms were wet, so I didn't completely believe her.

But the second night was better. Eli's oxygen level never left the normal range, and on the third day, on the verge of his birthday, the doctor disengaged the tube in his trach. For two more days he stayed in the hospital for observation. The day before they left the hospital to tour the city, a remarkable event took place. Eli was allowed to call me collect. I knew without knowing when the phone rang that day, it was Eli. I expected his voice to be different, but it sounded raspy like always.

"What does it feel like, Eli?" I asked.

"I don't know," he replied. "I guess it feels like you feel. Except I hold my hand over my throat when I cough so the hole won't blow open." Surely, I thought, he must be overjoyed to breathe as others did, but he didn't want to talk about it. Or the hole in his throat closing. I kept asking until finally he said dismissively that his throat didn't have stitches and would close up all on its own.

While I pondered the mystery of how a hole deep in human flesh could close without stitches, he raved about attending the upcoming Red Sox game at Fenway Park to celebrate his birthday. His parents had promised him the opportunity to see his beloved team after he got through the procedure. It was an incredible occasion, I knew, for my own father loved baseball but had never attended a major league game. Eli's desire to see his team play, even with the apprehension of the trach removal, had burned in him for weeks.

It seemed to me the approaching game overrode his fear of the whole procedure, but maybe that's not true at all. It's probably only what I thought, because Eli never spoke of his fears. I did not know if he let down his guard when he was alone or with his parents. I don't know it even now. In front of the world and me, he held in his pain—both physical and emotional—more and more as the years passed. It became second nature to him. Part of me was relieved Eli kept the intimacies of his pain to himself, but another part of me wished for him to release his feelings to me so that I could feel what he felt. But I didn't probe. I took my cues from him.

"I'm jazzed to see them play the Yankees," Eli declared. The connection had become scratchy, but the exhilaration in his voice trumpeted through the long-distance line. It made me feel happy.

Eli loved the Red Sox. He said he chose the team because it was in the city where he had lived for six months. But they had been a losing team our entire lives. It wasn't likely he'd see them beat the Yankees or anyone else. They were underdogs.

And then the association suddenly dawned on me—why had it not before—as I listened to him carry on about the approaching game. My cousin was not unlike the Red Sox with his own desperate need to be a winner, too.

"I'm going to see Yaz play," he continued. "Dad says I'm going to get his autograph." Yaz—Carl Yastrzemski—was Eli's favorite player whose position was left field. "I'll get to watch him play off the Green Monster. He knows the angles."

"What is the Green Monster?" I asked, curious, at least, at the word "monster," until he explained that it was only the nickname for a tall left-field wall made of concrete and tin.

"You're jazzed for Yaz," I said because I thought it sounded cute. We both knew I possessed no serious interest in baseball, Red Sox or otherwise. He laughed in his croaky way, and the sound comforted me. Soon after, Mary Lily came on the line to speak to Mama and my conversation with Eli ended.

The Red Sox lost to their arch rival, the Yankees, on June 5th that year, 5-3. Eli came home undaunted in his loyalty for his team, with souvenirs enough to fill a dresser drawer and with the prized autograph on a brand-new baseball. Determined to snag Yaz for Eli's benefit, Uncle Gene had purchased tickets for seats near the first-base line, making it easy for him and Eli to hover near the dugout before the game. The initial strategy didn't work, but Gene was unfazed. After the game, they waited on the players to leave from the parking area. Yaz not only signed Eli's ball; he reached down and tousled his hair.

Eli positioned his treasure—soon encased in a display cube—on the left back corner of the bare expanse of his dresser top. Later, this space would become crowded with teenage accoutrements: English Leather cologne, loose change, a rabbit's foot on a chain, a collection of bold watches with colorful faces, but the baseball never moved. It is likely there now.

Eli's loyalty finally paid off. The next year, after being near the bottom for so long, the Red Sox won the American League pennant and went to the World Series in 1967, where they lost to the St. Louis Cardinals, but barely, four games to three.

Carl Yastrzemski achieved a momentous peak that year, winning the Triple Crown by leading the league in home runs, runs batted in, and batting average. Eli tried to explain it all. Ignorant and indifferent as I was, even I could understand it was an amazing feat. Eli was ecstatic, and that's what mattered to me.

Not unlike his hero, Eli advanced toward his own remarkable season. He returned from Boston, as far as I could tell, a normal-breathing, normal-eating boy. An accomplishment every bit as commanding as Carl Yastrzemski carrying the entire Red Sox team on his back to earn the American League pennant.

It was through the Ouija board that I gleaned most of what little I knew of Eli's inner struggles. We had long toyed with my board, but then one day, soon after returning from Boston, Eli visited his grandmother, and poking around, discovered an old board in the closet underneath the stairs. Mimi said he could have it. She told Eli it had belonged to her deceased sister who once used it to find things that were lost.

"Really, Eli, really?" I asked.

"This is the real thing," he said. "It will tell us the truth." We were standing in the Winfields' solarium. He held the board up high in front of his face for me to see. Both of us knew, without ever admitting it to the other, that in all of our Ouija board sessions over the years, we had likely forced the words to appear under the power of our own fingers on the shiny new letters of my Parker Brothers game. It was just one of dozens like it on the shelf at Bundy's Toy Land. It had no distinction. Merely a commercial product, it was no different from the entertainment of Monopoly or Clue. But this one was different.

"Man, who would have thought old people played with a Ouija board," Eli said.

"She probably wasn't old when she played with it," I said. "Besides, why wouldn't old people play the board? Seems like they're closer to the other side than anybody else."

"'Cause they're nearly dead?" Eli said, nodding. "Could be. Makes sense."

The wood was chipped along the bottom of the board, and the letters faded. An odd and contemplative round moon face dominated the left top side; a crescent moon with a star balanced it on the right. Two circled stars anchored the bottom. Looking at this worn object, considering its authenticity—once in the hands of Eli's dead great-aunt—made me shiver. The directions on the back read in part, *Have no one at the table who will not sit seriously and respectfully. If you use it in a frivolous spirit, asking ridiculous questions, laughing over it, you naturally get undeveloped influences around you.*

No longer would we sail the planchette around the board willy-nilly as we were wont to do with my modern board, to spell the answers we wanted to see. This board turned us serious.

We waited until an afternoon of dark hanging clouds, a thunderstorm looming. It set the atmosphere, and it also cooled off the garret enough to make it bearable. At Eli's house, instead of only a low-ceilinged attic with a pull-down staircase, there was a real room under the high-angled eaves, tall enough for children and most adults to walk around. A room containing the glorious stained-glass window as well as two tiny windows we could open on opposite walls, offering a cross breeze.

We climbed the narrow stairway and closed the door behind us, walked toward the empty space we'd carved out long ago among the myriad stored belongings and taped-up dusty boxes. I sat cross-legged in my usual spot, a few feet in front of a portrait propped on the floor, the canvas split across the forehead of a young man wearing a mustache and an ascot. I supposed Mary Lily couldn't bring herself to discard a family image, especially one that to me looked awfully like Eli, but whoever it was, the painting was ruined, and so abided in what she called "the junk room," our haven.

Eli sat with his legs splayed on either side of my knees. We set the old board between us, balanced between his thighs and my lap. We did not turn on the bare bulb overhead. The diffused light coming through gray sky to the windows was enough to read by. We augmented the dark daylight with only a tall taper in a brass candlestick we had brought along with us.

"What do you want to ask?" I whispered.

"Is anyone here?" Eli called out. My fingertips rested lightly on one side of the heart-shaped planchette, his on the other. We sat very still. I closed my eyes. Nothing happened.

"Concentrate," Eli said.

"I am," I said.

"Shhhhh." We sat quietly. I squeezed my eyes shut tighter. I thought only of my fingers. The little table stuttered forward and stopped. It started again and began to move in earnest. I kept my eyes shut. It circled around and around, and finally rested. I opened my eyes to see Eli looking down, surveying the answer. The lens in the little table hovered over the word, "Yes."

Eli and I looked at each other. "Who are you?" he asked.

Again, we concentrated. Again, the table moved beneath our fingers, this time stopping over "No."

"What does that mean?" I asked.

"It's not going to tell us who is here," Eli said. "It doesn't matter. Ask a question, Delia."

"Who will be my teacher in fifth grade?" I asked.

"That's a dumb question," Eli mouthed.

"Let it tell us," I said. Our fingers began to move. M…Y…E…

I already knew my teacher would be either Mrs. Myers or Mrs. Tyler. Was it my subconscious that picked out letters in Mrs. Myers' name because she's who I wanted? Half of me thought yes and the other half thought no. The no half desperately wanted to believe.

"So, we will have Mrs. Myers this year," Eli announced definitively, but quietly. "Will I make friends this year? Will I be different now?" he asked all of a sudden. The candle flame blinked and came back.

I looked at Eli. I felt an electric tingle in my shoulders. "I'm a little bit scared," I confessed.

"Close your eyes," he ordered. I did what my cousin said.

Again, the tiny table moved in circles around the board, landing finally.

"Yes, it says yes," he said, excited, his voice rising. I opened my eyes to see his hands pumping the air above his head. The mysterious spell fell away, for my thoughts turned quickly away from the spirit world to Eli, to realize he had admitted, if indirectly, what I knew always in my heart, how badly he wanted to be in the world the same as the rest of us. He looked at me, grinning. The room had become brighter. I stood and walked to the nearer window. A crack of light had broken in a shimmering streak through the clouds.

8

AUGUST 1966

In the summer of Eli's transformation, our neighborhood began to change, too. Mrs. Smither's husband died, and she sold her house immediately in June and moved away to live with her daughter in North Carolina. The Viceroys moved in right away with their identical twin boys a year older than Eli and me: Dale and Drew. Until then, Eli, Helen, and I were the only children on the street. Then the Thomases decided to sell their house and retire to Myrtle Beach. A family named Duke from up north with a son in our grade named Craig moved into the Thomases' rambling house during July.

"At least I'm not the only only child now," Eli said. I had never heard him refer to being an only child. It hadn't occurred to me Eli might want a sibling, maybe because I never wondered why he was an only child. The reason seemed obvious. With all they had gone through to keep Eli in this world, Mary Lily had no need or energy to birth other children, and Uncle Gene had all the responsibility he could handle.

"What names," I exclaimed to Eli, ignoring his declaration, not knowing what to say. "Do you think they will act like royalty?" We laughed. Eli stuck his nose up in the air and pranced around, flinging his hand behind him as though he were adjusting a long robe. It was the first day of August. We'd not officially met the new neighbors, only seen them in their cars passing down the street.

"Let's knock on their doors," Eli suggested.

"To do what?" I asked.

"I don't know. We'll think of something."

"Not me," I said.

As it turned out, they came to us a few days later, an unusually mild day for August that coaxed Eli and me outside in his yard while Pot was gardening. He was moving loads of sand from a hauled-in pile, using it to help break up the hard Carolina red clay around Mary Lily's

59

daylilies. We coerced him into pushing us in the wheelbarrow between loads.

It was Pot's idea to dump us into the sand pile. Probably to get us out of his way so he could work. Eli wanted to bury me in sand up to my neck, and I decided to let him. He dug using a spade from Pot's supply of gardening tools, and when the spade wasn't fast enough, he tunneled with his hands. Damp sand sprayed out around us in clouds. "Lie down," he directed when he'd dug the shallow grave. I sat in the cavity where the sand was dark gray, not like the white surface. "Lie down," he said again, "so I can cover you." Cold goose bumps traveled my arms. It took all my willpower to lie prone, for I felt I might suffocate. Still, I accomplished a fair amount of shrieking, particularly when the sand reached my shoulders, in my terror of being buried alive, of being dead.

Perhaps the new boys heard me because I turned my head to see the three of them standing at the edge of Eli's backyard.

"Don't move, Delia. You're going to crack the sand," Eli commanded. He turned, picking up the spade and waving it toward the boys. "Come on over," he called. And they began to walk toward us. Eli stood and approached them. I remained buried.

The tallest boy—I would learn was Craig—led the twins, swinging his hefty arms in a swaggering gait. The four boys met midway, within spitting distance of Pot, who stopped his work and leaned one arm on his shovel.

I couldn't hear what they were saying, but I saw the furrow formed on Pot's forehead when he cocked back his straw hat, and I knew he didn't like something about these boys. I thought of Pot as my Raggedy Man from my and Daddy's favorite James Whitcomb Riley poem because he was "the goodest man you ever saw!" He had been the one to find Eli holding the Coca-Cola bottle filled with lye, and saved his life. And maybe because of that, and because he was a good and kind man, Pot had always been extra protective of him.

Eli turned toward Pot and asked something. Pot nodded, patted his hat back straight on his head, and picked up his shovel. He returned to heaping sand from the wheelbarrow and directing it underneath the foliage of a mound of daylilies. Eli looked at me and waved me toward the group. I sat up. The sand cracked a jagged seam down my middle.

I kicked out my legs and stood, coated with sand and sweat. I shook and wiped at my trunk and limbs, but much of the sand stuck like an extra layer of skin.

"Pot's going to push us in the wheelbarrow," Eli announced when I arrived and he introduced me. I looked at Pot. He tipped his hat.

The boys attempted to sit together in the bucket of the wheelbarrow, but no matter how they tried to configure themselves, only three would fit. Finally, Drew rolled out, landing with a thud in the grass. I would learn soon enough he was the kinder twin, aggressive only because he felt compelled to follow his brother. Pot rolled Eli, Craig, and Dale in a circle around the yard, returning to give Drew and me a turn. The rotation continued, all grand fun until Craig fell. He was sitting at the helm and leaned forward too far, falling face first into the dirt.

Pot pulled back hard on the wheelbarrow handles to keep from running over him. This strapping boy—a phrase Daddy would use— straggled up on his knees and brushed at his face. There was a spot of bright red next to his nose where he'd scratched his face in the gravelly dirt. He touched his finger to his cheek, and it came back tipped with blood. "This is a sissy game," he declared, rubbing his finger on his shirt before jamming his hands into the pockets of his shorts.

It was clear: Craig was a self-assured decision maker. As soon as he made the statement, I knew the wheelbarrow rides were over.

"Yep, this game is for little kids," Dale said. And with Dale's consent, Craig had both twins in tow.

"But it's fun," I intervened. Not one of them, including Eli, answered me.

"I b'lieve you chillun would have more fun if you played out yonder," Pot said. He pointed toward the gazebo and Eli's playground equipment we hadn't used in ages. "I gotta get back to my work, anyway." He jerked his shoulders and reached for the shovel. At six feet, three inches tall, Pot astonished me. He was the tallest man I knew, my own father being five feet, six inches. I watched the legs of his overalls rise to reveal narrow, bare ankles when he bent low to retrieve his shovel. I wondered how a man so tall and strong could be supported on those skinny ankles.

I concentrated on Pot, watching him scoop sand from the pile into the wheelbarrow because the boys were mumbling together, and it made me nervous. I think it made Pot nervous, too, because he kept glancing over at Eli and making a jumpy shoulder motion.

The three of them whispered for what seemed a long time. They wanted us to know they were making some kind of plan. Of course, Eli wanted in on it. Watching him, his attempt at nonchalance in approaching the group, made me feel his desire like I was in his own skin. Finally, when the three-headed clump did not break apart, he abandoned subtlety. He said too loudly, too brightly, "So, hey, what do y'all want to do?"

"We know a good game. It'll be a gas. Cowboys and Indians," Craig said, coming out of the huddle. He bumped Eli genially on the shoulder.

The three approached us, and Eli in particular, in a friendly way, but something was off. I couldn't have defined it then, the way I know now people can be: presenting themselves as friends as long as they hold sway. The new boys were out to stake their claim among the natives on Congress Street.

Right away, the game didn't sound good to me, because who didn't know the difference between cowboys and Indians. The good guys against the bad. Someone would lose. But I didn't say anything. No one would have listened anyway.

"Here's what we do," Craig explained. "Eli, you and Delia start out being the Indians. The rest of us are cowboys." He explained the big pecan tree—out of Pot's sight on the other side of the house in the wide side yard—would be base. We were safe as long as we could make it out of hiding and to the tree. If only one of us was tagged, we could try to free the other by running close enough to touch, but if we both were tagged, we were caught for good. Craig didn't elaborate on what "caught for good" meant.

I said I didn't want to play, but Eli placed his hand gently on my forearm and squeezed affectionately. We had to play the game, he said. He promised it would be okay. He would take care of me.

The first go-round, Eli was tagged almost immediately. Though in time he would build more stamina for running faster—it was still so early after the removal of the trach—he would never be able to run as fast and long as most boys could. There was too much scar tissue. He didn't have the breath. I hid inside a thick holly hedge—ignoring the thorn pricks on my legs and arms—and was able to dart out, tag Eli, and set him free. We dashed to base successfully, only because the boys, searching in places unknown to them around Eli's yard, were too far afield to catch up when they saw us running.

The game resumed, our turn to chase. I tagged Dale who froze in place, his face fixed angrily, but the other two escaped into hiding. Eli and I separated to search for the other two. While I hunted for Drew, Craig sped by Eli and tagged Dale who made it to base. I ran after Craig. He circled around in figure eights, eluding me. Eli ran toward me, trying to assist. But he arrived too late. We couldn't catch Craig as he followed the other two, already at base. In the next play, Eli and I both were tagged and lost the game.

The boys circled us around the tree, determining what our sentence would be. Craig decided. "We'll tickle them," he said.

I would rather all the pecans in the tree rain upon my head, and I screamed, "No," as loudly as I could.

My cry went unheeded. The cowboys searched around, procured a length of cotton rope from the gardening shed and tied us, Eli and me, side by side by the waist to the tree. My hands remained free, and desperately I reached up and grabbed a heavy branch. I shook it with all my might, and a few green-hulled—not yet ripe—pecans pelted our heads. The cowboys laughed.

"It's all right, shh," Eli said, his voice frog-throated, quiet, sweet. I wanted to take hold of his hand, but I dared not reach out. I knew it would humiliate him. And I needed both hands for what small defense I could muster.

They came at us, all three at once. They did not stop to let us catch our breath. It wasn't like the mischief I endured from Eli years before in the gazebo. Their hands weren't teasing and there was no way out. I was terrified.

Fingers went under my armpits, stabbed into my flesh. I tried to shove away the hands—flattened into my sides, punching at my ribs. Drew assailed me while the other boys took on Eli. His face came close to mine; his breath hit my chin. "Stop, stop, I want to quit," I screamed. I spit at him. Then, in spite of the meager protection my arms offered, I extended them from around my body and reached for a branch. I shook it in Drew's face. I didn't care if a stem poked him in the eye. Mercifully, he backed off. Not the other two. Dale took Drew's place. Craig assaulted Eli.

I begged for mercy. I screamed, hoping Pot would hear, but he didn't or he would have come running. Perhaps he had gone inside. Eli would not surrender. He remained mute. He panted with the effort. They continued.

Suddenly, Helen appeared, running from our yard across the street. No doubt, she heard my screams. "Tell her to go away," Eli gasped at me.

"No," I blubbered. I kicked a leg out at Dale, catching him on the knee.

"Youch," he exclaimed. He poked my chest. I kicked him again. "Stop hurting us," I yelled, but he did not.

"Dee, what are you doing?" Helen asked.

"Go get Mary Lily," I shouted to her. If Eli heard me, he didn't respond. By then, perhaps, he couldn't.

Helen flew off on her kindergarten feet. Thankfully, quickly, my aunt appeared, Helen trailing her. Perhaps the boys sensed her presence, for they slowed their assault.

"Mary Lily," I called. Craig and Dale immediately stopped, their hands arrested at their sides. No longer part of the melee, Drew grasped his hands behind his back.

I watched Mary Lily move one hand to her throat; the other gripped her beautiful hair, pulled it high off her head. I beckoned her with my eyes. She stepped forward, not twenty feet from us, her gauzy skirt pressed against her legs.

"Go away, it's just a game," Eli said to his mother.

"I want her to make them stop," I cried.

"What's going on out here?" she asked.

The boys spun around.

"Playing a game, Mama. We're fine," Eli answered. "Go back in the house." At first she ignored him. She inched forward, shoulders bent, leaning awkwardly toward us. "Go," Eli shouted. She did what Eli commanded. She backed away, but did not turn until she was nearly to the house.

Quickly, the boys untied us and scattered across the yard. For long minutes, Eli heaved from the exertion he'd endured. Helen stood staring. "Go home," I called to her.

"I don't have to," she snapped.

"Yes, you do," I said. "You have no business here."

Her head hanging, her toes scuffing reluctantly at every step, my sister retreated across the street.

The rope hung like a sash on the tree, caught by the bark from falling. Once he caught his breath, Eli couldn't be still. He walked around the tree, pulled the rope free, looped it between his arm and elbow like the cowboy he didn't get to be. He breathed in choppy gasps and muttered to himself about being a "candy ass."

Finally, I spoke. "You're wrong. You had no way to defend yourself. I'm never, ever going to speak to those boys again. They are mean." I hugged my arms across my chest.

Eli looked at me; I believe he had forgotten I was there. "They shouldn't have done it to a girl, not to you." He strode toward me and planted his hand between my tightened arms, trying to loosen them. "You're okay?" I remember his discerning tone, perceptive far beyond his years. I nodded, barely.

"It was a game to test us," he said. His focus shifted to himself again. His tone hardened. "A test to see if I could take it." He held the looped rope and pulled down hard, making it taut. "You don't understand how it is, Delia," he continued. He stretched the circle of rope so tightly it reddened his hands. His face reddened, too.

What I did understand was in the short space of the summer, things had changed. There was the Eli before Boston, and there was this Eli. I hated those boys for taking advantage of me, for humiliating me. I hated them more for tormenting Eli. He'd returned from Boston—the visible signs of his accident gone—resolved to prove himself. To start with a clean slate. And the way he saw it, these ignorant boys had defeated him.

◈

I knew somehow Mary Lily would be waiting on the front porch. I walked in that direction. Eli trailed me, saying nothing. My aunt sat on the white wicker settee in the curving crook of the porch. I touched the banister gently, testing my balance on the steps as I approached. Her hands folded primly one over the other, her airy skirt fluffed out formally around her. She didn't look our way. She gazed in the opposite direction toward her rose garden. She could have been posing for a portrait in the afternoon shadows slanting across the porch.

I hardly ever saw Mary Lily sit, and if I did, still she was occupied, likely at the piano with her skirt hiked out of the way, freeing her legs to work the pedals. Deliberately, I walked in front of her, not knowing what I was aiming for. I continued past her to the corner of the porch and stood. Eli remained on the steps. Barely, formally, my aunt moved her head toward me, as though to say she wasn't really there at all, merely a statue in my path.

Eli called to her. She swiveled her head toward him.

"Don't ever, ever do anything like that again. I can take care of myself," he said. His voice cracked. I believed he might cry.

"Ellison, please understand. Helen came to the door. And then I heard the screams. I didn't want you and Adeline to get hurt." Her voice was forceful even as her expression remained placid and her body still.

Eli exploded. Not directing anger at his mother, exactly, but out to the world. Out of control, he railed about taking care of himself. My body clenched. I felt every muscle in my neck and arms and legs.

The front screen door slammed. I watched Uncle Gene lunge in huge steps across the porch. The pale gold liquid in his glass splashed across his arm, dotted the porch floor. He banged the glass down on the table beside the settee where Mary Lily perched.

"Boy, what is this?" he growled. He grabbed Eli's shoulders, nearly lifting him. Eli's chin jutted out. "You must have lost your mind. I can hear you from the back of the house."

He let go of Eli, reached to the front of his pants, and unbuckled his belt. In one quick motion, he yanked. The strap of the belt lay across his thick palms. I recoiled at the sight. "You don't talk to your mother that way, you hear? Not ever." I wanted to flee but couldn't make myself move.

Eli's chin remained rigid, a stoic soldier. "She needs to know...," he began.

"I don't care what you want her to know. She's your mother. You don't talk to her that way."

"Yes sir," Eli answered, quiet and low. But he was seething. I saw his fingers twitch convulsively at his sides. He was fighting for control with all his might.

"Apologize before we go inside, and mean it, or the licks with this belt will be twice as many," he commanded.

"I'm sorry," Eli said stiffly. Then I saw him mouth to his mother, "Don't tell him; don't tell anyone what happened."

At that moment no one on the porch was the person I thought I knew. Not Eli compressed with anger, nor Mary Lily sitting statuesque, though clearly, I saw her eyes brimming. And especially not Gene, unyielding—his caterpillar eyebrows drawn together toward the bridge of his nose.

I had no concept of the beating that awaited Eli. The most I ever got was a couple of pops on the bottom with Mama's green hairbrush. My father's hand had spanked me only once. When I lied to him about emptying green peas from my plate—I detested them—behind the kitchen door next to my seat at the dining table. I insisted Helen had pitched the peas. I was spanked for lying, for blaming my sister, not for hating peas.

I thought Mary Lily would speak up on Eli's behalf, but she never moved or said a word. She sat in that same position until Eli walked ahead of Gene into the house. I realized this beating was not a first-time occurrence when she took a deep breath and exhaled very slowly. I didn't know what to do. I was frightened. If I am honest, though I had never been his victim and Eli never told me anything concrete, I knew Uncle Gene possessed an inclination to be cruel.

My aunt abruptly stood, reached out, took my hand. Shaking out her skirt, she asked me to walk with her to the back garden. She stood tall and straight, her willowy figure still composed. I wondered if she was taking me from the house so I wouldn't hear Eli react from inside. But I couldn't imagine my resolute cousin surrendering to screams. Nevertheless, she hurried me away and held my hand all the way as we walked, remarking she had late zinnias blooming and would cut some for my mother. "Ellison will be fine," she said finally and squeezed my hand.

I didn't think he would be fine at all. I didn't think Mary Lily was in some kind of denial; I thought she was scared, too, of Uncle Gene, who never even asked Eli to explain. Who was whipping my cousin with his belt.

She picked up a shallow basket and gardening shears from the shed. She directed me to cut fat blooms of gold, red, pink, and green zinnias blooming around the rectangular concrete fountain. "Cut Jeanette lots of green ones. She loves the green ones," she said. "They're uncommon." I waited for her to say more about what had happened on the porch, but she never did.

At home, Mama stood over the stove frying onions and peppers to start spaghetti sauce. It was awfully warm for spaghetti, but it was of my daddy's favorites. The front part of her hair formed a wet circle around her face, little brown curls smashed flat to her skin. "How lovely," she exclaimed on seeing the flowers. "Did Mary Lily send those to me?"

I nodded. Moments later, I began to cry.

She sat me at the table. I poured out the story to her: the boys, the tickling, Uncle Gene's belt...

She rose and turned down the stove. She walked to the white metal cabinet, my nemesis with its rusty, squeaking hinge because I could never sneak a snack without her knowing. It squeaked loudly now as she opened the door. She held out a small, green bottle, one of her coveted Coca-Colas. My heart leaped. Normally, I was allowed this luxury only at Sunday lunch and on occasion, after school.

She lifted the church key from the drawer and pried off the cap. She pursed her lips as she emptied ice cubes from the metal tray into a glass and poured the fizzing brown tonic over the ice. "You're growing up, Delia," she said, handing me the Coke. Her first words since I'd told the whole story. "Things will be different. It's hard for me to explain, but let me try."

"Boys play differently," she continued. "And it's other things, too. I know you love Eli, and you will always be close. It's just that..."

"You can't tell me not to play with Eli. He's my best friend," I interrupted her, all but shouting. Coke burned up my nose. I started to cry again.

"Of course. I don't mean that. But things have to change, Delia. They just do."

"But Eli isn't like other boys," I said. I love him more than my best friend, I started to say but didn't. "It was Dale and Drew and Craig who caused all the trouble," I said instead.

"Yes and no," she responded.

I didn't know what she meant. I only knew I felt worse than before. The Coke now felt like a bribe. "Never mind, Mama. Just never mind. I shouldn't have told you," I said and left the last few sips of Coke in the glass.

"Delia," she called, "when your daddy gets home, we can talk about this better." But I had already left the room and pretended I didn't hear. I passed by my sister in the den, watching *Dark Shadows*, a new show about a vampire named Barnabas Collins and other frightening creatures. She wasn't supposed to watch the show because though it didn't scare her during the day, it frightened her at night. Normally, I would have threatened to tattle, because whenever she couldn't sleep after she sneaked and watched the forbidden show, she came in my room, waking me. That day, I ignored her. I flung myself onto my bed. My mother liked to act like Daddy was the authority, but it was a cover. She mostly made the rules, and he went along. If I threw in her face how Daddy would let me make my own decisions if not for her, she reminded me, "He has to work like a dog in that mill and doesn't know how things are raising a child all day." It was one of her favorite lines. Probably because you couldn't make a comeback to something like that.

I make my mother sound intransigent. She wasn't. She was a worrier and obsessively protective, still is. And if I am honest, looking back, I see she perhaps fathomed the grown-up feelings developing between Eli and me.

As it happened, when Daddy came home, and we sat eating our spaghetti dinner, Mama didn't bring up the story of me tied to the pecan tree. My father seemed tired, and I guessed she decided not to trouble him.

That night, though, lying in wait for Helen to appear—not minding for once to be my little sister's comforter, for she had saved me—I could hear bits and pieces of my parents' conversation floating from the den, even with the television on. "Boys," and "older," I heard Mama say. Then, "I don't think things are…over there."

"Gene?" I heard Daddy say my uncle's name in a question.
"Drinking," I heard my mother answer.

9

AUGUST 1966

For a few days, my mother prevailed by keeping me occupied, so that Eli and I did not see each other. She suggested I invite both Nealy and Gloria to spend the night at the same time. She did other things she didn't often do. Like take Helen and me to the mill swimming pool without us begging. We swam—not just for an hour but all afternoon, eating moon pies on our breaks—while Mama sat in the hot sun, continually mopping her face and neck with a towel.

Another day, she took me to the cloth shop at Belk's where I chose a loud pink and lime green paisley print for a simple shift pattern with which—finally—she was going to teach me to sew. Eventually, though, my uneven seams and difficulty with facing and turning the armholes and neck of my dress tested her limits. Mama wore down, finished the dress herself, and let me loose to roam.

It was an afternoon when clouds had begun to darken and coalesce. I decided to scoot over to Eli's before the rain could start. The air steamed hot and heavy, like nature had cast a thick, wool blanket over our neighborhood. Maybe, though, without the sun beating down, it would be cool enough in the attic. Maybe Eli would be in the mood to consult the Ouija board. I had reached the fence gate and swung it open, ready to bound toward the house when I heard something— human sounds—somewhere. I stopped. I listened. Nothing. I was mistaken. I wiped at sweat dropping down my forehead.

I had stepped onto the bottom porch tread when I thought I heard voices again. I backed myself out into the front yard to listen. I heard nothing, and I didn't see anyone. Not Eli. Or Pot. Or Mary Lily. Not even Uncle Gene. Yet I walked around the corner of the house and turned toward Mary Lily's perennial gardens. Why, I don't know. Something drew me.

I hardly noticed the asters, their stunning purple stars coming into bloom along the path. Instead, I proceeded single-mindedly, until the voices, several voices—at first low, inaudible, intermittent—emerged.

I saw them, only partially hidden, in the tall joe-pye weed. Craig, Dale, and Drew stood over Eli, naked from the waist down. Craig's arms encircled Eli's stomach from the front, in a position that thrust his hips toward the dark sky. Dale stood behind my cousin, the jaws of a small crescent wrench in his hand. It was a common tool boys carried for bicycle repair in leather saddlebags beneath their seats. Eli had this tool in his own kit.

At first I stayed back, but close enough to see and to hear Dale's words, which during my approach had sounded mostly like animal growls. "This is what happens to a mama's boy who tattles," he snarled. "We got our asses beat to a pulp. Because you told your mama to rat on us, when we just were playing a regular game. Now, it's your turn."

I watched as Dale touched the smooth metal handle of the wrench to Eli's bottom, and I realized, without even knowing such acts existed, what Dale was about to do. I ran forward, yelling at them to stop. "Get out of here," I commanded when I reached the edge of the scene.

But instead of leaving, Craig motioned to Drew, and he came toward me—if reluctantly at first—and grabbed my wrists, dragging me forward into the group. I screamed.

"Cover her mouth," Craig said. He sneered in my direction.

Drew pinned my arms with one of his and cupped his other hand over my mouth. I tried to bite, but only my tongue could reach his fingers. They were too far away from my teeth.

"This is even better," Dale proclaimed. "Delia can watch what happens to sissies who tattletale."

Eli didn't look up. His head pointed toward the dirt. I saw his shoulders quivering beneath his shirt. I twisted and kicked at my oppressor, trying to break free, but Drew was far stronger than I.

Lightning lit the sky in a frightening, jagged line. "Watch what happens to blabbermouths, Delia," Dale said, looking directly at me. He maneuvered the end of the smooth, metal handle between Eli's buttocks and pushed. I saw my cousin jerk. I closed my eyes against Eli's pain, but I saw everything with my ears when I heard my cousin grunt. My stomach roiled in agony, both for Eli and out of my own fear.

"Eli, that you out there in the garden? Sounded like somebody screamed. Who you with? It's coming up a storm. Y'all need to get inside." It was Pot, his deep, expressive voice reverberating across the garden.

I heard the wrench thud onto the ground and opened my eyes to see the three boys fold over low and flee toward the back entrance of the garden. Eli had fallen onto his stomach.

"It's just us, Eli and me," I called to Pot. "We're coming on in a minute or two." My mouth became watery when I spoke; I held on to my stomach and took deep breaths. I sat and put my head between my knees, determined not to vomit.

"All right, then," Pot called back from the direction of the toolshed where he was likely putting things away. "'Cause you can't stay out with lightning shooting straight down like this, even if it don't rain."

I reached for Eli's shorts. "We've got to go inside," I said, heaving, yet somehow—miraculously—containing the churning contents of my stomach.

"I don't care," he mumbled. He kept his face toward the ground, his forehead buried into the backs of his hands.

"Please, Eli. Here. Put on your shorts. I'm not looking." He didn't move.

"You can't stay out here. It's dangerous," I said. Still he didn't move. "I'm not leaving without you, and if we don't go in, Pot will come get us."

"Shut up." He turned his face away from me. I touched him on the back, and he shuddered. "Leave—me—alone."

"They're gone. It's okay," I said, though I couldn't imagine anything ever being okay again.

Finally, Eli raised himself enough to sit, his back to me. "I told Mama not to tell anyone," he said, though I could barely hear him. "I told her." I stood and laid his shorts and underwear beside him. He grasped the shorts. At first he held them in his lap, and then, finally, he put both legs in at once and pulled them to his waist without ever standing.

"What about your underwear? You can't leave it in the garden," I said. He shook his head. His hair was matted from perspiration, and the clumps swung wetly together.

73

"I'm scared," I said.

He turned then, and I saw. He was weeping. Not a little, but in great streams flooding his face. I had never seen him cry, and I, too, began to cry, soon consumed with sobs. Thunder cracked around us.

"Eli," Pot called again. "You and Delia on the way? Come on in the house now."

"We're on the way," I called in return, choking out the words. I picked up Eli's underwear and stuffed it under my shirt.

I looked at my cousin sitting on the ground, his tears still spilling. I leaned down beside him and pulled at him by the arms. He rose. We walked side by side to the house. Eli used his shirttail to dry his eyes while I swiped clammy fingers across my own, hard, slanting rain pelting our skin.

10

SEPTEMBER 1966

I started fifth grade eagerly, ready to return to schoolwork and the activities that started back in the fall: Girl Scouts and church choir practice. But Eli shocked his parents by refusing to go to school. He wouldn't tell them why, and nothing they said, neither threat nor bribe, swayed him. The only activity he agreed to was his piano lessons with Miss Faulkenberry, an old maid and the second best pianist in town next to Mary Lily.

Eli loved playing the piano. He could play with a power and feeling like no young person I've heard before or since. Within a couple of years, he would perfect a high-spirited and difficult version of "Yankee Doodle," certain sections bringing him up off the piano bench and making my breath catch in my throat.

Only I knew it wasn't the idea of schoolwork affecting Eli's dark mood. I saw it in the way his feet moved—no hint of the turned-out jaunt, of slinging his feet at an angle that was his custom when he felt energetic. He couldn't stand the thought of seeing those boys at school. I tried to talk to him, declaring that no one—not the toughest boy on earth—could have beaten back three mean boys by himself, but he didn't want to hear anything I had to say. My attempts to help him feel better only made him feel worse. He told me to stop, ordered me not to mention it ever again, not to him or anyone, and I obeyed.

After a few days of his parents pressing him to know what was wrong and why he wouldn't go to school—I pleaded ignorance when questioned—Eli exploded. Uncle Gene exploded too. Mary Lily decided Eli should go out to Magnolia Manor and stay with Mimi for a while. She picked up his schoolwork every day from our teacher, Mrs. Myers, and Mimi supervised the lessons. Some afternoons I accompanied Mary Lily. In the evening, either Mama or Daddy came for me. At Mimi's old oak table in the kitchen, while Caro prepared dinner for us, I did my homework or read a book while Eli studied, occasionally asking me a question about something or other I had learned that day, a crazy makeshift version of school.

One night, an extra person appeared in Mimi's kitchen. It was a surprise to see a young woman open the door up the back steps at dusk and enter our midst. Mimi looked up from Eli's math book and turned toward her. Then she turned back to us. "This is Francie," she said matter-of-fact, while Eli and I gazed in amazement at this girl, surely not so many years older than us, who might have been pretty with her large, dark eyes and long, pale hair, but for her large fleshy body, its thick arms and heavy legs protruding from a formless sack dress.

Eli stood as he'd been taught to do. I decided to stand, too. "Goodness, have a seat," the girl said and laughed.

"Francie is going to help Caro and me in the house, going to help with some of Pot's work, too, while he's gone," Mimi explained. "He's been showing her around today." I knew Pot was planning to leave soon for St. Louis to care for a dying uncle who had left the South long ago during the Great Migration. But I wondered why Mimi needed someone else, especially a young woman, when she and Caro handled everything inside and there were a couple of men who worked regularly for Pot.

Mimi invited Francie to sit at the table with us. I glanced toward Caro, wondering if Francie would be eating dinner. Then, I saw Caro was indeed expecting Francie, because she'd stacked an extra dinner plate beside the stove. Sometimes Pot ate with us, and sometimes he didn't. But since no one ever knew whether to expect him, there was never a plate set out for him until he happened to appear.

"I'm about done in with New Math," Mimi said to all of us, exasperated. Before Francie arrived, she'd been studying Eli's math book. "Why do you have to figure out putting all these numbers into sets, when all you have to do is learn your multiplication tables? I excelled at mathematics in school, but that was before this silliness."

"Don't worry about it," Eli told his grandmother. "I'll figure it out." Both Eli and Mimi knew better than to ask me.

"Maybe I can help," Francie intervened. "I studied set theory in school." We learned she was a junior at Green Branch High School.

By the time Francie was through explaining and giving practice problems, the sets made sense even to me.

76

"Well now," Mimi said. "This is still too much candy for a nickel, but at least we've got it now." She leaned over and patted Francie affectionately on the arm.

୬

Back home on Congress Street, Uncle Gene fumed about Eli's absence from school. He wasn't having "his boy" act this way. And "what the hell was Eli afraid of," he bellowed to Mama in our den one Saturday morning, while I listened from around the corner.

"Have you thought about having someone talk to Eli? Maybe someone at the church?"

"You sound like Mary Lily. What is it with you women? No outsiders," he yelled. Mama shook her head. She didn't know what to say.

"I don't know what it is, but I'm going to change it."

"Remember, Eugene," my mother cautioned him. "You can always catch more flies with honey than vinegar." It was so typical of Mama to come up with one of her sayings. I almost moaned and gave myself away.

It was a mystery how, but somehow I believe my uncle knew. Not the specifics, but still the shadow monkey, he intuited something awful had happened to his son. I feared him, yet even as I had witnessed his cruel streak, I also knew he would do almost anything for Eli.

Gene's cookie route took him all over the state, and one afternoon in mid-September he came home with a two-foot alligator in the back of his van. Where it had come from he was never to tell. We questioned him repeatedly, but all he ever said was, "Below the fall line." That meant somewhere below Columbia. It could have been anywhere: a river, a marsh, a farm pond, or a drainage ditch. And for all I knew, even a pet store in Florida.

Like the gift of Fred the pig so long before, Gertrude the alligator brought Eli out of his shell and home to Congress Street. And unlike her predecessor, Gertrude—a gender guess, for who knew the sex of an alligator—made no loud noise. She didn't disturb the neighbors. The afternoon Eli returned, he and Gene put the alligator in the long concrete fountain surrounded now in early fall by chrysanthemums

77

(replacing the zinnias turned puny at the end of summer). The day before, Pot and Gene had strung four-foot-tall dog wire to enclose the area.

The spring returned to Eli's step. I watched father and son from a distance—for I had no desire to get close to the alligator—learn to handle the beast. Over and over, Gene picked up Gertrude, and eventually Eli held her, too. I shuddered when I saw the alligator twist her head back toward Eli's hand. I marveled when he held firm, and she gave up the fight. I watched Uncle Gene hold up his thumb in approval.

Predictably, living on our street, Craig and the twins learned of Gertrude. Surely it was Uncle Gene who put out the word. Shameless, they knocked on the Winfields' door after school one afternoon. Uncle Gene greeted them and escorted everyone to the yard.

Helen and I saw the crowd gathered at the fountain and arrived not long after the boys. Gene held the creature with one hand on the base of her tail and the other around her neck, his thumb under her chin. I kept my distance, Helen beside me.

"Step up close, fellas," Gene said to the boys, also hanging back. All except for Eli who stood close by his father. "Who wants to hold her?"

"Me," Eli exclaimed, and Gene handed the alligator over to him. Eli held Gertrude exactly as Gene had, with only one difference. Instead of gripping all his fingers around the reptile's neck, he stroked the back of her head with his index finger. The alligator appeared to smile and closed her protruding eyes.

"Come touch her," Gene coaxed the other boys. Eli thrust Gertrude toward them. He wasn't a bit afraid. Craig stepped forward. He laid his hand on the alligator's back.

"Want to hold her?" Eli asked.

"No, it feels like dry turd," Craig answered. He was trying to be tough. As if he'd ever picked up a turd.

Drew and Dale stepped up for a turn. Dale touched the tail. "It's just rough and bumpy," he proclaimed. Drew did the same and agreed. But like Craig, neither of them wanted to hold Gertrude.

I looked at the long snout, the tiny pointed teeth peeking out. I was intrigued by the darkish green-gray stripes, the little pyramid tips ridging the chalky hide, but not enough. "No thanks," I said when Uncle Gene asked if I wanted to hold her.

"Oh come on Delia, don't be a sissy," Eli said. He winked at me and flicked an index finger rakishly above his eyebrow, his signature charm emerging even then.

"Yeah, Dee," said Helen. "I'll do it."

"You're young and stupid. Go ahead," I told my sister.

"Well, now, how about that?" Uncle Gene chuckled.

I feared Gertrude would sense Helen's small hands, wriggle from the grip, and flip her head back to attack my sister. "Don't you dare," I shrieked at Helen. "It'll bite." For once, she listened to me.

"What say we feed Gertrude?" Uncle Gene suggested. He set her on the ground. Gertrude stood at attention, blinking at us, moving her tail back and forth.

Gene had carried out a canvas sack under his arm—rolled tight at the top—and laid it on the ground. Now, he opened the bag and pulled from it a live mouse, so young it had no hair. It was all pink skin.

Uncle Gene handed the mouse to Eli who held it in his palm. The boys gathered close to watch. I pulled Helen to me and backed us farther away.

"Do what I told you," Gene said to Eli. "Put it down and Gertrude will take care of it."

A sound like a hiss arose from the alligator, and then, in a millisecond, she darted forward, jaws open. She lifted the poor mouse in her teeth. I turned my head.

"I saw the blood," Craig hollered a minute later. The other boys laughed. Quickly, Craig recovered and joined them.

I thought I might be sick. But my reaction mattered not at all. What mattered was the boys and what they thought. And what they thought made all the difference. I saw it in their bearing. They would not trouble my cousin again.

Eli returned to school, and a kind boy named Tim Morris remarked first on my cousin's changed appearance. "Hey, Eli," he called exuberantly, getting Eli's attention and everyone else's marching in line from the auditorium to Mrs. Myers' classroom, "you look good. You don't have that thing in your throat anymore." Anyone could see something had been wrong with Eli's throat because the scar was still raw and red. But if you hadn't known him, you might have thought he'd simply cut it in an accident.

Later in the fall when the weather cooled, Gertrude had to go inside. She lived in Eli's bathtub. Every night before he bathed, he lifted her into a big galvanized tub residing in a corner of the bathroom. Afterward, he put her back. He handled his pet by himself, fearless.

Before the winter was out, though, the whole business of keeping a rapidly growing alligator in the bathroom and feeding it in the house overwhelmed Mary Lily. Arrangements were made to transport Gertrude in the cookie van to the nature museum a couple of hours away.

I thought Eli would fight harder to keep Gertrude. But he didn't much protest. For after all, I supposed, she had accomplished her mission. Eli had earned those boys' respect.

11

JANUARY 1967

Back in school and flourishing in Mrs. Myers' fifth-grade class at Chesterfield Grammar School, Eli still liked going out to Mimi's for what he called his "tutoring sessions" with Francie. He was taken with her, with how smart she was. He loved to ask her questions. Sometimes, I went too, and I have to say, there were few questions we asked, whether US history, New Math, or Earth Science, that Francie could not answer. And when on occasion she didn't know, it delighted Eli to catch her.

One cold Saturday morning in January, Mary Lily called our house to say Eli was bored and driving her crazy, so she was taking him out to Magnolia Manor for the day and would I like to go, too. Helen and I were watching television. Saturday morning cartoons grated on Mama's nerves. She'd asked me to lower the volume three times, but I hadn't. She was delighted for me to vacate the house and thereby redirect Helen to a quieter interest. On our drive to Magnolia Manor, Eli anticipated Francie being at the house, puttering around the kitchen. He had a question for her about the solar system. To see if she knew why the moon has more craters than the earth. Who knew how he came up with that one.

As soon as Mary Lily reached the bottom of the long drive, I strained to see the house through the branches of huge magnolias, no white popcorn flowers adoring them at this time of year, but beautiful still with their ice-glossy leaves. When the house popped into clear view, I sighed with pleasure, for it was a place I loved, an imposing Greek revival built before the Civil War by Lauderdale ancestors. It was shaded from the blazing sun by a two-tiered portico supported by Doric columns across the front. Old boxwoods crossed the front of the foundation.

Eli nearly fell into the hedge jumping out of the car to get to the door and ring the bell. Not an ordinary doorbell, this was a beautiful brass bell—etched with an intricate vine of flowers—hung on a pedestal by the door. My cousin loved the sounds of bells.

"Where's Francie?" he asked his grandmother as soon as she answered.

"She didn't come today." Mimi shrugged her shoulders nonchalantly, but I saw the concern in her eyes.

"Why not?" Eli asked, exasperated.

"I don't know," Mimi said. "She didn't come yesterday either." I don't think she meant to tell us the second part, because her hand flew up and touched her lips, but it had slipped out.

"Did you call her?"

"Well, yes, but she wasn't home and her father didn't know for sure where she was. He said he thought at a friend's house."

"That is very strange," Eli observed.

Mimi nodded pensively, vaguely twisting her hands into the skirt of her dress.

❧

Without Francie to keep us company and enlighten us, Eli decided we should walk to the river—not a real river but Cane Creek at the back of Mimi's property that we called a river because it ran deep—and look for crawfish.

"It's too cold," I exclaimed.

"Just right for catching crawfish," Eli said. The creatures slowed down in winter, making it possible to pick up rocks just inside the water's edge and find them huddled beneath. I liked the idea of staying indoors better.

Eli prevailed, and before we'd even taken off our coats since arriving, we were out the back door with a milk bucket.

The hardwoods were bare, but the evergreens and undergrowth grew thick once we reached the end of the pasture. I could have easily lost the way, but Eli led us forward. We stopped at a broad, open, bare spot of hard-packed clay near the shoreline where rocks lined the water's edge like a miniature wall. A place where the water swirled swiftly in eddies. Eli removed his gloves and sat the bucket on the ground. He squatted and picked up the biggest rock within his reach.

Sure enough, a sluggish brown-gray, nearly translucent crawfish lay beneath. The antennae moved first and then the reddish pinchers twitched. "This will be a breeze," Eli squealed. "We'll get a bucket full. Take off your gloves. Dig in."

"No, thanks," I said. Though I had gone so far as to squat beside my cousin, I was not about to pick up a crawfish.

"They're good to eat."

"Not to me," I responded. I couldn't imagine putting that creature into my mouth. "I'm too cold anyway. My hands would freeze in that water."

"Chicken," Eli said and laughed. But before he could stir up more rocks, we heard something coming through the trees and brush. Both of us jerked up to standing. The hood of my coat fell back. Eli grabbed up his gloves and the bucket with its lone crawfish scrambling noisily inside.

"Dump it out. Let's go," I hissed. "It could be a wild animal."

"There aren't any wild animals. Maybe a deer is all," Eli said. "It's the most open part of the creek where they would drink." Nevertheless, he followed my directive and tilted the bucket. The crawfish escaped. Then we ran, the bucket bumping against Eli's left knee, back into the trees in the opposite direction from the sound, but not far from the shore. Eli scuttled behind the trunk of a large, downed pine, covered with vines and scrub.

"Not here. There'll be snakes," I said.

"Not in winter."

"Are you sure?"

Eli touched his fingers to his lips, but I kept talking.

"Maybe it's people," I ventured. "But who would be out here?"

"No one. I'm telling you it's probably deer. Now, shush so we can see what's out there before it sees us." He peeked up over the fallen tree trunk and gazed toward the clearing by the creek where we'd been.

"What do you see?"

"Delia, look," he whispered.

"What?" I drew my head above the trunk and saw Francie standing at the bank. In almost the same place we had squatted minutes before. I squeezed Eli's arm. "What is she doing here? What's she carrying? Where did she come from?"

"Maybe she parked on the dirt road. That's the direction she came from through the woods. It doesn't matter. Shh. Don't talk. She might hear."

I had forgotten I was cold in the January air, for Francie wore nothing for warmth but a baggy cardigan sweater. We watched her place something on the ground, and then we heard soft human cries coming from the dirt. A baby, I realized. I rose up and squinted my eyes to see better. A just-born baby as tiny as Helen had been when she came home from the hospital.

Quietly, Eli slithered around to the front side of the tree and crawled forward on his stomach, staying under the jumbled pine branches. I grabbed his foot, but he shook off my hand and shooed me away. I almost shrieked, but I caught myself. Eli kept inching forward. I stayed behind the tree trunk, but I watched.

Francie held a burlap sack and bent down to the water's edge. She began to gather rocks, putting them in the sack. Why was she putting rocks in a bag and leaving a baby on the ground in the cold? Whose baby was it? The only possible answer hit me as I was still asking the questions in my head. This was Francie's baby. And no one had known because she was big all over. I put my own hands over my mouth to keep from crying out.

Eli realized at the same moment as I, for he turned his head back toward me, and I saw his eyes huge and alarmed. I was too terrified to stay back behind the tree by myself. I crawled slowly around the tree trunk same as Eli had done. I reached him, and we huddled together among pine needles and leaves, horizontal and motionless on our stomachs.

When the bag was heavy with rocks, Francie picked up her baby. We were close enough that I could see it wasn't a white baby, but it wasn't dark like a colored person either. I looked at Eli, wondering if he saw, too. I couldn't help myself. I opened my lips and mouthed the word, "How." And then Eli stopped me from going further by pulling my head up under his arm, afraid, I suppose, that I was going to speak. Or maybe it was that he didn't want me to see. I never asked, for what came after superseded everything.

For a few minutes, I lay still under Eli's arm. I did not want to see, and I did miss the worst of it. I missed seeing Francie put her now quiet child into the bag and tie it tight with twine from her sweater pocket. I missed seeing her lower the sack and its contents into the fast-moving frigid water. I missed watching the baby in the sack move a little ways downstream, then sink.

But when Eli began to shake beside me, and when I heard an awful wailing from the creek's edge, I came back into the world and opened my eyes. I moved my head from under my cousin's grasp and looked. I did not want to, but something, some dreadful human urge, impelled me. I saw Francie down on her knees by the bank. The sounds she made were not crying. They were primal howls.

It seemed like forever. Time stopped and there was only the tableau of Francie folded over and the sounds she made and Eli and me frozen in place. I couldn't have moved even if I'd wanted to. Finally, Francie rose and drew her arms around herself. Her long, loose hair was terribly tangled across her face. She looked around; she shook herself from side to side. It was a gruesome sight. I feared she would see us, even through the cover of the brush. But she didn't. And I realized she might not have seen us even if we were right in front of her. She was crazed.

❧

Eli and I never told anyone about the baby. My cousin decided it must remain a secret forever because Francie had told none of us she was pregnant, and she would be put in jail for what she had done. I didn't disagree. I wanted to forget.

After Francie walked away that day, her heavy body slow and unwieldy as she moved back toward the woods in the direction opposite us, Eli and I sat on the trunk of the fallen pine tree. We tried to fathom what he had seen and I had shut my eyes against—Francie drowning her newborn baby, neither colored nor white.

Strangely, our conversation came out more lucid then than it did later in the day. It was because the reality had not yet penetrated our whole selves, a kind of denial.

"Why did she drown her own baby?" Eli asked. "She could have given it up for adoption. Isn't that what unwed mothers do?"

"Maybe she didn't know how," I said. "And the daddy must be

colored. Who would adopt a baby like that?"

"How do you know?" he asked.

"I just do."

"Huh?" Eli inquired.

"Because its skin was light brown like cinnamon, not dark or white," I proclaimed. "A colored boy and a white girl would make a baby of a color in between." All of a sudden I thought of the crawfish dumped from the bucket and set free, nearly the same color.

"Oh," Eli said.

We might not have understood how genetics produced the color of a biracial child, but we understood the world in which we lived. We knew such a baby would fit nowhere, would be shunned by both colored and white. We knew Francie understood it, too.

"No one knew," Eli said. "Or she wouldn't have put her baby in the creek."

"No, she wouldn't," I agreed.

"I can't stop seeing it. I don't think she'll ever come back here."

Eli's hunch was right. Francie never returned to Mary Margaret's house. And no matter how he tried to approach the subject of Francie—that day when we returned to the house and in days or weeks to come—to find out more about her, Mimi was vague. She said only that she had known Francie's father for many years, and he suggested she hire his daughter to work after school. She added Francie's father thought she seemed restless and needed more of her time filled. "And, as you know, I needed help with Pot gone, so it was a good arrangement," she said.

"What about her mama?" Eli asked.

Mimi looked at both of us quizzically, and then her face turned down. "She's dead, honey," she said. "Family can be so hard," she whispered.

"What do you mean family is hard?" Eli asked quickly. "Was Francie's mama your family?"

"Oh no, darling, I didn't mean anything like that," her voice sort of sputtered. "No, I was thinking how it's sad that Francie lost her mother so young. I really didn't know her mother well. We were only acquaintances. Goodness." She fanned her hands fast like hummingbird wings at her face. The feeling I got from Mimi's flustered state was something more than a kind woman's normal concern for Francie's being motherless. Eli thought the same thing.

On the one hand, we could believe Mimi knew little more than what she told us. Because what difference would it make? On the other hand, after Eli asked what she meant about family, it was like pulling teeth that day for him to get his grandmother to tell us Francie's last name—for we had never been told, and it never occurred to us to ask.

He wouldn't let up about the name until, exasperated with her grandson, and likely worried, I thought at the time, about Francie not coming in to work for two days and not even calling, Mimi finally said her name was Turner to shut him up. She then shooed us off to the front porch bundled in our coats to wait on Mary Lily to pick us up.

"Why does it matter now? Her last name?" I asked Eli after we had settled uneasily on the front steps. "You said she's not coming back. How could she? How could she bear to come back here?"

"I want to know about her," he said.

"What do you want to know? Why? You can't change anything. You can't make it any different. The only thing that will be better is for us not to think about it."

"I'm going to find out about her. You saw how Mimi acted. It's a feeling I have. I can't explain it. There's a connection."

"You're thinking up crazy ideas about Francie," I wailed. Because it's like you're the baby that lived, I thought suddenly to myself. That's the real connection. Eli suffered for being different, and Francie's child, because it was dead, never would. Francie had made the decision to suffer instead.

The image of the wrench penetrating Eli rushed into my head. He never once talked about it. He buried that horror somewhere deep inside. Same as I'd tried to do because just like with Francie's baby, you can't make it any different, no matter how much you want to. All you can do is try to forget, not knowing then that you can never forget any of Eli's pain. That it will cultivate inside you like the purplish misshapen pearl Eli once found when he pried open a mussel in the creek, a treasure he'd brought home to show me—amazed at something beautiful originating from grit abrading the creature's inner shell.

"Don't think about any of it. Don't. You're not even making sense," I begged him that day, aching for him, for both of us. I felt sweat trickling down my back under my coat, though, with the sun waning late in the afternoon, it must have been nearly freezing outside.

He turned toward me. My cousin's face was pallid. And his eyes were huge as they'd been at the creek. I couldn't distinguish the pupils. "Francie didn't want her child to be shunned," he mumbled.

Instead of calming ourselves in the aftermath, instead of trying not to remember, Eli made it worse with his irrational resolve—going all over the place—wanting to know more about Francie, projecting his own experience into hers. My heart broke for Francie and for her baby, too, but it broke even more for Eli. I wanted to push it all away. I was too young to perceive how both of us were trying differently, desperately, to cope. And I had no idea then how long, or how far, he would pursue his suspicions.

12

MARCH 1968

In the passing weeks Eli persisted in his belief that Francie meant more to Mary Margaret than a girl she casually hired upon a father's request. He saw a difference in his grandmother's demeanor. He claimed she seemed disturbed, and knew it had to do with Francie. Surely, he determined, his grandmother would have called Francie's house to learn of her whereabouts. And if so, Francie would have made up a credible reason she couldn't return. So why, he continued to wonder, did Mimi seem anxious? It certainly wasn't the workload at Magnolia Manor because Pot had returned in late February.

Since it was us, not Mary Margaret, who knew the terrible truth, I thought my cousin was reading more into his grandmother's frame of mind than was warranted. He did not agree. I knew Mary Margaret well, but not like Eli. So I couldn't argue logically against his conclusion, though I wanted to. I wanted all thoughts of Francie to go away, but Eli wouldn't allow it. He wanted to talk about Francie. He wanted to find Francie.

But he wouldn't ask his mother anything. He figured Mary Lily knew nothing, or on the outside chance she did, he didn't want to put her on the alert because she might deter him. He decided to start with the only fact he knew: Francie's last name. He looked up Turner in the phone book and found fourteen entries.

"That's not too many," he said.

"Are you kidding? You're going to call fourteen people trying to find her?"

"Maybe I'll get lucky on the first or second try."

"And what if you do? What then? What would you say to her?" I asked.

"I don't know," he admitted. "I've got to find her first."

"Eli, let it go," I pleaded. "What good could come from your finding her?" But he didn't listen. In addition to believing in some unknown link between Mary Margaret and her employee, he felt an uncanny affinity with Francie.

Eli decided the calls must be made from my house so he wouldn't raise his mother's suspicion and create a shutout. I went along with him, thinking as soon as he actually confronted the reality of going to Francie's house, he would give up. We chose a Saturday morning when Daddy was at the plant, Mama was upstairs conducting spring cleaning, and Helen was safely entrenched in cartoons. It took six tries until Eli found Francie's house under the name Mace Turner.

"May I please speak to Francie?" Eli crooned as he'd done in the five previous calls.

"Who's calling?" The male voice rang out loud enough that sitting close to Eli, I could hear every word.

"I'm a friend of Francie's and would like to speak to her, please," Eli said.

"She's not here. Who's calling?"

"My name is Ellison. Francie helped me with schoolwork."

"She's not living here at present."

"Oh, then could you tell me where to find her?"

"I'm afraid I can't," the man said and hung up.

"We're going to his house," Eli announced as he replaced the receiver on the hook.

"No way," I said.

"Ah, Delia, come on. He'll talk to us if we're face to face. Look at the address. Not far at all. We can ride our bikes." My theory had been wrong.

"Please, let's see what he says." The plaintive look on my cousin's face did it. I caved in, thinking if I accompanied him to Mace Turner's house, finally he would be satisfied and let Francie go.

It took no more than ten minutes to reach the house at 161 Grove Street in the same old part of town as us. "This is where she lives," Eli murmured as we leaned our bikes against a large oak tree at the curb. It was an inauspicious dwelling, the shrubbery around the foundation overgrown and unkempt, the paint peeling on the columns, one lone rocking chair on the porch, yet the bungalow's aged bones exuded warmth.

We approached the porch. Eli rang the bell. Almost immediately, a man with hunched shoulders and wrinkly jowls dropping low on his face opened the door.

"Yes?" he inquired.

Eli stepped forward, unafraid. I hung back behind him. "My name is Ellison. I called a little while ago asking for Francie. Are you Mace Turner?"

"I am," the man said. "And I told you Francie is not here." His voice was direct but not unkind.

"Yes sir," Eli continued. "But would it be okay if my cousin here, Adeline," and he motioned toward me so that I had to step forward, "and I came in to say hello?"

"As long as you understand Francie is not here."

"Sure," Eli said.

Mr. Turner extended his arm and we entered a tidy if musty, dark living room. He walked to a floor lamp and turned it on. "I don't have company often," he said. "I haven't dusted lately." Eli nodded amiably.

Eli and I sat side by side on a camelback sofa. Mr. Turner lowered himself into a wingchair. "So, you are friends with my daughter?" he asked. "You're a good bit younger than she is." He smiled.

"Yes sir. She worked for my grandmother and helped both of us with our studies."

"Ah, I see. I know who you are. Mary Margaret Lauderdale's grandson." Again, Eli nodded.

"I don't have much to offer in the way of refreshments. I could offer you a glass of ice water." Simultaneously, Eli and I shook our heads, no.

"We miss Francie," Eli said. "We wonder when she might return."

"No time soon," Mr. Turner said. "She's gone to live with my sister to finish high school. She needed a woman's influence in her life instead of only an old widower like me."

Eli pinched his lips together. I knew he wanted to ask why, to see what Mace Turner would say, but he refrained.

"What town?" Eli asked. "I really miss her."

"I can't tell you that, son, but I can tell you Francie is in a good place." His voice sounded sad.

"So you're a widower," Eli prompted. My cousin amazed me. Unafraid to ask a complete stranger anything he wanted to know.

"Yes. My wife, Frances, died some years ago, only thirty-eight. She had kidney disease. She was sick for many years." He looked beyond us, his expression almost dreamy.

"I'm sorry to hear that," Eli said.

"Me, too," I said.

"Do you have other children?" Eli asked.

"Francie is our only child. We wanted more. The years go by, and you learn to get along," Mr. Turner said.

Though I did not move from my seat, I had the urge to comfort Francie's father, to walk over to him and put my arms around his neck. This man who looked older, I realized, than he likely was. His loneliness was palpable.

By asking what Mr. Turner did for a living, Eli landed on a subject he liked talking about. He was the head newspaper press operator at *The Examiner*, our local paper that came out three times a week. He told us all about the process, and it was pretty neat to learn how the ink went onto the paper through a roller to make words and pictures. Eli kept trying to return the conversation to Francie, but he never could.

"I wonder if he knows about Francie's baby," Eli said after Mr. Turner had closed the door behind us, and we were walking to our bikes.

"I don't guess we will ever know," I answered.

&

Instead of going home and bringing the investigation to an end, Eli said we were going to find the newspaper obituary for Francie's mother. Mr. Turner's talk about his job had given Eli that idea, and there was no deterring him. I didn't see what benefit an old obituary could be in discovering anything meaningful about Francie, but I went along to please Eli.

We rode our bikes to Meeting Street, parked them beside the stone steps of the two-story brick building that was our public library, and entered the place that always made me want to tiptoe.

At the circulation desk, Eli whispered to the librarian what he wanted. She whispered back that unless we knew how to use microfilm, no one was available on Saturdays to work the machine. We didn't even know what microfilm was. She suggested we come back on Wednesday, the day Miss Inez Wilson came in to help people researching material. Eli and I knew Miss Inez—as most people called her—our self-proclaimed town historian, because she had interviewed both our families for her books. She was an old busybody, but she did know a lot of things about Green Branch.

Eli anticipated Miss Inez asking questions he didn't want to answer about why he was looking for Frances Turner's obituary, so he dreamed up the idea of a school project in which our teacher assigned partners to choose a deceased person from Green Branch—but not in their own family—and research as much information as possible, then write up a report. He planned to tell Miss Inez we chose Frances Turner because she'd been a friend of his grandmother.

At first I told him to go on his own, that I didn't want to be in the partnership. That I never wanted to investigate Francie in the first place. But, as always, he cajoled, and once again, I went along that Wednesday after school.

By the time Eli finished explaining our project to Miss Inez, she had bought in hook, line and sinker. She asked if she might expect other children from our class to need her assistance, and Eli said he didn't know. I looked at him sideways, wondering what Miss Inez would think when no other kids came in for her help. I was thankful she didn't ask our teacher's name.

Miss Inez knew the name Frances Turner because she knew about everyone in town. She couldn't remember the exact year Mrs. Turner died, she said, but she thought around 1960. We watched as she efficiently clipped a reel on the left-hand side of a machine with a screen like a television. Miss Inez was in her element, her half-glasses down low on the edge of her nose. She threaded the film through a slot under what she said was a camera and secured the outer edge of the film into an empty reel on the right-hand side. Then, she pushed a button and images began to fly across the screen. News stories, advertisements, comics. Miss Inez slowed the pace when she was getting close to the obituary section of an issue. "It takes some getting used to," she explained, very official. I figured she knew the setup of the newspaper sections by heart.

"Wow," I exclaimed, not only because I was truly impressed but because I knew Miss Inez wanted me to be.

"Wow, indeed," intoned Miss Inez. "This school project is a fine idea to expose you young people to local history." I rolled my eyes, but of course she couldn't see. She was concentrating on the screen. She continued all the way through 1960, but we never saw Frances Turner.

"Well, now," Miss Inez muttered. "My memory needs some adjusting. Let's try 1959." And there it was, the write-up of Frances Turner's life and death on September 15, 1959. The same year as Eli's accident.

Miss Inez adjusted the focus so we could read more clearly. The deceased's given name was Frances Burchett Mobley Turner. Francie was listed as her only child, survived also by her husband, Mace Turner, and her mother, Louise Flynn Mobley. No siblings were listed, either dead or alive. We read Mrs. Turner was to be buried at Covenant Presbyterian Cemetery, and that's about all there was, except to say she was a homemaker. Eli started poking me in the side behind Miss Inez's back, annoying me. I pushed his hand away, and he started again. "What?" I finally said, rudely, making Miss Inez turn around.

"Yes?" Miss Inez inquired.

"Oh, excuse me," Eli said. "I was trying to tell Delia wouldn't it be a good idea to ask you to find Mrs. Mobley's obituary, and if you didn't, we would know she's still alive and could talk to her."

"No need in that, Ellison," Miss Inez responded. "She died a couple of years ago. But if you like, we can find her obituary, too."

"Oh, no," Eli said, disappointed. "That's okay."

"But here's something. You can check out my book that has a lot of history of the Mobley family, and you might find more information that way." Miss Inez nodded eagerly.

So Eli checked out the book, but I knew it was a ruse for Miss Inez's benefit. He wasn't interested in any Mobley history that far back.

"That was a lie you told Miss Inez," I said when we were out of the library and descending the steps. "You weren't trying to ask me if I thought we should look for Mrs. Mobley's obituary so we would know if she's alive or dead. You were going to ask Miss Inez that question all on your own. Why were you poking me so hard?"

"I thought the name would ring a bell with you. You know. Burchett."

"No." I shrugged my shoulders and threw up my hands.

"Yes you do. Think about it. Where have we seen that name?"

"I don't know. I give up. Give me a clue."

"Mimi's parlor," he said.

"Oh." I suddenly recalled. My cousin and I liked digging through the secretary, looking through old family papers, and Mimi had come into the room one day while we had a scroll of a family tree rolled out on the rug. I remarked that Eli might be kin to Carol Burnett and be invited onto her television show. Mary Margaret bent over to see what ancestor I was referring to.

She said we were looking at members of her family, the Castons, her maiden name. She corrected me and said the name I saw was Burchett, not Burnett, started to say something else but stopped midsentence and stood up straight. She said she had to get back to the kitchen. I hadn't thought about it at the time, but now her action seemed abrupt and therefore not like Mary Margaret at all. I didn't mention this detail to Eli.

"It's probably a coincidence," I suggested instead.

"I don't think so," Eli said.

"Just because Francie's mother was called Frances Burchett doesn't mean it has anything to do with the last name Burchett in Mimi's family."

"I don't think you'd name a girl Frances Burchett unless there was a family connection," Eli said. "I mean maybe Frances Jane or Sarah Frances, but Burchett is not a pretty name for a girl." He looked at me hard. I shrugged.

"Why don't you just ask Mimi about the name? Or ask your mama? Then we can have all this over with."

"No," Eli answered. "Whatever it is, Mimi wouldn't tell me. You know how she won't talk about Francie. And I don't want to ask Mama, because like I said before, if she doesn't know or doesn't want to tell me, then she'll get suspicious. And it might cause a big ruckus with Mimi."

"I'm hungry," I said. "It's got to be suppertime if you haven't noticed." I pointed at the darkening sky. "Mama will start having a fit worrying. And your mama will, too. I'm going to ride my bike home. Come on." Even if there was some distant family kinship between

Mary Margaret and Frances Burchett, I didn't care. I didn't see how it mattered, and I didn't see where there was any avenue for more information anyway. What mattered was getting Francie out of our heads, and I really was starving for supper.

13

JULY 1968

We were devoted Methodists. Eli's family hardly ever went to church. Mary Lily sometimes made a joke of it. She said they were lapsed Episcopalians. The way she said "lapsed" was supposed to be funny, but it always sounded sad.

Mama and Uncle Gene grew up Baptist. Mama started going to the Methodist church because of Daddy, but Mary Lily wasn't about to go to the Baptist Church with Uncle Gene. She said it was absurd because you had to be dunked in a pool of water in front of everyone to belong to their church. Eli said it wouldn't have made any difference if his mother had agreed to be Baptist. His old man wouldn't go to church anyway.

We had the church picnic on the lawn to celebrate the Sunday before July 4, and Nealy came home afterward with me. I suggested going over to Eli's to see what was happening on his side of the street. But Mama caught me by the arm and suggested cooking.

About the only time my mother had willingly let me into the kitchen was the year Sarah Wood and I made a meal for our families to earn our Girl Scout cooking badge. Mama stayed in view the whole time we prepared Shake and Bake Chicken, rice, and lima beans, with angel food cake for dessert. I'd like to say she feared we might burn down the house, but in reality it was all about the mess. She scurried around behind us, cleaning when I spilled sugar on the floor and when Sarah—my Catholic friend accustomed to disorder with seven siblings in her home—left greasy handprints everywhere.

Needless to say, the offer that Sunday afternoon to let Nealy and me untidy Mama's kitchen came as a surprise. She wasn't fooling me, though. It was a bribe to keep us occupied in the house instead of playing outdoors with the boys. Ever since the boys had tied me to the pecan tree, she'd been cautious about letting me loose on the street.

"Okay," I challenged her, "if we can make bananas Foster."

"Oh, Delia, don't be ridiculous," Mama said.

"It's you who suggested cooking," I said. I gave an exaggerated, puffed-up sigh.

"How about brownies? I've got all the ingredients for brownies," she countered. I acquiesced.

It must have been hard for her, but Mama retreated to the den and let us be. I put her to the test. I started a flour fight with Nealy. We got it on our faces, in each other's hair, and all over the floor. Mama looked in when she heard us squealing. But she stood staunch in the doorway, uncomplaining. I smeared chocolate batter on Nealy's ear. She retaliated with a daub on the back of my neck. "Girls," my mother began, but then she stopped.

As the timer beeped for the brownies to come out of the oven, the phone rang. We had just the one phone back then on the first floor in the kitchen, and even though Mama stretched the cord around the corner into the den, I could hear most of what she said. I knew immediately from her tone she was talking to Mary Lily.

"Oh, my, yes," she said. I looked around the corner and saw her wipe her hands on her skirt. Then, "Cooking. What was I thinking?"

After that, it was mostly "I know what you mean," and "ums," and "ahs" until she said, "Thank you for the invitation. I will talk to Will and let you know?" Her voice sounded too musical. Then I heard the hesitation: "Is that okay?"

As soon as she was off the phone, I pestered her. She was evasive. "You're being rude to Nealy," she said. "Enjoy your visit right now."

That evening I learned Mary Margaret had asked Mary Lily to invite me to accompany Eli out to Magnolia Manor the next weekend. My protective mother, meanwhile, got busy trying to think of a reason I should not go. I was nearly a teenager, she pointed out, and too old to be going on overnight excursions with boys. But it wasn't boys, I pointed out. It was Eli. She was undeterred. She even suggested I could have a campout in the backyard with Nealy and Gloria at home instead.

We were sitting in the den watching *The Ed Sullivan Show*. Helen had left to get ready for bed. She could only watch the first half before time for her bath. My mother took in a deep breath and let it out slowly. She adjusted the band on her skirt.

I'd been going to Magnolia Manor all my life. Even if it had been a very long time since I'd spent the night, my mother's reluctance was absurd. It was going to be a standoff.

I leaned up close to Mama and uttered the most soulful "please" I could muster. What I wanted to do was roll my eyes in disgust at having to beg. She tugged on her skirt, adjusted the waist again.

She looked at my father. He smiled and shrugged. He didn't see what Mama had to be concerned about. "Gracious sakes, Jeanette, she'll be in Mary Margaret's care," he said. "Romp the woods, wade in the creek. I wouldn't mind going myself."

"I'm not sure Mary Margaret can keep up with them," she said. "She only makes right turns now when she drives to town." I said Mimi's driving ability had nothing to do with Eli and me. Daddy said again we would have a good time in the country. Finally, my mother relented. If for no other reason, because she loved Mary Lily and Mimi and didn't want to offend them.

⁓

I packed everything I could possibly need in my hip bag—red patent leather. An extra pair of shorts for the day, and my new bell-bottom pants if it turned cool, unlikely but you never knew. I retrieved the bug repellant from under the bathroom counter because summertime chigger bites will make you itch like you've never itched before. I was excited, but I was uneasy at the same time because I'd not been out to Magnolia Manor since Francie.

About a half-mile from Mimi's house, like we usually did, we took the old dirt road used before the highway in front of the house was paved through to Columbia. It was the same road Mary Lily ran to when she eloped with Uncle Gene. Eli loved to take the old road instead of the highway. My aunt's enormous Chrysler New Yorker bounced wildly along the ruts, traveling through the green-shadowed tunnel created from the oak trees grown together across the way. I couldn't help but think somewhere near the end of this road Francie must have hidden her car the day she sank her baby.

Mary Lily stopped the Chrysler beside the apple tree at the bottom of the long drive. She peered up toward the house and then back at the tree. "It'll have a good crop this year," she said. But she wasn't really

99

interested in the green apples from this tree. Apples we all knew were sour and tart. She was gathering her courage to approach the house. She liked bringing us to Magnolia Manor, but you could always tell by something she said or did that she didn't much like being there herself.

"I'll get the bell," Eli yelled when Mary Lily pulled to a stop. He jumped the brick steps two at a time.

I followed more slowly with my aunt. I was never to visit this august house without a sense of reverence and mystery, for the glimmers of things and occasions gone, both sad and joyful, still hovering. I ran my hand along the tops of the green rocking chairs on the porch.

"Gene asked me to marry him here," Mary Lily said, blessedly distracting me from Francie, who had jumped hard into my thoughts. "I sat in the spot where you are." She pointed at the chair my hand was touching.

"Really?" I imagined Uncle Gene on bended knee when he knew the Lauderdales did not approve of him. I had learned long ago it was more than class difference and lack of education that tainted my uncle. There was also his father. My Grandfather Winfield, his nerves stunned by mustard gas in World War I, became a famous town drunkard. He never worked after the war; instead, my grandmother supported the family by toiling at the mill. She worked her way up to a nearly impossible position for a female mill worker. She became the overseer of the sewing room.

I'd not known my grandfather, but his infamy endured. One night he passed out by the side of the road on a walk home from town. His right foot jutted out too far, and a passing car bumped it. He went down in a ditch. It was morning before anyone saw him. For the rest of his life, when he walked, the maimed foot turned nearly backward. A reminder to the whole town.

I'd never known my Winfield grandmother, either. But I knew she must have been strong and stable to work and raise my mother and her brother the way she did.

"Right after I married," Mary Lily interrupted my thoughts, "Gene and I sat with my daddy on this porch. Just a few months before he died."

"I'm sorry. That must be sad to think about," I said.

"No, it's a sweet memory," she said. "Daddy didn't want us to marry, but then when we did… He was a good man. I miss him. I wish Mother could have accepted Eugene, even if…" She trailed off. Mary Lily was talking more to herself than to me.

"Well, Lordy be. Do look who's here!" Caro opened the door for us. She never changed. Her large eyes grabbed hold of you. The strong, prominent chin secured you. She was tall and thin, a wrinkled version of Pot. "Mimi's coming right out. Excuse us for taking so long. We was just having a little tea party in the kitchen before you all's got here. Maybe you'd like something to eat. Got some fresh blueberries and muffins I baked this morning." She waved us inside.

"No, Caro, I'm not staying," Mary Lily said. "You might tempt the children, though."

We stepped inside the entry hall, wider than any room in my house. I inhaled the rich, sweet, old wood smell. A leaded glass fixture overhead dimly illuminated dark furniture: the mahogany table, its ever-present candy dish filled to the top, the Regency side chairs and the hall tree. People long dead inside golden frames peered out straight-faced from the right wall—flanking the family shield and crossed swords—following us with their eyes. The stairs rose along the other side.

I felt it then; I feel it still, the command of this house. How it has stored up memories in the thick walls with a will of its own. How it can swallow the present. You remember everything when you return to this house. All it takes is the smell of old tea roses mingled with cedar boughs arranged in the hall. Or climbing the stairs of creaking treads worn smooth by generations of Lauderdale feet. Or most of all, the tinkle of glass from the kitchen, like the sound of little bells.

Mimi emerged from the shadows and into the pool of light where we stood near the opened door. She was nearly as tall as Mary Lily and as willowy. She wore a pale blue cotton dress, a shift tied loosely at the waist, and low heels on her slender feet. As always, a large, jeweled comb held her yellow hair tightly in a bun at the base of her neck, circled with a strand of pearls. She held out her arms, and Eli ran into them. She kept them out, and I knew she meant for me to come, too.

"Oh, Delia, I haven't seen you in such a long time. Since back in the winter." It seemed to me, also, a long time. "I'm so glad you've come to visit. Let's all go into the parlor."

"Mother, I'm not staying," Mary Lily said. "I have things to get back to."

"Can't stay? Can't stay? What is it always keeps you so busy?" Mimi said. As much as she was obviously drawn to the surroundings of her childhood home, my aunt usually found reason to leave almost as soon as she arrived. Between Mary Lily and her mother there existed a certain kind of estrangement, not overt, but under cover. I believed a lot of it had to do with Uncle Gene. I suspected Mimi only tolerated my uncle for Eli's sake and for Mary Lily's. Even if she loved me and my family.

Mimi turned to Caro. "She should stay a while. Isn't that so, Caro?"

"Oh, yes ma'am, I think so. Got to rest sometime. Mimi and me, we go strong, but we know when to slow down and rest," Caro answered.

"I'll be back late tomorrow," Mary Lily said. Even Caro's veiled appeal did not affect her.

"Certainly, certainly. They'll be fine. Get on back to town then," Mary Margaret said. Her long, thin arms floated up in the air and waved her daughter away.

Carrying our bags, we followed Caro to the second floor. She pointed to the room with the sleigh bed for Eli and the one with the spindle bed for me. "Now Mimi says you two come on back down when you put your things away, and she'll have the tea party ready, okay?"

"Aren't we a little old for a tea party," Eli said and crossed his eyes at me.

"You never too old for a tea party," Caro said. "Now, I got to get on back to my own house. Potter's hired a new man to help with the cows, and I got to see if he needs help settling in." At the Winfield house, Pot mostly gardened, but at Mimi's he ran the place and had since Eli's grandfather died. The farm was scaled down from when John Macon Lauderdale was alive, but it still took a lot of work.

I couldn't help but think how Mary Margaret hired Francie because Pot left to take care of his uncle in St. Louis. How his absence brought her presence to Magnolia Manor. At least, that's what I thought then. We had admired and looked up to Francie all those afternoons at Mimi's kitchen table when Eli wouldn't go to school. But I wished Eli and I had never met her, for the sorrow of her dead baby never completely let go.

Downstairs, we drank iced tea and ate muffins covered in sugared peaches. And even if we were too old—going into our thirteenth year—to call our snack a tea party, it tasted mighty good. Then Mimi asked us to come into the parlor and sit with her. It was my favorite room. The first thing you saw was the melodeon, a gilded mirror hanging over it by a thick silk cord. The melodeon wouldn't play because the bellows had holes, but one of these days, Mimi always said, she would get it repaired. I wished I could hear it play. She told of her mother-in-law playing only hymns on Sundays, but on Saturdays, people gathered to sing "Silver Threads Among the Gold," "Cushion, Bend," and "Susan Jane," songs from a far-off realm.

"Mimi, you don't need to entertain us," Eli said. I thought his tone a little stern.

"Why, of course, Ellison. But an old lady like me, I'm enjoying the company of youth. I won't keep you long." She reached over and squeezed her grandson's knee.

"There are things around here to know," she suggested mysteriously. I saw Eli roll his eyes, but I was ready to listen. "I've never told you Sherman's troops came through here and set fire to Magnolia Manor." We didn't have to be told who Sherman was. If you lived in Green Branch, you knew. Quickly, Eli leaned forward on his toes.

"Where was the fire?" he wanted to know.

"It was started in the very bedroom where you'll be sleeping," she replied. "The floor once had a charred circle in the middle. Your grandfather tore it out and replaced the boards."

"Why didn't the house burn down?" he asked. His eyes had grown huge, as they did when anything startled him.

"Because the fire was slow, and one of the soldiers confessed after he stumbled down the stairs and saw the family huddled in this parlor. When the Yankees left, your great-great-grandmother organized the servants and children to haul buckets of water from the river. She saved the house."

Mimi kept talking, telling us about the old days after the war. She told about cotton farming and how it sustained Eli's family until the boll weevil tried to destroy everything. Her husband's family outsmarted the insect, though, by taking away its dinner and planting other things.

"I'd like for you children to see some things," she said and led us over to the mahogany secretary, nearly as tall as the twelve-foot ceiling. "The old ledgers are here. You can see everything the Lauderdales farmed and how much came in and what everything cost. The name will be gone after me," she said, "but you carry it in you, Ellison." Mary Margaret had no other grandchildren. She had a son, but he had not married and lived far away in Alabama where he taught in a college.

"Mimi, you know we've looked in here a lot of times. We know," Eli said. He opened one of the books. The leather cover crackled. He sneezed twice. We saw entries like numerous ones we had seen before in faded pencil lines. Four bushels of corn, twenty bags of cotton meal, five bags of oats, smoked salmon and sardines.

"Perhaps many of these things came from your family's store," Mimi suggested to me. "One line of the Greens became merchants. Look in Miss Inez Wilson's book on the history of Green Branch, Adeline, and you'll know how important your ancestors were to this town," she continued. "Your people helped make this town a town." She nodded and patted the bun in back of her head. I nodded in response. "Of course, you must know that," she laughed. "It's in your name."

Eli picked up another ledger, began turning pages. It was dustier than the first and older. I kneeled behind him and looked over his shoulder. He stopped his finger on the purchase of a coffin. "Creepy," he said.

His finger stopped again at the top of the next page. The heading read, "Negroes bought in 1848." Listed were Charlotte for $475, Polly and child for $350, Robert for $500. Mimi saw what Eli saw. She caught her breath but didn't speak. Surely, she knew we had seen entries like these even if we had never inquired about them. "Our family owned slaves," Eli said quietly. His voice held no emotion.

"Yes, they did, Ellison. Life was that way. I'm glad that way is gone."

"Were these Pot and Caro's people?" he asked.

"I think so, yes," she said. "Some of them."

104

It was hard to take in. That the ancestors of Pot and Caro had lived here, in this very place, but not of their own volition. And yet Pot and Caro were here now, taking care of themselves and of Mary Margaret and her family. I had no map in my head for understanding.

"Oh, look, a Blue Black Speller," Mimi exclaimed. "How did that get here?"

But Eli didn't look up from the ledger. Finally, Mimi found something to distract him from staring at the names of slaves his ancestors had owned. It was a thin braid of straw-brown hair pressed into a small gold frame. It was in a box we'd never noticed before on the shelf behind some of the record books.

"Whose hair is it?" Eli asked.

"Well, some of your grandfather's people is all I know."

"Why would anyone save hair?" I asked. The ancient strands repulsed me, and yet, if I am honest, the idea fascinated me, too. I thought of the hair piles swept up in the dustpan from customers at the beauty parlor where Mama went every week. I ran my hand down my straight, copper hair falling down my back, trimmed only occasionally, usually at Mama's request. I liked the sensual touch of my hair, though I couldn't have described this feeling when I was twelve.

Mimi's pale eyebrows rose. A pleased look came over her face. "As a tangible reminder of a loved one," she said. "Why, I wouldn't be a bit surprised if this hair belonged to one of your ancestors, Adeline."

"Mine?" I asked incredulously.

"Why, of course. Your family has been here as long as Ellison's. People found good ground and stayed in one place. They married the people who lived nearby. They didn't have cars and such to travel like we do today."

"Are you sure?" I asked.

"Absolutely," she said, already digging again, this time into a drawer of the secretary for a chart of the Lauderdale family tree. She brought out a scroll tied with a worn black ribbon. It wasn't one we had examined before. The three of us unrolled the document and spread it across the needlepoint rug. We sat, all three, cross-legged and peering at the tiny print.

"Here, here," Eli shouted.

"Let me see." I nearly knocked him over. Sure enough, there were names from a marriage in 1854 when Griffin Green married Harriett Chisholm Lauderdale. They had five children who lived to adulthood: Wiley, Tazewell, Harriett, Thorne, and Madeline Rose.

"Wow," I exclaimed, though I knew this Griffin Green wasn't necessarily my relative. There were plenty of Greens in Green Branch we didn't claim kin to. But then again, perhaps we were, and didn't know it.

"So imagine that," Mimi said. She leaned forward, her arms spreading wide across the scroll. She smoothed at the corners. "And there could be others."

"So, we are cousins more than once," Eli said. "You and me, Delia."

I didn't think this was really true. Still, I wondered at the name Madeline Rose. My middle name is Rose, for a great-aunt on Daddy's side dead before I was born.

"Oh, kinship is a marvelous thing," Mimi said. She raised her eyebrows again and smiled. And then, suddenly the smile was gone. She stood quickly. "I'm going now and think about supper. Ellison, you be sure to put everything back."

"Wait, Mimi," he called. "Are there any cousins in our family who married each other?"

She hesitated before she answered. "Yes. Of course. It was common until after the Civil War. Look at the names to see," she said.

"Can cousins marry now?" he asked her.

"No, my darling, not now," she said, "though Queen Victoria married her first cousin Albert. And a whole lot of other famous people, too."

"But why not?" Eli asked, looking up at her from the floor.

"Medical people believe it's too risky. Cousins are too much alike and can pass on genetic diseases." Her voice was lively, but a strange look came over Mimi's face.

"Yes ma'am," he responded. After Mimi left the room, Eli squeezed his shoulders back. His Buster Brown bangs fell low over his forehead, nearly into his eyes. He needed a haircut. Spontaneously, with two fingers, I raked his bangs to the side. He smiled.

"I want a lock of your hair," he whispered near my cheek. "Cut one and give it to me."

"Why?" I asked.

"To have it," he said. "A reminder."

"A reminder of what?" I asked. "I'm not going anywhere." My stomach squirmed and heat flooded my face.

I was ready to go outside among living things. Away from lockets of dead hair, dead Lauderdales, dead songs, exotic dead names. And I didn't want Eli to start looking in documents for the Burchett name. I stood and thumped him on the back of the neck. "Let's go outside," I said.

"Don't you want to look for first cousins who married?" he countered, rubbing the back of his neck in an exaggerated fashion.

"No, really, Eli, let's go." I grabbed him by the hand and pulled. He pulled back and grinned. Fortunately, he was in a mood for teasing me and apparently not thinking about looking for people named Burchett.

"If you'll let me get the scissors now and cut a lock of your hair."

"No," I said. "Come on."

"Okay, okay," he finally gave in. "Let's walk through the back pasture to the creek."

"The bull," I said.

"The bull's not out right now."

"I don't want to go there." We both knew it wasn't the bull I was worried about. It was the creek.

"Trust me," he said. "We can do it. We have to do it."

"Okay." I breathed out slowly, realizing I'd been holding my breath.

We stopped in the kitchen to tell Mimi we were going outside, and she said to wait and she'd pack our supper to eat by the river. That's how she referred to Cane Creek too. It was as if unawares, she was in cahoots with Eli and telling us to tackle our inner demon. That we must go to the creek to confront our secret.

She was fixing cold things for supper anyway, she said. Eli swung our basket of supper over his arm. The basket rocked back and forth while he ran down the back porch steps until I thought everything would spill. "Slow down," I commanded. He didn't slow down. I scurried behind him.

"I don't see the bull, do you?" he said, stopping at the pasture gate to wait on me.

"That doesn't mean he's not here," I said, though both of us knew the bull wouldn't be out.

"We're fine." We looked at each other. "We can't let the bull stop us. You know what I mean, Dee." I knew. We were talking about the specter of Francie.

"Dad got in the pasture with the bull once when he didn't know it," Eli said out of the blue. "He turned from one direction to another, and saw the bull staring at him. Dad took off running toward the nearest tree, climbed up, and stayed until the bull wandered away."

"You're trying to scare me more than I already am."

"I'm warning you just in case. Keep your eye on a tree." I couldn't tell if he was trying to tell a joke to break me down, or whether he was directing me, or both of us. Maybe he didn't know either.

He opened the gate, the basket poised on his arm. He looked back at me. "I can't go there," I said. I set my lips tight.

"Come on." Eli knuckled my arm lightly.

"Stop, that hurts," I protested, though it didn't really.

He kept working at me, his expression firm but his manner light, tapping my arm, poking my shoulder. I pulled away. He grabbed the waistband of my shorts and pulled me toward him. He leaned over and kissed me, brushing my right cheek. "You're my kissing cousin," he said. "We can do this together."

"Oh," I said. I touched my cheek, forgetting for a moment he couldn't possibly protect either of us from a storming bull, real or figurative.

Barely, I nodded.

"Atta girl. We're going," he said. We walked then, silently, toward a stand of hardwoods along the creek.

We passed meandering cows, some with their wide noses close to the ground, biting and tearing off grass, others clumped together, huddled as though in communal thought. One wandered toward us, her neck and tongue sticking out.

"What does she want?" I asked Eli. It was the first thing either of us had said in a while.

"Nothing," he said. "She's just a curious one." He scratched her behind the ears.

We reached the tree line. The air seemed cooler, away from the thick, open heat.

Soon enough, we arrived at the flat bank of bare clay where Francie had lowered her baby into the water. We glanced at each other.

"We're here," Eli said. The spot was quiet except for the slender sound of water bubbling and swirling among the rocks. "Do you think her baby is still here or surfaced somewhere else?"

"There would have been a big story in the newspaper if a drowned newborn baby appeared," I said.

"Maybe no one would bother to open the sack."

"No, I think it is resting in its grave somewhere deep in the Broad River, or maybe even in the ocean." It was crazy to imagine a dead baby in a bag full of rocks as peaceful, but it was a way to cope.

"I like that idea," Eli said. And we both exhaled.

Eli reached out and took my hand. I squeezed hard. Incongruous as it sounds, because we shared the sad secret, because we were together, we had been able to confront our fear in coming here. I could feel it, an almost physical thing pulsing between the palms of our joined hands.

"But let's don't stay here," I said.

"No, let's don't. Let's make it a good day." Eli smiled and swung my hand up high.

We continued our journey under maples and sycamores along the water's edge. I wiped sweat trickling off my forehead. Eli's face was dripping, too.

"Let's go to the rocks," he said. "That's a good place." I was familiar with a small outcropping of granite jutting over the water in a narrow place on the creek. When the water level was high enough, you could sit and dangle your feet in the stream. The water was plenty high that day. All of a sudden, I relished the feel of the cool, clear water washing over my legs and feet.

و

At least an hour of light remained after we ate our supper—egg salad sandwiches kept cool with a plastic bag of ice, blueberries, chips, a thermos of tea—and packed the plastic dishes and flatware back into the basket. Eli wanted to walk back by way of the barn. It housed horses once upon a time but was now entirely storage, full of hay.

Eli set the basket on the ground at the entrance. "Let's climb into the loft. It's a great lookout from up there. You can see all over." He meant looking out of the opening at the south gable end. The other sides were walled in. I'd never climbed the ladder into the loft.

"You go first. I'm behind you," he directed.

I am not afraid of heights. But I did wonder if the old ladder would hold, if it might be rotten. I tested the bottom rung by jumping on it.

"Well, there's hay stored up there, so people like Pot go up and down it all the time," Eli said.

I climbed up and piled into the itchy hay.

"This is great," Eli said, heaving himself over the last rung and plopping down beside me. "Feel the breeze coming in? Look and you can see all the way past the tree line to the creek and beyond."

And I could. It was marvelous. A place above that seemed a world belonging only to Eli and me.

He moved close beside me and peered out into the late light. We sat on our knees, looking out into the world his ancestors had farmed starting more than a hundred years before.

He put his hand in my hair, startling me. I jumped. His hand remained. "Like bright pennies," he said. He pulled my hair playfully. He grasped it in his fist. "You're beautiful, Delia." Clumsily, he turned me toward him.

I remained on my knees, bewildered, awkward. Without words to respond. I was no longer gazing out on the open pasture but facing him. "Your eyes are like cat's eyes," he said. There was no teasing in his voice. "The color changes. Sometimes green. Sometimes sort of gold." He moved his hands to my face. He put his thumbs on my eyebrows. "Not only that. You always look determined."

He paused. "Let me kiss you," he said. "On the lips."

"Cousins aren't supposed to kiss like that," I said.

"They used to," he said.

I nodded. Inside my heart beat fast, feathers flurrying in my chest.

He cupped a hand on either side of my face and leaned toward me. He was shaking. But when his lips covered mine, they were firm and soft at the same time, without a tremor. What a strange and wonderful sensation it was, the feel of his lips in that kiss, his warmth covering me.

The sky was still light with the moon risen too, nearly full, when we ascended the rear porch steps leading to the kitchen, a large added room jutting off the back. Originally, the kitchen had been its own separate building, long torn down. We saw Mimi through the window, sitting at the table, her back folded forward. She was reading the newspaper, or pretending to be. Mainly, I knew she was waiting on Eli and me.

Eli opened the door. "Hello, Mimi," he said quietly.

"There you are," she said. She folded the newspaper and set it on the table. "Did you get enough to eat?"

"Yes," Eli said. I nodded.

"Do you young people like to watch television?" she asked. "I like *The Jackie Gleason Show*." She glanced at the clock above the stove. "Ah, it's nearly over now."

Still, we accompanied Mimi to the small den where she turned on the television set for the last few minutes of the show. When it ended, she said it was her bedtime and did we need anything before she retired.

"We're fine," Eli said. "Goodnight, Mimi."

We watched *My Three Sons*. Then, I went up to the bath at the top of the stairs. Though I was nearly a teenager, I was anxious as I had ever been about sleeping alone in a bed not my own.

Eli remained in the den for *Hogan's Heroes*, a show I detested for its silliness, its deception, even as I heard Eli laughing.

I sat in the old claw-foot tub, luxuriating in the bath oil beads I found in the jar on the shelf above the sink. I tried not to think about being scared to sleep alone.

Out of the bath, I called to Eli to ask if he was coming upstairs soon.

"On my way," he called.

With the windows open in my bedroom, it wasn't stifling, but warm enough to push the crocheted spread to the end of the bed, even wearing my coolest night clothes, baby doll pajamas with puffed sleeves and lace around the scooped neck. I lay beneath only the sheet, feeling exposed. For a moment I thought I saw the antique cradle rocking on its own in the corner of the room. I closed my eyes. I clutched the second pillow to my chest. I heard Eli climb the stairs and go into the bathroom. I tried to fall asleep, but I smelled the old smell of the room, wondered at the shadows, feared its ghosts in the dark.

I heard my cousin pad toward his room across the hall and called to him. He appeared at my doorway. "Are you sleepy, Eli?" I asked.

"I am sleepy," he said.

"Promise to stay awake until I fall asleep," I said.

"If I can," he said. "Are you scared?" he asked.

"Do you believe in ghosts?" I asked.

"You know I do, but they don't scare me," he said.

"They scare me at night but not in the day," I said. "Will you lie down with me until I fall asleep?"

He walked into the room and climbed into the space beside me. "The ghosts here won't hurt you," he said. "Don't worry. This is their home. They don't mind us being here. We're family."

I handed the pillow I clutched to Eli. He smoothed it. He placed it beside my head and lay next to me. I watched the breeze toss the white organdy curtains. "I wish they'd stop moving," I said.

"Close your eyes," Eli said. "Turn your pillow over to the cool side, and it will feel good against your face."

I did what he said. "Do you want to cuddle?" he asked. He reached his arm out across my stomach.

The word unsettled me. It made me squeamish. But it soothed me, too. I didn't know what I felt. I ignored the anxiety the word produced, for Eli's presence was the stronger pull. I fell asleep comforted with his arm around me.

14

JULY 1968, NEXT DAY

I woke in the morning to find my cousin in bed with me, still asleep. He'd never moved to his room. The word "cuddle" came back to me, and with it the unsettled feeling. It suggested an act of great intimacy, an overwhelming word.

"Eli," I whispered. I jostled his shoulder.

"Yeah?" He opened one eye beneath the long bangs.

"Your hair is everywhere," I said, suddenly realizing that, darkened now from the butterscotch of childhood to a hue more like brown sugar, his hair was disheveled all over his head, not only his bangs growing into his eyes but strands of hair splitting across the tops of his ears.

"I'm growing it," he said.

"Really? You're going to be a hippie?"

"I think so," he said. "Come here." He reached over and grabbed me around the waist. "I've got you," he said. His arms gripped around me. The blousy top of my pajamas rode up above my navel. Inside my stomach softened, muddling me again.

"We have to get up, Eli," I said, squirming away.

"Why?" he said.

"Because the day has started." I pointed to the yellow glow at the windows.

"Okay, I've got to pee anyway," he said, rising.

"I don't have to know that, gross," I said.

"You don't have bodily functions?" he asked. He was laughing.

I picked up my pillow and slammed it into his back. He laughed harder.

"You can be so prissy," he said, his feet hitting the floor. I wanted to call him back, to hold on to his body, warm next to mine, as I watched him leave our room.

I made up the bed, righting myself, and changed into my second pair of shorts and a peasant blouse.

"You going down?" Eli called. I looked around the bedroom door to see him standing at the top of the stairs, still wearing his shorts and T-shirt from yesterday. The clothes he'd slept in.

"I'm hungry," I said.

"Me, too," he said. We galloped with elephantine noise down the long, straight run of stairs.

"Don't have to wonder if you all are awake," Caro said when we entered the kitchen. "Mimi done traipsed out in the field with Pot to help with the new man. I'm cooking breakfast. We having grits, eggs, and bacon. Toast if you want it."

"I'll have it all," Eli said.

"Toast won't scratch your throat?" Caro asked. He shook his head.

"Very well, and you, Miss?" Caro looked at me with one eye squinted shut, spatula in hand.

"Me, too," I said.

"Growing young'uns." She smiled and turned to the stove.

I ate grits all the time for breakfast, usually with a sausage sandwich, made by folding a piece of buttered toast around a sausage patty. But the grits we ate at home were white. These were yellow and richer. "Where do yellow grits come from?" I asked Caro.

"Same place as any grits. Corn. It's just the kind of corn. Yellow grits come from yellow corn. White grits from white corn. 'Course some say yellow grits is sweeter and stronger."

"They are," I agreed and asked for a second helping.

"Hurry up, little pig," Eli said, "so we can go out to the bell tower before it gets too hot."

"You can be so nasty," I said. He grinned, blew on his fingernails and rubbed them along the top of his day-old T-shirt.

"Nah, I'm cool," he said.

"You're corny, too," I said.

"Let's go," he said.

"Wait, wait, wait just a minute," Caro hollered as we were headed out the door to the back steps. "Mimi don't want you all's going up that old metal tower without her knowing. You gonna have to wait on her."

"Oh for Pete's sake," Eli said.

"Pete, or nobody, you not going up that bell tower without Mimi's permission." Caro was firm. "Might as well go upstairs and brush your teeth while you wait."

We retreated to brush our teeth. Then we rocked on the front porch waiting for Mimi to return from meeting with Pot. We didn't wait long. She walked around the corner from the old store that once provided goods for the tenant farmers, now a storage building that held tools and supplies.

"Good morning, lovely loves," she called. She wore a pale lavender blouse and skirt. Though no comb adorned her bun this morning, her hair was neatly coiffed as ever.

"Mimi, we're waiting on you to say we can go up the tower." Eli jumped up and ran down the steps to meet his grandmother.

"Oh, Ellison, that old tower. I don't know how much longer it might be stable for you to climb. And I worry about you walking around up there at the top."

"I've done it a lot of times. We'll be fine," my fearless cousin assured her. "Besides, maybe some of the scuppernongs are ready, and I know you want some." He presented a wide, knowing grin, referring to the vines that grew at least halfway up along the steel beams of the octagonal sixty-foot tower. Vines that produced the grapes for the sweet scuppernong wine Mimi made if someone picked the harvest for her.

"Oh, goodness," Mimi said. Then, she looked over at me. "No, I don't think so."

"Why not?" Eli demanded.

"We don't have permission from Delia's parents."

"Then call them," Eli insisted. He stomped one foot in front of the other.

"Not this trip," she said. "There are other things you can do."

I knew the tower's original purpose. It was built in the days when fire could quickly destroy a family's entire life, in the same days kitchens were separate buildings outside, days before fire trucks and hydrants. In case of fire a family member was to climb to the top and ring the enormous bell for help. Neighbors lived far away across acres of farmland, and it would take a loud bell to notify them of fire or any other emergency.

Suddenly I wondered if the bell had been rung when Sherman's troops set fire in the bedroom, but recalled Mimi told us the tower wasn't built until after the war, after the scare.

For a while, Eli kept trying to wear her down. He wanted very much to climb the tower and ring the bell. I wanted to climb it, too, even if it did look scary. But I wasn't about to challenge Mimi.

"That's not fair, Mimi. You know I can climb the tower," he insisted.

"Of course, I know you can, but you're not," she said. "Not today, and that's final. No need for either of you to take that risk." She patted her bun with one hand and shook her pointer finger in front of her face with the other.

Eli stubbed his toe into the ground in frustration but Mimi stood unwavering, saying quietly, "Right now, you're your daddy's son, aren't you?"

&

Two of my failings came into play after I arrived home Saturday afternoon from my trip to the country with Eli: the tendency to wear my feelings on my sleeve, as my mother likes to put it, and the impulse to speak before I think. I could blame it on my senses being quickened, and that is surely true, but also it was solely my mistake.

Mama was home from a garden club event, her lips bright with her distinctive ruby red lipstick. Daddy had gone to check on a malfunction in the weave room and taken Helen with him. I walked in and set my red patent bag on the coffee table.

"How was your visit?" Mama asked.

"It was wonderful," I answered. "We could have stayed longer, but Eli had to go to Little League practice."

He played now in the summer league, usually at first base. The coach was smart, Daddy said, to position him there because though Eli couldn't run fast, he had quick hand-eye coordination. Daddy said it made him a good hitter. Eli's best friend Paul Robbins in Little League was a good hitter, too. Sometimes, Paul came over to Eli's and they pitched balls to each other in Eli's side yard.

Daddy, Helen, and I went to the games sometimes. Mama rarely went. The team's blue jerseys said "Steele's Grocery" across the shoulders with the players' numbers printed front and back. Eli wore number 8, Carl Yastrzemski's number.

I liked watching my cousin play, especially when he was at bat—I once saw him hit a triple—but I found the game itself generally boring. Frankly, it mystified me how hitting a ball into space could matter so much.

"Tell me what you did out at Mary Margaret's," Mama said.

I told about looking at the old ledgers in the parlor, walking the pasture, eating supper by the creek. Purposefully, I passed over the hayloft. And then, not thinking, I slipped. I told her I'd gotten scared alone in my bedroom and asked Eli to stay with me.

"What do you mean?" Mama asked. Her red lips compressed. "Eli lay in bed with you? This isn't proper. We've talked about the birds and the bees, Delia. You are too old to be in this situation."

I hated that silly phrase, the birds and the bees. And we hadn't really talked about it. Mama had given me a book to read about sex and conversed only on the subject of how my body would change, about the blood that would come each month, and what that blood meant. Most of what I knew—even if inexplicable—came from Gloria's older sister. I doubted Mama would ever really tell me details concerning sex, and that was okay by me. It made me queasy even thinking about trying to hear her tell the things Gloria's sister Bridget had told.

"I was scared. And Eli's not some boy," I said. "It's an old, spooky house. It wasn't improper." I was ready to explode with indignation. If I could only take it back, but I couldn't. I could only hide the full truth of Eli staying the whole night with me.

I have no recollection of the time that passed before Daddy and Helen came home. I must have gone to my room and unpacked, hoping my mother's reaction would blow over. What I do recall is my parents telling me that evening after Helen went to bed they would have to call Eli's parents and discuss the matter.

"No, don't you dare," I shrieked. "It isn't Eli's fault. It's mine. He'll get in trouble."

"Delia, mind your tone," Mama said. "It's best you stay in your room." She was distressed, wrapping one hand around the other.

"Mama, don't, please," I begged.

"Go now," she said.

"Jeanette?" my father questioned. "Perhaps we're making too much of this."

"It has to be nipped in the bud," Mama said. My father hunched his shoulders together. He didn't want to confront Mary Lily and Gene; that much was clear. Mama gave me a stern look and I retreated, irate, to my room.

I lay awake much of the night, both angry and shamed, knowing my parents had called Gene and Mary Lily. Knowing what would surely happen to Eli when nothing was his fault. Imagining the scene. Fearing the beating. Knowing our days had now divided between childhood and the beyond. I tried to understand what could and could not be. Loving Eli.

15

AUGUST 1968

I lay low for a while before I attempted to see Eli. I figured letting time pass would put our night at Magnolia Manor to the back of the grown-ups' minds. It wasn't that my parents had outright forbidden me to see him, but Mama, especially, was keeping tabs on me. Also, I was afraid to call Eli's house. I didn't know what to say if Aunt Mary Lily or Uncle Gene answered the phone. And I knew Eli didn't want to call my house either, because one of my parents might pick up.

I was into sunbathing in those days, and one afternoon I donned my bathing suit and pulled a chaise lounge into the side yard. Every few minutes I turned the garden hose on myself to keep from burning up. I knew Eli would emerge. Even if he didn't look out the window, he would still know I was waiting for him. We were intuitive that way.

"What took you so long?" I asked when he sauntered across the street and sat on the grass beside me. He shrugged.

"What are you trying to do, fry?" he muttered.

"I'm getting a tan," I said.

"Girls," he said. We grinned at each other. I threw my legs over the recliner and sat up.

"Did you get in trouble?" I asked.

"Not too much," he said. "Just a big lecture from Mama about proper behavior." He furrowed his brow in a phony frown and threw back his head.

"No whipping? Your daddy can be... I didn't mean to tell."

"Forget about it. You're my kissing cousin," he said, and grabbed hold of my foot and began to tickle.

"Quit," I said, trying to pull away, shoving the other foot in his face.

"Q..ui...t," he mocked me, then smacked the balls of my feet and let go. "Listen, seriously. I've been thinking we should go to the graveyard where Frances Burchett is buried."

"Eli, no," I exclaimed. "Why can't you stop? This whole time since we came back from the creek have you been holed up brooding? When you didn't look for Burchetts in the parlor papers when Mimi was showing us everything, I thought you had decided to let it go. There's nothing else to know."

"We don't know what we don't know. I didn't look for Burchett names because I've seen them all already. Names on an old document. So what good are names if I don't know how they fit? All I know is Francie's mama and Mimi meant something more to each other that Mimi won't tell. Or she wouldn't have acted so nervous that day."

"Oh, please. You're being melodramatic. Of course, Mimi was upset that day because Francie had left without a word. She said 'family is hard' because Francie has no mother. She feels sorry for her. And, after we saw Francie at the creek...we were out of our minds, Eli, seeing what we saw. It would be simpler if you'd just go back to your grandmother and ask about Francie's mother again. She'd probably tell you now."

Eli shook his head, no. "Tried it," he said.

"Well, what do you think a graveyard will tell you?"

"Maybe nothing, but a graveyard is full of people buried together by names. We can see who is in the ground near Frances Burchett Mobley Turner."

"And how do you propose we get out to Covenant Presbyterian Church? It's probably ten miles from here. Who knows?" We were familiar with the church because, in fact, it was on the highway leading out to Magnolia Manor. "You're so clever. Are you going to ask your mother to drive us? Or Uncle Gene? Or what?"

Eli pondered my question. He squinted one eye at me before he spoke. "I guess not," he said. "But you don't have to be sarcastic."

"Well, then," I answered. "How would we get there?"

"Does your bicycle have good tires?"

"It's too far."

"That's garbage. It wouldn't take much more than an hour."

"Mama would shoot me if she found out I rode my bike that far out."

"She doesn't have to know. We should go soon before school starts. Which Saturday is Aunt Jeanette's garden club?"

"Even if Daddy doesn't pay attention, Helen will tell Mama if I'm gone a long time."

"So what? Say you're riding to the drugstore for a candy run and afterward to the library or something."

I shook my head.

"I'm going with or without you," he said. It was easier for boys, or at least it was for Eli. He could take off for hours without questions.

I was quiet for a few moments. "Garden club is this Saturday," I said.

&

Mama left for garden club at the community center at 10:00 am. To get on her good side, I hung out the clothes before she left without being asked. I hated this chore because I was too short for the job and had to pull the picnic bench underneath the clothesline and slide it along to reach the clothespins. I would be so happy if Mama finally got a clothes dryer like Mary Lily had.

By 10:15, I was on my bike, leaving Helen in her room playing with the new rubbery Creepy Crawlers I had helped her cook the evening before in the Thingmaker—she was too young to operate the oven by herself. I was confident she would be occupied for a while. I sneaked off without telling Daddy, who was out mowing the grass. I told Helen that if either parent asked, she should say I'd gone on a long bike ride with Nealy that included several stops.

I brought my Girl Scout canteen of frozen water and candy bars for the long ride, stowed in my basket. "That's my girl," Eli said when he saw my supplies.

I'd never ridden so far at once, and our land could be hilly. Several times we got off our bikes and walked them up hills because Eli, and sometimes I, too, started breathing so hard. There was one stiff climb just off Main Street heading onto the highway where both of us got so short of breath we had to set our bikes down off the shoulder and stop for a while. "Should we go back?" I asked, for I was more than a little miserable pumping these hills.

"No," he wheezed. "Just give it a few minutes. We'll fly down this bad boy going back." We rested. The frozen water in my canteen had already melted, but blessedly, was still cool. Eventually, we got our second wind and walked our bikes to the top.

We arrived at the church soaking wet from humidity and heat. Eli and I took turns gulping more water. "Save some," I cautioned when it looked like Eli would never stop.

We parked our bikes beside the gate and entered the churchyard with no idea where to find the grave of Frances Burchett Mobley Turner.

"It's not so big. We'll find her," Eli said.

"This place is packed," I remarked. "The graves go right up to the church door."

We walked along, looking at names and dates. Most of the graves were old, many from the 1800s. "I don't think there's any room for new occupants," Eli remarked.

"Hello," we heard a male voice call and looked up from our scrutiny.

"Oh, hello sir," Eli said to an elderly, stooped man approaching us. He was thin as a stick, his shirt collar open and his sleeves rolled up.

"May I help you locate someone?" he inquired.

"Oh, yes sir," Eli answered. "My name is Ellison and this is my cousin, Adeline. We're looking for the grave of Frances Burchett Mobley Turner."

"I'm Hoyt Greer, the minister here," he responded. "I can certainly help you. Is there a particular reason you are looking for Mrs. Turner?"

"Oh, yes sir," Eli said. "We're friends with her daughter who recently moved out of town. And since Adeline and I are whiling away our time before school starts, we said we would check on her mother's grave for our friend." I shot a sidelong glance to Eli at his absurd lie.

But the minister didn't question him. "You must mean Francie. I haven't seen her for some time. Her father tells me she's gone to finish her schooling elsewhere. Living with her aunt."

"Yes sir," we concurred simultaneously.

"Did someone bring you all?" he asked.

"We rode our bikes," I answered.

"I see. Well, young people, follow me," the minister said. "Frances Burchett Turner has a beautiful stone."

We turned right and followed a path behind the church. "Here she is," Mr. Greer announced, stopping abruptly. Eli and I stared at the large marble gravestone. The words were carved in large letters, "Beloved Daughter of Herbert Gray Mobley and Louise Flynn Mobley." And then below: "Cherished wife of Mace Ferguson Turner."

"Are her parents buried here?" Eli asked.

"Indeed, they are," Mr. Greer answered. "Right above her. Over here. Herbert died at Carnes Crossroads when he was still in his prime. His automobile overturned and hit a tree. People were still getting accustomed to cars in those days." He shook his head gently.

We took a couple of steps forward to see the graves. "Louise loved her daughter very much. Loved her like she had birthed her. They were always close. Even more after Herbert died. It broke her heart for Frances to get sick and die so young. Her only child. Louise herself didn't live but just a few years after. Tragic."

Eli and I looked warily at each other. My cousin recovered quickly. "Yes, we knew Mrs. Turner was adopted. Our friend Francie told us. Are her biological parents buried here also?"

"Oh, I don't believe so," the minister said. "Or if they are, we don't know the association. And though they would be far up in years, perhaps they are still living."

"I see," Eli said, echoing Mr. Greer. He sounded very grown up.

"The adoption would have been a private thing. Of course, there are public agencies now, but then, well…it was kept very quiet among well-respected families. And the Mobleys, maybe you know, were a wealthy and long-standing family. All gone now, though. At least in these parts. Still, there's plenty of them buried here." The minister pointed a long arm and began to walk in the direction of more Mobley stones.

"Thank you, sir," Eli said. "You've been really kind to point us in the right direction. You seem to know everyone in the graveyard."

Mr. Greer chuckled. "Why I guess I do," he said. "I'm with them every day."

"We'll look around a bit more and then take off."

"You just make yourself at home," he said. "Young lady," he tipped his head to me. "A pleasure to meet you. I'll get on back indoors out of the heat, but you have any questions, come in that side door. It leads to my study."

"Would there be any records inside the church about Mrs. Turner's birth parents?" Eli asked.

"We have baptism records, and such, but nothing about adoptions. Like I said, back then those kinds of arrangements tended to be very private. Families didn't want scandal. Sorry I can't help you."

Mr. Greer retreated. Eli and I peered at the graves of Frances Burchett Mobley Turner and her parents. Her *adopted* parents. "What did I tell you?" Eli said. "Francie's mama was adopted by well-to-do people around here. I knew there was a secret. And what do you want to bet the birth mother's name was Burchett?"

"So you think some woman whose last name was Burchett of some distant kin to Mimi had a baby, and Mimi helped arrange for the Mobleys to adopt her? And that's why Mimi knows of Francie and hired her?"

"Could be," Eli said. "It would make sense. If Mimi was the go-between for the Mobleys to adopt Francie's mother who is now dead, she would care about Francie's welfare. You know she's very caring about everyone. But Mimi is so proper, too. She wouldn't tell us because it might lead to her revealing a scandal. Because maybe the Burchett woman who birthed her is still living around here. And maybe Francie doesn't even know."

"I think you're jumping to some wild conclusions. And, oh, okay, so what?" I said. And then it occurred to me that the best thing for both of us was for me to agree with my cousin, and this whole investigation could end. "Actually," I offered, changing my tone to serious, "I think you are correct. You've solved the mystery of Francie's presence at Magnolia Manor. We know she felt desperate and had no mother to turn to. We don't have to wonder anymore."

"Maybe," Eli mused, but I heard the question hanging in his tone. He still clung to the word "family" we'd heard Mary Margaret utter at the mention of Francie's mother that awful drowning day.

16

JUNE 1970

By the time of Eli's fourteenth birthday, he looked nearly grown. Unlike me, still waiting—the only girl left in our grade without her period—he matured early. He'd grown taller than most of the other boys, and his voice, though still froggy, had deepened. Brown fuzz grew on his chin, and he let it stay there. His hair, not a hint of curl in it, reached nearly to his shoulders. So much hair, yet he looked every bit as beautiful with his perfect prince nose as he'd been at half this age. His extraordinary eyes, thickly lashed and shifting at times from olive to forest green, presented a hint of melancholy that made him all the more appealing. The eyes made you wonder. And unlike the gangly disproportion often present in other growing adolescent boys, his features fit his frame.

A surprise party took place in Paul Robbins' basement, planned by Mary Lily and Paul's mother, Eli's friend since the days of Little League. Though Eli's interests no longer much included baseball, either playing or intently following his once beloved Red Sox, Paul—hair cropped close above his ears—represented one faction of Eli's friends. My cousin lived between two worlds then: mainstream, mostly compliant ninth grade boys, and those following the counterculture.

You could separate the two camps, both boys and girls, by the music we listened to. Influenced by her older sister Bridget, whose mantras were "Do your own thing" and "Blow the mind of every straight person you can reach," my friend Gloria had gone the way of Grand Funk Railroad, the Grateful Dead, Janis Joplin, and The Who. This was Eli's penchant, too. Yet he exhibited a duality of vision. "A Whiter Shade of Pale"—his favorite song—perhaps best defined him, the words a psychedelic kaleidoscope of fragments while the sound was derived from Bach.

Nealy and I listened to the Beach Boys, the Lettermen, the Temptations. We didn't broadcast it too loudly, but we even liked Bubble Gum songs. Mostly, we loved beach tunes and shagging, having learned the basic steps in obligatory ballroom dance lessons in eighth grade. Our heaviest music was Three Dog Night. I'd played the song "Eli's Coming," on the album *Suitable for Framing*, until that track changed color from so much wear.

That fall, I got my driver's permit after turning fifteen. While my forbidden fun involved sneaking across the railroad track to Shorty's on the other side of town with Gloria, commandeering Mama's Valiant station wagon for a pack of cigarettes and a single Budweiser, it was the year drugs would begin for Eli.

My cousin Nancy from my daddy's side rode the bus from Norfolk the week of Eli's birthday. Her stay wasn't planned around the party. It was her annual visit, and it simply coincided. In some ways, Nancy and I resembled each other. Same coppery hair and fair skin. Same ample curve to our chin. But Nancy was a year older, very developed, and with me already lagging behind other girls, I marveled at her breasts, the biggest on any girl near our age.

Paul's basement was dim, lit mainly by a black light creating a fluorescent, surreal glow. It illuminated colors in funky ways, especially on the posters hanging on the walls. I especially dug Snoopy's "Feelin' Groovy" and had the same poster on the wall above my bed.

We were hiding behind furniture, around corners, under the bar when Eli walked unsuspectingly down the basement steps with Paul. His ruse had been taking Eli downstairs to listen to records. We screamed, "Happy Birthday," our teeth lighting up the room, floating like so many tiny bridges in space, making a bright, white glow.

"Oh my God," Eli exclaimed. "This is too much." His own teeth lit up. He was very pleased.

He walked around slapping his guy friends on the shoulders, hugging the girls. He shook Paul's hand and embraced him at the same time. He looked over at the parents and grinned. Mary Lily, Gene, and Paul's parents had hidden with us for the surprise and now retreated upstairs.

Nealy, Nancy, Gloria, and I pulled matchbooks from our purses and lit our homemade table lights. Much to my mother's dismay, we had collected empty wine bottles from various parental sources and inserted tapers inside. My mother had wanted no suggestion of alcohol at the party, but she was outnumbered.

We were still young enough that for a while, the girls stayed mostly on one side of the room, the boys on the other. Eventually, the braver boys began asking the most popular girls to dance. During the fast songs, we all joined in, a free-for-all. Then someone put slow music on the record player: "Jean" by Oliver and then "The Long and Winding Road." No one asked me to dance. I did my best to act nonchalant, to make it not matter. I busied myself, filling a bowl with chips, pulling more drinks out of the icebox, pretending to be engaged in important conversation with Nealy—also not dancing.

I watched as Eli caught Nancy by the hand and pulled her into the middle of the floor during "Love (Can Make You Happy)" by Mercy, a song that made my heart swoon whenever I heard it. I watched her arms stretch around his shoulders. I watched her melt into him, his arms enfolding her waist. They barely moved, just swayed back and forth. And who could blame him? What boy wouldn't be taken with my voluptuous cousin?

Nealy caught me staring as Nancy and Eli embraced. "I know what you're thinking," she said.

"How would you know what I'm thinking?" I asked, turning quickly from the direction of the dancers to face my friend standing beside me.

"I can see the rejection on your face."

"He's my cousin, Nealy. Don't be ridiculous."

"You're in love with him," she said. "You always have been."

I stared hard at her. "You don't know what you're talking about, Nealy Simmons," I admonished her. "You'd better watch what you say."

She raised her eyebrows and cocked her head at me. "I know you better than you know yourself," she said, all pleased. I ignored her.

Toward the end of the evening, finally, I did get asked to dance. Sweet Tim Morris tapped me on the shoulder. Had he felt sorry for me? Or did he really want to dance with me? I don't know. Gratefully, I put a hand on each of his shoulders. He touched his hands to my waist. We moved as others moved, to the soulful pace of "I'll Be There" by the Jackson 5. And though his shirt smelled like mothballs in the sticky warmth of a June night in Paul Robbins' basement, I was happy. When it ended—last song of the evening—bright lights flicked on suddenly, bringing us back in a shock to real life. The parents had turned on the lights. Boys and girls let go of one another. The party, and what part of young innocence still lingered that evening, would soon be over.

∾

For the remainder of the week while Nancy was with us, Eli was smitten. He stayed at our house constantly. He held her hand while we watched television. They snuck out on the stoop while I remained inside. She giggled in the evenings after Eli left, saying things like, "Your cousin Eli is really cute," and "He surely has changed."

Why was I resentful? I couldn't blame Eli for being attracted to my lovely and bosomy cousin. She wasn't kin to him, and I was. She was available. Still, I felt invisible.

Eli decided the three of us should slip downtown to the clock tower on Nancy's last night. He had long wanted to see the bells we heard chime four times every hour, every day. Their constancy captivated him. "What if we get caught?" I asked. "It's one thing to climb up Mimi's tower. It belongs to her. But if we climb this one, we could get in trouble."

"We won't," he said. "It's easy. Who's going to know? The door to the tower isn't locked. It's public property." I shook my head slowly, not quite buying the legitimacy of it.

"Come on, Delia, this is the real best. Mimi's tower was my warmup. You'll be astonished. Wait till Aunt Jeanette and Uncle Will go to sleep and come out. Come over to my porch and we'll walk to town. I'll be there waiting."

I figured his risky decision had something to do with showing off for Nancy, but I also knew he would make the climb sooner or later. Eli's childhood accident had long ago given him a heightened sensitivity to the potentials of life. He trusted his struggles somehow made him invincible.

Certainly, he yearned to touch the bells, to take them in, but it was more. It was the ever-present specter of his self-doubt, since that dreadful day with the boys in the joe-pye weed, to prove his bravery.

I looked at my cousin, his wide grin, standing with his feet flung out in opposite directions at their characteristic angle. He was sure of his mission. Suddenly, I wanted to see the bells, too. I wanted to feel fascinated as Eli was.

Nancy was reluctant. She didn't have much of the daredevil in her. After a while though, Eli sweet-talked her into it. He could talk almost anyone into almost anything.

We wore dark clothes and carried my flashlight to Eli's porch. He sat, rocking gently in the swing. He smiled a little. "Ready?" he said.

"Ready," I said, though I was plenty nervous.

He put his arm around my shoulders. He swayed a little. "Don't worry, little Dee," he said. "This is going to be an adventure." He looked at my lovely cousin. "Nancy, girl. What about you?"

"Okay," she said, but she was jumpy.

Eli grabbed one of us on each side and linked his arms through ours. A faint sweet, oaky scent wafted from his shirt and maybe his hair. I didn't know then I was smelling weed. I shined my Girl Scout flashlight in front of us along the sidewalk, guiding us to the tower.

We stood in plain sight under the streetlights at the bottom of the tower. The last movie at the Parr Theatre a few blocks away had let out, so Green Branch had pretty much closed down. We saw no one. "Prepare to be amazed," Eli said. He began to cough. He kept coughing, like something had gone the wrong way down his windpipe. I slapped him between his shoulders.

"I'm okay, I'm okay, let up," he sputtered between breaths. Finally, he quieted. "I got choked on air," he said, laughing, but still catching his breath, frightening me.

"There's eight bells up there," he continued, pointing upward. "Played manually at first. Now, it's automatic. It's sort of like inside a music box. But not like a music box, too." Eli was talking nonstop, intense. "What time is it?" he asked suddenly.

"Hello, Earth to Eli," I said. "Are your ears working? We heard the chimes for 11:00 a few minutes ago."

"So let's get going. If we hurry, we'll see them chime the first quarter."

129

I looked up at the brick structure resembling an enormous three-tiered cake. "Are you sure we should do this?" I asked.

"Am I sure? Are you kidding?" He opened the double wooden doors, large and ominous as church doors—indeed, unlocked. We stepped into a large, cavernous space.

"Come on," Eli said. It was dark, but slants of faint light coming through the windows from outside helped us get our bearings. My eyes adjusted. I shone my flashlight around.

"Over here, the stairs," Eli called, walking toward the spiraling metal staircase. "I'll go first. You follow." I handed the light to him.

We began to climb. We'd climbed maybe twenty steps when he leaned back and said, "Hey, Nancy, we're going to pass behind time." All of a sudden, maybe because he'd leaned back to show off with his metaphor—passing behind the clock mechanics on our journey to the bells—his right foot slid off the step. I threw my hands upward as though to catch him. Nancy, behind me, gasped. Eli caught himself.

"Eli, concentrate. Quit talking, or you're going to trip." He shook his head and laughed. Nancy began counting the steps out loud. When she reached seventy-five she said, "How much farther?"

"About halfway," Eli called.

"Not me," Nancy said. "I'm going back. This scares me. It's too high."

"Ah, come on," Eli urged.

"No, I'll wait outside," she said. She turned and retreated. I followed Eli.

We didn't quite make it to the top before the first quarter chimed. It was a splendid and deafening sound from our nearness in the stairway. Then we reached the turret, open on all sides, surrounded by a metal catwalk. I thought of walking the perimeter to see what the town looked like from this height. We could see our way around now without the flashlight. I expected the bells to be neatly organized according to size, all in a line. Instead, they hung on cables in what seemed random space. Eli walked from bell to bell, touching the ones he could reach. His hand came to rest on the smallest bell.

"Don't you dare, Eli," I cried out. "We'll be heard." He didn't acknowledge me. With both hands he swung the bell forward. It tolled into the night.

"Eli, stop," I said. I pulled frantically at his arm until finally, he ceased. The flashlight sat on the floor beside him. I picked it up, went to the stairs. "I'm leaving," I called, forgetting any interest in the catwalk. I descended the first few steps and waited.

"Yeah, coming," he called. I continued descending after I heard him on the stairs. I counted the steps in my head. At the bottom, I breathed relief, not knowing two policemen waited. We exited the clock tower onto the street to see Nancy standing between them, her hands clasped in a V below her waist, her lips deathly white in the streetlight.

Why the policemen didn't come inside to confront us, I do not know. Perhaps they feared a scramble on the stairs. Perhaps knowing we would exit eventually.

"What's going on here?" the larger policeman asked. His stomach swung in a heavy arc over his pants.

"We wanted to see the bells," Eli said, striking a pose, one foot thrust forward, the other behind as though he might sprint. I said nothing.

After the dark of the tower, the street seemed inordinately bright. The second officer, younger, thin, shined his light directly onto us, blinding me.

"I see," he said to Eli. "But you're trespassing."

"It's a public clock," Eli said. I flinched.

"To look at, not to climb," the skinny officer said. He shone his light onto Eli's face. "Your eyes are mighty red, son," he observed.

I looked at my cousin. I could see his eyes were laced with veins of red.

"Want to tell us what's going on?" the fat officer asked.

"Nothing but what I told you," Eli said.

"Let's get in the car," he said. "We'll straighten this out at the station."

❧

They called our parents. Uncle Gene arrived drunk and furious. Mary Lily stood behind him, hands raking through her hair. My own parents arrived in a stupor.

"What the goddamn hell is all this?" Uncle Gene demanded to the officer at the desk.

"Hush and listen," Mama commanded. My uncle turned on her and glared.

"You're not helping," Mama said. "You're making things worse."

Soon enough, though, we were released to the discipline of our parents.

Nancy came out smelling like a rose, an innocent bystander. She headed home the next day on a Greyhound. No need to notify her parents.

I never understood exactly what law Eli and I had broken, but it didn't matter. We were caught. I was grounded for a week. No television, no telephone, nothing. I was admonished and threatened with far worse if I ever did such a thing again. I don't know what happened to Eli, and he never said. I did not see him for two weeks. I don't know if the officer suggested to his parents Eli had been smoking pot. I knew little about pot or had any notion Eli did either until the officer posed the idea that night. In time, looking back, I would realize, of course, Eli had been stoned.

17

OCTOBER 1971

I started tenth grade at Green Branch High School without Eli. In the late spring his parents had sent him to St. Joseph, an Episcopal boys' boarding school far away in Connecticut. There was great opposition on Eli's part. He tried cajoling, and when that didn't work, he fought. He said he would not go to classes. He said he would run away from that forlorn place. They couldn't make him go, he said. But in the end, he went. It wasn't Uncle Gene who was adamant; mostly he thought Eli was being adventurous, experimenting, he said, as boys do, and chuckling as he said it. It was Aunt Mary Lily who stood firm, bucking her husband's attitude. She told Mama she chose the school for its discipline, its remote location in the Berkshire Hills, and its music.

The decision was made after Eli—along with two fringe friends, Philip Gates and Neal Brewer—got busted at the City Cemetery duck pond. It was stupid to be smoking out in the open, but I suppose the pond was as secluded a location as they could think up. And Eli couldn't smoke at home (though in later years he would light up abundantly, boldly, up in the garret, albeit with the windows open). All he was thinking that night was getting stoned. He wasn't thinking about being careful.

Somehow, it was determined Eli provided the marijuana for the group. Though he would give no explanation for where he'd gotten his stash, several ounces, more than simple possession. He acted like he found it lying on the street, and no one could make him say otherwise. It was a first offense, Eli was underage, and his family had influence, so he was pretty much off the hook with the law. He promised his parents he would never smoke again, but he was back at it within a week. Mary Lily was no fool. She had a nose and eyes.

Eli remained at St. Joseph School through the summer. He had not returned home since the day he left. He could communicate with me by letters, but he wasn't allowed to call. His parents phoned him occasionally, but they were the only ones permitted.

His early letters spoke of rules and regulations robbing him of his *individuality*, such an Eli hippie word. He told how they scalped his head and made him wear a coat and tie to class every day. He claimed the boys there were a sorry lot, and he was nothing like them. Then, suddenly, the tone of the letters changed. He wrote in glowing generalities—of learning to be responsible and enjoying his classmates and teachers. I suspect he learned authorities at the school were "reading over his shoulder," and he decided to play the game. Thinking, I'm sure, he might at least earn a visit home for a positive attitude. It didn't happen, and eventually, his letters became more open again.

My own life shifted dramatically too, if differently. At fifteen, at last, I sprouted breasts. Always one of the shortest girls in my class, I sometimes felt sorry for myself, though Mama was a great champion of my self-esteem. She worked at convincing me that petite (her euphemism for short) girls were not limited like gawky tall girls were. She mostly meant the realm of boys. Shorter girls could date boys of any height, she finally proclaimed when at sixteen I was still sitting—humiliated—on a pillow to see over the steering wheel to drive her Chrysler Town and Country station wagon.

I did grow nearly two inches in a matter of months in my fifteenth year and watched my body change from artless straight lines into curves and rounded places. I wore bikini underwear to better observe my waistline—a pleasing inward bowing—in the mirror. And miracle of miracles, I went to the bathroom one blistering afternoon in July to discover blood on the toilet paper.

I have wondered if Mama willed me to stay a child for so long. She certainly tried her best to deter me from adolescent interests as long as she could. I was the last girl (or at least I believed so) to shave her legs and was unspeakably embarrassed at my mother's refusal to allow this rite of passage. I begged; I yelled; I rolled my eyes and made fun of my mother's prim beliefs. None of it worked. As for Daddy, his overabundance of propriety caused him to steer clear of any conversation involving "female matters" altogether, so I could not appeal to him. He adopted an ongoing line, usually accompanied by his right hand rubbing vigorously across the bald of his head, "I don't know about these things. You'll have to ask your mother."

If I hadn't been invited to join the Junior Honor Society at the end of seventh grade, I might still be wearing tights over hairy legs. Desperate, I used blackmail. I announced to my mother I would not walk across the stage to receive my membership pen unless I could shave my legs and wear nylons over hairless skin like the other girls.

I believed my mother would be unable to bear my threat not to join the prestigious group, and this would be her tipping point. But when I'd still not gotten the go-ahead a few days before the ceremony, I took matters into my own hands behind her back. I didn't know how to use a double-edge razor or how to shave my legs. I stripped off my shorts and gripped the Gillette, dragging it up my dry shins, first one, then the other. I've no idea why I didn't finish with one leg to consider the results before starting on the other.

A burning sensation surfaced, not pain at first, not really, until I saw beads of blood appear along my bony shins. Quickly, blood began to trickle in narrow streams down both legs. My legs stung and throbbed. I started breathing fast.

I pulled off squares of toilet paper and stuck them onto the wounds as I'd seen Mama do. But there were too many, and the blood came too fast. Band-Aids were in the hall closet, but I would ruin the thick, shag carpet getting there. I had no choice but to seek assistance. I called loudly from where I sat on the edge of the tub, legs hanging over, dripping small, black-red puddles. Footsteps clambered quickly up the stairs, then another set—Helen tagging along behind my mother.

"Ooh, Dee, what did you do?" Helen squealed. She ran around Mama and was the first to see the mess.

"Go away, you," I hollered. "This is none of your business."

"She's bleeding everywhere, Mama," Helen declared, but by then Mama had assessed the situation for herself.

"Go on now, Helen," Mama said. "Go find something to do while I take care of your sister."

"That's not fair," Helen said. "I want to take care of her, too."

"This doesn't concern you. There's nothing for you to do. Off, now!"

"Yes, there is," Helen mumbled as she sulked out of the bathroom.

"Well, let's see here," Mama said, bending down on her knees to inspect my legs. I described what I had done.

"Never shave your legs without lotion or soap or something to soften the skin," she said. "And don't dig with the blade. Just barely skim the surface."

"It hurts," I said, wishing my mother had told me these things before I gouged holes in my legs. "I'm going to have scars."

She bit her lips together, but she was not angry. "Let's start with cold water and then apply some pressure. It just looks bad; that's all. The wounds aren't deep. You're going to be fine."

When the bleeding finally stopped, revealing a series of evenly spaced indentations—destined to become permanent white spots decorating my shins—Mama filled the bathtub partway with warm water and instructed me to remove my underwear and sit. The top of me remained clothed. She leaned over and rubbed suds into my right leg with the bar of Safeguard and set it back in the dish. She lifted my leg and guided the razor up and around my right calf, across the front and back of my knee, and along my thigh to the midway point. She shaved every inch except my shin, already quite bare of both hair and skin.

"Easy does it, see? I don't know why you wanted to shave your legs so soon," she said as she watched me tackle the left leg. "Once you start, there's no going back. You have the rest of your life for this chore."

"I don't care," I said, stepping out of the tub. Mama handed me my towel.

"Why do you want to grow up so fast?" she asked, squeezing lotion from the Jergens bottle under the sink, rubbing it on my legs.

"I've told you," I said. "The other girls make fun of me. No one else has long brown hair all over her legs."

"Well, they are all foolish to start so young," she said. "Pushing time. Believe me, the hair never stops growing. And it will never be soft again. It grows out bristly, so whether you want to or not, you'll have to shave it."

It would be this way with nearly everything. When I wanted to wear heels, apply makeup, pluck my eyebrows. Each time Mama said I should enjoy the freedoms of youth. That I had the rest of my life for these burdens. Even if she knew she wasn't going to convince me, her goal was to detain me. Then when push came to shove, she would concede and steer me forward.

136

I believe Mama was frightened of pregnancy, because she told me once if I became pregnant out of wedlock I would be disowned. She didn't mean what she said. She tried to scare me because she was anxious about my impending womanhood.

↵

Sporting new breasts and miniskirts (another battle), I looked the part of a bona fide teenage girl when I entered tenth grade, but no boy asked me out. The most popular girl in our class, Katie Crenshaw, had bulging saddlebags, but this feature did not dissuade the boys. They'd been watching Katie a long time because she'd looked like a woman by the beginning of sixth grade. Who was going to notice me this late in the game—even with good legs—when all the girls had matured long before me and gathered all the attention? There was also the matter of Nealy, my prudish best friend who acted scared of boys. I'd been labeled a stick in the mud right along with her.

Home from school and restless on a Thursday afternoon in mid-October, I sat to watch a rerun of *Gilligan's Island* and drink a Coke before starting my homework. But I couldn't settle down. I looked out the plate window in our den to see the red maple transformed into its full glory, leaves blazing in the sunlight. Suddenly, I had to move. I called Nealy to meet me at the top of Hawthorne Lane to ride downtown on our bikes to Smith's Drugstore where kids hung out.

It was a mostly uphill ride and we arrived hot and thirsty. We tethered our bikes to the light pole out front. Later, if someone had asked me, I might have said I noticed two broad male backs on the barstools as we entered the store, but I'm not sure. I didn't really have a chance because Nealy did it for me, hitting me vigorously on the arm as we passed the counter to a booth at the back. "The new boy," she mouthed as I glided onto the red vinyl seat. "In my biology class, fifth period. That's him sitting at the counter with the man in an Army uniform."

"Yeah?" I said.

"Yeah," she repeated. "Look." I leaned far out into the aisle and nearly collided with Josie, coming for our order.

"Whoa," she said, backing up, snatching the yellow pencil behind her ear.

"I'm sorry," I said. "Her fault," and pointed at Nealy.

"Cute new boy at the counter?" she said, unflustered. "Cherry Coke?"

"Yes," I said. "Please."

"Me, too," Nealy said. "And a bag of Lays."

"Coming," she answered.

"He's definitely cute," I said, peering out again. We were not subtle, leaning out and looking toward the counter, our heads bending together heart-like.

"Where did he come from? Look at his hair. What boy wears hair that short?" I continued. This new boy had striking straw-blond hair, and I wondered what texture it might be if he didn't practically have a crew cut.

"Maryland, maybe. You think that's his father in the Army uniform?"

"Would make sense with the hair," I said.

We pulled ourselves back into the booth, our view now blocked by the tall wooden back.

"Here are your Cokes," a male voice announced. I jumped in confusion and looked up to see the new boy, tall in an Army green T-shirt and gray polyester pants.

"Oh!" The exclamation bubbled in my throat.

Nealy said nothing. She stared straight at me.

"My name is Rad Fulmer," he said, each hand holding a drink, the bag of chips crimped under his arm. "Conrad, really, but only my old man calls me that anymore. I saw you come in. I asked the waitress if I could bring these to you. Who gets the chips?"

"Oh," I said again.

He turned sideways and pointed the bag of chips in my direction. "They're hers," I said. "Nealy's. I'm Delia." He leaned the other way, and Nealy pulled the chips from under his arm.

"Aren't you in my biology class?" Conrad said to Nealy.

"Yes, Miss Fergie's class."

"She's a trip," Conrad said. (I couldn't yet think familiarly of someone with a name as cryptic as Rad.)

"She's Miss Fergie," I said. "She's an institution. You pass her

138

class, and you'll be set for college biology. That's the word."

"Maybe so, but talking about how bone structures are different in different races? Calling that black boy to the front of the room to demonstrate? Does she know what decade it is? Is she for real?"

"She's old," Nealy said.

"Sure," I said. My hands were sweating. I wrapped them around my cold glass.

Abruptly, Rad changed the subject. "Hey, Delia, you like football games? You want to go to the game with me Friday night? My old man would have to drive us. I don't have my night license yet. That's him up at the counter." He stopped for breath, looked at me. His eyes were so blue they dazzled me, and if eyes could be said to smile, that's what his did.

"I might could," I said. I didn't even pretend to pause before I answered. I did try to think of something more to say, something mindful, but words failed me.

"Is that a yes?"

I nodded.

"Where's your locker?" he asked.

"First floor, A-wing."

"That's where I am. Good fortune." He showed a row of gleaming white teeth, the eye tooth on the left side barely crooked. "I'll see you there tomorrow at ten-minute break. You can tell me where you live. So, I'll see ya?" He didn't expect an answer. He just threw a little wave at us. I watched him retreat in long, loping strides, his feet striking out at an angle. The way Eli walked.

"Delia!" Nealy exclaimed. "You just told him you'd go on a date."

"I know. He's really cute, right?"

"The pants are weird," she said. "Polyester, really?"

I sucked Cherry Coke through my straw. I squeezed my forehead into wrinkles.

Nealy shrugged her shoulders. "You're the one who said you'd go to the game with him."

"Yeah, I know. Did you see how blue his eyes are? They're like bluebird blue."

"Who knows about you," Nealy answered.

"But he's really cute."

"I guess," Nealy said, distant.

⮑

Mama scurried around, tidying the den, anticipating Conrad's arrival. I couldn't wrap my head around her excitement. Now that I'd been formally invited out on a date, she seemed a different mother; she couldn't wait to meet Conrad, all the more intriguing because she knew nothing about him or his family.

I wished they would stay upstairs, but my parents sat on the sofa, watching television, pretending nonchalance, nosy Helen between them. I was mortified to see my entire family waiting.

Daddy answered the door when Conrad knocked.

"Hello, sir," Conrad said.

"Yes, hello," Daddy said. "I'm William Green, Delia's father." They shook hands.

"Yes sir. My dad is in the driveway. To take us to eat and then to the game."

"Well, fine," Daddy said. "Just fine."

Mama jumped up then from the sofa. She was wearing her new bonded knit pants suit, as bright red as her lipstick. It was a hip outfit, and I liked it, definitely not something she would normally have worn around the house.

"Hello," Mama said, smiling broadly, something she rarely did.

"This is my mama," I said to Conrad, hoping he didn't think she was overdoing it. "And my little sister." I pointed toward Helen. He glanced in her direction, and smiled.

"I'm pleased to meet you, Mrs. Green," he said. He took her hand. "I'm Rad." His head dropped a little toward his waist.

"I know you and Delia will have a lovely time," she said. "Would you like to ask your father to come in?"

"Oh, he's fine," Conrad said. "He's got the car running."

I looked at Helen, willing her not to say a word. She locked eyes with me. I glowered at her. Thankfully, she didn't move.

"Well, then, you all have a good time," Mama said.

"Yes ma'am, we will," he said. "Sir." Conrad put his hand to his forehead and saluted toward Daddy.

His father sat erect as an arrow in the front seat when Conrad opened the back door of the sedan for me. Yet when he introduced us, Sergeant Fulmer turned and smiled before he put the Plymouth Fury in gear. He remained in the car at Hermies Hamburgers. Kids I'd known all my life were there. Most of them knew I had never been to Hermies, or anywhere else, with a date. Eyes were on me and the new boy in town. Katie Crenshaw strolled over to our table with her current steady, Bill Sinclair.

I and just about every other girl mooned over Bill Sinclair. My one chance with him had come during a game of Spin the Bottle at Gloria's house on a Saturday night in eighth grade. With girls outnumbered four to three, it was inevitable one of the boys would land on me. When I got Bill, I was scared but thrilled. I thought it was a sign he really liked me, ignoring the fact the game was pure chance. We stood under the chandelier in Gloria's foyer for the kiss. He leaned toward me and perfunctorily, briefly, put his lips over mine. When he pulled away, he said, "Guess it's time to get back to the others."

I knew better than to think he was being shy. He had played the game hoping for Gloria, and even better, Bridget, but ended up with me. I felt crushed and embarrassed. I had wished for Eli's comfort that night. I thought of our kiss in Mimi's hayloft. Instead of the hard lump lodged in my stomach, I longed to feel wanted, desired, to experience the miracle of that sensation again.

"Why did you move here, Conrad?" I asked as we walked in one direction to the student section of the bleachers while his father headed ninety degrees to the right to find a seat.

"Rad, please. I don't like Conrad."

"Okay," I said.

"My old man did four tours in Vietnam," Rad said. "The Army made him a recruiter here. It's like a rest."

"Oh," I said. I didn't even know Green Branch had an Army recruiting office.

"I'm here with him, and my two sisters are back in Maryland with my mother. My parents are divorced."

"Oh," I said again, aware this utterance was fast becoming my trademark response. I didn't know any divorced parents, but I didn't tell him this.

"Yeah, I guess he deserves a rest in a small town with no stress," Rad said. I nodded.

"I kicked for JV back in Maryland," he said when a senior kicked a field goal, putting us six points ahead in the second quarter. "I'm not too bad. I'll try out next year. It was too late this year by the time we moved." I felt a swell of pride to be dating a football player. Usually, they reserved themselves for the cheerleaders and the Silver Belles.

At halftime, the band marched onto the field, followed by the beautiful Belles. Lined up in their uniforms—really one-piece bathing suits with a lot of silver sequins and headbands with a single blue feather to signify our team, the Blue Hornets. Now it was Rad who exclaimed, "Oh!"

"They don't have dancers with the band where you come from?" I asked.

"Oh, wow, no, not like this. Maybe a few fat majorettes who twirl batons, but not this. Why aren't you one of them?" he asked suddenly. "You should be."

"Not my thing," I said dismissively.

We watched as the twenty-five girls—spread from ninth grade through seniors and aligned by height—linked arms and danced in perfect precision to the band's rendition of "Mame." At the end of the piece, the Silver Belles did what they always did: an eye-high leg kick in unison, just like the Rockettes. It was this kick, largely, that caused my father to forbid me to try out for the line. In a way, I had been relieved, for his decision saved me from the prospect of failure and disappointment. But it made me angry too.

I had asked my mother during the summer about trying out to be a Silver Belle. She had looked at me incredulously. "A lot of tenth-grade girls are on the line," I told her. "A lot of my friends."

Mama hemmed and hawed, putting her hands on her hips, tossing herself around the kitchen. "I'll have to talk to your father," was all she said.

The next day, with the same hands-on-hips stance in the middle of the kitchen, she announced, "Your father says it isn't proper."

"What do you mean it isn't proper? It's part of the school. It shows school spirit," I declared. Helen stood in the doorway listening.

"Go away, Helen," I demanded. She didn't move.

"Why can't Dee be a Silver Belle?" Helen asked. "She's pretty enough." All of a sudden I looked at my little sister with compassion. I realized she was on my side, and I realized it would be her turn soon enough to face these same parents and their antiquated attitudes.

"Thank you, Helen," I said.

Mama shook her head. "The subject is closed," she said. "Your father doesn't want you kicking up your legs to every Tom, Dick, and Harry in the stadium."

"Is that what he said?" I shouted. "Every Tom, Dick, and Harry?"

"It isn't proper, is what he said. You can lower your voice, Miss." Her own voice remained flat and calm.

"I don't know how much longer I can take this," I had said, clenching my teeth and pulling at my hair. I stormed from the room to vent my frustration in my diary, calling my mother a bitch and my father an old-fashioned nut.

"Me, either," Helen declared and followed me to my bedroom where I flung myself across my bed in misery.

As I watched the Silver Belles perform that night, sitting beside Rad, I felt hot with jealousy. Because I would never know if I could be a high-kick dancer. Because though I could finally fill out one of the sequined suits, I would never be one of these goddesses that boys idolized.

Sergeant Fulmer did not cut the headlights, nor did he turn off his car when he brought me home. Rad walked around and opened my door. He touched my back as he walked me, in the twin spotlights casting across the asphalt, through the carport to the door. He paused and leaned an arm onto the storm door while I stood beneath him, sheltered, I thought, from his father's gaze, private enough for Rad to kiss me. He had a good time, he claimed, but he did not kiss me. I went to bed feeling cast off.

I wrote to Eli, telling him I'd officially gone on a date, even if I hadn't been kissed. Even if it took the new boy in town for me to be asked out, I added glibly. I informed him Rad sported tacky polyester pants and wore his hair in an outmoded crew cut, but that he was awfully cute. I explained he had moved south with his divorced father, a four-tour Vietnam War veteran who'd become an Army recruiter in Green Branch.

And then I remembered in my letter to say—for Mary Lily had reminded me—I was glad Eli was in the orchestra again for the semester, playing percussion. I said how wonderful because he loved bells and could play them all the time.

Before I could wait for Eli's response, I wrote him again the next day after Rad passed me a note in the hall that I crammed in my sweater pocket and later pulled out in history class where I almost gagged. I summed up my letter to Eli by quoting Rad's words proclaiming he was "wearing out my fingers, writing the one I love." I told Eli the note asked me to meet Rad in the parking lot, but I did not.

As Rad's pursuit continued I wrote to Eli, unprecedented, for a third day in a row:

Tuesday, October 19

Dear Eli,
Okay, this is serious. Today at morning break Stuart Denby (he's made quarterback this year) walked up to me and said Rad wanted to see me. Would I come outside and talk to him. It made me think Rad is hanging out with normal guys, so I said okay and followed Stuart outside to the courtyard where a bunch of football players were standing around.
Rad stepped out and asked me to walk over to one of the

concrete benches with him, which I did. Then, he pulls out this little jewelry box and hands it to me and walks off before I can even try to give it back to him. I'm standing all by myself out there with all the football players, holding this black box, and turning redder than a beet. Then dumb Willard Timms lumbers out from the group (he could tackle a whole football team by himself) to see what I have in my hand. Thank God the bell rang.

I didn't open the box until after school at my locker with Nealy standing there hovering over me, breathing down my neck. I opened it and there was this little diamond ring blinking at me. I slammed the lid shut fast. Eli, it's a pre-engagement ring. Like girls who get married at 17 wear! For once, Nealy kept her mouth shut. I brought the ring home, because I couldn't leave it at school, but I don't want it. I wish you were here to give it back to him for me.

Love, your cousin,
Delia

Thursday, October 21
Dear Delia,

You're having a lot of excitement, my girl. Of course, I don't blame the guy for giving you the rush. Granted, he's somewhat out of the ordinary, but he obviously knows a good thing when he sees it. As for my advice, give him a chance. You don't know how rings and things might be different where he's from. Pennsylvania, you said? Definitely give him the ring back, though. Tell him it means something serious to you, and you're not ready for serious. But don't give up on him if you like him. Hair and clothes, they don't matter. Hell, if I walked into school at home right now with my own crew cut and outfit I have to wear, I'd be a laughingstock for sure.

You asked about orchestra. It is the one redeeming part of being at this school. I'm playing a lot of different instruments like the xylophone, the cymbals, the triangle, and I'm mean on the tambourine. But the tubular bells are it. So cool to play. We give a concert about once a month here to the community. It's free, so a lot of people come. I wish you could hear us play. We're pretty good.

Nothing new to report. I eat; I study (you know how I hate to study); I go to class. Other than the music, there's not much to rev me. I miss girls, especially you! I'm so damn tired of looking at all these guys. We all look alike.

Let me know how the love story progresses, my sweet Little Dee. And please, do anything you can to persuade my parents to get me out of here.

Yours forever,
Eli

The following Saturday, midmorning, Rad called, asking to come over. I begged Mama to return his ring for me. She finally gave in when the doorbell rang, and I hid in my room. I watched from my window as my suitor backed out of the drive in his father's car. Mama didn't think I should keep a pre-engagement ring either, but she wasn't happy with me.

She called in a high-pitched shrill for me to get myself downstairs. She stood on the bottom step, hands on her hips, brown curls springing out around her face. "Adeline, don't you ever ask me to do your dirty work again. Those were the bluest, saddest eyes I've ever seen."

Thus began my mother's affection for Rad. My own attraction would be rekindled soon on a beautiful, moonlit Friday night. I described it all to Eli:

Monday, November 1
Dear Eli,

As you know, I thought Rad and I were finished after I gave back the ring. But we're not finished after all. It all happened because I was embarrassingly dateless for the big Halloween Honor Society hayride this past Friday night—even Nealy mustered the nerve to ask nerdy George Hollis—so I was desperate and invited Rad.

I got cold, and he took off his Army jacket and put it across my shoulders and wrapped his arm around me. As soon as the moon dipped behind the clouds and everything was dark, that's when he kissed me the first time. I found out what a French kiss is. I forgot about his stupid wingtip shoes and plaid pants. He

146

kissed me three times.

Nealy said in front of everyone yesterday at the Doughnut Hut where we were playing hooky from church that she saw Rad making out with me, and he acted like an octopus. I think she's jealous. She and George Hollis sat side by side doing nothing the whole trip to the state park and back.

Yesterday, Rad drove to my house and we went to the park. After we swung on the swings like little kids, we sat in the grass, and he asked me to go steady with him. I said okay. It's now or never, I guess, right?

I want you to come home, too, Eli. I promise to screw up my courage like you asked and beg your parents this week.

Love,
Delia

Wednesday, November 3
Dear Delia,

I'm glad you're giving this guy a chance. Get out in the dating world, have fun, be part of things. And if you like this Rad, try to overlook the kinks. Go with the flow, Little Dee. He's one damn lucky guy if you do. Oh, to be Rad.

They don't do much to celebrate Halloween around here. We did have a haunted trail the faculty created in the woods. You walked around in the dark and saw a noose in a tree, an open coffin, shit like that. It was all right. I'd love to have been on that hayride with you instead.

What I said before about all us looking alike up here isn't quite true now because a new guy who is biracial arrived a couple of weeks ago. Mostly these Yankee white boys don't have much to do with him. He's the only other Southerner besides me, and we've become friends. He got expelled from his high school in North Carolina because he wouldn't stop fighting. I don't have to be told why. His name is Blease Singleton. Can you believe the law has never let his parents marry, even though his daddy is a rich white man who owns a huge tobacco farm. But he just found out in a letter from his mama that the first biracial couple in North Carolina were legally married a few weeks ago, on Oct. 6. She told him to expect wedding bells. Hallelujah.

Hey, we're practicing an amazing piece. It's "Sabre Dance" from Gayane Ballet. Ask Mama to play it for you or see if she has a recording. I get to do the xylophone solo and some other percussion. It's fast and wild. It pulses you out of your seat. We'll perform it at the Thanksgiving concert.

Thank you for agreeing to talk to Mama and my old man. I gotta come home. Tell them it's going to get cold as shit up here, and I want to be in my warm bed at home. Tell them I might break a leg if I have to ski like these Northern guys. Try anything you can think of. I need all the help I can get.

Yours always, and don't think I've forgotten your Sweet 16, sweet Dee! Happy birthday,
Eli

I didn't relish the role of trying to sway Eli's parents, of stepping in where they would likely think I didn't belong, but I couldn't stand how he felt trapped and isolated. I didn't ask for my parents' advice because I knew they would tell me to stay out of the Winfields' business. Instead, I forged ahead because I knew my cousin counted on me. And I missed him terribly.

I approached Mary Lily one afternoon when she walked to their mailbox at the curb. I began by elaborating on—and embellishing on—all the happenings at school and otherwise that Eli was missing. I clinched my plea by vouching for Eli's promise to toe the line and be responsible if she and Uncle Gene would bring him home for good at Christmas.

Though Mary Lily's countenance was restrained, and she offered no answer one way or the other, she hugged my shoulders. "Thank you, Adeline. Ellison has a champion in you," she said.

Before I could pen a letter to Eli describing my plea to his mother, and her response, I received another letter from him.

Friday, November 5
Dear Delia,
I wish I could be with you today on your birthday. Instead, it's been a bad time up here. I have to tell you what happened in

the bathroom this morning with Blease. Ever since he arrived, he gets up earlier than everyone on the hall so he can shower alone. No one else rises before the damn courtyard bell—the only bell I don't like—rings us awake. By the time the rest of us stagger into the bathroom, he's already wearing his towel and shaving at a sink. We're friends but it's not my business to ask why. Anyway, I know why. He's spring loaded from his whole life. Being naked in the showers with us white boys would make him feel too vulnerable. It would be a prime shot for these guys to rag him about the color of his skin or the kinkiness in his hair and how it doesn't flatten when it gets wet, even when his eyes are blue.

He doesn't realize he's calling more attention to himself. That doing something different from the crowd makes you stand out more, but then I get this, too. You want to be invisible and sometimes you go at it ass-backwards. Why am I telling you all this crap? You know. Still, I figured even if they have their own society, these Yankee boys couldn't care less about somebody's skin color being half colored and half white. I was wrong.

I had just stepped out of the shower, dripping, pulling my towel across my back, when this hard ass named Arnie from New Jersey popped a towel and caught Blease on the calf. For a second there was silence—'cause everyone heard the snap—until Blease turned to Arnie and said, "What's eating you?" He was standing stiff as a ramrod. He was pissed.

"What you hiding under that towel, zebra?" Arnie snorted. I mean what the hell, Dee, it came out of nowhere. Blease hasn't done anything to ruffle anybody since he's been here.

"Why you interested in what's under this towel, white boy?" he snapped back at Arnie. And that did it. Maybe it had been too long since Arnie flexed his muscles. Who the hell knows what triggered him. Mean, bigoted son of a bitch.

"Want to see if your ass is striped," Arnie smarted off again. He had no idea what he was up against. Blease pulled back his left shoulder and threw his right fist in a straight punch into Arnie's nose. It was some kind of terrible. Blood gushed in a river down his chest. Arnie staggered back while a big red blotch soaked into the towel wrapped around his waist. His roommate Karl rushed

in to assist. Only he didn't have a chance because I threw my foot out and caught Karl's left shin. He didn't know what happened when he fell facedown on the tile. I'm sorry, Dee, I couldn't help it.

We scattered then because no one wants the punishment they dream up and dole out up here for fights. Karl didn't know who tripped him, and no one told. Too scared of having something pinned on them, too, I guess. So only Blease and Arnie are getting the treatment. Four days of confinement for Blease in this empty dorm space above the dining hall. I've heard they will probably detain Arnie in a storage area of the infirmary after they patch up his nose. And unless the brass change the penalty from the last time a couple of guys got in a fight, Blease and Arnie will be digging holes all day for four days, somewhere on campus for all to see. Those frigging holes will be deep as graves before it's over.

I've got to get out of here.

Love you,

Eli

My cousin had never written me such a long and detailed letter, so I knew how deeply the incident affected him. He knew what it felt like to be where Blease was. And Eli's inherent compassion had worked to dishearten him. When I wrote to say I was sorry for Blease, I did not mention the obvious. I knew he'd be thinking what I was thinking anyway. How this was proof—even up North where I'd thought people more open-minded and accepting—of what Francie knew too well when she drowned her own child. Of what Eli knew too well: the cruelty people could inflict to make themselves feel bigger.

The days crept by. My sixteenth birthday came and went with a quiet celebration. Daddy took our family to an expensive steak house in Columbia. Had Eli been home, he'd have insisted on painting the town red.

Thanksgiving approached. No one mentioned the possibility of Eli's return at semester's end. I worried about him not only because I knew he hated the school, but because I feared him dwelling on Francie after the incident with Blease. My cousin's terse letter at over the holiday confirmed my suspicions and saddened me further. The addendum alarmed me.

Wednesday, November 24
Dear Delia,

I am jealous. You'll be eating all the good stuff with everyone. Tomorrow is Thanksgiving in the dining hall at St. Joseph. Whoopee.

Still here,
Eli

P.S. You know Mama and the old man pay attention to everything you say. Keep working on them.

P.P. S. By the way, don't get your panties in a wad, but I wrote to Miss Inez to ask if she knows who Frances Burchett Mobley Turner's birth parents were, or maybe still are. I'm sending you her response with this letter. As you can see, she doesn't know, or won't tell. I already know what you're going to tell me: stop thinking about Francie and her baby. But I've never stopped thinking about them, and seeing how Blease was treated brings it back close. I want to know about her. I want you to be our eyes and ears while I'm away. Think hard about anyone in town you could talk to. There has to be someone.

Thursday, November 18
Dear Ellison,

Of course, I remember you. In fact, I saw your mama earlier in the fall at an arts benefit luncheon, and she mentioned you'd gone off for your schooling for a while. I hope it is a pleasant and invigorating experience.

Ah, my dear, I suspected long ago that perhaps your interest in Mrs. Frances Burchett Turner's history was more than a school-inspired research project when none of your classmates ever came to the library for assistance on this project. I would help you if I could, but in this case, I cannot. Even if you were willing to confide your reasons for searching into Mrs. Turner's background, I don't know any more about who the birth parents are than you do. I know the Mobleys adopted Frances Burchett and would have told you so at the time, if you had asked. I wonder how you learned

It is quite true that I know about many families in Green Branch, and I can tell you the Mobleys were of the highest order. But adoptions among such families in those days were very hush-hush. They usually came about because of an unwed mother, and secrecy was necessary to avoid scandal. If I had to guess, I would say Frances Burchett's birth parents lived in or around Green Branch, for adoption agencies were barely developing back then. I would also say the birth parents were likely from well-respected families.

I wish you the best of luck in your endeavors, both academic and genealogical.

Most sincerely,
Miss Inez Wilson

Of course, Blease's trouble would remind Eli of Francie. It reminded me. But that didn't mean we had to bring it all back to the present. Why wouldn't Eli let it go? If I'd been face to face with my cousin, I might have prevailed. I might have convinced him not to go back to his search. And everything might have been different. As it was, I had only the mail, and though my abrupt response—*As for looking for Frances Burchett Mobley Turner's parents, no thank you, and I mean it*—would be enough for him to "officially release" me, as he put it, it would not be enough to stop him. I said I didn't want to go digging for answers that people wanted to keep hidden. He responded that I must accept he would never stop trying to figure out a connection to Francie.

On a better subject, I was able to tell Eli that, at Thanksgiving dinner with everyone gathered, I had asked outright whether there was a chance my cousin would be home for Christmas, and not just for the holiday but for good. Uncle Gene had been slurring his words all over the place, but he was the one to answer loud and clear when I asked. "Damn right," I quoted him to Eli.

What happened next, I explained to Eli, was his mother held up her hand like she was going to stop a tirade before it started. Uncle Gene stared at her. Mama made a hemming and hawing sound in her throat. I knew I should keep my mouth shut, but I went right on. I said

I knew Eli wanted to come home and they did, too. And then, I wrote to Eli, all of a sudden his mama turned to me, nodded and said, "I know." I wasn't positive—but the wistful look on her face—I believed there was a good chance he'd be home after the semester ended, I told Eli.

About a week after my letter following Thanksgiving, I heard from Eli, addressing me as "Sweet Dee," exuberant at the possibility of coming home. I worried I had gotten his hopes up, and it might not come to pass at all. He would be crushed. But my worries soon died:

> Monday, December 13
> *Dear Eli,*
> *It's official! You're coming home. Mama and Daddy told me. You're flying into the Columbia airport this Friday.*
> *I'm sure you already know. I knew before they told me because I worked the Ouija board with Helen after your letter came Saturday. I had to know if you were really coming home. I have to admit, for her first time, my ditzy sister was serious and paid attention. We went to the basement. I lit two candles. I asked if you are coming home, and in no time, our hands moved across the board to "yes."*
> *Afterward, Helen said, "It's real, Dee." Of course it is, I told her. She wasn't a bit scared. She's growing up.*
> *I've told everyone at school, and everyone can't wait to see you. And I can't wait for you to meet Rad.*
> *Your cousin in person soon,*
> *Delia*

19

DECEMBER 1971

A week before Christmas we rode in Uncle Gene's cookie van—the only vehicle with enough space for all of us—to the Columbia airport to welcome Eli home from Connecticut. I felt almost shy when I spotted him coming out of the gate, his hair cropped close to his head, a black leather satchel slung on his back, for I had not seen my cousin in nearly nine months. Helen dashed out immediately and reached Eli first.

She stretched her arms high around his chest. He ruffled her hair.

Mary Lily wasn't far off Helen's heels. I heard her whisper, "Ellison," as she reached up to put her hand on his face—for he was now taller than his elegantly tall mother. I guessed he'd grown to nearly six feet. Her adoration was palpable as her hand skimmed a path from his temple to his cheek. They embraced.

And then I reached him. Eli removed one arm from around his mother at my approach. My heart swelled. He hugged me to his side, and in that way held us both. The three of us—Helen heralding ahead—walked as one body toward the others in the waiting area.

"He's home," my sister announced loudly. "And he's all grown up." She looked around to see who else in the airport might take notice. Eli grinned. Daddy stuck out his hand, and Eli released his arms from Mary Lily and me. They shook hands with formality. Mama gave him a firm, quick squeeze. I could tell she was working hard not to let her eyes fill up. Finally, there was Uncle Gene. He clapped his son on the shoulder. He stood back then, looking square on at Eli. "Good to see you home, son," Uncle Gene said. He was nearly sober that night.

❧

On Christmas Eve, Rad gave me an oval onyx ring with a small diamond set twinkling in the middle. It came in a red velvet box from

Robinson's Jewelry, purchased with wages from his new part-time job at, of all places, Bernard's Clothing Store for Men. (I never asked how he'd afforded the earlier pre-engagement ring. I secretly thought he originally bought it for a girl back home in Maryland.) The store was within walking distance of his house in Wadewood Heights. I helped him pick out flared cords and khaki chinos with his employee discount to replace his abhorrent polyester pants—his suggestion. I felt it was because he wanted to please me.

My Christmas gift to him was a chunky cable sweater bought with earnings from my own part-time seasonal job wrapping packages at Belk's Department Store. The sweater's color, size large to go around his wide shoulders, matched the brilliant blue of his eyes.

I bought Eli a sweater, too. His was soft green cashmere, also to match his eyes. Also size large for his broad shoulders. Eli presented me with a Lady Hamilton watch on Christmas Eve. I felt quite extravagant and elegant wearing Rad's ring on my finger and Eli's watch on my wrist.

Eli's gift from his parents trumped everything, though. He woke on Christmas morning to find a 1971 sunflower yellow Camaro with bucket seats parked under their porte cochere. My first thought about the car was not so much of its wonder but of its wondrous significance. I concluded the lavish gift meant Eli was home for good, and I was right.

Besides my pleas to Mary Lily and Gene to bring Eli home for keeps at Christmas, Eli had lobbied through letters, quite successfully it turned out, on his own. From the start, I was surprised Mary Lily had ever mustered the willpower to send Eli off to school when he fought so hard to the contrary. Because when it came to Eli, she was putty.

Eli knocked at our side door mid-morning that Christmas day of our tenth-grade year, twirling a four-leaf clover keychain. "Let's go for a spin, Delia girl," he said. Daddy stood behind me at the door.

"What are you talking about?" I said, for I hadn't yet seen the car.

"Take a look," he said and swept one arm in a flourish, holding the door wide with the other. I peered through to the driveway to see his gorgeous yellow car, a blinding blaze in the winter sunlight.

Daddy leaned over my shoulder and peered out, too. "Well," he said, "how about that?"

Mama was in the kitchen preparing our Christmas meal and waved to Eli across the expanse between kitchen and den. She hadn't quite picked up on the excitement.

"You don't have your license yet," I whispered, but why I bothered to whisper I don't know. Daddy knew this fact as well as I did.

"Doesn't matter. I know how to drive. I have a permit," he said, flipping the keys into the air. "I'll get it soon enough." Eli actually winked at Daddy.

I turned around to my father. "Daddy?" I questioned. "Please."

"Go," he commanded, quietly so Mama wouldn't hear. "But don't go too far. And bring her on back within the hour, Eli. Delia is picking up her grandmother for Christmas dinner."

"Yes sir, Uncle Will," Eli said. "I'll have her back. Promise."

"Delia, don't go off with Eli," Mama called from the kitchen. "You have jobs to do." She motioned to me toward the kettle to make tea. After these chores, I was to drive to the mill village to pick up Grandmama Loula, my father's mother. I looked again with pleading eyes at my father.

"Let her go for a little while," Daddy called back to Mama, still stirring something at the stove. "I'll set the table for you." He didn't mention Eli's new car in the driveway and that he'd given me permission to ride with my cousin who possessed only a permit. We both knew what Mama would say.

"Let's go to Rad's," I said soon as we were planted on the leather seats. "He'll love your car."

Eli had met Rad on his second day home. My boyfriend drove over in the late afternoon when he could borrow his father's car. It was important to me for them to meet, for Eli to approve. Eli was at my house, waiting when Rad arrived.

They seemed to get along fine. But it was brief and all small talk of football. And then motorcycles, an obvious topic around my house because Daddy—much to my mother's dismay—was going through a phase and had purchased a 1970 Honda Motorsport in the fall. So far, no one had driven the motorcycle but Daddy. Helen and I had ridden exactly one time each on the seat behind him along the oak-canopied dirt road out at Mimi's. Mama was not pleased. She said, "Oh, Will,

156

hurry and get this over with." She didn't mean just the ride at Mimi's that day. She meant the whole motorcycle affair.

❧

"Hello, sir, this is my cousin Eli," I exclaimed to Rad's father who met us at the door leading into the small kitchen. Sergeant Fulmer's stiff manner always made me nervous, but I was terribly excited, and there was the odor of turkey cooking to give me a pleasant feeling. "We've come to show Eli's new car to Rad. A brand-new Camaro."

"Well, son, nice to meet you," he responded, shaking Eli's hand. "Let's see this beauty." He wiped his hands on a dish towel slung over his shoulder, laid it over the back of a chair, and accompanied us outside.

"Hello there," Rad said, coming out of the house. When he saw Eli was with me, he tipped two fingers toward him in a mock salute.

Rad whistled, looking at the car. "Whew," he said. "Don't mind if I do take a ride."

"Good enough," Eli said. I climbed into the tight back seat with the boys up front. Sergeant Fulmer walked around the car, patted the hood, and waved us off. I wondered whether he would have objected if he'd known Eli lacked a full license. He was a very strict man.

I knew Uncle Gene wouldn't care about this technicality. He had three licenses himself, each in a different state—I have no idea how he accomplished such a feat. Eli explained if his dad got stopped enough times to lose one license, he had fallbacks. As far as Mary Lily, I figured Eli sweet-talked her into letting him drive. Immediately, Eli decided to show off. He drove out to Redcedar Lake and let it loose. We flew around the curving road surrounding the water. "Work the gears," Eli commanded Rad. "I'll steer."

"Slow down, Eli," I said, leaning forward between the seats. "Don't be crazy." I wasn't even trying to sound cool.

"Just call us The General and Mr. Motors," Rad said, laughing. His left hand gripped the central gearshift.

"How fast you want to take her?" Eli asked Rad. I sat back and held on—never mind my fear we might overturn.

"Fast as you want to go," he answered.

"No way," I said. "Not me. You can let me out at the stop sign and come back for me." I tried to sound offhanded, but it didn't come out that way. They weren't listening. So I kept my mouth shut, caught between terrified and not wanting to be a total pansy. We squealed across the narrow bridge at the dam and kept zooming, the cedar trees lining the lake spinning in a green blur. I concentrated on survival.

"Whoo wee," Rad exclaimed. An oncoming car appeared. It swerved to the shoulder to give us the road. I sat forward and glanced at the speedometer on a long, straight stretch. The needle hovered at 85.

"Enough, Eli," I finally screamed. "If you want to kill yourself, you can do it when I'm not included." I had never worn a seatbelt, but now I grabbed the strap and clipped it in place.

"Oh, Little Dee, where's your adventurous spirit?" he asked. He cocked his head toward me.

"Back where we left my stomach on the bridge," I said, without humor.

He caught my tone. "All right, just for you. We'll cruise our way back. Let's slow her down, Rad," Eli said, and Rad brought the gear down to second.

Eli promised to come back for another ride when I wasn't in the car to slow them down.

"I hope you enjoy your dinner," I said to Rad when he was climbing out. Small talk was all I could manage. I was trying to regain calm.

"Hey, I'll call you later. Maybe I can come over and eat leftovers at your house. Your mama likes to feed me." His blue eyes sparkled.

⁊

"Why did you have to drive like a bat out of hell?" I asked soon as Rad was gone. Part of me wished Eli actually had skidded the Camaro's back end into a tree to damage the car enough to wake him up. He had obviously forgotten that taking risks was the reason he was sent to boarding school. Or didn't care because nothing mattered when it came to Eli proving himself to other boys.

"You want me to impress your boyfriend, don't you?" he

158

responded.

"Not like that," I said.

"Look Dee, the last thing I'd ever do is hurt you, but life is short. You have to take a few chances in order to live it, to feel it. You have to trust I can handle things. Hey, I'm making up for lost time sitting on my duff at St. Joseph's." I stared at him. "Think of it that way." He took his hand from the gearshift, reached for mine, and squeezed.

I wanted to believe him, so I ignored the little warning voice edging at my ear, especially when he laced his fingers through mine and said, "You know I love you, Little Dee. I'll take care of you."

When we arrived back home, it was past time for me to drive over to Grandmama Loula's and pick her up, oxygen tank and all. And Eli needed to get home so they could go to Magnolia Manor for the Winfield/Lauderdale Christmas meal.

But Eli lingered. "I'll go with you to Loula's," he said.

Of course he dreaded the undercurrent of discord between Uncle Gene and his grandmother. But it was Christmas, after all, when Uncle Gene was generally on his good behavior, especially at his mother-in-law's table. And wasn't there joy in that? And in eating in the same place on the same plates where his Lauderdale ancestors had eaten for decades of Christmases before him?

I had promised Helen she could ride with me, but miraculously—caught up in her new tabletop pinball machine—she didn't want to go.

"Good," Eli said as we walked out the door. Vaguely, I wondered why he didn't want Helen with us, but then, my sister could certainly be a pest.

I drove Mama's Town and Country wagon. Eli's Camaro was out of the question, not only because of the license problem but because the seat would be too low for my grandmother to negotiate.

At five miles over the speed limit, but not fast enough to attract the cops, I'd nearly be on time. Eli told me to slow down. "You of all people are telling me to slow down?" I asked incredulously.

"I want to talk to you, Delia," he said. "In fact, pull off at the park and let's sit for a few minutes."

"I'm already late picking Grandmama up," I reminded him.

"A few minutes won't matter."

"What's this about?"

"You, mostly," he said. I pulled into the grassy parking area, less than a mile from our house, off Forest Lane Park where Rad had asked me to go steady with him. I looked across at the tennis courts, vacant on Christmas day. Only dry, brown leaves scattered the surface.

"What's this about?" I asked again. I put the car in park and cut the engine.

"I like Rad, don't get me wrong," he started. "But there are a lot of things you don't know about boys, Delia."

"How do you know what I know and don't know?" I said. He was catching me completely off guard, on purpose; that much registered, if nothing else.

"Let me talk," he said. "It's not that guys don't care, but they want to run the bases and score," he said. "Has Rad put pressure on you?"

"Is this really any of your business, Eli?" I asked, irritated now at his waylaying me out of the blue.

"How far has he gone?"

"This is really not your business," I answered.

"Has he touched your breasts?"

"Eli, I'm not answering that question. We have to get to Grandmama Loula's." I reached for the ignition, but he put his hand over mine and stopped me from turning the key.

"You just answered the question for me, Dee," he said. He continued to hold my hand. "Look, nothing wrong with it. You do what you feel. I just want you to be careful. I don't want you hurt. That's all."

"You of all people are telling me to be careful!" I exclaimed, not only irritated now but insulted.

"Yeah, me of all people. It takes one to know one," he said. "Look, I wasn't going to tell you because I knew it would upset you, but here goes nothing. My old man took me to a whore a few days ago. I hadn't been home three days when he got the idea."

"Oh my God," I gasped. I put my hands to my ears.

"I'm not going to fill you in on the details, Dee. I'm telling you the basic situation so you understand how men think."

"Not all males go to prostitutes," I declared. "I know that much."

"Maybe Dad thought I'm behind in my development, since I've been with nothing but guys for so many months." The words hadn't

160

come out right. I watched my cousin wince. And then he caught himself. "It's what guys do," he said.

"That doesn't make it right," I said. "It's gross." I didn't want to envision Uncle Gene driving Eli to some seedy part of town, offering his son a choice among pathetic women sitting out like fish bait in a room. But then I found myself picturing women in tight miniskirts over garter-stocking legs, poised in platform shoes, open blouses pouring out their breasts. Or had the woman been purchased ahead of time and lay waiting for Eli? I envisioned a room at the rundown Witherspoon Inn.

"Why, Eli?"

"So I would know what it feels like to be a man. I guess that's it. I don't know. You know Dad. Who knows why he does things sometimes?" I imagined Uncle Gene self-satisfied in his van, pulling out his flask. I knew my uncle was capable of outlandish conduct, but never would have dreamed he would send his son to a prostitute.

"I'm not talking about Uncle Gene," I said. "I'm talking about you. This isn't just a thing." A shudder ran through me.

"Delia, I didn't tell you for you to get all upset. Dad didn't strong-arm me, but he wanted me to go."

"And you went."

"Yes, I went."

"How did my mother and your father come from the same gene pool? How are they siblings." It was a statement more than a question. And I meant it. Eugene Winfield's impulses were as far afield from my mother's as humanly possible.

"Look, we're not talking about whether what my old man did is right or wrong here," Eli said. "Or whether Aunt Jeanette's choices are right or wrong. We're talking about guys and urges. And don't you ever tell Mama any of this. She would be beside herself."

"I would never tell Mary Lily," I said. "It would break her heart."

"Yeah, it might," he agreed.

I didn't ask my cousin if he'd lost his virginity to a prostitute; the answer seemed obvious. I felt sick.

"Let me get back to the beginning," Eli said. "The reason for telling you. That guys have needs, and they hope girls do, too. You need to take care of yourself. I know Rad."

"You don't know Rad," I said. "You met him exactly a week ago."

"But I do know him, Dee," he insisted. "I know. I can tell he operates like me."

The first time I let Rad touch my breasts had been in late November. On a walk in early evening, and he ducked us into a home under construction a few streets from my house. We walked through the framed-up spaces, guessing which room was which in the near dark, until he stopped to kiss me.

He slid one hand between my blouse and skin, up my back, and under my bra strap. I did not stop him. On the contrary, I kissed him harder. I'd grown bold at pushing my tongue between his lips. His fingers slipped under the rim of my bra and traveled until they reached the front seam between my breasts. I did not move his hand. Still kissing me, Rad pushed my bra up high, out of the way, and held my naked breast. He rolled the pad of a finger around the nipple. A delicious new feeling rippled through me, warming me.

"Does it feel good?" he asked quietly. He moved his hand to the other breast.

I'd been raised by Jeanette Green, and I knew I should be squirming with culpability. But I wasn't. I liked what I felt. Yet I didn't answer him. I'd had that much self-possession, at least. We continued, leaning for many minutes against a stud in some unsuspecting soon-to-be homeowner's kitchen. The liquid warmth continued through me, rolling, collecting in the most private place of me. And then, without any talk at all, Rad pulled my bra back in place. I straightened my blouse reflexively. He held my hand, and we walked back to the house.

And since then, yes, he wanted more. When we were standing together, embraced, he sometimes reached beneath my pants or skirt and smoothed his hands down over my hips. I felt tremors in my legs travel up through my body, a feeling that tingled like electricity. But I stopped him. And when we lay on the sofa after Mama and Daddy and Helen went upstairs, he had tried more than once to reach a hand deep into my panties. I felt desire, but I also felt exposed, and I hadn't let him touch me there. Rad wasn't happy. Now, somehow Eli sensed these things.

"What makes you so smart? Makes you think you know everything about Rad and how I feel?" I snapped. I would have loved to pour out my heart to Eli about my wants and fears, but I couldn't. Because when I was with Rad, I often imagined Eli. So, instead, I got angry. Who was he to instruct me in the ways of boys, I declared. I didn't need him to watch over me. I could tell him a thing or two about girls he'd never learn from a whore.

20

FEBRUARY 1972

Nealy tried not to like Rad. In spite of his charm—not unlike Eli's, and she adored Eli—she was jealous of my time with my boyfriend. Nealy and I had been joined at the hip for most of our lives, but I had a new life. She didn't.

A few weeks after Christmas, Nealy came downstairs into their kitchen before school one morning to hear her father talking to the police about a burlap sack of cow manure left on her front stoop. It was a hideous affront, and I felt very sorry for her. Thank God, her father dragged it off before she could see it firsthand. Or at least she said she didn't.

It wasn't the only prank to be played that winter around town—there was a rash. Cherry bombs were set off in several mailboxes. Two teachers' cars got keyed, after which Mr. Claiborne, our principal, came over the intercom and threatened the whole student body. And one morning, the sun rose on shrubs and trees resplendent with toilet paper garlands at about a dozen houses. The only common denominator seemed to be that teenagers—male and female—lived in each residence where the pranks were played.

I figured I knew why Nealy had been targeted first and worst. Not only was she a prude; she had the highest grade average in our class and got needled a lot because of it. Especially because she was so intense about everything. Like when skinny, acne-faced Jimbo McGimpsey called her a genius one day after math class in a mocking tone. Anyone knew if you taunted Nealy, she would spring back with a reaction. Laughing if off would have been the smart thing to do, but no, Nealy didn't know how to brush it off (or maybe she didn't want to). She could not be cool. She said stupidly, "It wouldn't hurt you to study. But you're so dumb you'd fail geometry anyway."

I was there when she said it, and I could see the mean come over Jimbo's face, his eyes slitting like knife blades. I happened to walk not far behind him in the hall going toward his next class. He mumbled "bitch" a few times, loud enough for anyone within ten feet to hear— even with the roar in the hallway. He waved over his good buddy Dale Viceroy going in the other direction, and pulled him out of the crowd by the shoulder. "Get this," he said at the top of his lungs. "That nasty bitch Cornelia Simmons just told me off."

I walked around them holding up the traffic and heard Dale say in a piercing voice, "We'll show her. She always acts like her shit don't stink."

Hearing Dale's comment took me all the way back to that awful day when he and the others tied Eli and me to the pecan tree. And though I was mostly cordial to his twin, Drew, who did not align himself with his brother's antics now, I didn't like Dale. I could still see those boys coming at us, hands clawing the air as they reached for our ribs. I thought about Eli's response to our tormentors. How he'd done all he could to hang on, to pretend their cruelty didn't matter. He'd remained stoic, determined to prove himself, the opposite of Nealy's approach.

Dale was an attention-seeking intimidator and, like Jimbo, used sarcasm to zing others. He reveled in the notice it brought him. It had been his idea to taunt poor Miss Dickert, our Latin teacher who wore old-lady jersey jacket dresses of pale blue, pink, or lavender, her face a festival of wrinkles. She had no notion—nor did I guess she wanted to know—what teenagers thought about. But she was a nice lady, and she sure as hell knew Latin.

Dale scribbled a message on a piece of notebook paper one Friday afternoon, our last class of the day, all of us building energy toward the weekend's release: "When old lady Dickert turns around from the board, everyone lean to the right. Let's see what she does." The note circulated through the whole class.

When Miss Dickert turned around a little while later after conjugating irregular verbs on the board, most of us leaned to the right. I am ashamed to say I leaned, too. I did it because I didn't want to be singled out as a stick in the mud. Nealy sat upright, her face prim and fixed, asking to be taunted.

Miss Dickert surprised us. She tilted her head; then she leaned far to the right herself, her hand braced on her desk for balance. "I can look at the world slanted, too, if I've a mind to do so," she said. She chuckled before continuing right on with the lesson.

So the joke was on Dale that day. But he never stopped trying. Anything he could do to impress other boys was a go for him. I was pretty sure he was one of the leaders in the juvenile delinquent ring playing all the pranks around town. Likely the manure, cherry bombs, and rolled yards and trees were all his brainchild, and he'd rounded up his buddies to assist. Or maybe a gang of them took turns deciding what stupidity to enact next. Who knew? The police never determined the culprits for any of the acts. By March when the weather began to warm and spring activities surfaced, the pranks were long gone.

Nealy was determined, though, to make someone pay for humiliating her. Perhaps resentful of my time spent with Rad, or simply jealous I had acquired a boyfriend and she hadn't, she accused him of dumping the bag. I boiled with anger. "What would he gain by humiliating you?" I protested over the telephone the night after the debacle, my voice raised at least an octave. "He wants you to like him, and you refuse."

"Then who?" Her voice quivered. She began to cry. Eventually, she cried so hard her words were unintelligible, only snorts.

Lowering my voice, I said, "You're never going to know. Ignore it and it'll blow over much faster." It made me sad she'd been a target, but it also made me want to pull away from her. I thought of my own reputation. It was self-centered, but I was tired of being branded a prude with her.

Talk of the incident took its toll on Nealy. She became more sensitive than ever. She lay in wait for a scapegoat. One freezing day in late February, six of us—Rad and five girls—sat at a corner table at first lunch, unfortunately close to the draft of the double glass doors. A constant blast of Arctic chill hit us from the stream of fools going to the courtyard to smoke. I smoked occasionally, like a lot of my girlfriends, when we sneaked to Shorty's and bought beer, but we didn't smoke in the daytime on the school grounds where the world could see.

None of us much ate the cafeteria food. I'm not sure if the food was really all that bad, but we believed it was and packed our sandwiches, chips, apples, and thermoses of tea from home. I had a Snoopy lunchbox, shaped like a doghouse. At the time, I was mad for anything Peanuts. Nealy had a Bobby Sherman lunchbox, and so it went, each of our boxes related to a craze. Rad brought his lunch in a brown paper bag. Often, he ate the cafeteria food—I suppose because there was no mother to make his lunch—and when he did, usually proclaimed it perfectly edible.

With an audience of five girls that cold day, my boyfriend was particularly tuned in, intent on getting noticed (like any of us could not notice him, blue eyes dancing and blond hair grown out now nearly to his ears). In the beginning, with his odd family life, odder clothing, and no car at his ready disposal, the girls paid him little attention. I'd become Rad's girlfriend before he got much notice. Now, with his long-range bombs on the basketball court always bringing the crowd to their feet, girls swooned.

Besides Nealy and me, at the table were Gloria and two other girlfriends, Sarah Wood and Julie Benning. Rad started teasing Nealy about her lunchbox, asking if she had a crush on Bobby Sherman. He wasn't trying to be hurtful. He was trying to get her to loosen up. He was flirting.

"Leave me alone, Rad," Nealy said. She snapped the lunchbox shut and pulled it to her chest.

"Come on, Nealy," he said. "Cut me a break." He leaned across the round table and grabbed the handle of her lunchbox. Gently, he began to tug.

"Let go," she said. "I mean it."

He continued the challenge. He wanted to win her over.

"If you let go, you'll enjoy yourself more," he said. He smiled at Nealy. The dimple in his left cheek showed.

"I mean it, Rad, let go," she said again. Finally, in frustration, he did. His hand relinquished the handle and the box popped back as though on a spring. Each had been pulling harder than I thought. The corner of the lunchbox—a rounded corner, but a corner just the same—bounced against Nealy's left cheek.

Her hand flew to her face. She stood. "I'm telling," she said, like a spoiled five-year-old.

"Oh God, I'm sorry," Rad said. "I didn't mean to. Can I see?" He jumped up to examine her face, but she hauled it out of there before he got around the table.

Icy air blew around us as she opened the glass doors and exited, though what she was going to do by herself in the courtyard with the smoking crowd—the only people willingly out in the cold—I could not imagine.

"Uh-oh," Rad said.

"Oh, don't worry about it," Gloria assured him. "Nealy likes to get her panties in a wad. She'll get over it."

"Sure, don't worry," Julie concurred. She lifted her blonde mane and swung it across one shoulder. Julie knew how pretty she was, head cheerleader and all. But she wasn't stuck up. Our mothers were friends. Sarah nodded in her deliberate, measured way.

"All I wanted was a bite of her apple," Rad joked, trying to lighten the mood.

But I was pretty sure there would be fallout, and it would not be good.

That evening, sure enough, Mr. Simmons called Sergeant Fulmer and relayed the whole lunchtime saga. His daughter had been wronged by Rad Fulmer, and Mr. Simmons wanted Rad to pay. My boyfriend was grounded for six weeks. No driving the ragtag station wagon his father had recently bought for $350 to transport Rad to school, a Rolls Royce as far as I was concerned, since the vehicle was also an unhindered means of seeing me. Six damn weeks.

The next morning at school, I did not look at or speak to Nealy. Our lockers were spitting distance from each other, but I looked through her as though she were thin air. I thought I would never in my life speak to her again. I honestly felt my blood pumping—hot—in my veins when I saw her, wearing a new Laura Ashley peasant dress I knew cost a fortune. Her parents bought her everything she desired, and the dress was surely compensation for Rad's supposed ill-treatment. She had no mark on her cheek, not even the faintest bruise.

My boycott—girlcott?—continued for more than three weeks. When I saw Nealy walking the halls alone, even when she looked at me in passing, hopeful, I turned my head aside. Even when she got bold enough as we exited English class a few days later, to say, "Hello, Delia, how are you?" wistful like a hungry puppy, I did not answer. It wasn't only Rad being punished because she acted like a baby. It was me.

I don't think Rad cared one way or another whether I spoke to Nealy ever again. He was not a mean-spirited person, but his life outside school and basketball games had been brought to a halt. Finally, it was Eli, in spite of having second lunch and thus no firsthand knowledge of the instigating event, who intervened. Looking back, I realize it was because he inherently understood. He had so often experienced what Nealy now felt.

Rad, Eli, and I often met in the library during fourth period. Eli and I got legitimate passes out of study hall, but Rad was in P.E. That posed no problem, however. Rad could easily convince his teacher— one of the assistant football coaches who anticipated his being the starting kicker in the fall—to let him "study in the library" instead of bounce the basketball around the gym.

We were sitting at a back table, hiding behind open magazines, whispering, when Eli made a startling statement. "I'm going to ask Nealy on a date," he announced quietly.

"You're what?" I exclaimed.

Starchy Mrs. Wilkerson heard me all the way at the front desk and let out a big, "Sshhh."

"You're what?" I asked again, whispering.

"I just told you. I'm asking Nealy on a date."

"I'm not believing this, Eli," I said. Rad reared back in his chair and grinned. He raked both hands through his hair. "You know what she did to me. Besides, you've known Nealy all her life. You know she's never been on a real date, and you're going to ask her out?"

"Yep," he mused. "It might help."

"And just how is dating you going to help?"

Eli had not stopped for breath since arriving back home, dating first one girl and then another. Any girl he asked wanted to go out with him, and the more untried they were, the more interested he was, at least initially. None of them stuck. No girl had won his heart. I shouldn't have been, but I was glad. And he'd decided to take my oldest friend and now my enemy on a date? What was he doing?

"She's got a sad reputation, Dee," he said. "And her uptight parents haven't helped anything. God, Mr. and Mrs. Simmons are from another century. And that nerd of a brother who does nothing but take radios apart and put them back together. Jeeze. I feel for her. I can help, for the very reason I *have* known her forever. She won't turn me down."

I looked at my handsome cousin. I considered his magnetism, his confidence. Nealy would accept, even if she was terrified. I thought of the prostitute and Eli's experience, but I hated her so much, I didn't care if Eli toyed with her. It would serve her right to be swept off her feet and left out in the wind. But then, a smidgen of conscience got me.

"She's your friend, Eli. It doesn't seem like it would work to try to change that now."

"I'm not going to change it," he declared. "I'm still her friend. I'm going to help her by being her friend. She's got to climb out of that shell sooner or later. Might as well be with me." If it hadn't been Eli talking, I'd have been dumbfounded at the smug ego.

"Let's do a double date," Rad suggested.

"You can't go anywhere," I reminded him.

"Well, damn, let's think about it. What about if Eli calls the house and asks me over to work on a school project? My old man would go for that."

"On a Saturday night?" I asked.

"Okay, then let's go for Sunday night. The drive-in. It's open on Sunday, isn't it?" Eli asked.

"I guess so," I said. Eli could always stay out as late as he pleased. My curfew was 10:00 on school nights. But it got dark early this time of year, so that the first showing would likely start about 6:00, giving us plenty of time. If Rad could convince Sergeant Fulmer to let him "study" with Eli, we could easily pull it off. I didn't worry about whether Nealy could get permission; Eli would figure that out.

He called Nealy that evening. Later, he told me they talked about school for a while, and she got in a chatty mood before he sprang. He told her it was high time they went out together. He said dead silence followed, so he called out her name and asked again. And as he predicted—for Eli had long ago honed his skills at getting his way—she eventually agreed to the date. Even when he told her they would be double dating to the drive-in with Rad and me, she didn't back down or ask how Rad was breaking out of the house.

170

Lovers and Other Strangers was playing, and though I'd seen it the year before with Mama on first release at the Parr Theatre downtown, it had so many storylines with different relationships, I hadn't kept up completely the first go-round. I didn't know if Nealy had seen the picture. I knew the boys hadn't. The movie didn't usually matter much at the drive-in anyway.

Eli talked Mama into letting us take her station wagon. He wanted more space for making out—a thought that made me absurdly envious. What he told Mama was we'd be much more comfortable with legroom than in his sports car.

It was cold, so after Rad hooked the speaker through the driver's window, he rolled the window up tight. We'd brought army blankets to keep us warm. The screen opened with boxes of popcorn, Coca-Colas, and hot dogs in fat buns dancing on stick legs and waving stick arms to the concession stand jingle. The commercial made Eli plunge out of the car and head toward the snack building in the middle of the lot. "Snacks for everyone," he called, "my treat." The blast of cold air made Rad reach for a blanket.

Of course, Eli had the munchies, for the sweet corn odor of marijuana came clinging to him when Rad honked, and he jumped in the backseat before we picked up Nealy. If the others noticed the smell, they were mum.

For a while we watched the movie, Eli eating Raisinets, the rest of us devouring popcorn. Nealy and I sipped Cokes and the boys drank Pabst Blue Ribbon that Eli confiscated from home. I wanted a beer, but Nealy would have freaked, so I stole swallows of Rad's when I didn't think she was looking. I'd started speaking to her a few days earlier, barely, after Eli devised this double date. I determined to be civil even if I despised what she did to Rad, and by association, to me.

Two beers in, Rad reached over and pulled me to him. He lifted the blanket from across our laps and raised it behind our backs and around our shoulders. He rubbed my left earlobe. Then he leaned over and kissed inside my ear with his tongue. A shiver shot through me, and I turned toward him, hungry for his mouth. It's strange how at that age, not so many years ago but a lifetime ago just the same, we could carry on as though no one were watching.

When we came up for air and I could think, I moved over toward the middle of the seat. My shoulder touched Rad's, but I was no longer glued to his body. I glanced in the rearview mirror, aware suddenly of our unseemliness. What I saw astounded me. Eli's sweatered back took up most of the space in the mirror, but I could tell he was kissing Nealy enthusiastically, their blanket pushed aside. I couldn't help myself. I glanced back. Nealy's cardigan had been removed, and Eli's right arm had disappeared under her blouse. I imagined Nealy's eyes popped out like the brown metal buttons on the fly of her jeans.

I poked Rad. He looked up at the mirror and nodded. "I don't believe this," I said, quietly as I could—repeating my words from when Eli first suggested the date. My lips lay against Rad's ear. I fought the ache in my heart, wishing for once to be Nealy.

"Believe it," Rad whispered back. "It's a new day, baby."

21

MARCH 1972

Eli had delivered handily on his promise to initiate Nealy into the world of sexuality. And from my front-seat perspective in the rearview mirror, she had seemed receptive to Eli's advances, lying back as if on a magic carpet. But they never dated again. Before she could fall in love with him and moon away forever, Eli somehow smooth-talked her into believing they were better off as friends and convinced Paul Robbins to ask her out.

Paul took Nealy to Tiffany's Pizza Parlor, a quirky place we loved for its fake Tiffany chandeliers and Budweiser mirrors. Eli thought his old friend from baseball days—a straight shooter—would be the right fit for Nealy. In spite of Eli's assistance, however, a match was not made. Paul did not ask for another date. Nealy never quite got the knack of boys in high school. Nor did we completely return to the bond we once had. Still, Eli, in his magnetic way, had made it all better. Because he disliked seeing people in pain.

In mid-March, I got the worst strep throat ever. I am prone to them still, but this one surpassed all others I could recollect. Mama blamed it on the season changing, and even Dr. Crawford's powerful Bicillin shot took its sweet time in making me better. My temperature shot above 103 at the worst of it on the third day. I lay miserable on the couch, wrapped in my old pink flannel blanket, drooling gray patches onto the white case of the pillow I had dragged from my bed. Helen wanted to nurse me, but Mama kept her away on the other side of the room. She didn't need two sick children, she said.

I had been out of school all week when Rad cut last period and sneaked over on Thursday—his grounding not yet ended. Sergeant Fulmer had recently decided to let him drive to school (likely tired of toting his son all the way from the lake), but he wasn't supposed to go anywhere else. He sat on the sofa and hoisted my foul pillow onto his lap. He patted it, beckoning me, and I gladly succumbed. He pulled my damp hair from across my neck, laid it across the front of my shoulder. I felt a blessed cool puff of air. I situated my top arm along Rad's leg and felt his thigh muscles flexing.

Mama walked by and cautioned him about my contagious state, but it didn't matter, he said. He wanted to "pet" me. My mother thought his attitude endearing and allowed him to stay. She didn't say anything about his skipping class.

I was still lying in this position when Daddy came home early from work. I hurt so badly I couldn't swallow my own saliva without tears springing and hardly noticed until Rad leaped up, and my face fell from my pillow onto the couch. I opened my eyes to see him shaking my father's hand.

"Nice of you to be here with Adeline," my father said. "But she's mighty sick." His words were cordial but his tone was stiff. Of course, it was my head in Rad's lap bothering him.

"Yes sir, just trying to give her a little tender loving care," Rad replied.

"Yes, I see," Daddy said.

Rad remained standing. "Mr. Green, I wouldn't mind taking your motorcycle for a spin if it's all right with you." He often talked to me of wanting to ride the Honda, but who knew he would pick such a time to ask. Maybe he thought it would shift the focus from the intimacy in which my father had found us. I didn't know. At any rate, my father seemed delighted. He pulled the ring of keys from his pocket and removed one.

"You know how?" Daddy asked, passing the small key from palm to palm.

"Oh, yes sir," Rad assured him.

My boyfriend stayed gone a long time. I wondered what excuse he would give his father for arriving home so late. It had been dark a half hour. Mama had set chicken and rice soup in front of me on the coffee table for supper by the time he returned. "Sorry," he said to me, handing Daddy—absorbed in watching the news—the key. "Time got away."

"Glad you enjoyed it," said Daddy.

Rad sat beside me and kissed me on the cheek. "Feel better," he said. "You'll come around soon." I didn't ask where he'd been. At the time, I was too sick to care.

୬

Thanks to Eli, I found out soon enough the destination of Rad's
joyride. He waited until Saturday, until I was mostly well, to tell me.
He walked in the side door, not bothering to knock. I was glued to a
rerun of *Lost in Space*, listening to Robot scream, "Danger, Danger,
Will Robinson," when I looked up and saw my cousin.

I turned my attention from the space colonists. "Do you think
Angela Cartwright is cute?" I asked Eli. She was the actress who played
Will's sister Penny on the show.

He nodded. "Yeah, an innocent kind of sexy. It's the eyes—wide
set, sleepy. And the bangs that make you think she's a little girl when
she's not."

"Rad told me I look like her."

"We need to talk," Eli said. His face turned serious, his voice
especially raspy. At times, he sounded terribly hoarse and then,
overnight, he would improve.

"What's the matter?" I asked. I walked to the television to turn it
off.

"Where's Helen and your folks?"

"Mama and Helen went to the Winn Dixie. I think Daddy's out
back trimming some bushes. Want me to go see?"

"No, I want us to be alone."

"Okay," I said, sitting again on the sofa. Eli plopped down across
from me in the stuffed swivel chair.

"You remember in the beginning what I told you, right?"

"What are you talking about?"

"Rad's a playboy, Delia. He came here more streetwise than you
should ever be."

"Thanks a lot," I said. "Thanks a lot for your confidence." I stood.
"What is this? Attack Delia Day?"

"Hold on." He put his hand out, motioning me to sit. I remained
standing. "I don't mean it to sound like I'm putting you down. You
know that isn't it. I'm sure Rad is crazy about you in his own way. I
mean, why wouldn't he be? You're the all-American girl, Dee. Red hair

and rosy cheeks. But Rad is who he is. He's been around the block. You don't change a guy."

Eli told me how he'd spotted Daddy's motorcycle parked at the bottom of Julie Benning's driveway on Hunter Circle, two blocks away. He claimed to be cruising the neighborhood and noticed the Honda. I suspect it more likely he heard the engine crank and looked out to see Rad pulling away from our house. With Daddy normally at work and me sick—curious, Eli likely followed at a distance.

Eli started coughing. "Damn," he said. "I get so sick of this." For a moment, he was unable to speak. A common occurrence when he was upset. Then he caught his breath, heaving heavily several times before he said, "He's cutting out on you. You don't deserve that." He put his hands on his knees, folded over and took some more deep breaths. He looked up. "It's time to let him go," he finally managed to say. "He was in Julie's house."

"Been in Julie's house?" I echoed. "You don't know that. You're assuming."

"Yeah, I do." The words bubbled from his throat.

"Why are you telling me this?" I thought how wrong to jump to his conclusion. That if it was because he didn't want me to be with Rad in the first place, it was unfair torture.

Then, I looked at Eli's face, sober and straight. My stomach started to twist. A wrench tightened around the crown of my head.

"It isn't true," I said boldly, even as I grabbed my arms across my stomach.

"It is," he said.

"How do you know?" I asked. I felt like Judy Garland's Dorothy in her pigtails and blue gingham pinafore, landing in Oz. I couldn't comprehend.

"Do you know where Uncle Will's motorcycle was two days ago?" he continued. "I'm guessing it wasn't Uncle Will at Julie's house, and you were sick, and Helen surely isn't riding the bike, much less Aunt Jeanette." He smiled oddly at his little aside.

"You think this is funny?" I said, turning spiteful. He didn't flinch.

"Hell, no, I don't think it's funny," he barked. "I'm telling you because you need to take care of yourself. You need to look out for yourself." I felt tears begin a line down both my cheeks.

176

"He's not worth this," Eli said. "Please don't cry. But I'm not sorry I told you."

"And what about you? Who are you to talk? You don't stick with one girl for more than a week or two." I rubbed at my cheeks.

"This isn't about me. It's about you."

"You're mean, Eli," I said. "You don't know anything. You've never wanted me to go steady with Rad when it was you who first told me to give him a second chance."

"Hitting below the belt doesn't change anything. And I like Rad fine. But not as your boyfriend. I've never made any bones about it. It's nothing against Conrad Fulmer. It's caring about you. I won't see you hurt."

"I don't believe you," I said. I wanted to remain calm. I swallowed the rising sobs back down my throat. But the tears reached my chin and began to drip. Eli pulled his handkerchief from his pocket and attempted to wipe my cheeks. I shoved his hand away.

"Go home, Eli," I said, my voice beginning—finally—to break and in so doing, to snarl. I was crushed. Instead of admitting to myself my cousin would never purposefully hurt me, I slammed my anger onto the boy who wanted to protect me.

"Okay," he said and rose. "Fuck it." I fell into the sofa and buried my head in my arms as he walked out the door, slamming it.

I had not moved from my position—turned toward the back of the sofa, half lying and half sitting—when Mama and Helen came home, laden with grocery bags.

"Dee, what's the matter, Dee?" Helen came and sat beside me. She noticed right away I'd been crying. She put her hand on my arm. My sister, on the cusp of adolescence herself by then, regarded me as the pinnacle of teenage glory and paid more attention to me than ever.

"I'm fine," I told her. "Go help Mama." Normally, my mother would have hollered for me to get to my feet and help unload, but I guess because I was still recuperating from the sick bed, she left me alone.

"Why goodness, Delia, what's got you? I thought you were feeling better," Mama said after Helen called attention to my state. I didn't think my mother could possibly understand the numbness settling into me as I watched her fiddle inanely with the long, pointy collar of her white blouse.

"I'm not," I said and retreated upstairs to my room. I was sixteen years old, and I didn't have a clue what to do or how to address the angry band of pain squeezing me around my middle. I believed I loved Rad. I trusted him. And now, Eli had told me, so simply, to "let him go."

Upstairs, flat on my back, as I stared at the ceiling for a long time, and my anger shifted to Julie. She was my friend, for God's sake, or I had thought so. She was also a beautiful blonde flirt, especially with a good-looking boy, and she had stepped out with Rad.

Eventually, I got worked up enough to call her. I felt very proud of myself for confronting the problem at its source from my yellow princess telephone.

She answered with a breathy hello, all light and glory. When she heard my voice, though, her tone changed. "Oh, Delia, hi. Oh. Are you feeling better? We've missed you at school." Her uneasiness was alive. So I knew it was true. I pressed forward.

"Was Rad at your house on Thursday?" I asked, for what was the point of small talk? Though I forced decorum into my tone.

"Yes." She paused. "On your daddy's motorcycle, so I thought you knew he came by."

"Came by?" I echoed. "You thought I knew?" My head felt fuzzy and stupid, padded with cotton.

"He asked if I wanted to ride on the back with him around the block. But I didn't. I promise, Delia."

"Why didn't you call to tell me?" I asked.

"I told you. I thought you knew. And you were sick. I didn't want to bother you."

"Bother me? Bother me? You're hanging out with my boyfriend. I guess you *didn't* want to bother me." My tone was no longer a pretense of civility.

"Delia, stop. I don't deserve this. Rad showed up out of the blue. I swear."

For some reason I believed her. Maybe it was Eli's words haunting me. But it didn't change the facts. Even if she wasn't overtly coming on to my boyfriend, subconsciously she was, or why had he made a beeline for her house when I was safely sick? "Okay," I said. "So?"

"So, don't be mad at me. Okay?"

I didn't answer.

"Delia, can I tell you something without you blowing a gasket?"

No, go to hell, I wanted to say, but I said, "Yes."

"He did ask me if I wanted to go out last night, and I didn't go. He said we could drive over to Ridgeland to the new hamburger place, but I told him no. I did it because of you. I wouldn't hurt you that way."

Ridgeland is about thirty miles from Green Branch. I surmised Rad thought no one was likely to see them that far away. It infuriated me doubly to know he would have come up with some excuse for his father to get out of restriction and drive Julie to Ridgeland.

"You don't have to do me any favors, Julie," I countered.

"This isn't fair, Delia, when I'm being truthful with you."

"I get the picture," I said. "Thank you for talking to me."

I broke up with Rad in the parking lot before school on Monday. By lunchtime, he had shoved a love note through the slats of my locker, begging me not to break up with him, proclaiming he loved only me. He said he was sorry he had ever looked at another girl. Julie was the only girl I knew about. His remark implied there were others.

I held my ground for a week, but just as my physical strength returned from strep throat, conversely, Rad wore me down emotionally. I was a teenager who didn't know any better and didn't want to lose her boyfriend.

I agreed to go back with him.

&

Eli and I sat facing each other in Mary Lily's rocking chairs on the wraparound side of his porch in the dark when I told him. He was high. A few minutes earlier, he had taken several tokes from a joint, snuffed it out, and put it in a little pouch in his pocket. He reached his arms across to me and groped for my hands. I clasped his hands and rested them with mine on my knees. He shook his head and said, "It's your life, sweetheart. We'll see. What I'm thinking is it might do you some good to get high. It'll make the world go away. It can give you peace."

I shook my head, no, but I doubted if he could see.

22

MAY 1972

Our youth leaders at the Methodist Church planned an excursion to Myrtle Beach to celebrate the upcoming end of the school year. Each of us could invite a guest. Naturally, I invited Rad. We loaded up the church bus and traveled to an inexpensive place owned by Bratton Mill, a recreational benefit for its employees. My daddy, being an employee, arranged for our accommodations in flat-roofed dormitories—the girls in one and the boys in another. The chaperones got private rooms.

Sitting on the bus beside Rad on the three-hour trip to the coast, I considered his expectations. I'd continued to put him off, not going to "third base," the boys called it. He'd made it clear, not so much in words but in his constant attempts, that he was frustrated. He had needs, and I wasn't forthcoming. He expected things to happen at the beach. I believed we could continue as we were.

Friday night after dinner in the cafeteria at our compound on South Myrtle Beach, we streamed out to the strand and went crazy under a full moon, nearly thirty of us. We ran down the beach roaring like children, driven by the escape from home and parents, and intoxicated with the joy of impending summer. Some of us ran fully clothed into the surf, leaving only our shoes in the sand. A few boys shucked their shirts. I hung back for a moment, and Rad picked me up and carried me, screaming. I said my watch would be waterlogged and ruined. "You only live once," he shouted back over the noise of the waves, white capped, cuffing the shore.

"Sharks come out at night," I shrieked.

"Lucky sharks," he said and tossed me under the waves. I came up sputtering, my watch forgotten. He grabbed me around the waist, hoisted me—for he was so much taller—above the breakers. "My sweet Delia," he proclaimed.

Later, saturated with ocean, we retreated into the dunes. I was shivering. Everyone scattered, many paired off in couples, all calmer now after the exertion of bracing cold water. Some walked down the beach wrapped in towels, or wandered toward the grounds. Others slipped into the dunes like us. Our chaperones must have been in their rooms. They were certainly not outside with us.

Caught up in the raw emotion of the crowd running toward the shore, I hadn't thought of towels or a blanket.

"We don't need a blanket," Rad said. "I can keep you warm." I lay on my back, spread full beneath him on the sand. He reached underneath my soaking shirt and unhooked the wet fabric of my bra. He began to knead my breasts. The sensation overwhelmed me. I moaned. "Feels good?" he asked.

"Yes," I murmured. I sat up and removed my shirt and bra.

"You're beautiful," he said. "Beautiful in the moonlight."

His hands traveled to my shorts. He kissed me as he pulled them, and my panties—sopping and sticky from the surf—below my hips to my thighs. He parted my legs with his hand. Again, I moaned. I knew we had reached third base.

"Rad, I can't," I said. My breath was shallow.

"Why can't you?" he said.

"I just can't," I replied. He put his hand between my legs. He stroked with one finger back and forth across the soft tip of me. Making me want to cry out. Not wanting him to stop. But I was young, and my mother had indoctrinated me well. Even if it wasn't true, I remembered her words: I'd be disowned if I got pregnant.

"You're wet there. I know you feel it," he said. "I have a condom in my pocket."

"I can't," I said again. Knowing it wasn't really pregnancy I feared, but something I couldn't name, some missing thing. Even as I desired the painful ecstasy of his finger stroking insistently, urging me, between my legs, I wanted to stop.

He put my hand on the crotch of his cutoffs. "Feel it?" he asked. "You know what that means?" I felt the hard lump beneath the layers of soaked denim and underwear.

The wind picked up, blowing sand onto us. He kissed deep into my mouth. I felt grains of grit between our teeth. He ground his pelvis into mine.

"That's all I can do," I whispered. Rad stopped. He rolled off of me. He didn't seem upset or frustrated. On the contrary, he took me by the hand and pulled me up. He brushed the sand from my arms and shoulders as I fastened my bra and pulled my wet shirt back over my head. He waited.

I was not yet ready to cross over and change who I was. As I tugged up my shorts, I could hear Eli's words back in the car on Christmas Day. *You need to take care of yourself.*

Rad and I held hands, not talking, as he walked me to the girls' building. He put one elbow nonchalantly on the doorframe and leaned in to kiss me goodnight.

❧

We were two girls to a room. Gloria had the bed near the double window looking out onto the wide grassy grounds between us and dunes. "What kind of day is it?" I asked when I woke. She was holding *That Was Then, This Is Now* in front of her face. The novel was all the rage, and she'd been reading while I slept in, the frosted louvers of the window still rolled tightly shut. Gloria hadn't invited a boy on the trip. She played the field, declaring she had a long time before she had to tie herself down.

"I think it's sunny. I was waiting on you to wake up. It's nearly 9:00. I'm hungry." She reached over to the window ledge and turned the crank. The panes squeaked open. "Wow," she said. "It'll blind you."

Our room looked out onto a playground complete with swings, sliding board, see-saw, and merry-go-round. "People are already outside," she said. "I see Rad whirling the merry-go-round."

"Are you kidding?" I said. "Let me see." I jumped across the concrete floor onto Gloria's bed and peered out.

Sure enough, there he was, blond hair electric in the sun, one arm extended, spinning a lone girl squatting on the floor of the merry-go-round. It made me dizzy to watch.

I'd not even gotten out of bed before he began. This time with a girl in the grade below us, Jackie, her androgynous name befitting her appearance. She was on the girls' basketball team and had shoulder muscles nearly as big as Rad's. I watched her bulky arms grip the rail as she whizzed around. Insecure teenager that I was, it hurt me even more

182

that she was a mannish girl. At least with Julie, I understood.

I searched for my white hot pants, finding them, finally, crumpled amid underwear in the bottom of my bag. Quickly, I pulled on my plaid halter top and tied it at my neck. I could at least look like a girl. I ran my brush through my hair and pulled it into a high ponytail. I dashed cold water onto my face from the sink, stuck a toothbrush in my mouth. I asked Gloria to hurry and dress while I ran down the hall to pee. "Delia," she began. "Maybe it's nothing."

"It's not nothing," I said.

"Don't embarrass yourself," she said when I returned.

"What?" I exclaimed. "I'm not the one who should be embarrassed."

"You know what I mean," Gloria said. She stood at the sink, carefully brushing her perfect teeth. "Be cool."

I sashayed out into the brilliant sunlight, Gloria at my side, as though I had no idea Rad dallied on the playground with Jackie. They'd moved to the see-saw. He faced the ocean and didn't see us right away. Jackie saw us immediately, for we were in her line of sight. She planted her feet on the ground, leaving Rad hanging in the air.

"Hey," he called to her. She nodded in our direction. He turned toward us.

My boyfriend reacted nimbly. "Good morning, sleepyheads," he said. "Late start on the day?"

Jackie let go of her feet and Rad came sailing to the ground, bumping hard.

"Youch," he exclaimed. Then he laughed nonchalantly, recovering. "You girls know Jackie, don't you?" he asked.

"Sure we do," Gloria answered. "Hello, Jackie."

Jackie threw us an awkward half-wave. I thought if she had any decency at all, she should be shamefaced. But she wasn't. She looked like she was sorry we'd stopped her fun.

"I'm loving this sunshine," Rad said, voice slippery smooth.

"I can see that," I said, toneless.

"Hey, I'm hungry," Gloria said. "Y'all had breakfast?" She pointed toward Jackie and Rad. "I'm thinking about pancakes."

I glowered at her, and she returned my stare.

"Not hungry," Rad pronounced. "You guys go ahead. Pour on

double syrup for me."

I didn't look at Rad and he didn't look at me.

Gloria knew what she was doing. If Rad were capable of feeling guilt, of realizing he was my guest and therefore owed me the courtesy of not running off with another girl during this trip, he would have felt it then.

Instead, he stayed glued to Jackie for the remainder of the weekend. Gloria yanked hard on Rad's ear as we walked past him sitting on an aisle seat for the return trip Sunday afternoon, his arm wrapped protectively around his new interest, she huddled into him. He raised his hand as though swatting a fly, but I saw Gloria pull hard. I was glad for this small victory on my behalf, because, humiliated, I was aware every kid watched me pass by Rad to the back of the bus. Perhaps finding my misfortune humorous or pitying me.

23

DECEMBER 1972

After my second breakup with Rad, I tried to let go. I really did, but even after many months, I had not completely succeeded. In the beginning, I cried many nights in my bed while I wrote in my journal, dramatizing my crushed heart. My boyfriend did not want me unless I was willing to have sex. He once called it proving myself to him. I felt belittled and insignificant. One night, finally—I'd thought my parents asleep—my father tapped lightly on my door. I didn't respond, so he pushed it open and walked in. I sank quickly from my writing position, sitting upright in the middle of my bed. I clicked off my flashlight and stuffed it under my coverlet. I'd wrongly believed—in using faint light—I'd kept my agony-filled prose a secret.

"Your mother and I hear you through the walls, sweetheart," he said. "We see the light in the hallway." Why had I not considered our rooms adjoined, my bed against the very wall connecting to theirs? "I know this is hard on you. I remember my first girlfriend. The loss. It takes a while. But it will get better."

It was the first time in my adolescence my father talked to me directly instead of using my mother as the medium. I took notice. "I see you're writing your thoughts. Nothing wrong with that," he continued. "Please try to think of events that are good in your life too. Write about some of those things. And you might remember you have a little sister who likes to get into your belongings. Be careful what you say." He walked over and patted me on my shoulder.

By the time school started in August, Rad had moved on to yet another girlfriend, also in the grade below me, named Patricia. She was a nondescript girl with whitish, thin hair and a pale complexion to match. Maybe, I thought, Jackie was not the fast girl he had hoped for and Patricia would be the one to fill his needs. By then, I'd gotten more control over myself, but I still felt demeaned. And absurdly, I missed him. Or I missed having a boyfriend. I looked the other way when I saw him and Patricia walking the halls together. It was too painful. Thankfully, I didn't have their lunch block.

Eli never said I told you so. And for that I loved him profoundly.

One rainy November day after school, Rad blew two tires on the bypass and walked to our house to use the telephone. I was sitting at the kitchen table struggling with trigonometry homework when I heard the knock and looked up to see him, hair stuck flat to his head, through the storm door leading into the den. The same door where he'd kissed me a hundred times.

Mama stood at the stove kneading the ingredients to make meatloaf. Her view was obscured by the partial wall jutting out beside the oven. "It's Rad," I said. I'm sure my voice sounded stunned. She wiped her hands on the dish towel on her shoulder, stepped around, and looked across the den to the door.

"What in the world?" she pronounced. Though my mother was disgusted by Rad's cavalier behavior toward me, she had a soft spot for him. I think partly it was because he was motherless, but also he'd spent a lot of time being polite and charming her. "He's drenched," she said, walking quickly to the door.

"Oh, Mrs. Green," Rad began when he stepped inside, making a show of wiping his wet shoes on the welcome mat. "Bad luck. I had two flat tires out on the bypass. May I call my father?" I found myself rather delighted at his misfortune. I wanted to snicker, but controlled myself.

"Well, goodness, of course," Mama said. "Sit at the table here." She pointed to the captain's chair beside me and pulled the telephone from the shelf, stretching the cord as far as it would go, onto our well-worn cherry table. "Let me grab a dish towel so you can dry your hair," Mama exclaimed.

"Oh, I'm fine. Thank you, though. The telephone is what I need."

"Mama, please," I said. I rolled my eyes at her. I turned, finally, toward Rad. "Hello," I said. "How does a person get two flat tires at once?"

"By driving too fast and bumping off the road over a sharp curb."

186

"I see," I said.

"Could you...would you mind driving me back out to my car after I call Dad?" he asked. "If it's okay with your mom?"

"Oh certainly," my mother answered.

"I can do that," I said. Of course, I wondered why he came to our house when he could have walked to the homes of other people he knew who lived closer than two miles from the bypass. At a spot—I was soon to discover—not far from the Chinese restaurant which certainly had a telephone.

"I miss you, Delia," he said when we got into Mama's station wagon. "I've made some bad mistakes." I realized I was not surprised to hear this proclamation. I had almost expected it to happen sooner or later. Somehow, I had known he would come back.

We arrived at his car and I pulled onto the sloping shoulder where the curb ended—a muddy ditch. "Do you want me to wait with you until your dad gets here?" I asked.

"Sure, would you? You're the sweetest, Delia. I'm not getting out in this rain to put on the spare. There's no point when I'd still have one flat." It was pouring, rain sheeting the windshield. I nodded.

We sat in Mama's car, the engine off. The windows began to fog. Rad drummed his fingers on the dashboard. We were silent.

"I think about you all the time," he said after a minute, out of the blue. "Could you ever let me start over?"

"I thought this was about flat tires," I said.

"It is," he said. "But I've wanted a chance to talk to you, too. Maybe we could see each other sometimes. See where it would lead."

I am ashamed to say I even listened.

*

I called Eli and said I needed to talk. After dinner, we sat on the Winfields' porch. The rain had stopped, but it was still a dark night, not a piece of moon or glimmer of star. Eli didn't turn on the porchlight. As we'd done the last time we talked about Rad, we sat in shadows facing each other. The only light filtered from behind the closed drapes of his living room. I told Eli about Rad's coming to my house, about the flat tires, about his desire to see me again.

Even in the near darkness, I could tell he looked at me incredulously, for he leaned forward and stuck out his head toward me.

"What?" I said.

"You're pulling my leg, right? Come on, Dee, be real."

"Maybe he's ready to be serious," I said.

"Yeah, he's serious all right. For God's sake, Delia."

Eli's anger was rising, but I continued. "Why can't you let me live my own life? And support me? And maybe consider that Rad realizes how much he misses me?" Since Eli could not be my boyfriend, I wanted the next most impossible thing: for him to sanction Rad, as if that would make everything work out.

"Jesus," Eli said. "No more. I can't sit around and watch you be a doormat."

"Are you jealous?" I asked. It was a preposterous thing to say. I said it because my feelings were twisted all crazy around.

"Maybe I am," he said. "But that's neither here nor there."

Eli was a member—with his grandmother Mary Margaret as his sponsor—of an exclusive dance club in Columbia for young men, The Grover Association. He'd attended his first Christmas ball the year before and taken a date. This year, I received in the mail an invitation to the illustrious occasion, engraved on heavy cream paper. It was because of the stag line, a kind of antiquated ritual to teach the boys how to "cut in" on dances and to keep the attention on the girls. Eli was consigned to the stag line, and though he couldn't invite a bona fide date, it turned out he could invite me, his cousin.

I wrote back to accept the invitation on specially folded stationery Mama bought. Mary Lily called Mama to suggest what I should wear. "All this training to be in society is sort of a lot of bullshit, " Eli said, when I called to say I was excited to accompany him to his fancy party, "but it's cool, too. Keeps us civilized. And one thing's for sure, this dance will make you forget about Rad."

Mama took me to the expensive Diane Shop to purchase a semi-formal outfit. Helen sat on the small bench in the dressing room beside me while I tried on possibilities. When I tucked a star-filled burgundy blouse into a velvet skirt of the same rich color, my sister oohed and aahed.

"You think?" I said to her. I looked at my reflection. I could see my sister in the mirror, too, inspecting me.

"You look so beautiful, Dee," she answered. "Like a princess."

"Thank you," I said. I turned and smiled at her. "You can wear it sometime if Mama buys it." Though Helen was so many years younger, unlike me at her age, she was maturing already; she wore a training bra to cover her tiny buds. It wouldn't be much more than a year, I predicted, before she could wear my clothes.

I promenaded out to the three-way mirror where Mama waited in a chair. The skirt was probably shorter than she would have liked, but she didn't protest. I rubbed the slinky material of the blouse, adorned with its plethora of tiny embroidered white stars. "I love it," I said.

"It's yours," Mama answered, standing up. "You're so grown up. It's hard for me to believe." Her voice was soft. I took the few steps to my mother and hugged her. Helen joined in, hugging Mama from the other side, the two of us branches on her tree.

I would have liked a new pair of shoes—black patent pumps—but I couldn't have everything, I suppose. I would wear my navy Sunday shoes with grosgrain bows and a decent heel.

❧

We sat in the car—pulled to the curb so others could pass—for a few minutes before Eli eased beneath the porte cochere at the Capital Club in Columbia. He removed a small silver flask from the inside pocket of his suit jacket, unscrewed the top, and took a long swig. My cousin, persuasive and charming but needing his drink. Hiding the insecurities that lay beneath. "You want?" he looked at me and asked.

"What is it?"

"Bourbon."

"Nah, I'm okay," I answered.

"It'll loosen you up," he said.

"All right, maybe a little," I said. Eli handed me the flask, and I turned it to my lips. The liquor filled my mouth, strong and sweet, a taste like caramel, burning my throat as I swallowed.

I returned the container and Eli drove forward. A valet knocked on his window, and Eli handed him the keys. I stayed in my seat while he walked around to open the passenger side of the Camaro. He tucked my right arm under his left one. "Get ready to enjoy yourself, beautiful girl in burgundy," he said against my ear. He wore a new worsted gray suit, accented with the zing of a fat-knotted tie spiked with apple-green paisleys. "We make a damn good-looking couple," he said as he opened the right half of the heavy wooden front doors to the club.

In the foyer, brilliant chandeliers bounced crystal light. I removed Mama's angora shawl and handed it to Eli to check. In the ballroom, the light dimmed. An elegant middle-aged black woman was singing "The First Time Ever I Saw Your Face," accompanied by a five-piece band. "Impressive voice," I said.

"Yeah, the band will probably be pretty good. Mostly top-40 stuff, though. Nothing hard. And some old stuff you've never heard of, too. Let's camp out here," he said, walking toward a small table where another couple sat. "John Cleveland, this is my cousin Adeline Greene," Eli said. "Call her Dee. Or Delia if you're going to be serious."

"And this is Margaret Breelong, my date," John said, curving his arm toward a girl bedecked in an emerald dress, the v-shaped bodice tied at the neck. A teardrop diamond pendant—dazzling—hung at her cleavage. With short, fawn-colored hair cut in a wavy angle against her chin, and large, round eyes, she would have been striking if not for her prominent aquiline nose.

"Our grandmothers know each other," Eli said. He gestured toward John, a boy with no distinguishing features I could note. Eli explained John lived in Columbia and attended Dorchester Academy. Even the rural kids in Green Branch knew of this school, private and expensive.

"Yep, we can thank Mrs. Lauderdale and Mrs. Cleveland for this lovely evening," John said. I didn't miss the trace of cynical humor in his tone. "Let's live it up."

"Pass me your cup," Eli directed. My cousin slipped the flask from his pocket and poured bourbon into John's punch. Eli looked at Margaret who smiled approvingly, so he spiked her cup, too.

"Hold on, you need some pink punch," John said and dashed off.

A boy named Richard appeared and asked me to dance. Tall and thin with hair so black it shone indigo blue. And while I danced with Richard, a guy who said to call him Joe-Joe with long, kinky-brown curls cut in. I danced song after song with one boy and then another until the band took a break. The phrase "swept off my feet" occurred to me.

When I finally came back to the table, Eli had just returned himself. Sweat drenched his face. How many girls had he danced with? "Not bad, little Dee," he said. "You're holding up well. It's fun to watch you."

"Did you ask all these boys to dance with me?" I asked.

"Not at all," he said, but I didn't believe him. Margaret rose to go to the ladies' room, and I followed.

"Girls can never go to the bathroom alone. What do they do in there?" I heard John say to Eli as we retreated.

"Things we don't want to know about," Eli said loudly, to make sure I could hear.

Whether Eli asked all the boys to dance with me or not, the evening worked the magic he had predicted. I did not once think about Rad.

We stayed until the last song when I danced finally with my cousin to the band's rendition of "My Girl." I approached him sitting at our table and held out my hand. Of course, I'd felt like a princess dancing with so many unknown admirers, and I knew this was what Eli wanted, but mostly I'd wanted all evening to dance with him. He was more or less drunk, yet he led me beautifully in a slow shag to my favorite Temptations song.

When the lights came up and Eli called to have the Camaro brought around, I asked if I should drive. Even though I did not know how to drive a stick shift.

"Should you drive? No, sweet cousin, I'm fine. Do you not think I know how to handle myself?" He opened my door in a show of gallantry. I knew the futility of asking again.

"Then hurry around and turn on the car. I'm freezing," I said.

"Have fun?" he asked as he wheeled onto Highway 21, turning up the heat full blast.

"What do you think?"

"I think you did," he said as he turned and winked at me.

"Keep your eyes on the road, Eli," I said.

"It's all right, Little Dee," he said and reached over to pat my leg.

"And both hands, too," I admonished. For a second, I thought he was going to start one of his coughing jags, but he caught it. He cleared his throat hard several times.

"Okay, I'm good. Hey, you want to go parking when we get back to Green Branch?"

"Don't be ridiculous," I said. "Why in the world would we go parking?"

"I dunno. It'll be a surprise. I'll get you home before Jeannette and Will call the police. They know this is a special night." I raised my eyebrows and shook my head, mock dubious.

Sure enough, Eli pulled the Camaro onto one of the dirt spaces carved out long ago by parkers at the pond. There were a couple of other cars around but none close by. Most of the crowd was gone.

Eli cut the engine and pushed his bucket seat as far back as it would go. He reached over and opened the glove compartment, pulling out a baggie with a partly smoked joint and a lighter.

"Eli," I exclaimed.

"Eli," he mocked. "Look, try it, why don't you? You worry too much. I've told you. It brings peace."

My cousin inhaled deeply and passed the reefer to me. I'd taken tokes before but to no avail.

"Marijuana doesn't work for me," I said. I'd told Eli this many times.

"That's because you've never smoked right," he countered.

I put the cigarette to my lips and drew in.

"Deeper," Eli said. "You don't know how to inhale."

"That's bullshit. I know how to smoke tobacco." I pulled in the smoke as hard as I could. I sputtered.

"Better," he said.

Still, after the joint was nearly spent and I passed the roach back to him to extinguish, I felt nothing, or at least nothing I could detect.

"Man, I'm going to have to get some better shit, then," Eli said. He was certainly feeling no pain.

"I'll stick to beer and Boone's Farm wine," I said. "I like the wild cherry flavor." Though in truth, I was now feeling a pleasant sense of relaxation.

He laughed and said, "No wonder you're irresistible. You're such an innocent. And you're so sexy." Then he moved toward me. He turned my shoulders toward him.

"I know I'm near wasted, but what I'm telling you is the truth. I love you, and I don't want anything bad ever to happen to you." He put his hands in my hair and kissed me lightly on the mouth. I clung to his kiss. I believe he felt what I felt, a paradox of intensity and quiet comfort. For a moment afterward, we were silent, and then I said, "Do you remember when we were little, out at Mimi's house? When she told us about how first cousins used to marry?"

"Sure, I do," he said. "I said your hair was the color of copper pennies." He leaned toward me again and kissed the top of my head. The gesture felt wistful. His voice was pensive.

"We will always have each other," I whispered. All of a sudden I felt shy in the presence of the person I believed I knew better than anyone on earth. I looked down at the floorboard, saw my feet flexing in my high-heeled shoes.

"Look at me," he said, his tone shifting, almost stern, so quickly.

"I'm looking," I answered, recovering, reaching out, giving his chest a playful shove.

"Seriously, there's something I haven't told you. I wasn't going to, but I decided I need to tell you. It's one reason I stopped here to be alone."

All sorts of thoughts began to run through my head. Was he being sent off again to boarding school? Had he gotten in trouble with the law again for smoking marijuana or more? Was Aunt Mary Lily finally going to separate from Uncle Gene?

"I got a girl pregnant," he continued. The tracks of my mind stopped cold. I stared at my cousin. "My old man paid for the abortion."

"Who?" I managed to stammer.

"No one you know well, Delia. Who is not important."

"I imagine it's important to her," I shot back.

"That's not what I meant." He shook his head fiercely, as though trying to shake out one thought so he could grab on to another. "I'm not proud of it. It was an accident. I think she's okay with everything. I check on her."

193

"My God, Eli," I said. I knew my cousin's attraction to inexperienced girls. I cringed to think of it. "Was she a virgin?" I asked.

"No, no, this is a girl who gets around."

"It's still an awful thing. She will never forget. When will you be convinced, Eli? How much does it take to prove you're a man?"

He shook his head.

"Does your mama know?"

"I don't think so. Not unless Dad told her. I hope not." Eli put his hands to his head. He pulled hard on his hair with both fists. When he let go, brown sugar tufts stuck out at wild angles. "My whole point in telling you—because I didn't want to—is about you, Delia. I don't want this or anything like it to happen to you. I didn't love her, Dee. And when you make love with a boy, when it happens for you, it should be when you're ready. It should be with a guy who loves you like crazy. Or it would destroy you."

"You think Rad would get me pregnant? Is that what this is all about?"

"Not on purpose. But did you ever hear that phrase, 'It takes one to know one'?"

"Yes," I said.

"No more going back to him. Promise? You're over him now, right?"

I nodded.

Eli reached into the console and retrieved a tape. He turned the ignition and inserted his 8-track of *Led Zeppelin IV*. It started on "Black Dog." I knew what was coming soon, the favorite song of Eli's life: "Stairway to Heaven." He loved its aggression and emotion, unresolved and mystical. He loved it, too, because it was lonely.

The tender opening chords began on the guitar. The recorders followed with their sweet and expectant melody, reminiscent of time long ago. I imagined Elizabethan maidens in brocade gowns, tiptoeing about on a mossy forest floor.

"The radio will play this song forever. Other bands will play it," Eli said. "It will last. Mark my words. Not because of the lyrics. They're imprinted on your brain, but they're bullshit pompous. It's the music that matters. Listen."

We leaned back into our seats. I closed my eyes, Eli reached for my hand. "A minor," he whispered. "Haunting. It's the unknown flirting with you. Like our Ouija board."

I waited for the crescendo to build toward the long and dramatic guitar. And then the comedown at the end, the near silence as the song faded.

"It's like life," Eli said when the song ended. "Tension and release." He squeezed my hand and let it go. He ejected the tape.

The music resonated inside me.

"Eli," I said.

"Hmm?"

"I love you."

"I love you like crazy," he said.

"You said it."

"What?"

"That you love me like crazy."

"That's nothing new."

"But you just said when I make love, it should be with a boy who loves me like crazy." For a moment I was still, waiting for Eli to respond. When he didn't, I leaned my body toward his and took his face in my hands. I touched my lips to his, and he grabbed me hard, pulling me into him.

"Delia," he exhaled, my name muffled, for he had begun to kiss me deeply. I closed my eyes. I focused on the sensation of his lips, of his tongue meeting mine.

He pulled back suddenly then and looked at me. "I love you like crazy, too," I said.

His hands fell to the buttons of my star-filled blouse. When he'd undone half the row, I slipped the sleeves from my shoulders. My blouse pooled around the top of my skirt.

Eli reached around my back and deftly unfastened my bra. My breasts fell free and he cupped them in his hands. "Dee," he whimpered.

"I want to," I said.

He kissed each breast. "So beautiful," he murmured. Everything inside my body throbbed. Moved to the center of me in a pulsing current. Instinctively, I reached down and placed my hand over Eli's hard groin. I squeezed my fingers along the length of him. He groaned.

195

He put his hand over mine, I thought to encourage me, but he pulled my hand away and held it in his.

"Let's get in the back seat," I said.

"Dear God," he said. "There is nothing I want more, that I'll ever want more than this, but we can't," he said.

"Please, Eli."

"We can't," he said again.

"You've made love with girls you don't love, and you love me. Isn't that more reason? Why not me? You said you love me."

"That's right. You said it. I love you. I didn't, I don't, love those girls. We've had sex; I didn't make love with them."

"Then, I'll take sex," I said.

"No. It wouldn't be possible. For us it would be love. Making love. And then where would we be?"

I put my arms around his shoulders and buried my face in his neck. "Why can't we?" I begged, ignoring the truth of his words. Tears began to leak onto my cheeks.

"You know why."

"We would keep it a secret."

"And how long do you think we could keep that secret?" he asked. "We would want to be together. A couple. How long before people—our parents—figured it out?"

"We are already a couple," I said. "You said it earlier tonight."

"You know what I mean, Delia. We wouldn't be able to stand it, keeping it all bottled up, because the world says it's depraved."

"It doesn't seem immoral when you're living with the feelings, and they feel right," I cried. "It didn't used to be wrong. I read Albert Einstein married his cousin. We can't help that we're kin."

"Precious Dee," he murmured. "You've always the stable, steady one. But now. What if? What if you got pregnant?"

"I wouldn't," I exclaimed. "We would be careful."

"You are such my innocent," he said and kissed my hair. "I didn't plan to get a girl pregnant and her have to get an abortion. And if that happened to you... It's not going to."

"We love each other; we would figure it out without abortion."

"No Delia, we wouldn't. A baby born of first cousins would be shunned as much as Francie knew her baby would be—maybe despised

196

more. We saw Francie's desperation. We saw her baby die."

"We would find a way," I sobbed. Eli pulled his arms around my naked back and pressed me to his chest. "When we were children in the hayloft, it was you who kissed me. It was you who started," I mumbled into his shirt.

"We were children, Dee. We had no grasp of what it could mean."

I felt his heart beating beneath my breasts. I wanted Eli with me always, for him to meld into me.

He loosened one arm and pulled his handkerchief from his pocket. He reached between us and wiped my wet face with the folded square. "Don't cry," he pleaded. "You said we will always have each other. And we will."

"It isn't fair," I said.

"It isn't," he said. I found myself looking at the scar on Eli's throat. I touched its horizontal ridge. It was the only outward sign that he had swallowed lye as a child, of what he'd lived through. And I realized, as I fingered the delicate scar, that Eli's fate had taken with one hand and given with the other. If not for his accident, we might have been familiar cousins, friends—close no doubt—living across the street from each other, but Eli's accident changed the ordinary relationship we might have had. Instead, it grew into an incomparable love.

I refastened my bra. I pulled on my blouse and rebuttoned it. My heart was full of this boy I loved, and I yearned for the parts of him I could not reach or fully know.

Eli bowed his head in my direction. "Ah, my love. My joy," he said. Then he cranked the car to drive us home.

24

APRIL 1974

Eli continued to date first one and then another girl through high school. They didn't mean anything real, he told me. He called them a "fix" for what he could not have. And so I coped, by knowing he loved me even if I could not have him in the way these other girls could.

But in the spring of our senior year, Eli fell in love. Her name was Isabel Shepherd. Eli gave her the nickname Izzy, and she loved it. I thought Isabel soft and gracious like her name, not at all snobby like I might have imagined a girl from Columbia, attending the exclusive Dorchester Academy. Eli met her—a senior like us—at the Grover Association spring dance that year.

He invited a date from home but told me once he saw Isabel, she shone out among the other girls in the dim light of the ballroom, and he couldn't take his eyes off her, not once the whole night. He described her as not quite human but ethereal—I thought of the night-blooming cereus I'd seen on rare occasion with Mary Lily, penlight in hand, guiding the way into her darkened garden—a creature existing in some beatific realm.

Perhaps it was because Eli and I stood in Mary Lily's perennial beds that day after the dance that I imagined Izzy as flower-like. I was gazing at the peonies beginning to bloom—gorgeous, profuse blossoms. Lovely tissue paper flowers that have never seemed to me quite real. I pictured her skin like those blossoms: pale, pinkish, luminous. "Alabaster" was Eli's word.

"What color is her hair?" I asked. I bent over to inhale a blossom, attempting nonchalance.

"Honey," he said, and I was reminded of the butterscotch blond of Eli's hair when we were children.

"Eyes?" I asked.

"A pale tint of azure."

"Heavens," I remarked. "This girl has turned you into a poet."

"Ah," he said, the exclamation emerging in a long throaty sigh. "I am a poet because my heart jumped when I saw her, and it jumped harder when she left."

"How can you be lovesick when you've been around a girl for all of four hours?" I shook my head, attempting mock disbelief, but I couldn't carry it off. I picked a large flower head. I stroked it across my arm.

"What?" he questioned. "You don't believe me?"

I did believe him, and he knew I did. He searched my eyes, his own pleading with me. It was all there in his bearing, his need for me to accept the inevitable. My emotions clashed, how I felt them powerfully and instantaneously—the joy and the jealousy—as I held the pale pink peony beneath my nose, the fragrance fresh and citrus.

I wanted to rage and scream at the unfairness of it, that this beautiful girl should capture the heart of the boy I'd loved all my life. How could I be happy for him when I wanted to be Izzy? But I couldn't, so how could I not be happy for him? Here was a girl, at last, who might settle Eli, who might help him forget his self-doubts, if she felt the same way toward him. And why would she not? Eli possessed something unusual, a keen sensitivity I've not known in another human being. For all the years of being excluded, of being ridiculed, molested, had not hardened him but had made him deeply aware and responsive to the feelings of others.

I put out my arms, and Eli walked into them. We held each other tightly for a long time. I don't know if it was only I who trembled or if it was both of us.

Finally, Eli released me. "It's the only way," he said. "You know it, too, Dee. We can't change our heredity. Nor would we want to. Or how would I love you like I do?"

"It's a mixed blessing, isn't it?" I smiled. I worked from the inside out to create that smile and make it real for both our sakes. "So tell me everything," I said.

And he did. Every detail, while I kept the smile pasted on my face. Each time a guy cut in on his date, Eli cut in on Isabel's partner. He described her Carolina shag as sublime, and Eli was a shagging fool. "I'll be dancing with her at Ocean Drive this summer," he proclaimed. I rubbed the velvet petals of the flower between my fingers. My cousin loved another girl. I felt removed from the world.

&

Eli wooed Isabel elegantly and relentlessly that spring, his Camaro constantly on the road between Green Branch and Columbia. He courted her family, too, especially her mother. The piano was his savior. He played for Mrs. Shepherd and Isabel on their Steinway baby grand, well-known pieces they would recognize. Some jolted your energy, like Rimsky-Korsakov's "Flight of the Bumblebee." Others, like Beethoven's "Moonlight Sonata," soothed. And there was Rachmaninoff's "Rhapsody on the Theme of Paganini" that could make me weep. I was certain no human hearing Eli play this piece would not be similarly moved. It was simply too beautiful.

He surprised Isabel with elegant gifts, too, one I remember in particular, a dragonfly pin, a piece among other treasures Mimi gave him. I loved this brooch with its twinkling tourmalines setting the insect's lustrous eyes. Eli was like a dragonfly himself during that time—wing strokes full of power and poise, always in agile flight, as though skimming across water.

He played golf with Isabel's father, his tee time at the country club set at 9:00 am on those Saturdays. Though Eli had played little golf in his lifetime, he was not embarrassed by his embarrassing scores. He was too smitten with Izzy to care.

As for me senior year, I began dating a sincere boy I met when Gloria and I visited Clemson University in the fall. We went on a weekend to case the campus as prospective students, sleeping on the floor in Bridget's room. A junior then, Bridget called up friends in the Pi Kappa Phi fraternity to find her sister and me blind dates. How Kelly Foster from Green Branch volunteered, and whether his being a hometown boy was a coincidence or not, I've no idea. Kelly and his buddy Grady Malone—Gloria's date from the lower part of the state—treated us to pizza and beer on College Avenue. Gloria liked Grady quite a bit, but for reasons unknown, Grady did not follow up. For a few weeks, Gloria complained about Grady's not calling her, especially, I supposed, since Kelly pursued me. But then Gloria, being Gloria, moved on.

Kelly was the presence of stability after my tempestuous time with Rad. I'd known him only by name back home because three years older is a lifetime when you're in high school. Frankly, I was surprised my parents accepted my dating a twenty-one-year-old—especially a Catholic, for the religion inspired great fear in my Protestant mother. But my mother knew his mother, an art teacher who had instructed Helen when she was in grammar school—an acrylic patchwork Helen painted under her instruction still hangs in our kitchen. And I guess my folks were willing to endorse any reasonable relationship that would help me move beyond the impossible relationship with Rad, never knowing Rad had been the stand-in, and it was the impossible relationship with my beloved cousin I had to move beyond. I had to follow Eli's lead.

Kelly shared a car with his younger brother, a freshman, and since I didn't have a car at all in high school, we didn't see each other every weekend. But he was persistent. He came home a couple of times a month, and if it wasn't his weekend to have the car and he couldn't find a ride home with someone he knew, he hitchhiked. I was pleased Kelly would go to such trouble to be with me. But I also found the prospect of thumbing out on the highway a terror. What if a serial killer picked him up, I asked once after he described his ride home with a long-bearded farmer. But he laughed and patted me on the arm. "There are things to worry about, but not a ride home from Clemson with a man taking his chickens to market," he assured me.

Kelly treated me like a queen. He was studying to be an engineer—like my father—and could sketch anything freehand. I admired his talent. In the letters he wrote faithfully each week, he often included a caricature of someone or something attention worthy around the Clemson campus. As Eli loved Izzy, I wanted to fall in love with Kelly.

The third weekend of April was junior-senior, and Eli determined the four of us would attend the dance together. "Why would Kelly want to go back to high school?" I asked my cousin.

"Because we will make it a hell of a lot of fun," he said. He was standing in our kitchen, leaning against the table, his feet slung out at their jaunty, slue-footed angle. "And because he will do anything for you. Come on, Little Dee, you know you want to go. And I need you with me. You keep me straight."

"No one keeps you straight, Eli," I said, and laughed as though I didn't mean it.

On top of hefty alcohol consumption, my cousin smoked a lot of pot, and though he worked an after-school job dispensing equipment at the Bratton Recreation Center, no way did it provide enough income for Eli's activities. When I asked where he got the money to buy so much weed and take Izzy on so many fancy dates—the alcohol he easily stole from Uncle Gene's stash—he said he grew it in the attic with fluorescent lights and a fan to ventilate, and sold what he didn't keep for himself. When I expressed shock, he said his dad knew.

"This isn't good," I warned him. "In fact, it's crazy. What parent sanctions his kid growing marijuana in plastic pots in the attic? Have you thought what could happen?"

"It's under control," he said. "Do you think the Green Branch police are going to come looking?" He chuckled. "The old man isn't against my bringing in a little revenue to provide for entertainment. Sometimes, he smokes a joint with me."

"What about your mama? What would she think? You know she can smell the plants."

"She doesn't know," he said.

How could she not, I wondered. Aunt Mary Lily was not stupid. Even if she miraculously didn't pick up on the smell, she took things back and forth from the attic from time to time, and she was very observant. "She's pretending not to know," I said.

He shrugged.

"Why, Eli?" It's not that I thought smoking pot was so bad. Lots of kids did it. The police weren't so much after the smokers. But growing that much stash, and growing it to sell, was another matter.

"Why not?" he responded.

"Are you hooked?" I asked.

"You don't get hooked on it. But do I like dope? Hell, yeah, I like it. It's all mellow. No worries, no pain, no problems."

What problems did Eli really have? What did he need to escape? He made good grades without studying. He attracted girls like honeybees to pollen. He had a supply of friends. He was in love. Did anyone even remember the infirm child who'd been harassed and bullied? Tall, handsome, lithe, he'd overcome his handicap. Hadn't he? I tunneled my fingers through my hair in frustration. Eli harvesting marijuana, and Uncle Gene partaking. I cupped my ears, leaned my head forward, and closed my eyes.

I was sure Aunt Mary Lily didn't know what to do any more than I did—the supposed solution of an isolated boarding school now far in the distance, and who knew how she put up with Uncle Gene. If Mama found out, I shuddered to think. I watched Eli watching my reaction, half-smiling at my consternation.

෨

The night of the dance, I rode in the back seat of the Camaro with Eli and Isabel out to the Fosters' house at Partridge Hill where Kelly waited. Eli had picked up Izzy in Columbia in the afternoon. Mr. and Mrs. Foster hosted a little pre-party for us on their patio, lanterns lit and a festive floral cloth on the round wrought-iron table. The Fosters were what my mother referred to—uneasily—as strong social drinkers, a bonus for us, of course, getting in the mood for the dance.

"Pictures," Kelly's mama exclaimed when we arrived. Ever the artist, Mrs. Foster affixed her complicated camera to a tripod and took myriad shots in various poses and angles. "You could all be magazine models," she said. The blue trim on Eli's ruffled tuxedo shirt matched the dark blue lace on the bodice of Izzy's gown. Kelly's shirt was ordinary white, unruffled, but the heart of the orchid he presented— now on my wrist—was the same lavender of my gown.

By the time we pulled away from the Fosters' house, both Eli and Kelly were on the way to drunk. Eli drove. We'd imbibed—beer for the boys and me, chilled white wine for Isabel—for perhaps an hour. But I wasn't worried. It was a short distance, less than three miles to the high school gym where the dance was being held, and I paid little attention. I was feeling good.

It was Kelly who became aware of the spinning glow behind us, who turned and saw the blue light bearing down. "Let up," he said to Eli. "We've got a situation." As fate would have it, we were approaching the intersection at Congress Street. At first, it seemed like Eli was about to speed up, but Kelly leaned forward and put his hand on my

203

cousin's shoulder. Eli turned onto our street and pulled into my drive, not his.

He rolled down the driver's window and offered his hand to the officer to shake. "Yes sir, I'm Ellison Winfield, how are you this evening?" Eli said as the man reached the car.

"I'm fine," the policeman said, "but you're not. You've been swerving."

"Really?" Eli exclaimed. He threw his head back, as though he were stunned.

"Really," the officer answered, deadpan. "License. Registration. Insurance card." Eli twisted theatrically and pulled his wallet from his pocket. He handed over his license.

"And the others?" the policeman asked. I heard his heavy boots shuffle on the pavement. Eli's brow compressed ever so slightly. He reached toward the glove compartment. I sensed his reluctance.

"Want me to find them?" Isabel asked.

"No, no, too much junk in there," he said. "I'll get them." Eli fumbled around without looking or opening the compartment all the way. Eventually, he pulled out a plastic folder containing the car registration and insurance information. He expelled air, a muffled huff. I recognized the sound of relief. Perhaps the others, if they noticed at all, assumed it was his fear of being caught behind the wheel after drinking. For her part, Isabel sat nonchalantly staring out the passenger window, as if pretending she was somewhere else. Kelly fidgeted in the backseat. The policeman, seemingly oblivious, never asked to search the car.

But I knew my cousin. Alcohol alone wouldn't affect his manner. After all, Eli was almost legal, and everyone knew cops looked the other way when you were close. I would have expected him to throw open the glove compartment and make a big show of finding the documents, keeping up banter with the officer as though they were friends. He was a master at dissuading authority. And indeed, as far as any objective person could see, he was absolutely composed, considering he'd been caught driving with several beers under his belt. Only I knew something was off.

The policeman inspected Eli's credentials and asked him to step outside the car. "Where were you headed?" he asked.

"The junior-senior dance, sir, at the high school. I apologize for getting a bit carried away on this festive evening."

"No need to apologize to me, but you're not driving anywhere right now." A little gasp escaped Izzy then, and she looked toward Eli who leaned into the car and whispered something to her.

"You got somewhere you can go to sober up?" the officer asked.

"Of course, officer." Eli stopped and squinted at the policeman's nametag. "There's nothing to worry about, Mr. Mahaffey. We will all exit this vehicle right now." I looked out to see Daddy walking down the driveway. The policeman sauntered over to him.

"You know these young people?" he asked my father.

"Yes, I do," Daddy said. "That's my nephew driving. And my daughter in the back."

"Then, I can leave them in your care?"

"Certainly," Daddy answered.

When we shuffled inside, the crepe of my gown swishing about my ankles, Mama was still standing at the window where she'd watched the spectacle. She frowned and looked hard at us as she poured water into the coffeepot. She told Eli he should be ashamed of himself, and when she realized Kelly's speech was thick with drink, she admonished him as well. She said little to Isabel and me, but then we weren't so tipsy as the boys.

Daddy sat stoic in the den with us. At one point, he removed his pocketknife from his pants and began opening and closing it in nervous concentration.

Mama made Eli drink nearly a pot of coffee, and then, eventually, my parents allowed us to leave. Perhaps it was the rareness of the occasion that prompted them to let us go. I don't know. Certainly, I was surprised to be released. During the short drive to the dance—half over when we finally arrived—Eli hummed merrily while Kelly stewed, rocking from one hip to the other beside me in the backseat.

A thought struck me on that drive, the irony and the absurdity. How Kelly, the older, experienced college student, should have been at ease. He wasn't even driving. How Eli should have been at least a little discomfited about drinking and driving but wasn't whatsoever. But then, was I surprised? Not at all, for I knew my cousin and his confidence.

At the dance, Eli and Isabel appeared to have a glorious time in spite of the upset. I knew Eli had charmed Izzy and made her forget all about being stopped. I watched them laughing, spinning to the music of the Georgia Prophets, a band I loved and had lobbied for on student council.

But Kelly would not stop fretting. He feared my parents would never let me date him again after this night. I kept assuring him all would be well, but he wouldn't relax. As we danced close to the blended duet of voices in "For the First Time," my arms around his neck, he whispered in my ear, "Are you sure your mom doesn't hate me?"

"Stop," I whispered back. "Can't we just enjoy this song?" Then abruptly, I stopped dancing, for in that moment, I glanced at Eli and Isabel dancing. I was reminded again of the contrast that had struck me on the drive: Eli, younger, barely legal, still at home, and Kelly, free at college. Yet it was Eli who acted unrestricted.

"I thought you wanted to keep dancing," he said.

"Yes," I answered, and began to move my feet again, but my mind was elsewhere, across the room with Eli, watching him hold Isabel by the waist, his head bent to her shoulder. My handsome cousin was completely relaxed, an image I was accustomed to, yet something was different. Not in him but in me. I realized that, impervious to objection, relying on personality, he believed himself absolutely invulnerable. Consequences be damned.

&

Often, I caught a ride with Eli to school, and I made sure to do so the Monday morning after the dance. I told him a lie when I called on Sunday night and said I needed to leave early to work on a biology project with my lab partner.

As soon as we exited Congress Street, I leaned over my books and opened the Camaro's glove compartment. Eli reached over and grabbed my left arm hard. In doing so, his foot pushed the gas and the car lurched wildly forward. "What the hell are you doing?" he asked. The car swerved. He twisted the steering wheel hard back left with one hand.

"What's in here that you don't want me to see?"

"Nothing. Close the door, Delia. Now," he commanded, but he couldn't stop me because the car overcorrected and swung back to the right, bumping onto the shoulder. Eli couldn't squeeze my arm and control the car at the same time. He had to use both hands to pull the car back onto the road.

With both hands free, I quickly shuffled through the contents. I removed the only unusual thing I saw: a sheet of paper consisting of little perforated squares, a yellow peace symbol centering each one. Two squares were missing from one edge. "What is this?" I held the paper up in clear view.

"Jesus, Delia," he yelled. He pulled off the road into the abandoned parking lot at Monty's Tire Service. "Put it back."

"You don't want anyone to see this?" I taunted him, waving the paper around. "What is it?"

He threw the car into park, left it running. His knees jumped up and down in place. His hands opened and closed on the steering wheel. For a moment, I wondered why Eli didn't simply grab the paper from me. Then I realized he didn't want it to tear. I lowered the sheet of paper and set it back in the glove compartment. I closed the door. I placed my hands across my books. "So tell me," I said. I didn't look at him. I looked out the windshield at a dump pile of old tires. I stared at the ugly, useless waste.

"Okay," he said. "It's a blotter sheet."

"That doesn't mean anything to me," I said. I continued to stare at the grotesque mountain of rubber.

"It's a way to ingest acid."

"Acid. You mean LSD? What would you be doing with LSD?" I turned to him.

"I'd be taking a trip," he said.

"Eli, no," I exclaimed.

"Don't get all worked up. It's not addictive. It's an experience."

"No, no, no!" I shrieked.

"Sshh, calm down. If you'll let me tell you about it, you won't be so upset."

I made no attempt to stifle my alarm, for by then I'd realized a whole sheet of squares meant a whole lot of trips, and it was unlikely Eli was taking all those trips himself. That meant it likely he was also dealing LSD.

"You don't give a damn about yourself or me," I cried. "Where does it stop?" Eli cut off the car. His knees continued to jerk nervously up and down. "Because I would be in trouble, too, if a policeman came right now. We all would have been the other night. No wonder you didn't want Izzy to look in the glove compartment," I hissed.

I opened my door as though to exit, but what did I think I was going to do? Walk two miles to school and haul twenty pounds of books?

"I'm sorry," he said.

"Sorry about what? Sorry you're dropping acid? Sorry you're selling it? Sorry you're oblivious to the danger?"

"I'm sorry I put you and the others at risk," he said. "I know I've got to be careful."

I shook my head wildly. "Careful means getting rid of this paper, and I don't mean by selling it."

"Okay, I make you a promise. I'll never ask you or let you ride in the car again with something like this."

"Well, that solves everything," I said. The sun shone into the car, and I watched fine globules of spit spray when I spoke, magnified in the light. I wiped my hand across my mouth.

"Delia, please," he said and reached his hand across the seat, tentative. "Close the door so we can talk."

I pulled the door toward me but didn't close it all the way.

"You're right to be scared about getting caught," he said. "But not about the drug. You don't know anything about it. That's why you're scared of it."

"What I know is what I hear. People have bad trips. They have flashbacks that won't go away."

"It's all about the set and the setting," he said. "The drug is only a catalyst. You have to be in the right frame of mind. It wouldn't work for you. I wouldn't want you to try it. You're too uptight. Weed, on the other hand, weed you need. It would make you feel loose."

"You're crazy," I said. "How many times, Eli? How many trips? Don't you know I would probably die if anything happened to you?"

"A few. It's not something I do repeatedly. Hear me out," he said.

"Who are you with when you drop acid?"

"I'm alone. It's a solitary thing."

"How? Why?" I asked the boy I thought I knew, who now possessed an underground life, not known to me. My head spun.

"It's something to expand my mind."

I looked at him in disbelief.

"Listen. I'll describe it. Hear me out," he said again. "First is a sense of euphoria and then images appear. On my best trip I could see bells. Little by little I began to enjoy the color of golden bells, so many of them gleaming high in a tower by a lake. The sizes and shapes changed and shifted constantly. A kaleidoscope of bells. They circled each other. They spiraled around and around. So glorious." His voice continued to rise through the telling. "I could taste the gold. I could see the sound as the surfaces rippled and the bells melted in a puddle of molten metal. Music louder, richer than I've ever heard. The sound of heaven come down to earth."

I sat mute. Vaguely, I tried to perceive senses mixing, tasting gold, seeing sounds. It seemed absurd. And yet, was Eli's perception so surprising? I looked at my cousin, his face animated and flushed. Hadn't we always dabbled in the mystical from the time we were small children? It was a way, where Eli was concerned, to cope with the fears of the known world. I thought of the Ouija board on the shelf in my closet, unused now for years.

"Hey," Eli said. "Are you there?"

"I'm here."

"I think you've missed your meeting with your lab partner."

I looked at my watch, pretending for a moment. Then, I looked at Eli. "I didn't have a meeting with my lab partner," I said. "I told you that to buy time."

"What do you know? My cousin is a deceiver," he declared.

"I learned from a pro."

"Touché," he said, a yowl rumbling from his throat. He started the car. I sat silent beside him on the drive to school.

25

MAY 1974

I could think it was a bad dream, finding out Eli dropped acid, because life proceeded on its expected course, graduation approaching.

Mama and Mary Lily were abuzz, planning a grand dinner at Eli's house to celebrate after our 5:00 pm graduation in the high school gym. Eli left early in the afternoon to rehearse his part on the glockenspiel and other percussion instruments with the Green Branch High School Marching Band, which would perform the music for our ceremony. Eli had studied not at all through high school but still donned a white sash over his gown, showing he was an honor student. Had he been of a mind to, he could have been valedictorian.

Mama dropped me off at 3:30 to get in line. I wore a gold stole, having worked hard enough to make it into the top ten of our graduating class. I felt both elated and sad that day. I looked forward to leaving home, to living without my parents' constant oversight, but I hated to leave Eli. And there were my girlfriends. I would miss even Helen.

I was headed to an all-girls school—Tulloh College—upstate, at my parents' urging. I could go to a coed and larger school, they said, after I got my feet wet. For a while, I protested at my lack of choice, but in the end I didn't fight it. I was happy enough at the prospect of being on my own, of sitting in a real college classroom, of meeting new people, even at a school outdated with its curfews and ban on boys visiting in the dorms.

Eli was bound for the University of South Carolina in Columbia. He wanted to stay close to Isabel, also going to the university but as a day student because her parents—like mine—were reluctant to let her completely loose (a phrase my parents liked to use) the first year into the world of open dorms, Greek life, and wild parties. Little did they know their daughter's boyfriend likely surpassed any riotous influence lurking at USC.

Isabel was what boys refer to as a nice girl, as I suppose was the epithet designated to me. We weren't averse to a certain degree of risk; we liked excitement, but we were amply guarded—the parental influence a damper on both of us. Eli's reaction in the car on the night of junior-senior was enough to tell me he hid the wildest side of himself from Isabel, if not completely, then nearly so.

Our event went as all graduations go. Applause, gushing joy, syrupy tears. The truly amazing part of the evening came during the musical interlude between the valedictorian's speech and diplomas, when the band played "Tubular Bells" from *The Exorcist*, a movie I'd been afraid to see. Eli had not told me he would play the solo. Sitting transfixed, watching him, mallets in a blur along the keys, I knew he wanted me to be surprised. But it wasn't surprise I felt so much as transported, traveling back to a world belonging to Eli and me in his attic so long ago. A dark, cloudy day lit by candle, my cousin and me in shadow, the Ouija board moving unbidden beneath our fingers, foretelling the future of our young lives. Briefly, I thought of Francie's horror just months after her own graduation. But I shivered with the thrill of the music, of the diploma awaiting me, of the future now present.

❧

Our mothers outdid themselves preparing Chateaubriand, potatoes au gratin, asparagus salad, and strawberry-topped cheesecake. The lavish dinner included my family and Eli's as well as Mimi, Pot, Caro, and Isabel and her family. Kelly and his parents did not attend, for I had broken off my relationship with him three weeks earlier.

I missed Kelly, and I was sad without him. But I was not in love with him, and I did not think it fair to either of us to continue. For all these months, I had tried because he loved me, and was as kind and attentive a partner as I am ever likely to encounter. But he saw the future planned in front of us, a relationship I could not commit to. I cried for a long time the night I told him, sobs muffled into my pillow, because I hurt someone I cared about, who had been good to me.

Isabel was especially beautiful that night at dinner, and her presence reminded me of my aloneness. She wore a romantic floral prairie dress. A Jessica McClintock design. The pale blue hues illuminated her skin. A glittering heart pendant—tiny sapphires perhaps—hung on a silver chain just below the hollow of her throat. She had straightened her naturally wavy hair. It hung flat and long down her back, parted in the middle, as I wore mine. Eli never stopped looking at her. I could hardly stop looking at her myself. She glowed.

After dinner, when the Shepherds had left to drive back to Columbia, when Mimi, Pot, and Caro had retreated to the country, when my parents and Helen had assisted with the dishes, when Mary Lily had finally collapsed into her mohair chair in the living room and Uncle Gene had poured one more glass of brandy, Eli and I retreated to the porch.

"We've arrived," he said, settling into the swing, pulling me beside him.

"Have we now?" I responded.

"The world is our oyster," he said.

"I like that," I said.

Eli put his arm around me and pumped his feet on the floorboards. We began to swing. I leaned my head back. The wine from dinner swirled—mellow—through my head.

"The night's not over," Eli said into my ear, his breath hot and insistent.

"No, Eli, I'm done," I said.

"On the contrary," he said.

"What?" I asked.

"In a minute. But first I need to tell you. Never see *The Exorcist*. Will you promise me that?"

Images from the previews and posters I'd seen that spring emerged in my mind: a picture of Regan—a normal little girl's body in a sweet, lace-necked nightgown, with her face destroyed. The haunting, open-mouthed grimace. The blood between her teeth. The staring glass marble eyes beneath the mop of witch's hair. A face as frightening as anything I had ever seen. But why not tough it out for the sake of the music, incredible and irresistible. Music I'd heard Eli play tonight. "It's only a movie," I said.

"It's not only a movie. She's a victim for the spirit to enter so he can get back at some priests. He uses her. She's an innocent kid. She's done nothing wrong. It's pure evil."

"How do you know all this?" I asked.

"Because I've seen it."

"Why didn't you tell me?"

"I went when it opened in Columbia, but not with Izzy. I was glad I didn't take her. I went with a couple of guys because I wanted to hear the music. That's all. It's too scary, Dee. I don't want you to see it. The demon deceives her and gets to her with the Ouija board."

"The Ouija board? Like our Ouija board?"

"Yeah," he said. "Maybe we were lucky to connect with good spirits."

"But it's a make-believe horror movie," I said. "Of course, there would be a bad spirit."

"No, in a regular horror movie, you know it isn't real. It's not that way."

"Doesn't she get possessed? That doesn't seem too real," I said.

"Maybe so, maybe not. The scary thing is the questions that get raised. And how Regan's possession affects you. It's the almighty fear of losing control. Promise me, Dee. You won't see it." I felt his body go stiff next to me; his fingers gripped tight on my shoulder.

It seemed silly, this vehemence, the panicky tone. But it was Eli, and no matter what strange ideas affected him, I agreed. He liked being my protector, and in truth, I liked it, too.

"Ok. I promise. I won't see the movie."

"Not ever? Not in reruns years from now?"

"Not ever," I proclaimed.

"Good, all settled. Now, we can enjoy ourselves," he said. He raised his eyebrows as high as he could, his mood shifting quickly.

Together we pumped the swing. I flung my arms akimbo. "You!" I exclaimed.

"Us!" he said and caught my left arm midair. "Ready for an adventure?"

"Eli, we aren't kids anymore. We've graduated. No adventure."

"Last chance," he said. He bumped my shoulder, cajoling.

"You win," I conceded after the third bump.

We drove to the Pit Stop, into the smell you tasted on your tongue of grilled burgers and greasy onions. The barstools and red vinyl chairs flanking tables at the back were filled with kids in graduation revelry. I had assumed everyone was spending the evening at home, my parents insisting graduation night was reserved for family. What had been my gullibility abruptly turned into unexpected glee. "See what we might have missed," I said. I giggled wholeheartedly at my sudden feeling of freedom.

Noting my mood, Eli nodded approvingly. I gravitated toward a table of girls, the popular Katie Crenshaw and my friend Sarah Wood among them. Like me, they'd had their own graduation dinners at home and so were drinking Cokes and beers to hold the table. I ordered a beer.

I looked around for Eli. He stood beside his hippie friends Philip Gates and Ladd Brewer, hanging out at the bar next to the ubiquitous giant jar of pickled eggs swimming in vinegar. A half-eaten egg—greenish and grotesque—rested on a plate in front of them, Budweisers on either side. Eli would not be eighteen for a couple more weeks, but these pals had come of age. Philip was joined at the hip with Ladd, who gave him rides everywhere since Philip had never bothered to acquire a driver's license. I marveled at the identical lank dishwater hair flowing down their backs.

I motioned to Eli and he joined us. Philip and Ladd followed. "Squeeze in," Eli told them, dragging chairs over. "There's room for everyone." His fingers thumped the linoleum surface, piano playing.

"Whatcha playing?" someone asked.

"Lucy in the Sky with Diamonds." He grinned.

A couple of beers later (beers I ordered for him on my ID), my cousin announced, "Let's blow this place. Night to remember."

"Where to?" Philip asked.

"Anywhere we want to go. Take my wheels. Who wants to go?"

"Your car fits five people," I said.

"Au contraire, many more," he countered.

I sighed, conceding.

"OK," he said, "then we'll squeeze in until we get to the house and take Mama's wagon." Mary Lily had an almost new Oldsmobile Custom Cruiser, a burgundy beauty with matching leather seats and woodgrain sides.

"I don't know, Eli, what if...," I began. My cautionary tone was

214

foolish, for it made him more adamant.

"What if? I'll take care of it. Mama doesn't care." He scowled at me. And that was that. The three boys, Sarah, Katie, wild child Gilda Rhodes (Katie's best friend), and I headed out to the parking lot.

Philip and Ladd squashed themselves into the passenger bucket seat, Philip's legs dangling over Ladd's lap. The three girls packed into the backseat. Fated because I was shortest, I lay horizontal across their laps. My head fell into the gap between Sarah's legs. My behind settled on Katie's thighs. Gilda held my ankles. It was most unpleasant.

As soon as Eli pulled into his drive and threw the car in park, he bounded toward the house. The rest of us peeled out and shook ourselves like dogs. We waited beside the Camaro.

My cousin returned holding the station wagon keys aloft. "Let's go," he shouted.

"Where?" I shouted back, though shouting was not necessary.

"Wherever we want to go."

I sat in front with Eli; the girls took the backseat; the hippies sat on the floor in the way back. We journeyed out to who knew where. The guys asked Eli to lower the tailgate window. Katie tapped me on the shoulder, and I turned around. The boys had opened the bottom of the tailgate and were kneeling on its hard metal surface, reaching up to the luggage rack for support.

"Oh for God's sake," I gasped.

Eli craned his neck to see what was going on. What he saw was his friends' torsos—faces out of view, legs folded beneath their knees. "You guys have it figured out," he called. He hooted with laughter.

"Yee, ho," one of them answered.

Eli drove the station wagon to the graveyard and parked. It was a cloudless night with the barest sliver of a moon. Not enough for the Carolina crescent on our flag, but stunning in its perfect arc. Stars shimmered, a dotted sparkling blanket across the sky. The night was warm, but I felt a cool shiver when I stepped out of the car.

"Why are we here?" I asked.

"The grave's a fine and private place," he said. He knew I would catch the Marvell allusion. We'd studied that poem in class.

"Seriously," I said.

"Old times' sake, right, guys?" He turned to Ladd and Philip. The

215

boys nodded in agreement. "And it definitely appears private this evening."

We hiked a short distance to twin cement benches near the edge of the duck pond.

"Let's relax," Eli said. He pulled a joint from his pocket and sat.

Ladd provided a light and the joint passed among us. "Whoo," Gilda said. "What a hit. Good shit." I took a toke when it passed to me. I felt nothing.

I walked to the edge of the pond. The water was as still and quiet as the graves. Where did the ducks go at night? Maybe a cove somewhere we couldn't see, maybe under trees. A cool breeze caught the air, ruffled the pond's grass edge. I hugged my arms across myself. I turned. An audience of gray headstones gazed at me. A jagged group of sentinels, blocking any stir of air across the dead. The graves sat more still than still while I shivered.

"Come on back over here," Eli called. "What are you doing over there? Looking for sleeping ducks?"

"Nothing," I answered. I wandered back to the benches. He lit a second joint and it passed again. I took another hit. Still nothing. "I don't feel a damn thing," I exclaimed. "What's wrong with me?" Katie cackled at my remark.

"Oh, now, little Dee, got to let yourself go. Pull it in, hold it, exhale," Eli instructed. "You know how." He kept his eyes on me. With the third toke, I became both relaxed and aware. Briefly, time shifted out of order, and for a moment I returned to that beautiful, sad night, "Stairway to Heaven" playing in my ears, my cousin's arms grasped tightly around my naked back.

Then, stories of high school lore began to pass back and forth and mercifully, the past refocused. The time Ladd got in trouble for mooning the librarian when she sent him back to study hall. The paddling he got. The time Katie's too-loose cheerleader sweater rose up and her boob fell out during a high jump on the football field. Laughter rose louder at each new episode.

"We're out of dope," Eli said in the middle of Katie's story about a former boyfriend Bradley—drunk—mistaking the streetlight in front of her house for the moon in an attempt at romance.

"That won't do," Philip said.

216

"Bradley?" Katie asked.

"Hell, no, lack of dope," he said. "No insult intended. Of course, Bradley did not deserve you."

"Agreed on both," Sarah said. She swooned forward on the bench. Katie caught her by the hair and pulled her upright before the tipping point. It was the first I knew my Girl Scout friend smoked pot. Or maybe it was her first time. Who knew?

"Hey, where's Joseph tonight?" Ladd asked. "He'll have plenty of dope." Joseph Ramsey was another hippie. He tended to be a loner.

"He's probably holed up at home. Let's go get him," Eli declared.

We piled back into the car. Again, the boys rode with the tailgate open, hands clenching the luggage rack to hold on.

"Hang on, y'all," Eli called. "I'll rev it up." He began to accelerate.

"Let her rip," one of them called.

I looked back to see their faces, two round moons, skin reflecting yellow, as headlights passed. "Maybe you ought to slow down," I suggested.

"Turn back around. Let them be," Eli commanded me. "Let go, sweetheart." From the backseat, the other girls didn't discourage him, but they didn't encourage him either. I looked at the speedometer: 55 miles an hour.

All of a sudden a hand slid down from the top of the windshield. It slapped the glass. Then it waved. I screamed. Female voices from the back screamed, too.

"What the fuck?" Eli yelled and then realized the prank. He turned on the windshield wipers. The hand disappeared. He laughed out loud and pulled to the shoulder of the road. He tapped the brake, purposefully, a little too hard.

It turned out Philip had somehow pulled himself up onto the luggage rack and crawled toward the windshield, reaching the slope.

"He's...too...much, crazy," Ladd said, laughing so hard he could barely speak. Philip slid off the roof and back to the tailgate. I sat dazed. The other girls seemed dazed too, for they didn't so much as murmur.

"All right, we get it," Eli said to Philip, "cool, outrageous, but stay in the fucking car, how about it? I don't need trouble with a dude on top of Mama's car." He pulled back on the road and continued toward Joseph's house.

We reached our destination and Eli shot out toward Joseph's front door. He left the car running. Before I knew what was happening, Philip sprang into the driver's seat. None of us had time to react before he put the car—perched at the top of an uphill drive—in reverse. It began to roll. It took me a moment to remember that Philip didn't have a license, and wonder what the hell he was doing. I had no idea whether he could drive. The car bumped hard off the pavement, two wheels in the yard, and I had my answer. The car continued to roll. I couldn't look to see how far we were from pine trees lining either side of the bottom of the drive.

"Do something," Sarah shrieked. Philip's hands twisted, turning the wheel. Instinctively, I reached toward the gearshift, but before I could throw the car into park, Eli's face appeared at the driver's window—running alongside—causing Philip to slam the brake. How had Eli arrived? Superhuman will and speed?

His palms pounded on the window. "Open the window, you stupid fuck," he yelled. "No, open the damned door. Now." Philip stared at the window, his foot remaining on the brake. Calmly—I thought under the circumstances—I eased the car into park.

I don't know whether Philip or Eli opened the door, but in an instant the two of them were outside the car, face to face. Without warning, still gasping for air from running, Eli punched Philip, whose hands flew to cover his face.

"You stupid fuck," Eli said again, his hand falling to his side, his fist still clenched. "You could have wrecked this car. You could have hurt people. You could have killed Delia." Tears sprang in my eyes at the mention of my name.

I'd never seen Eli throw a punch. Likely he would have tried if not for the recess bell—frail though he was—on the playground that day in second grade against Willard Timms. But that was the only time I knew he had come close. And Willard was a bully. Philip was his friend. It was then I noticed Joseph Ramsey standing dumbfounded near Eli in the drive.

"Party's over," Eli said. "Sorry, Joseph. Sorry, buddy. Next time." Joseph gave him a little salute, and Eli took his place in the driver's seat. Philip retreated to the rear. Wordless, we returned to the Pit Stop in Mary Lily's car, it and us all in one piece.

On the way back to Congress Street, just Eli and me, he drove slowly, solemnly. At the last red light before home, he turned to me. "I'm sorry," he said. "That scared the shit out of me. God knows. You could have been hurt. I had no idea Philip would be such a stupid fuck."

"It's okay, Eli," I said. "You saved the day. How did you run that fast? You were at Joseph's front door." He reached over the console and gave me a hug.

"I saw the car moving. God, if I know. I got lucky."

26

SEPTEMBER 1976

Eli hung on by a thread at USC, his grades abysmal. Though he'd been able to get by fine in high school without studying, now he not only didn't study, he frequently cut classes. His priorities lay with fraternity life, Izzy, and who knew what else. Aunt Mary Lily was a mess over his grades, and Uncle Gene complained about the money being spent for nothing. She didn't have to say it in so many words, but I knew Isabel wasn't particularly pleased either. She wanted a boyfriend who showed signs of making something of himself.

Somehow, though, and at no surprise to me, Eli continued to charm them all. He told his parents not to worry about probationary status on his account. That he'd pull it out in the end. He'd gone into great detail at the end of sophomore year describing how he'd declared himself a business major and had classes all lined up for the fall. I'm not sure how he placated Isabel, but she stuck with him, attending fraternity functions, going to football games and the like.

Eli hadn't confirmed it—it was too strange for us for him to say so outright—but I knew he and Isabel slept together. For a long time, he used to protest—albeit playfully—about "good" girls and how he'd gone and fallen for one. And in so doing never missed the opportunity to say—his expression always blank, never letting on whether he was serious or not—how I should stay a "good" girl.

I was aware Isabel sneaked off with tales to her parents of studying and staying over with girlfriends when she slept overnight with Eli. She wanted her own college dorm life, but her parents remained reluctant to let their only daughter live on campus at USC. However, they became amenable to her attending a private school in an environment more controlled than the university. She decided to transfer to Tulloh and continue her major in art education.

Meanwhile, I thought to transfer to the university after sophomore year. I announced to my beloved gray-haired advisor Dr.

Charles that I intended to transfer to USC and major in journalism (for there was no such major at Tulloh). He responded by waving an aged hand dismissively, the knuckles bluish and gnarled.

We sat in his light-filled corner office, my chair facing him across his wide oak desk. A blue and yellow striped bow tie clutched the collar of his neatly starched shirt, pulling wrinkles into pleats at his throat. It was the last week of classes, and I believed my decision made. Dr. Charles picked up my can of Tab from the desk, drank a swallow, set it back down in front of me, smiled. That kind of familiarity was his trademark.

"You want to major in journalism? You think you want to be a reporter? Or maybe a news anchor? Much wiser to stay here in the liberal arts. Major in English," he said. "You excelled in my Southern Lit class. You'll gain more in literature classes than any journalism major, I assure you. Stay. Next spring, I'll set up an internship at any newspaper or television station you want. You'll get all the experience you need."

"Really, Dr. C?" I asked.

"Of course, little buddy," he said, the endearment an assurance he often used with his students. He took another swig of my Tab. "You'll get a full semester's academic credit."

I walked the scant five minutes under the oak trees along the bricked path back to my dorm. I sat on my bed. I recalled the trip Mama and I had made several weeks before during spring break to USC. Determined, I'd called admissions and been assigned an appointment with a professor in the School of Journalism to talk about the curriculum and transfer of credits. It took me ten minutes to find a parking place remotely close to the building. We walked another ten minutes to my destination. We wandered yet another ten minutes looking for the right office.

After my appointment, I walked into the hallway where Mama waited on a bench. She looked up expectantly. "They have four different majors in the journalism department," I said. "It's huge. The professor didn't remember my name."

She nodded. "It's your choice, Adeline," she said.

Tulloh was a suitcase college. And if you had nowhere else to go and stayed on campus, even the coffee seemed stale on Saturday

221

mornings. To get a date, it had to be blind with somebody's brother, or you had to know someone to set you up with a boy from Henries, the private, all-male college across town. I thought of Dr. Charles who not only knew my name but cared about my future. I decided to stay at Tulloh.

෴

Monday, September 6
Dear Delia,

What in the hell am I doing still down here, helping move pledges into the fraternity quadrangle in Columbia, when the two girls I love are upstate? I could be up there helping you and Izzy move into your dorm. There's something wrong with this picture.
Love,
Eli

Thursday, September 9
Dear Eli,

Isn't it a little late to be thinking about transferring? Our classes started Monday. What about yours? Shouldn't you be thinking about starting the semester and pulling up your grades instead of helping Isabel and me move in?

We are fine. I'm sure Isabel told you that she's on the bottom floor of Brindley Hall and I'm on third. I can't believe I'm over here in this place with no air-conditioning. Tricia—ever the campus-involved roommate that she is—talked me into it because she ran for dorm president and won. Unopposed, I might add! Did I tell you this already? At least we get the big end room with lots of windows looking onto front campus and a private bath. If we don't melt before the temperatures drop, we'll be just dandy.

Has Isabel told you about her roommate? A wild child named Mignon Parks whose former roommate transferred to University of Georgia. Mignon stays out nights with her crowd of hoity toity friends casing bars for Henries guys, forever missing curfew and climbing in through the fire escape, but she's okay. She's an art ed major like Isabel, so they should get along fine. Mignon generally

222

hangs out on back campus in the studio when she's not out cruising or getting up a bridge game in the hall. Isabel could do worse.

  Your cuz,
  Delia

Tuesday, September 14
Dear Delia,

  I'm moving up to Hagood with y'all to go to school at Henries next semester. I can see you now, flipping out with joy. And why not? Me at an all-boys' school, I can introduce you to lots of guys.

  Okay, I know what you're really thinking. Why would they accept a student on probation? Hey, all I can say is they know a good thing when they see it. Seriously, they've accepted me, probationary status and all. All I have to do is get my GPA up to 2.0 by the end of this semester. No sweat. I guess they need the money. At any rate, I'll be there next semester.

  Soon,
  Eli

Friday, September 17
Dear Eli,

  Are you kidding? You're really coming up here? I went running to Isabel's room when I got your letter, but she was in class. Of course, though, I knew she knew. Ha! I caught up with her that night in the dining hall. She seems very pleased. I love the idea of us going to school in the same town.

  And sure, you can set me up with some guys at Henries once you're in the know. But not like the last blind date I had from there. Dear Lord, he was nice as could be but acted dumber than dirt (sorry, but it's true). Also, he looked like a caveman, black brillo hair complete with matching woolly beard. I thanked Gorilla Man—real name Ricky Troop—for a pleasant evening and said goodbye at the dorm door. No kiss, not with that beard.

  I thought that was it, but a few days later he called to go out again. I put him off. He called again. It was really awkward. The third time he called, he wanted to know if we could study together. He needed help with a history paper. I caved in (sorry, bad pun).

Somehow, after I helped him organize a bunch of notes on railroad expansion in South Carolina for a paper, I managed to tell him I wasn't in the market for dating at present.

Isabel and I eat breakfast together sometimes. She drinks her coffee black, and now I'm working toward that goal! So I can also skip those cream and sugar calories, too.

I guess you've got to make some A's this semester to pull up your GPA. Let me know how you like it going to class regularly.
Your cousin in waiting,
Delia

Monday, October 4
Dear Delia,

No way, can't believe you dated Troop because I met this guy at Izzy's country club. From a little community right outside Columbia, right? Family is loaded with banking money. What a small world. He's really okay, even if he's not the sharpest tack in the box. I'm sure you handled yourself just fine. And don't worry about Troop. With all his family money, he'll find a girl who is perfectly delighted with an ordinary mind and a grizzly beard. You, my darling, are such a highbrow. But a really cute highbrow.

Listen, I called Izzy on her hall pay phone last night, and the girl who answered said she wasn't on the hall. Library closes at 10, doesn't it, and it was after 11:00. You don't know where she might have been, do you? I'll try again tonight. She's coming down this weekend. Why don't you come, too? If her fine Audi is on the blink again (she told me something is clanking under the hood), y'all can always come in the Green Pea. Your Plymouth Duster never fails. You know I named it that not just because of your name; it's one awful shade of electric green. But by God your daddy was right when he bought it new for you off the lot and said its slant-6 engine would never fail.

I can get you a date, or you can just hang out with us if you want and go to the football game. We're playing Virginia. Should be a winner.

Izzy's parents don't know she's coming home this weekend, so mum's the word. She's going to stay with me. Our dorms have

*the living space between the bedrooms. You can sleep on the foldout
there. It's not bad. I might even wash the sheets.*

*You'll be proud to know I went to all my classes last week.
Bout wore me out.*

Love you,

Eli

*P.S. I'm glad you like Izzy. In lots of ways, she reminds me
of you.*

Thursday, October 7

Dear Eli,

*This will be quick. I'm overloaded with reading for
tomorrow. Thanks for inviting me to Columbia, but I can't come
this weekend. I have a paper due in Victorian Poetry that is
killing me. I have to turn it in Monday.*

*I told Isabel when I saw her in the cafeteria if her car is
acting up, she can borrow the Green Pea. It's cool beans. She'll get
there, maybe even before this letter gets to you. I didn't ask her
where she was Sunday night. Not my business to pry. Probably
out with Mignon and her crowd somewhere. The two of them
have become fast friends.*

Y'all have fun this weekend. I'll check you on the flip side.

Love,

Delia

Thursday, November 11

Dear Dee,

*Sorry about waking you up with that phone call. I don't
blame you for being mad at me. Yeah, I know I freaked. I still
don't get where Izzy was, and I just thought you'd know. I mean,
a Tuesday night? Where in the hell was she? Will you ask her? I'm
going nuts down here.*

*Just a couple of weeks until Thanksgiving and then
Christmas, and next semester when I'll be in Hagood. Thank
God.*

*Mimi told Mama she isn't feeling herself, so we aren't going
out to Magnolia Manor for Thanksgiving. Makes me sad. How*

did she get old without my knowing? I still see her sitting on the picnic bench keeping us off the bell alarm tower. How can she be 84 years old? Are your cousins coming down from Virginia for the holiday? Will they still come even though your Grandmama Loula is gone? I know you miss her, Dee. We haven't really talked about it, have we? She died so fast this summer, after being sick for so long. I'm sorry. I want you to know. Thinking about not going to Mimi's makes me realize your loss. I'm sorry.

I can't wait to see you in two weeks. Watch out for Izzy for me, will you?

Love you,
Eli

Wednesday, November 17
Dear Eli,

It's not so much that I'm mad about the phone call, but you woke me and half the hall. And people weren't too happy with me. When the phone rings, it rings down the whole hall, you know? It was after midnight. The phone's in the middle of our hall, and I'm at the far end. Meg and Donna's room is right by the phone, and one of them has to get up to answer late at night, unless someone just happens to be walking down the hall to the bathroom. I wish Tricia and I had a private phone in the room, but it's expensive. Not something Mama and Daddy, or Tricia's parents either, have wanted to spring for. So until and unless we get our own phone, don't call late.

And what could I do anyway in the middle of the night? You've got to calm down, Eli. Isabel doesn't even live on my hall. How would I know where she is? And it's not my business to ask her, either. That's between you and her.

I'll see you next week, cousin. All will be well.
Until then,
Delia

Sunday, December 5
Dear Delia,
Great to see Glenn and Nancy and have Thanksgiving

dinner with the Greens. Aunt Jeanette is the best. Asking us over to be with y'all. It meant the world to Mama.

Two more weeks. That's all. The semester will be over. I won't be separated from Izzy any longer, but, damn, now you'll be gone. Off to Charleston to work at the News and Courier. *Your big internship. So why do I not hear about this until Thanksgiving? Can't believe Aunt Jeanette found you a bedroom to sublet. What's the deal again? One of the roommates in this carriage house apartment is out of the country for the semester and you can take her place? Pretty lucky, girl. Aunt Jeanette is amazing. How in the world did she find this place for you?*

I'll miss you next term, but really, I know it's good for you. I can see you now, famous investigative reporter, uncovering the dirty dealings of some rotten mayor, putting him behind bars. Hey, maybe I can come down there a weekend or two? Who doesn't love Charleston? We'll work it out. You'll be hanging out with Gloria, too. Can't believe that girl is a pre-med major at College of Charleston. Never would have guessed it.

My cousin is cool.

Love her,

Eli

27

MARCH–APRIL 1977

Eli enrolled at Henries, and I left for Charleston. I missed my cousin during the semester, but in truth, I was glad for the reprieve from his long-distance telephone calls. We had letters to stay in touch. His fervor for Isabel had changed my nonchalant cousin. He'd become apprehensive, constantly worrying about his girlfriend's whereabouts. And he absurdly believed I could somehow solve his anxiety by spying for him. I hoped with the two of them together in Hagood, matters would resolve themselves.

Isabel and I were friends, but she had never shared her intimate thoughts about Eli with me. Nor did I want her to. She also did not tell me she often joined Mignon's group barhopping in the evenings. But she had to know I knew. And I knew the reason, for what else was there besides scouting for boys? If all one wanted was a beer or a glass of cheap wine, either could be purchased on campus.

&

Sunday, March 27
Dear Eli,

I'm glad Daylight Savings Time is coming. Days that get dark so early were okay when we were kids prowling around the neighborhood, playing Kick the Can, but I don't like them now. Makes me think time is slipping away. I get this crazy and impossible desire to pull back the light.

Thanks for filling me in on all the happenings at Tulloh. I'm sure Isabel's friends are enjoying you immensely, especially when you buy all the girls drinks! But you haven't written at all about your classes. What gives? Tell me how they're going.

I am still having an amazing time in Charleston. Like I wrote before, the first few weeks I was delegated to office work, mostly copyediting, writing cutlines and headlines. I didn't mind it. But then obits. Not my idea of the kind of writing I want to do. I was glad to get rotated onto photography assignments. Took a fabulous picture of a seagull perched on a post at The Battery. They ran it on the front page! Really, frameable art! Who knew? I'm sort of seeing the photographer who trained me. He's nearly 30 and lives on a houseboat. It's just a lark. Nothing serious. But Mama would probably blow a gasket if she knew.

Starting last week, I'm going out on my own assignments. The city editor, Lester Robinson—he's so nice to me—decided I've spent enough time going to meetings and interviews along with reporters, and I am ready to fly. I love it. Can you believe this? I get to interview General Westmoreland this week about his new memoir: A Soldier Reports. I'm nervous. I'm thrilled. I've been reading up on the war, the general's views, especially the Tet Offensive. What it must be like to be the man who commanded the forces in Vietnam... Wish me luck.

Your reporting cousin,
Delia

Thursday, March 31
Dear Delia,

Eli called as soon as he got your letter today about your interview with General Westmoreland. He is so excited for you. He knows all that military stuff. He started talking all about how America won the Tet Offensive, but how the whole thing scared the American public and turned the war. I don't know much about the psychology of Vietnam, but I do know who General Westmoreland is! By the time you get this letter, I guess you might have interviewed him.

I should have written you before now to get the scoop on all you're doing. But it's clear from what Eli tells me, you're loving it. When I go out into the world, it will be to practice teach with little kids and watch them smear paint everywhere. Definitely a different kind of excitement. Ha!

One reason I'm writing—the main reason, to be frank—is to talk about Eli. I hope you don't mind, Delia. I hope you can *help. He's not focused on school at all, and he thinks he's hiding it from me, but I know he's using a lot. We fight about it. He smokes too much dope, and I think he's taking Quaaludes. He denies it, but why else is he sometimes drunk, sleepy high when he's had maybe one or two beers? I found a bag with white pills behind some books on his desk and asked what they were. He said they were aspirin. Aspirin in a baggie? I don't think so. I care about him, Delia. I don't know what I'm going to do, but I do care about him and don't want anything bad to happen. I say all this because he listens to you.*

    Please don't tell Eli I wrote about my concerns. He'd flip. You know how he is. I look forward to seeing you asap.

    Sincerely,

    Isabel

Monday, April 14

Dear Isabel,

    Thank you for your letter. My interview was amazing. General Westmoreland's quite imposing—silver hair and heavy staunch brow. A tiny lady with a gray bun—maid's outfit, with white apron and all—answered the door. I had to pretend I wasn't myself but someone important and experienced to stay calm and ask my questions. Although I could never support the war myself, I got a different idea of the conflict from him. The general believes America could have won the war, but the powers in Washington did not provide the necessary means. I'm the first to say I don't understand the intricacies he tried to explain, but I came away understanding some of his frustration as commander. He had ideas about bringing the war to an end, driving into Laos and Cambodia, but those plans were disapproved. It's all in the book. I plan to read it.

    Thank you for confiding to me about Eli. I don't really know what to say. I've tried to talk to him. He sloughs it off, tells me I'm a worrier. I think he doesn't fully realize how much he uses any substance because he wants to escape things in childhood he can't forget when he's sober. Living through his accident was hard on him. I probably shouldn't be saying this, so don't bring anything like that up to him. He doesn't talk about or want anyone to know—especially you—any grim details from the past. I'm telling you because I know you care. You and I have never shared our concerns until now, and I'm glad we're being open. Over spring break, I'll try again to talk to him, try to get through. One thing I know is he loves you like crazy.

See you soon in the big town of Green Branch.

Hopeful thoughts,

Delia

℘

Spring break, which coincided with Easter, was not the respite any of us expected. On April 7, the Thursday before Good Friday, Mary Margaret Lauderdale died suddenly. In her own words, for some time, she'd not felt herself, yet when she visited Dr. Crawford in March, he found nothing wrong that hadn't existed before. He renewed her prescription for nitroglycerin for the angina she'd experienced for years.

That bright April morning, Mimi and Caro planned to drive upstate to the farming town of Millwood to buy strawberries, the first of the season. She sat at her dressing table preparing for the day; she pulled her long, cream-colored hair into a twist. She applied powder and rouge. We knew, because afterward, Mary Lily noticed the cosmetic containers and leftover hairpins still sitting out. But at some point—perhaps only seconds—after rising from her dressing table, Mimi collapsed.

Caro found her balled into herself like a baby on the hard oak floor between the dressing table and the door, not breathing. Just that quickly, she was gone. Because it was Easter weekend, Mary Lily waited an extra day until Monday for the funeral. Her bachelor brother Hall Lauderdale arrived from Alabama on Saturday. I knew him, but barely, because he came back to Green Branch to visit not more than once a year. He was a quiet, reserved person. A professor of economics at a small liberal arts college where he had been most of his adult life.

At the visitation Saturday afternoon, we beheld Mary Margaret Lauderdale laid out in her mahogany casket, wearing a flowing blue crepe dress, looking peaceful. I hadn't wanted to look—I'd never seen a dead body—but Eli took me by the hand. "Grandmama Loula was cremated," I said. "I didn't have to see."

"It'll be okay," he said. "I'm with you. It's what we're supposed to do." I squeezed my cousin's hand. I thought he was brave. I thanked God life awaited me.

の

Isabel and her parents attended the morning funeral and family lunch at the Winfield house. Mr. and Mrs. Shepherd left at the end of the meal with Eli's promise to drive Isabel to Columbia in the evening since we were on spring break.

The table was cleared, and the three of us sat facing the expanse of empty white linen, feeling at loose ends: Eli, Isabel, and me. For a little while none of us spoke. Then Eli announced unexpectedly, "Let's go out to the country."

"That's too sad," I responded. "It'll make me cry."

"What's wrong with crying?" he asked. Isabel reached over and touched his damp cheek. He took hold of her hand. I thought it an odd thing for Eli to say, for until now I had seen him cry only once. The day lived in us, yet we had not spoken of it since that long-ago afternoon when Dale dropped the wrench and the boys ran. But I knew the horror of that day compelled Eli. In his desperation to prove himself a man. In the challenge of an undue risk.

I realized, though, his crying at that moment was related to another feeling entirely, grief. And though I'd felt it at Grandmama Loula's death, Eli was experiencing sorrow for someone he loved, and loved immeasurably, for the first time.

"We're going to Magnolia Manor," he said.

Isabel peered at her platform sandals.

"You got some extra tennis shoes, Keds, whatever, that Izzy can fit into?" he asked me. I looked down at my own espadrilles with their two-inch wedge heels.

"Are you sure you're ready?" I asked.

"Please," he responded. "Do this for me."

When we arrived back at Eli's from my house, he was waiting on the porch. Or I should say he was pacing the porch. His olive eyes were glassy. And not just because he'd gotten buzzed while we changed shoes. He'd been crying again.

℘

Eli eased the Camaro up the long gravel drive. I felt my own tears swelling, ready to spill, even before the Lauderdale house came into view. It was the sight of the magnolias in all their glossy majesty lining the way. Eli pulled the car close, edging the long flight of front steps, like he always did. Like it was any other trip and Mary Margaret would arrive at the door to greet us. Only instead of ringing the brass bell, he walked behind the bushes and retrieved the key from under an empty flowerpot. Isabel and I stood behind as he twisted the large key—the lock stiff—until it finally turned.

Inside, the house was cool and brown in the late afternoon light. For a few minutes, we wandered aimlessly. No one turned on lights. Occasionally, I swiped at my eyes to clear my vision. Isabel followed Eli down the wide hall toward the dining room. I went my own way into the parlor. The room felt alive and lifeless at the same time. Light danced in the long windows; it played across the gilded mirror above the melodeon, reflecting no one. Crinkles in the needlework rug exposed the past presence of walking feet. The walnut secretary gleamed from polishing with human hands, departed.

I sank onto one of the twin brocade settees. I stared at the whorled grain of the ancient secretary. From here, Mary Margaret pulled out the old ledgers when Eli and I were children. I saw us on the floor kneeling beside her, absorbing the past. Records of genealogy, of first cousins who married, of slaves. How was it possible, the time so shortly gone, she was dead and we were all but grown?

I started from my eerie reverie at a hand on my shoulder. "Just me," Isabel said. I jumped again. I twisted my neck. I looked down at her manicured fingernails spread apart.

"Where's Eli," I asked. "Is he okay?"

"He said for me to come find you because he needed to go to the bathroom and would be along in a little bit. I think he just needs to pull himself together."

Maybe, I thought, but I knew my cousin. The company of Isabel

233

and me surrounding him would help him more than anything.

We sat waiting in the parlor, neither of us talking. Then I said, "She's here but she's not here."

"Mrs. Lauderdale?" she asked.

"She liked being called Mimi," I said.

"The little I knew her, she was a lovely person," Isabel responded. "Mimi."

I nodded. We sat, mostly quiet a few more minutes, waiting on Eli, until Isabel said she was going to look for him.

"That's a good idea. I'll go with you," I agreed, feeling peculiar and lonely.

Once in the the front hall, we heard scrapes and bumping, like things being moved about. We followed the sounds into Mimi's bedroom. Eli's back was to us. He was bent over, his head stuck inside his grandmother's armoire. A few boxes—perhaps from under the bed—had been pulled out into view.

"What are you doing, Eli?" I asked.

"Exploring," he answered, jumpy, and poked his head around toward us, his arms still in the wardrobe.

"For what?" Isabel asked.

"I don't know. Nothing. Just looking at her things to remember my grandmother." He stood. He meant to be surreptitious, and it worked with Isabel. She paid no notice, but I saw him crush paper into a tight wad and jam it in his pocket.

"Let's go outside now and breathe," Eli said, gesturing his arms outward. Isabel walked up beside him, and he put his arm around her.

I followed them through the back door and down the wooden steps. Wild dogwood trees—creamy-white petals at their peak—dotted the backyard, interlaced among the hardwoods budding with lime-green spring. Mimi's beautiful world.

"I'm going up," Eli said, looking toward the rescue tower.

"You're what?" Isabel exclaimed.

"I'm going up," Eli said again.

"Up what? That old metal tower? No, you're not. It might collapse on you." I knew Isabel had visited Mimi any number of times, but it seemed clear she had never climbed the tower.

"I've climbed it a hundred times," Eli assured her.

"Why?" she asked. "Why would you want to go up there?"

"To toll the bell," he said.

"Don't, Eli," I said. I looked directly at my cousin. "You've been smoking. You won't be steady."

"I'm fine," he said.

"Then, I'll come, too. Behind you."

"No, just me."

"Eli, please," I urged him.

"I'm doing this alone," he said. He flipped his head in that way he had, shaking his bangs back from his forehead. His hands pushed into his trouser pockets. He stood resolute.

I knew to protest further was futile. I looked at Isabel. "Let's don't worry," I said.

"This is crazy," she said. Her hand went to her forehead, pinching the skin together. Her face crumpled. Gently, Eli removed her hand. He rubbed his own hand across the creases.

"Do you know of John Donne?" he asked her. She shook her head. "He was a metaphysical poet. He believed when anyone dies, we all die a little. He was right."

"Metaphysical?"

"It means after the physical," he explained. "What exists beyond our senses, which we know exists but can only feel inside."

I knew, the gist of it anyway, what Eli meant. From Donne's poem in a meditation he wrote when he was ill. He heard the death bells tolling and thought they might be for him. When had Eli read Donne? I was bemused, for he'd never mentioned any interest in the gifted poet, and shouldn't he? Knowing I studied poetry?

"No, I don't know the poem," Isabel responded.

"No man is an island, entire of itself," he quoted. Isabel looked at him mystified.

He enfolded her in his arms. "We are all involved in death, sweetheart. It's what Donne means at the end when he says, 'For whom the bell tolls;/ It tolls for thee.' Thee is him and it's all of us."

I wished I were the girl in my cousin's arms.

"Are you trying to say we're all dying?" Isabel asked. "And you want to risk your life to climb that tower to ring the bell to say we're all dying?" She toed my canvas shoes into the ground, digging out tufts of grass.

"Yes, that's part of it, but it's more than mortality." He tried to pull her to him again, but she resisted. Isabel did not understand. But I did. I knew his thoughts.

"You're talking about the counterpoint," I intervened. Eli and Isabel turned toward me. I continued. "That there is some part of the living in the dead. Because Donne says all of us are 'part of the main.'"

Eli's hands extended outward. His eyes widened. "You understand. Of course, sweet Delia, you do. Of course, you would."

"I want to believe Donne," I said.

"Do," he said, and reached out to me, put his arm around me. I felt myself loosen into his touch. Isabel remained close beside Eli too— her stance at once hopeful and confused.

༒

Isabel and I stood on the lawn beside Mimi's henhouse, waiting. I inhaled deeply, watching Eli approach the tower. The air seemed redolent with straw and fowl, but that was impossible, for there had been no chickens for several years. In his dress slacks and white shirt, my cousin climbed. Isabel reached out and gripped my forearm. She looked away nervously toward the south end of the pasture.

I observed Eli intently. I watched him pass through the small opening onto the narrow, spaced slats of the platform around the bell. I watched him right himself at the top, walk the perimeter. I waved, but he did not see me, or if he did, he did not respond.

He began to swing the bell. The rings—hard and powerful— vibrated into the ground around us. Eight tolls, a pause, and four more. Mimi's life, I understood, eighty-four years. The echoing sound moved through me, like the bell had rung out from heaven. I turned toward Isabel.

"He's okay, see?" I said. "You can look." Hesitantly, she eyed the tower. Eli stood beside the bell. Isabel motioned him down in big sweeping waves of her arm. He understood and mimicked the action. Damn him. Ever the performer. I threw my own hand in the air and pointed my index finger down in a strong jerking gesture.

I couldn't hear him, of course, but if I could, I suspected he might

236

be laughing at our agitation.

All of a sudden, he collapsed onto the grated platform surrounding the bell.

"What is he doing?" Isabel shrieked.

"Not sure," I said. Eli had never sat on the slats before, at least not when I was around. It made me nervous. I squinted upward, my eyes watering against the intensity of the sun. I could see him sitting cross-legged and looking at something in his hands. It dawned on me quickly. He was reading whatever was on the paper he had stuffed in his pocket. Reading it while he was alone.

"Jesus, what is he doing sitting down?" Isabel asked again. "Is he trying to torture us?"

No way could I see eye to eye with my cousin from that distance, but it was as though I could. Still as stone, I stared up at him.

Isabel began flailing her arms, and I grabbed her to keep her still. I continued to stare, hoping if Isabel and I did not react, he would come down. I could no longer see the paper and assumed it was back in his pocket. He continued to sit. Minutes passed. His inertia scared me.

Finally, he stood and rotated his arms in a windmill toward us. The bizarre standoff ended. I determined to know what he'd been reading as soon as he reached the ground.

He planted his feet on the slats, withdrew to the opening, passed through, and began to descend. Isabel and I strolled toward the bottom of the ladder, our chatter marking our relief, when I heard a grinding pop and then a clank of metal. It wasn't loud, but it was distinct. I looked up to see my cousin dangling on rungs come loose from their connection to the tower, maybe twenty feet above us. He'd not swung far, but clearly the ladder was no longer anchored below him. Eli had come unmoored.

I opened my mouth involuntarily to scream, but what came out was a dry, hollow gag. Isabel screamed with as much might as I've ever heard in a human being before or since.

"Stop," I croaked at her. "Please stop." But she continued. "You've got to stop. You're making it worse," I said, but she couldn't help it. Her instincts had taken over. I don't think she heard me. I ran from her, spanning the few remaining yards to the ladder.

"Don't touch it," Eli yelled down, his voice trembling, and I knew he, too, feared the loose section would break off. I shielded my eyes with my hand and looked up again into the sun's glare. The white soles of his tennis shoes quivered on the swaying ladder.

"Listen to me, Eli. You've gotta get off the ladder, *now*. I can see from here what you have to do." Before it falls all the way, I thought. My throat clogged tight. I coughed hard and spoke again. "Put your left foot on the cross-support beside you and then your right. Hold on above and inch both feet into the corner at the steel column."

"I'm going to jump," he called.

"It's too far!" I warned, my voice suddenly returned.

Isabel arrived beside me, no longer screaming, but breathing hard in spasms.

"I've got to jump. I can't stay up here," he said, leaning out, making the ladder shudder. Herculean as he was in aspect, he believed he could leap safely to the ground. I knew he'd kill himself.

"No, Eli, don't you dare," Isabel called to him, panting but clear. "Be still."

"He's got to get off the ladder," I told her. She looked at me dumbfounded.

"I've got to jump," Eli called again.

"No, no, no, you'll break your neck." I remember trying to make my voice calm, knowing it was close to hysterical.

Eli put one leg out into the air, as though testing the distance. Isabel and I gasped in unison.

I could tell from the way he held his body—stiffly crouched on the dangling ladder—my cousin was more afraid to move sideways than he was to jump. Finally, though, with our coaxing, he raised his leg. He moved the foot to the narrow cross-support. His right foot followed, and he was off the ladder. He slid his feet toward the column and lodged himself there, hands clutching the x-shaped bars above.

"Throw your keys down," I said.

"We're going for help," Isabel declared. Now that Eli was out of immediate danger, she had miraculously gained self-control. The keys landed in a clump of clover.

"Can you drive a stick shift?" I asked, because I wanted to be the one to stay with Eli.

"Not really."

"What does that mean?"

"Eli has tried to teach me."

"Then, you know something. Stay in first gear if you have to. Drive to a phone. Mimi's is disconnected. Call the fire department."

"Okay," she said, retrieving the keys.

Isabel drove off, and Eli and I waited. We were mostly quiet until he said, "My arms are tired. How much longer?"

His question worried me. "Not much," I assured him. I tried to get his mind off his fatigue by asking, "Do you know what happened?"

"I think the bolts fell out," he said, though I couldn't imagine how the bolts on either side of the loosened section of the ladder could dislodge at the same time.

"Maybe one was already missing," I suggested.

"Don't talk, Dee," he said, his voice very hoarse. "The metal is cutting my feet. I'm tired."

Pretending composure, I sat on the ground. I picked at the grass. Sweat jetted down my face and into my eyes, soaked my back. I wished I could fly up and rescue him.

It seemed forever and then mercifully, the siren trilling up the drive, the truck maneuvering the tight corner between the house and the ancient crepe myrtle. Three firemen directing an extension ladder onto the tower. One went up to help Eli who waved him off. He remained until Eli grabbed on and started down.

One of the firemen found a rusted bolt on the ground and wove yellow caution tape around the tower. Eli explained how he thought the bolt wedged free at his approach down the ladder. He talked matter-of-fact, but I saw—barely—his body shaking.

Eventually Isabel returned with Gene and Mary Lily. And it was over. My uncle, taking quick, anxious drags on his cigarette, joked to the firemen about the rescue from the rescue tower.

Later—as dispassionately as possible—I asked Eli what he'd been examining at the top of the tower for so long. He claimed it was a drawing of Magnolia Manor he'd done as a child, something Mimi had saved. He insisted that finding it unexpectedly like that upset him, so he crammed it in his pocket to look at later. And why was it so important to open it at the top of the tower when he was alone, I questioned. He shrugged nonchalantly, but with fervor commanded,

"Don't mention the picture to Mama. It was something I drew only for Mimi and me, and I want to keep it that way." He never produced the crumpled drawing, though I asked more than once.

28

OCTOBER 1977

Isabel broke up with Eli in September. I knew it was coming since the awful scare at Mimi's tower after her funeral. Though she was attracted to his edginess, Isabel also yearned for a level of stability Eli could not seem to provide.

She planned how and where to tell him. The lobby of our dorm after they'd gone to eat Italian on a Friday night. A public place where she thought he wouldn't explode. But he exploded anyway. He hurdled out of his seat and paced around the parlor furniture, nearly knocking over an alabaster lamp. She tried to soothe him by saying they would remain friends. They could hang out, go to games, parties, whatever he wanted. Even if she *had* meant these concessions (she hadn't), they were of no use in calming Eli because she'd said she couldn't be exclusive any longer.

He pulled her then by the arm outside onto the dark front steps. He said he could not accept that arrangement. He would do whatever she needed him to do. He would calm down, let up on the drugs, whatever she wanted.

She told me it was hard to shake his hand from her arm. He didn't want to let go. But Eli couldn't change her mind, for Isabel had met Lane. Encountered him at an opening mixer—an event I skipped—on the front lawn at Tulloh in early September. A tall, gangly senior, Lane was a biology major at Henries aiming for medical school. His stringy black hair split over his ears, and his face bore the pocked scars of adolescent pimples. He wore dorky black ankle boots that crested over his jeans. But his goals presented stability.

Eli went crazy. He called me late at night, many nights, asking me if Isabel was in. We both lived in the same senior dorm, but just as it had been the year before, we lived on different floors. Eli wanted me to observe her comings and goings up the stairs and down between first floor and second. Why did he want to know? So that he could be more tortured? I wouldn't do it.

Now that it wasn't long distance, Eli called the line in my room many nights, waking Tricia and me. Sometimes I got sympathetic looks from her. Sometimes the opposite. I muttered apologies. Tried to explain that my cousin was going through a hard time. Even if I hadn't explained, she knew anyway. Everyone did. Tulloh was a small place, and Eli had made himself known.

I would drag the blue cord of the wall phone as far as it would go out into the hall and pull the door shut so that Tricia could go back to sleep. The conversations were always the same. Eli begged me to go to Isabel's room, to see if she was in when he called at midnight or later. I refused.

I sat on that hard floor, counseling him, trying to convince him to let go, promising until the wee hours he would be okay. Mostly, I was unsuccessful. He could not or would not accept Isabel had forsaken him, particularly for a person he constantly called "that turkey." It took many nights of Tricia and me listening to the line ring over and over late at night before the calls ceased.

"Why are you worsening this agony?" I asked him one night before I stopped answering his calls.

"I wanted Izzy to be you," he said, his voice breaking. I could not respond for fear of breaking, too.

By late October, I believed things were improving after a beautiful Sunday afternoon when Eli borrowed a friend's red convertible so we could ride open air—wind blowing—for an hour's trip to the mountains. I packed a late-lunch picnic and we hiked to a small waterfall. We marveled at tiny, brilliant yellow leaves falling like pieces of gold into the bowl at the bottom of the falls. We dipped our hands in the freezing water and exclaimed. On the way back, I asked him to stop at a pay phone to call Mary Lily and tell her about our outing, because I knew she was worried. He did and told her he liked living at the lake. Then, he said he loved her.

Eli no longer lived on campus at Henries. I didn't like to think in terms of "kicked out," but that's what it was. His GPA had fallen too low again. He enrolled that semester at the community college to earn some credits so he could return to Henries. He'd moved into an A-frame house at Lake Alastor about ten miles out of town, along with four male roommates, students at Henries. Eli resided in the loft; three guys had bedrooms on the main floor; and his good buddy Kyle Dunes occupied the basement. To me, stuck living in a dorm, it seemed like the coolest place on earth, decorated with Salvation Army furniture.

I especially loved Eli's chair, a shabby, overstuffed thing covered with huge red poppies in the vestibule of his loft, his reading spot. It was a messy corner, but comfortable. Beside the chair was a small table with a cracked Formica top. A stack of books always lay about. And beer cans. Lots of beer cans. It was easy to imagine him there, reading, musing. His brow crinkled when he read, his John Lennon glasses slipping down his nose. He always pushed them with one finger, back up his nose, over and over when he concentrated.

 ❧

The fall dance at Tulloh came late in October, and I invited a boy from a small liberal arts college thirty miles down the interstate to be my date. I'd been set up with Kurt Riehl at the beginning of the school year, and he'd taken me out a few times. I wasn't crazy about Kurt, but I wanted to go to the dance. The Embers—as fine a beach band as any around—were playing. I remember the moment Eli appeared. Kurt and I were dancing to "Far Away Places" when Eli tapped Kurt on the shoulder. Startled, Kurt stepped aside.

Eli picked me up and swirled me around and around. I trembled a little in his grasp. From the surprise of Eli's presence, perhaps, of the physical touch of him, but also from fear that he'd come looking for Isabel. "My favorite girl," he said close to my ear, his breath coming short with the effort of holding me.

"Why are you here?" I asked when he set me down and we retreated from the shaggers on the dance floor toward Kurt, waiting. My date hardly knew what to make of my cousin breaking in and making this grand display. But Eli quickly won him over. Especially when he invited us to come to the lake house after the dance.

"If you're looking for Isabel, she's not here," I announced after he'd successfully played up to Kurt.

"Really? She likes a dance. And the Embers." If he thought he sounded nonchalant, he was wrong. His voice was strident.

"A great-aunt died. In Virginia, I think. She's gone to the funeral." You could see the relief fold into his posture when he learned Isabel was off with family and not with Lane. Since she wasn't at the dance with him, somehow Eli believed he had another chance.

At the lake house that night, Kurt got drunk, very drunk. Eli directed him into one of the bedrooms on the main floor, its occupant away for the weekend. It got late, too late to think about going back into town. When I looked for another empty bed, I found none, all full of roommates and girlfriends. I ended up on the other side of the bed from Kurt.

Eli followed me into the room, somehow still on his feet. "Now, you be careful with Dee," he told Kurt, though Kurt couldn't have been listening. "She's my cousin. Nothing can happen to her."

"Go to bed, Eli," I said. "I don't know who's drunker, you or him. Go on. I can take care of myself." Reluctantly, it seemed, he stumbled out.

Sure enough, after a while, Kurt came to. I'd been dead asleep. He must have thought—finding me in bed with him—it would be okay to see where it would lead, because I woke to feel his hand kneading my thigh.

"Go back to sleep," I said and inched away from him. My put-off did not work. Too much alcohol involved. He rolled toward me, now pushed to the mattress edge. A hand groped at my breasts. I scrambled off the bed, landing, amazingly, on my feet. I didn't bother to announce my departure.

I climbed up to the loft and considered folding into Eli's chair. But I knew I'd never sleep soundly there. Instead, I slipped into bed beside my cousin. I was cold and rolled my body into his warmth, my back against his chest. He never stirred.

In the morning, he woke me making noise at the sink in the room. Brushing his teeth, he said through a mouth of paste and foam—seeing in the mirror I suppose that my eyes had cracked open—that Kurt said to say goodbye.

"He's gone?" I asked, sitting up, rubbing away sleep from the corners of both eyes.

"Yeah. I told him I would take you back into town. When I woke and found you, I knew he acted like a clown."

244

"Eli, that's not your business."

"Ha, if you're in my bed, it becomes my business," he retorted.

I looked at him hard, and he grinned.

"You need a toothbrush?" he asked before rinsing his mouth with one hand full of water and waving his toothbrush behind his back with the other. "Use mine. I'll remember to buy you one for next time you're out here."

❧

Isabel's absence from the dance spurred Eli. He chose to ignore the fact she'd not been present because of her aunt's funeral. The next week he called her. She talked to him, he said, but would not agree to see him. "It's that damn turkey," he proclaimed. "That greasy little turkey Lane has his hooks in Izzy and she can't get away."

"Please, Eli," I tried to reason with him. "If Isabel didn't want to be with him, she wouldn't be. She's free to make her own choices."

"I don't think so," he said. He was totally irrational.

The Friday of that week, the last Friday in October, when he supposed Lane would come on campus to take Isabel out, Eli came to our dorm, but initially I didn't know it. He waited in the dark, in the bushes—hiding like a thief—for Lane to appear. And appear he did. Once Lane walked inside to wait in the parlor for Isabel to meet him, Eli attacked. I didn't see the beginning, but I saw the end.

Eli's foe stood in the corner of the parlor by a desk, facing away from the front door. Before Lane knew what was happening, Eli grabbed the nearest object, a full trashcan, and hurled it at him. The trashcan cracked Lane from behind on the shoulder. Papers scattered across the rug.

"Man, you're some kind of crazy fuck," someone told me Lane yelled, whirling around and shoving Eli in the chest. Eli tumbled backward but he didn't fall. He came forward again and shoved back at Lane, his fists pressing in below Lane's bony shoulders. Lane kicked him in the knee. By then our dorm mother had been alerted. She was ancient and rarely seen, but she came stammering into the room, risen from her basement apartment. She held a walkie talkie and upon seeing the scene, talked furiously into the device.

By then, I had been informed and arrived in time to see our rotund night security officer lumber through the door, belly joggling over his belt. He caught sight of Eli and Lane and scurried forward. He grabbed them both by an arm, until he soon determined Lane was not the one at fault and released him. Eli began to fight for all he was worth. He lurched low, trying to get out of the guard's grasp, and kicked at Lane. Biting my lip, trying not to scream, I watched my cousin struggle. And when the guard pulled out his baton and whacked it across Eli's stomach, I screamed. As it had been on the afternoon with the boys in the joe-pye weed, he couldn't triumph over forces stronger than himself. Eli doubled over.

Lane shook himself off. I saw him sneer when Eli was escorted out of the building. I bolted back up the stairs to my room, successfully somehow, avoiding exchange with any of the dozen or so witnesses dispersing behind me, faces in dumb amazement.

The next day the assistant dean of students called me into her office to inform me Eli had been forbidden to come on campus. The whole episode struck me as a farce: nice boy from small town attacks ex-girlfriend's innocent beau on college campus. I hoped Eli and I would look back on this confrontation one day and laugh at the absurdity. Along with the embarrassment.

29

APERIL 1978

APRIL 1978

Eli's interest in the opposite sex descended into furious animal frenzy. He bounced from one girl to another. He wanted me to set him up with Tricia, not only my roommate but my best friend at Tulloh. I didn't, and he moved on. I was relieved.

Eli had not yet re-enrolled at Henries but remained at the community college. The classes were undemanding, so his grades were adequate. He lived only in the moment. In early April he disappeared from Hagood for two weeks. He didn't tell me he was leaving. I realized he was missing only after it occurred to me he'd not phoned in several days. I called out at the lake. None of the guys had a clue, they swore, other than he might have gone to see some "people" in Columbia.

The night he returned he called my room as though he hadn't been anywhere. Like he didn't know himself he'd been gone two weeks from school.

"Hey, Little Dee," he began.

"Where the hell have you been?" I snapped.

"Whoa," he said. "Anger not needed. Not a big deal."

"Not a big deal?" I interrupted. "No one knows where you are. You skip classes for two weeks, and it's not a big deal?"

"Come on. Cut me some slack. Drive out here tonight. We're having a party, kissing cousin. Pack an overnight bag. You can't drive that dark road back into town late at night." One sentence piled on top of another. Barely 7:00 pm, and he was already buzzed.

"What have you been doing all this time?" I asked, though I guessed. It didn't take a genius to comprehend: buying and selling and bringing back the surplus to consume.

"I had things to do," he said.

"What do you think about, Eli? What happens when you get caught? How are you going to pass the semester?"

"Probably, not," he said—a nonsensical answer to my barrage of

247

questions. He chuckled low and muffled in his frog-throated way, undisturbed. "So why worry about it now? I'll work it out."

A part of me wanted to get in the Green Pea right then and drive to the lake. I missed him. But if I didn't go, it would make a statement, wouldn't it? Show him what I thought of his doings. I stared down into my lap. I sat on my bed cross-legged, feet on my thighs, the way I did when I studied and concentrated. I ran my fingers along the creases that formed in my jeans. I wandered off, thinking, my ego indulging in inflated expectation.

"Hey, Dee, are you there? Where'd you go? You know I've got that extra toothbrush for you," he said, completely ignoring my distress.

I returned to his voice. I held the receiver between my ear and chin, balancing it, while I pulled with the fingers of both hands through my hair. I thought of him smiling, the line of straight squared teeth.

"The things you do for me," I said. I hadn't meant the words to come out that sharp, but they did. He was trying to break me down.

"Will you come?" he asked, his tone gone timid.

"I can't," I said.

"Why not?"

"Because, I just can't."

"I need to be with you," he said, his voice turned to yearning. I wanted to see him. Who did I think I was, believing my solemn stance mattered when a party was underway?

"I miss you, Eli," I admitted.

"So, see me," he yelped exuberantly.

≈

I arrived at the lake house to find Eli with his four roommates and a freshman from Tulloh I had seen around campus—no idea of her name—sitting in a circle on the floor in the living room, a bong passing among them. A bottle of Jack Daniels sat beside Kyle, Eli's closest pal at Henries. How Kyle stayed enrolled at the school, I had no notion, because he was interested mostly in drugs.

"It's Dee," Eli howled when I walked in without knocking. "Come join us, my love." He moved over to make room for me in the circle, but I remained standing, surveying the scene. Everyone getting wasted—hadn't I known this?—like it was the best and only thing on earth to do. "Hey," Eli called to me. He patted the space beside him. "You know everyone. Maybe not Rebecca?"

"Hey, Rebecca," I said. She sort of bounced her head of frizzy hair at me, gave me a dopey, wide smile. One eye drooped more than the other.

I sat. Eli was still sober enough to note my mood—prickly—and he pulled me to his side, my shoulder under his arm. I passed when the bong came to me, and Eli frowned. "Let it happen," he coaxed, but I shook my head. I had no desire. I did take a long swig from the Jack Daniels bottle each time it came around to me, my feeble attempt to release frustration.

No one talked much. There was the occasional hum or exclamation, Lynyrd Skynyrd's *Street Survivors* playing in the background. Until two of the roommates, Marshall and Kenny, began laughing hysterically over nothing. Then, "You farted," Kenny squealed.

"What the hell," Marshall answered and laughed harder. Eventually, Cody, the fourth and youngest roommate, pulled Rebecca to her feet, and they left for his bedroom.

"Shit, must be nice," Kyle remarked, his long locks bobbing as he shook his head, loose on his neck.

"Hey, watch it. My cousin's in the room," Eli said. He chuckled and swung his head from side to side, mocking Kyle.

"Delia, why don't you tell him he's full of crap?" Kyle asked and stood. "You weren't born yesterday. Idn'at right?" He cocked his head toward me. Then he stumbled toward the bathroom. I laughed uneasily.

"Hey, Eli, what'd you bring us? Time for the goody bag," Kenny shouted.

"All right! Let's check out the inventory," Marshall said. "Where's the good stuff?" They stood simultaneously.

I looked at my cousin, saw him cut his hand across his neck.

"What's the deal with the neck?" I asked. "Something you don't want me to know?"

"Shut the fuck up," Eli said to Kenny and Marshall, but they were too spaced out to heed his warning.

"Probably in the kitchen," Kenny said to Marshall. They half-shuffled, half-waddled toward the room.

"Yo, not now," Eli called, rising too slowly to impede me, for I was already on their heels, catching up in time to see them dig into drawers and cabinets. Soon enough, they found what they sought, each immediately vying to twist open the neck of a paper sack shoved into a corner behind the grimy toaster. The top of the bag tore, and the contents of smaller plastic bags dumped on the counter.

"Ooh-wee, ain't they purty? Pink, white, yellow. Darvon, Valium, Quaaludes. What's what?" Kenny asked. "What good is a 'lude without a girl?" he laughed and poked Marshall.

I stared at the small bags of pills. I glowered at Eli. "What's this shit?"

"Whoops," Marshall said, turning toward me. "Later." He hunkered his long body and slunk toward the door, but not before his hand dug into a bag and grabbed up who knew what pills. Kenny was oblivious. He had opened a baggie and was sniffing the contents.

"Get out of here," Eli yelled at Kenny who looked up confused. He held on to the bag he'd stuck his nose in. "Leave it," Eli said. Kenny shrugged. He set the bag down. He looked from Eli to me.

"So this is two weeks in Columbia," I said.

"Come on, Delia," Eli said.

"Come on? Like it's okay to be a drug dealer?" Even if I guessed his activities, until confronted with the evidence, it was possible on some level to pretend it wasn't entirely real.

"I'm not a drug dealer," Eli said.

"Really? What do you call it then?"

"Can we…?" he started.

I cut him off. "No. Whatever you're going to say, no." His arms extended toward me. I stepped back from his reach. "I'm leaving," I said.

"No, Dee, please. It's a party. Just a party. Stay with me."

"You're dreaming, Eli. I'm going back to school," I said.

"You brought your bag. Don't leave," he begged.

"I'm angry with you," I said. "You're being stupid."

"I'm sorry," he said. "We'll work this out. I love you."

Two days later, Tricia drove me to the lake house where Eli died. I asked her to leave because I didn't want her clucking over me, uneasy about what to say or do. There was nothing to say or do. Everything was gone except the chimney without a stain of smoke on it. How could one thing remain like that? I stood on charred wood and debris where the house had been, where five boys and one girl from Tulloh had died, everybody who had stayed the night. I thought it wouldn't have happened if I'd been there. I wouldn't have let it. Though how I would have stopped Kyle from lighting a cigarette in his tranquilized state in his basement bed, turning over, falling asleep, forgetting about the red tip of the cylinder burning in a house where everyone was drugged out, I don't know.

I hadn't wanted to see but Mary Lily asked me to pick up Eli's car. She couldn't bear it, and Gene was out of his mind, and she needed me. I bent and picked up a handful of lumps and ashes. In the debris I clutched, some remaining part of an object, something pointed, stuck my palm. It jabbed into soft flesh. I clenched my blackened hand and opened it. A shard of glass, the color of an old Coca-Cola bottle. A single full and perfectly round drop of blood formed and then another.

I felt disconnected from myself, strange and unreal, in the smoky dustiness of a crumbled world around me. I existed only as drops of accumulating blood. I stared again at my hand, the blood pooling now, running over, a stream down my wrist. I wiped my palm against my jeans.

I stepped around in the open space and walked through where a wall had stood between kitchen and den. I stepped over metal springs. My feet dropped into soft soot that swirled in little gray clouds. I stood still. The springs of Eli's fat armchair, surely, the bright red poppy cushions now ashes. I gasped. My injured hand dangled. I reached out to air where the little table beside the chair had sat. Where Eli always left his glasses and ring, his grandfather Lauderdale's signet ring.

Please, oh please—the words twisted in my head. Had Eli been in bed when he died? Had he known the fire surrounded him and he couldn't escape? A neighbor testified she heard a scream coming from the house and ran out to see the structure flaming from every window.

Was it Eli's scream she heard? Did she really hear a scream? The firemen claimed all had died without pain, of smoke inhalation. And it was impossible, they said, to know where any of the victims had been at the moment of death, for the charred skeletons had lain among the other ruins on the ground. An image emerged of Eli without tissue, without face, maybe even the bones of his hands and feet burned to ash.

I pulled the car keys from my pocket, saw my hand still oozing blood. I swiped my jeans again. I gripped the keys hard. My hand throbbed. I concentrated on the pain. I liked feeling the pain. I liked seeing the blood continue to flow. It was real. It made me cry out.

What was real and what was unreal ran together in my head. I cried in trembling noises. No tears came. I held my aching hand and stared into the grimy world of nothing before me. "Damn you, Eli," I said. I looked up at a dour gray-blue sky, layered with clouds. "Damn you, Eli," I said again.

Before I cranked Eli's car, some mystifying part of me—how and why I'll never understand—decided to look inside the glove compartment. Presumably, I was looking for drugs because I didn't want to be caught with any of Eli's stash. Looking back, I realize I did not have that much presence of mind. It was something else. You can call it intuition, clairvoyance, or whatever word fits. It doesn't matter. I unlocked that door and opened the glove compartment.

There were no drugs. Of course not, because Eli had taken everything inside the house for the party. What I found—beyond his car registration and insurance card—was a wrinkled, awkwardly folded letter from Frances Burchett Mobley Turner to Mary Margaret Lauderdale.

In the letter, Frances Burchett wrote about her incurable illness of the kidneys and thanked Mary Margaret for recently visiting her. She addressed Mary Margaret in the letter as her natural mother and thanked her for naming Gentry Burchett as her biological father.

I was not so much aware at that moment of the reality presented in the letter as I was by Eli's silence. He had known ever since the day of Mimi's funeral when he found this letter in her armoire. Why hadn't he told me? Because I'd said I wanted to forget about Francie and her history? Because I'd told him once in a letter I didn't want to know

252

secrets intended to remain hidden? Because he thought it would change the way I felt about his family? About us? None of these questions mattered so much as this: Did he ever plan to tell me?

I refolded the letter and placed it in my purse. I sat numb behind the wheel. I pulled the letter out again and reread it, the truth firmly taking hold. My heart began beating very fast, and I had the sensation I might choke. Eli's genteel and elegant grandmother had borne Frances Burchett out of wedlock in her youth, and Francie was her granddaughter. Eli had another first cousin. It seemed clear to me that Francie did not know, for in the letter Frances Burchett agreed Mary Margaret might see Francie if she promised never to tell her granddaughter or Mace Turner the truth.

I don't know what all I felt. Abandoned, helpless, shocked. I was never supposed to know, and now the secret was mine only. Or was it? What about Mary Lily? It could be a reason besides Uncle Gene that my aunt's relationship with her mother always had an underlying strain. And there was Caro, who'd been with Mimi forever. If anyone knew, she did. What was I supposed to do? I made myself breathe very slowly to calm my heart. I had to wait for a long time before I could drive.

I had little awareness of my whereabouts when I returned to campus to pack my bags. My senses were dumb. I discovered later when I opened my suitcase at home that I'd packed a winter jacket and dress for the warm April weather. I packed no nightgown but included ten pairs of underwear. Eli's car seemed to drive itself home. Sometime after the funeral, my parents drove to Tulloh to collect the Green Pea and the remainder of my belongings. I refused to return.

I also have no recollection of dressing myself the morning of the funeral, though I do recall what I wore: a pale pink sleeveless dress bought new for Easter the year before and still hanging in my closet— for there was no Easter when Mimi died.

I sat between Helen and my father on a hard Episcopal pew in a packed church. Seats ran out. People stood in the back and in corners, but Isabel was not there. She had called Mary Lily to say she was too upset to come. My oldest friends, Nealy and Gloria, sat in the row behind me. I stared ahead at the profuse blanket of white tulips wrapping the coffin, the edges dangling with lily of the valley. Deceitful blooms in their symbolism of hope and renewal, concealing a coffin of blackened bones. So little of Eli left that his skeleton would have gone unidentified if not for dental records.

I started out of my torpor when the church bells began to toll. Bong, Bing, Bong, Bing: a deep, warm chime from above, followed by a hollow brash rejoinder. At what count in the twenty-one years of Eli's life did I begin to cry? Noisy, inappropriate, crushing sobs. For three days nothing, and now I couldn't stop. Daddy put his arm around me. I continued. He leaned toward my ear, urging, "Get hold of yourself, Delia. You've got to stop so people can hear the service." I saw Mary Lily's back in front of me, stoic straight, a broad-brimmed hat reaching past the nape of her neck, her posture regal. I wasn't strong like that.

Daddy's hand tightened on my shoulder. I held my breath trying to stop. I wanted to do what my father asked. Still, my tears were audible. My sister's hand encircled mine. She squeezed hard. I looked at her.

"You're going to make it, Dee," she said. "Hold on."

"For what?" I asked her. "For what?"

30

AUGUST 1978

I'd walked away the morning and early afternoon, along the way encountering Miss Inez Wilson and the DAR ladies at the Lauderdale graves. Now, I strolled home from the cemetery—reluctantly—toward Congress Street, dreading the anxiety on my mother's face.

I was all too aware of my parents' increasing consternation as fall semester approached. In the last two weeks they had pounded into overdrive, imploring my return to Tulloh. They reminded me constantly all I had to do was tie up loose ends, study for my exams, and pass those exams to graduate. Dr. Charles had been kind, arranging for an incomplete in all my classes.

I rounded the little curve toward our house. The Green Pea sat in our gravel drive, gleaming in the sun. I'd hardly driven it all summer. I'd gone nowhere.

I felt the urge to cross the street and seat myself beneath the triangular window of stained glass set into the large front gable of Eli's porch. The blue and red jewels would be alive and dancing in the penetrating, cloudless sunlight.

I could have sat alone, quietly, on the porch, and Mary Lily—had she noticed me from a window—would have let me be. But on that August afternoon, two weeks before the semester at Tulloh would begin—a monstrous dread—I rang the bell. For what I really wanted was to talk to my aunt.

Uncle Gene answered the door.

"Adeline, hello," he said. He swayed. Drunk in mid-afternoon. "What do you need?" He opened the screen door and swept his arm wide. The cookie truck left the driveway only on occasion now. I thought he must drive only substitute routes, because no one could have a real job working as seldom as he did. I felt sorry for him at the same time I didn't feel sorry for him. He'd lost his only child, his son, whom he loved greatly, but I also partly blamed him. Maybe it wasn't fair, but I couldn't help but think early on he encouraged Eli to live recklessly, making him think that's what made a man.

"I'd like to see Mary Lily, if she's here," I said.

"I think she's here," he responded. "Hold on. Mary L," he called loudly. Then silence while we waited.

"It's okay," I said. "I'll sit out here a little while and wait, if that's okay."

"Of course," he said. "Still taking those pretty pills, I see." He was trying to be charming—he'd been making that same statement all my life to get a smile out of me. I was too old for it now. It seemed pathetic.

"Yes, Uncle Gene. I take a pretty pill every day," I said, giving him the expected answer. I shook my head slowly, sadly, but he did not appear to notice. He gave me the thumbs-up sign and withdrew to whatever corner he'd been sitting in with his tumbler.

"Hello darling," Mary Lily called from behind Gene's retreating back. "How lovely to see you. I'm coming out. Give me a moment to turn on the fans and pour us some iced tea. You'd like a glass? It's awfully hot."

"Yes ma'am, I would," I said. I sat in a wooden rocker directly under the stained-glass window, facing the street. I couldn't see the window from my position, of course, but I could see the sun play it reflected. Little beams shooting in angles around me.

The screen door squeaked open, and I jumped up to help my aunt carry the tray. She set it on the little table between us and reached over to smooth my hair before she sat in an identical rocker—the same places Eli and I had sat so many nights in the dark. Her own hair, strung with gray threads, rarely graced her shoulders now. It was pulled tight with a tortoise-shell comb cinched behind her head. It reminded me of the way Mimi often wore her hair.

Since Eli's death, what I should and shouldn't say, and pretend was or wasn't true, seemed absurd. His death changed life. I spoke my mind. I would work my way through until I reached the subject I'd most come to talk about. I'd gone back and forth about it long enough.

"Uncle Gene is a wreck," I announced sharply. I did not possess my aunt's gentility.

"Yes," she responded.

"Why, Mary Lily?"

"Why what, Adeline?" I could tell she thought I meant his grief, and was asking the obvious.

"No, I don't mean Eli," I said. "I mean Uncle Gene drinks all the time."

"It's part of the grief," she said.

"It might be worse now," I conceded, "but he's been this way as long as I can remember. Why have you stayed with him?" I'd never asked her such a personal and abrupt question. Mary Lily looked at me. "You're beautiful and so smart. You could have been a famous musician, but you married Uncle Gene. You stayed with him." For a moment she did not speak.

"Your uncle," she started then and stopped. "You've been under our roof all your life. You know his weaknesses. But we all have weaknesses. He is a good man in his way, Adeline. And he's my husband. For better or for worse."

"He ruined Eli," I cried out.

"Adeline!" she exclaimed. "He loved Eli."

"He took him to a prostitute when he was just a boy," I said. "Did you know that? He helped him grow pot in the attic...and then Eli started dealing."

"Stop, sweetheart. Please stop. Listen to me."

"What?"

"It's true that Gene pressed Ellison and also indulged him. After the accident, once our son's trach was gone, and even before, his father wanted him...wanted him to be normal. He pushed him hard. And who can blame a father for wanting his son to be as other sons?"

"Prostitutes aren't a *normal* father and son outing," I said. "Cultivating and smoking weed with your son is not a *normal* indulgence. Parents don't do that. It's like he wanted Eli to—"

"No. Many things your uncle did were not right," she interjected. "But he wanted Ellison to be... He couldn't accept the reality." She picked up her glass of tea, removed the lemon slice from the rim, dropped it into the glass. She took a sip.

"What reality? Eli *was* normal except for going wild." I was aware of being irrational for singling out Uncle Gene when, in his own desperate way, I knew he'd loved his son. And when the childhood torments living inside Eli weren't Uncle Gene's doing, at least not directly.

Mary Lily set her glass on the table. With her napkin, she patted her brow, where the tiniest beads of perspiration glistened. "No, darling, he wasn't. He kept things from you. And now—I've debated these months—I've wondered about telling you. I want him to remain as he always was in your heart. But now, I see. You need to understand. For your sake."

What else hadn't Eli told me? I wrapped my hand around my own glass of tea, skated it back and forth across the table. Mary Lily put her hand over mine and stopped me. I looked across at my aunt, warm olive eyes glistening—Eli's eyes.

"He was always in pain, Adeline. Always."

"What pain?" I asked. Did my aunt know, after all, what had happened to Eli in her garden so many years ago? Had he told her and not informed me? Had he done the same with Francie and her baby?

"To the day he died, Ellison had to swallow that excruciating tube. Every couple of weeks. He abhorred it so much that he would wait until his throat nearly closed and he couldn't swallow another bite of food. He would go hungry before he forced the tube down his throat."

"Why? Why did he have to do that? He'd been well for so long." I picked up my glass. I tried to take a swallow, but the muscles in my throat had constricted. I hadn't known about Eli's physical pain.

"He was never well, Adeline," she said. "The scar tissue would close his throat if he didn't keep it open. The tube was the only remedy."

"Oh, my God," I muttered. "I didn't know. I didn't help him."

"There wasn't anything you could do," she said. "Please believe that. He didn't want you to know. What good would it have done for you to know, to worry about that awful procedure?" she asked. "He hated the tube most of all, but there were other issues. The unrelenting heartburn. Choking. Foods he couldn't eat."

I looked at her. All of a sudden I realized I'd never seen my cousin eat popcorn. Not at the movies, not watching television, not ever. How could I not have realized? I sat bewildered. Mary Lily maybe didn't know all I knew, and yet she knew other things Eli had never told me.

"And there were fears," she continued. "Ellison's esophagus was severely damaged from the sodium hydroxide. The doctors were frank about cancer statistics. There was a high likelihood he would develop esophageal cancer, and likely as a young man."

My cousin had taken so many risks. Become a train wreck on drugs. And no wonder. It wasn't just the torment in his head. He lived in physical pain. It was all so clear now. That he escaped any way he could. I bent and held my head in my hands. "I could have done more to make him feel better," I cried.

"He wanted you to see him at his best, sweetheart. Please don't be hurt by that. I tell you these things because you're beating yourself up, Adeline. You're blaming yourself for his death and you're not to blame. Not the tiniest bit."

It hit me all at once. Eli kept things from me to protect me. Not telling me Frances Burchett was Mimi's daughter was a part of it.

"I left the lake house that night," I said, looking up. I could hardly speak. "I was angry because he was out of control. But I didn't know…all he was going through. I could have…" My words caught in my throat, squeaking. Breath poured out of me, like helium escaping a balloon. Leaving me a flat cardboard figure suspended in the chair.

"You did not stay and die, Adeline."

I began to shake uncontrollably. I thought my cousin and I knew each other as well as any two people ever could. But now that wasn't true. While I unburdened everything to him, taking his love and support for granted, Eli had not wanted to burden me.

My aunt stood and walked behind my chair. She rubbed my shaking shoulders. "This is why I didn't want to tell you. But you must understand, Adeline. He wanted you to love him for who he was, not for the troubles he couldn't control."

"I did," I whimpered.

"Of course you did. And Eli loved you with all his heart. He wanted to be strong for you."

"Yes, he wanted to be strong," I repeated.

She gave my shoulders a final squeeze and moved back to her seat. "Better," she said and nodded. I pulled in my breath, held it, my body still shaking but less now. I watched the sweat roll down my glass of tea. I traced the cold beads with my fingertip.

"He took care of me. He wouldn't take care of himself; he took care of me," I whispered.

"It went both ways, Adeline. He needed you, and you never failed him," my aunt said.

"I loved him like crazy," I said. Mary Lily reached across the little table and took my hand in hers. She bowed her head.

"Mary Lily," I said her name quietly. She looked up at me expectantly. "Do you know the name Burchett in your family?" She looked at me quizzically, yet her expression was blank.

"Eli asked me one time about the Burchetts, too," she said. Her straightforward tone made me nearly certain she had no knowledge Frances Burchett Mobley Turner was her half-sister.

I had no idea what story Eli might have made up along with the true part, that he had seen the name in Mimi's ancestral documents. "I'm not sure why Eli asked," I lied. "Maybe because as children, we saw the name when we occupied ourselves inspecting family papers in Mimi's parlor."

"That's what he said," Mary Lily concurred. "Goodness knows, Mother kept every record of everything related to family. I have boxes stacked in the attic I haven't yet shuffled through."

All but one, I thought. I clamped my hands together to keep them still. Had Eli not found Frances Burchett's letter that day, Mary Lily would one day have discovered it instead. And Eli might never have known. How many steps along the way could have prevented him from knowing? I focused hard to keep going.

"One of my friends at school has the last name Burchett," I invented my story as I spoke. "She called the other day, to check on me, just being nice, so the name got on my mind. It's unusual, so I wondered if maybe my friend could be kin to you." It wasn't a very believable story, but I hadn't planned out anything ahead of time to say.

Mary Lily frowned, barely. I was sure she didn't believe me—I wouldn't believe something so commonplace after the intensity of our conversation moments before—but she didn't push it. Instead, she answered my question.

"I had a great-grandfather James Burchett. I don't know much about him. He didn't live in Green Branch, but he must not have been too far away, because two of his children lived here. His daughter Gladys was my grandmother, and she came to Green Branch when she married Lewis Caston, my grandfather who farmed here. He died of gall bladder infection while Mother was still a young girl. My grandmother sold their large farm to one of her brothers who lived in Green Branch. He was Malcolm Burchett." Mary Lily wiped her brow. "He and my grandfather had been good friends. Grandmother often said his purchase enabled her and her children to survive." Mary Lily stopped. "Is this helpful?"

I nodded and she continued. "Malcolm and his wife Paula had three sons, but the whole family moved away before I was born. I know what I'm telling you only secondhand from Grandmother. I never met any of them. I don't even know where they moved."

"Did you know the sons' names?" I asked. I held my breath.

"One was Wyatt. Another was Samuel." She paused. "The other brother was Gentry. But I never heard Grandmother mention him. I wouldn't know he existed except for Caro sometimes talking about the Burchett boys when I was a girl, how she missed them running through the house like bulls, and calling them all by name. She loved their high-spirited nature."

My chest grew tight, my breathing shallow. I gulped to take a deep breath, but it wouldn't come. The name "Gentry" appeared visible in my mind, a flashing array of letters.

"You could ask Caro, I suppose, if you want to know more about Mother's Burchett cousins. She might know more." I wanted to nod my head, to be responsive, but I couldn't move just then.

Mary Lily's hand floated out toward me. "Delia, drink some tea. Your face is very red. I think you're overheated." Her fingers fluttered at my face. I closed my eyes, squeezed, opened them again. I picked up the glass beside me. I drank. "I'm going in for more ice." My aunt's voice sounded far away, but she was right next to me. "Won't be long."

I closed my eyes again. Eli's grandmother, our beloved and proper Mimi, had loved her first cousin Gentry and given birth to their child, Frances Burchett. A name she must have insisted on when the Mobleys adopted her to preserve in Mary Margaret's daughter the memory of the man she loved but could not marry. I saw Mimi behind my eyes, alive again, patting the comb holding her hair in the parlor that day.

261

Smiling as she told us how first cousins used to marry before the Civil War. The smile quickly disappearing as she explained how first cousins could no longer marry. How abruptly she left the room.

And now I knew, and I felt all she meant when she said, "Family is hard," on the day the baby drowned. How it must have troubled Mimi to watch Eli and me grapple with our feelings and accept the impossibility, having to relive her own emotions through us. Most surely her heart broke all over again. I felt tears begin to slide beneath my closed lids. I let them fall. I did not try to wipe them away.

I realized Eli might never have told me of Mary Margaret's love for her cousin Gentry Burchett. For all the joy we'd been to one another, he wouldn't want to rekindle the pain of what we could never change, the futility of being born first cousins who loved each other in an age that would reject us for such a love. Instead, he suffered the knowledge alone when he had already far too much to bear. How much had this secret cost him? A secret he'd known intuitively, at least in part, long before he found its proof.

I heard the screen door slam. I opened my eyes. Mary Lily walked toward me, a bucket of ice between her hands. "Darling, you've been crying," she said and set the bucket on the floorboards at my feet.

"I know," I answered.

"It doesn't seem like it now, but..." I stopped her sentence, put my hand on her arm. After a minute or more had passed, she squeezed my hand and released it. She smiled bravely at me, and I smiled back. My tears, for the present, gone.

"I'm glad you came today," she said. "We needed to talk about everything. There's something else I want to discuss with you, if that's okay? I was going to call you." Her tone was suddenly businesslike. "I've made some decisions about my mother's house."

"Oh," I responded. Of course, I had wondered about the future of Mary Margaret's house. Even when Eli and I were children, we talked of what he'd do with Magnolia Manor one day.

"Before I finalize my plan, I wanted to ask you."

"Me?"

"Because you are the next generation, my dear, and if you are interested in my mother's home, we should discuss the possibilities." It was Francie who was the true next generation. Mary Margaret's blood.

262

I'd not seen her since the day at the creek. As far as I knew, she never moved back to Green Branch after high school. Magnolia Manor was rightfully hers, even if I knew she would never want it. She wouldn't return to the place where she drowned her baby. Still, I wondered if it was my responsibility to tell Mary Lily and to locate Francie somehow and tell her who she was. The weight of my layered secret lay heavy in my heart.

"Adeline?" Mary Lily forced me from my daunting thoughts.

"I love Mimi's home," I said. "Such a fine home. I mean, I'm honored, but…"

"It's a lovely home. Historic. Valuable," Mary Lily reminded me.

"I couldn't," I said. "It would—"

She broke into my sentence. "You might feel different when you're a bit older."

"I won't," I said. I thought of memories overwhelming me. Of feeling forlorn in that big antebellum house, even if I had a family. I did not want to live among the ghosts. I knew in that moment I would honor the secret, just as Eli had done. I didn't believe any good could come from revealing it. If on the far-fetched assumption Mary Lily knew, it was clear she was keeping the secret also.

"Couldn't you live there?" I asked. She shook her head. "Why?" I implored.

"For likely the same reasons as you, my dear," she said and sighed.

"But I don't want a stranger living there," I said. "What about your brother?"

"He will not return to Green Branch. He has given me permission to do as I please. So let me tell you what I think." She crossed and uncrossed her legs. I looked at her intently.

"If not you, I want Pot to have the house. In fact, I've already discussed an arrangement with him, saying only if you were not interested."

"Pot?" I asked. It was a stunning thought. "What did he say?"

Mary Lily laughed. "He said, 'Now wouldn't that be something? Me in the big house.' She told me he put his hands on his knees and bent to her eye level. 'Lord, what white folks around here would think, black folks, too'." She said he chuckled when he said it, and it made her happy.

"I don't care what they think," she had told him. "You saved my son's life. You are part of this family and have always been part of this family." She said Pot worried "Mr. Gene" would not be happy, and she'd responded it didn't matter what "Mr. Gene" thought. It was not his house.

Though he still watched after Caro, Pot had finally, late in his forties, found a love of his own and married her. We had thought him a bachelor forever, a responsible man who would care for his mother until her death and then live out his years in quietude. Odessa was a young widow with a little boy, her husband killed in a helicopter crash late in the Vietnam War, at the end of his second tour. They met at the AME Church on the lawn after a homecoming Sunday service. Pot was simply a kind friend at first, helping around Odessa's house. Climbing the tall ladder to clean the gutters. Installing a fence for her little boy's dog. Pot took quickly to eight-year-old Alvin.

"I like to think of little Alvin growing up out in the country. He's a darling boy," Mary Lily said. "Where he can run and play and enjoy the world."

"Like Eli and me," I said. Maybe like Francie's baby, had it lived, I thought.

"Yes, indeed," she said.

31

AUGUST 31, 1978

The end of summer was upon me. I knew I should be packing to return to Tulloh the day after Labor Day. Within a few weeks, if I put my mind to it, I would be ready for exams. My professors were sympathetic. All had written to me, willing to help me prepare.

My parents stayed worried; they did not understand why I didn't appreciate my opportunity. I didn't want to worry them sick, but I felt no inclination or direction. I had no notion of what I'd do if I did graduate. Meanwhile, Helen was fired up about starting tenth grade, her first year of high school. She'd become quite a beauty and boy crazy. It made me think of meeting Rad at the same age. It made me think how Eli looked after me then.

I went to bed that Thursday night wishing, at least, for the motivation to follow through. It was unusually cool that evening, an early breath of fall, and Mama decided to turn off the air-conditioning and run the attic fan. We'd slept with the attic fan—windows open wide, curtains blown horizontal all night long—summers when I was a child, but since AC had been installed, the fan was rarely used. It felt nostalgic to turn it on.

The breeze cooled my room so much I pulled a blanket from my closet. It was cozy lying under the layers of cover. The moon was not present, but the pinpricks of stars—visible through the windows—shone everywhere. A silver aura filled my room, giving me a strange and unexpected comfort. The wind blowing over me felt imbued with something alive. I fell asleep to the hypnotizing effect of the dramatic flutter of the opened curtains.

I dreamed I was swimming in the deep end of a pool. I stroked my arms through blue water. I was alone. I wanted to reach the ledge at the other end; I swam toward it, but I couldn't get there. It didn't matter. I was content swimming. Then, the water clouded. I came up for breath and coughed. The air above the water appeared as foggy as the water itself.

"Get out," a voice called.

"Who's there?" I asked.

"Get out, now! Wake up, Delia." I heard the voice again. It was Eli's voice. Unexpectedly, the edge of the pool appeared before me, and I pulled myself up onto the concrete ledge.

"Hurry," he said.

"I'm wet and cold," I replied. "Give me time to find my towel."

"No time," he said. I saw Eli then. Through the fog. He came close. I could see only his face, nothing more. His eyebrows knit together, his mouth forming an open hole.

"Why is it so foggy?" I asked.

"It isn't fog. It's smoke. There's going to be a fire if you don't wake up now." His voice was calm, convincing, but his face looked panicked.

"Come on, Delia," his voice urged again. I felt something tugging me upward in the bed. Forcing me to sit up. I opened my eyes. The room was cloudy as in my dream, the air thick in spite of the breeze blowing in. I tried to clear my throat.

"Now, move quick," Eli said. I was no longer dreaming. I was awake.

I stepped barefooted onto the floor and walked out into the hall. The air was even hazier here. It seemed to stick to me. I struggled to take in breath; my lungs regurgitated the air. Something was wrong. I entered my parents' bedroom and woke them. My father jumped to his feet. "Smoke," he yelled. "Get your sister, Delia. Get down the stairs and out of the house. Quickly!"

Mama was in the hall now, too. "What is it, Will?" she asked, still nearly asleep, holding her hands over her nose and mouth.

"I don't know. There's smoldering somewhere. Go out with the girls. Outside. Away from the house." His voice was clipped. Demanding. In our thin short summer nightgowns, without shoes, exposed, Helen and I exited the house. Mama came behind us and ran across the street—her long gown flapping at her bare heels—to wake the Winfields and call for the fire department.

Helen and I stood on the front walkway holding hands. We watched the doors—front and side—waiting for Daddy to emerge. "He needs to get out," I said. "I'll go back in and tell him."

266

"No, Dee," she said. "He knows what he's doing. Wait." She pulled on my arm. And with that, our father materialized through the den door into the carport.

"It's the attic fan," he said, walking quickly toward us. "Got to be an electrical short. The wall was hot beside the switch. It's off now."

The firemen arrived, thankfully to find no fire. The hose remained coiled on the side of the truck. Two firemen, one a friend of my father's from his youth, went inside to inspect the house.

"Mighty lucky night, Will Green," my Daddy's friend Mack said when the two firemen returned to the street. "Mighty lucky. Much longer and the insulation behind that switch would have ignited. It was ready. Hot as a firecracker."

"Mighty lucky, Mack," Daddy repeated. "Thank you." He stepped back and forth, stopped, stuck out his hand for Mack to shake.

"What alerted you? People don't usually wake in a case like this. The smoke comes in, takes over before the flames start."

"It was Delia," Daddy said. "She woke up."

Everyone looked at me, expectant.

I opened my mouth to speak, but I didn't say anything. Had the smoke in the house infiltrated my dream, causing me to conjure an image of Eli because of the fire, or had Eli appeared to rescue us? The answer was clear to me. But if I confessed Eli came to warn me, everyone would think I had indeed gone crazy. I couldn't tell them the truth. I hesitated, determining what to say. I was trembling a little.

"Delia," Daddy asked. "Are you okay?" He walked toward me and put his hand on my back. "Everything's going to be fine. I know how this must have scared you. Reminded you. I'm so sorry." Mary Lily had brought sweaters for Helen and me, and I pulled the fabric tightly around me.

"I woke up because I had to go to the bathroom," I muttered. "I dreamed I was submerged in water and it made me have to go badly. When I walked out in the hall, I was surrounded by the smoke."

"Well, it's over now," Mama said, her voice as kind as any voice can be. She walked over and put her arm around my waist so that both parents surrounded me. Helen joined them, making us a family cocoon.

My parents then walked over to thank the men, six of them on two trucks, before returning to the house.

267

"We're going inside, girls," Mama called. "They say it's safe."

"Coming in a minute," Helen answered. I remained, standing on the walk. Helen stayed with me. "Poor Dee, it's scary. But it's all okay," she said. Yet, I didn't feel scared at all. I'm not sure what I felt. Amazed, certainly. Heartened, perhaps. Awakened. Eli had saved me and my family. He came to rescue us. As he had protected me during his life. I recited the lines in my head. Lines he quoted the day of Mimi's funeral, before he climbed her tower: "For whom the bell tolls;/ It tolls for thee."

"It's not just the living being part of the dead," I said to Helen. She looked at me quizzically. "The dead are also part of the living." She didn't understand what I meant. How would she? She thought I was upset and rambling. Her face softened. She wanted to comfort me.

"It's something from John Donne," I tried to explain. "A poet I need to review for my exams."

"Oh, you're going back to school!" My sister's face went suddenly joyful. She leaned over—when had she grown so much taller than me—and squeezed me around the shoulders, jumping to a conclusion I hadn't at all intended. But I squeezed her back affectionately. My kind and tender sister.

I gazed up at the mantle of black sky, studded with its various constellations of stars and the luminous band of the Milky Way, stretching from horizon to horizon. At the vast and mysterious workings of the heavens. Eli. A passage I had memorized in my Donne class came to me. Lines then I barely grasped but which now I surely knew: "But we by a love so much refined, / That our selves know not what it is, / Inter-assured of the mind, / Care less, eyes, lips, and hands to miss."

Helen touched me on the shoulder. "Ready?" she asked.

"Ready," I said.

AUTHOR

Susan Beckham Zurenda taught college and high school English for
many years and now works as a book publicist for Magic Time Literary
Publicity. A recipient of several regional awards for her fiction, including The South Carolina Fiction Project, The Alabama Writers Con-
clave First Novel Chapter, The Porter Fleming Literary Competition,
and The Southern Writers Symposium, she has also published numerous stories and nonfiction pieces in literary journals. Zurenda lives in
Spartanburg, South Carolina, with her husband Wayne.